INTRIGUE

Seek thrills. Solve crimes. Justice served.

Cold Case Discovery
Nicole Helm

Shadowing Her Stalker
Maggie Wells

T0359524

MILLS & BOON

COLD CASE DISCOVERY
© 2025 by Nicole Helm
Philippine Copyright 2025
Australian Copyright 2025
New Zealand Copyright 2025

First Published 2025
First Australian Paperback Edition 2025
ISBN 978 1 038 94054 4

SHADOWING HER STALKER
© 2025 by Margaret Ethridge
Philippine Copyright 2025
Australian Copyright 2025
New Zealand Copyright 2025

First Published 2025
First Australian Paperback Edition 2025
ISBN 978 1 038 94054 4

MIX
Paper | Supporting
responsible forestry
FSC® C001695
www.fsc.org

Published by
Harlequin Mills & Boon
An imprint of Harlequin Enterprises (Australia) Pty Limited
(ABN 47 001 180 918), a subsidiary of HarperCollins
Publishers Australia Pty Limited
(ABN 36 009 913 517)
Level 19, 201 Elizabeth Street
SYDNEY NSW 2000 AUSTRALIA

Cover art used by arrangement with Harlequin Books S.A.. All rights reserved.

Printed and bound in Australia by McPherson's Printing Group

Cold Case Discovery

Nicole Helm

MILLS & BOON

Nicole Helm grew up with her nose in a book and the dream of one day becoming a writer. Luckily, after a few failed career choices, she gets to follow that dream—writing down-to-earth contemporary romance and romantic suspense. From farmers to cowboys, Midwest to *the* West, Nicole writes stories about people finding themselves and finding love in the process. She lives in Missouri with her husband and two sons, and dreams of someday owning a barn.

Books by Nicole Helm

Harlequin Intrigue

Hudson Sibling Solutions

Cold Case Kidnapping
Cold Case Identity
Cold Case Investigation
Cold Case Scandal
Cold Case Protection
Cold Case Discovery

Covert Cowboy Soldiers

The Lost Hart Triplet
Small Town Vanishing
One Night Standoff
Shot in the Dark
Casing the Copycat
Clandestine Baby

Visit the Author Profile page at millsandboon.com.au.

For anyone who has made something good
in the midst of tragedy.

CAST OF CHARACTERS

Jack Hudson—Oldest Hudson sibling, sheriff of Sunrise and leader of Hudson Sibling Solutions.

Chloe Brink—Sheriff's deputy of Sunrise.

Ry Brink—Chloe's brother.

Mary & Walker Daniels—Jack's sister, who handles admin at HSS, and her husband, who also works for HSS.

Cash & Izzy Hudson—Jack's brother and niece. Cash trains dogs for a living.

Carlyle Daniels—Walker's sister, who is dating Cash.

Zeke Daniels—Walker's brother.

Anna, Hawk & Caroline Steele—Jack's youngest sister, who also works for HSS, her husband, who is a fire investigator, and their baby.

Grant & Dahlia Hudson—Jack's brother and his wife. Grant works for HSS, and Dahlia is a librarian.

Palmer & Louisa Hudson—Jack's brother and his wife. Palmer works for HSS, and Louisa works at her parents' orchard.

Chapter One

Her phone trilled in the dark.

Chloe Brink rolled over to find the other side of the bed empty, which was good. *Best.* Considering the screen on her phone read *Do Not Answer.*

In other words, it wasn't work or something important. It was her brother calling her. At two in the morning.

She loved her baby brother and wished she could save him, but he was an addict. And until he accepted that, until *he* decided he wanted to change, her relationship with him had to be distant.

She was a sheriff's deputy. She couldn't rush in to save him from every problem. It would only get them both in trouble.

So she didn't answer.

The first time.

After the ringing paused, only to immediately begin ringing again, she sighed and did the inevitable. Maybe one of these days all the steps she'd taken to try to insulate herself from this need to be his—or anyone's—savior would actually work.

But not tonight.

She closed her eyes, let her head flop back onto the pillow and took a deep breath. "Ry, what is it?"

"I need your help."

She counted to three, inhaled deeply. Let it out. He didn't *sound* high, but that didn't mean anything. "We've been over this."

"Chloe, you don't understand. This is serious. It wasn't me. I don't know what to do. There's bones. It wasn't me. It's too old. Too deep. Chlo, I don't know what to *do*."

Panicked, clearly. But *bones* didn't make sense. She pushed up into a sitting position on the bed, tried to clear her mind. "What do you mean, Ry? I don't understand."

"By the barn. I've been digging for that new addition, right?"

She didn't say what she wanted to: *At two in the morning?* She let him blabber on only half making sense. At least it was just some jumbled talk about bones, not actual trouble with the law.

"You have to come. What am I supposed to do? I didn't do this. This isn't mine. It's *bones*."

Chloe went over everything her therapist had told her. It wasn't her job to clean up Ry's messes. He had to be responsible for his own choices.

But this wasn't the *exact* same thing. He wasn't in a fight with someone. He wasn't asking her to get him out of a ticket or an arrest. He'd just stumbled upon some bones— animal, probably—and convinced himself, perhaps with the aid of an illegal substance, it was a bigger deal than it was.

If she went over there, told him everything was fine, he'd stop bothering her for a few days. "Fine. Listen. I'll come over. But just to look at these bones, okay? But you have to stay put. And sober."

There was a pause on the other end of the line.

"I mean it, Ry. Not even a sip of beer. If I can't trust you to—"

"Okay. I promise. Nothing. Nothing else. If you just come over. Quick. I don't know what to do."

"Just don't move, and don't touch anything. Or *take* anything," she muttered, before hitting End and tossing her phone onto the empty side of the bed.

This was what her therapist didn't understand. Sometimes going over to help was the better course of action. She'd nip it in the bud and then be free of him for a few days. Best all around.

Best or easiest?

She groaned.

"Bad news?"

She didn't jolt, didn't open her eyes right away. She'd woken to an empty bed, so she figured he'd gone, because that was how this worked. Usually, that caused an ache around her heart, one she was determined to stop and never did—but tonight, him still being here was the last thing she wanted.

Just another one of her very own choices she had to face. She opened her eyes.

Jack Hudson stood, leaning his shoulder against the doorframe of her bedroom. He was dressed now, in the clothes they'd left work in: Khakis that weren't so perfectly pressed like they had been all through his workday. A Sunrise Sheriff's Department polo—untucked now.

But she knew what he looked like without all those clothes. *Hot.*

Maybe his hair was a little rumpled, but no one would think or even believe that it was *sex*-rumpled hair. Jack Hudson, the upstanding sheriff and uptight head of the

Hudson clan, engaging in a clandestine affair with one of his deputies? *Impossible.*

She still hadn't spoken, and now she watched as Tiger wound her way between Jack's long legs like she always did. Because that animal was just as foolish and weak as she was when it came to Jack.

"Chloe," he said in that half-empathetic, half-scolding tone.

He only ever used her first name *here*, what they were—and weren't—perfectly compartmentalized. Her fault as much as his, she knew, though she wished she could blame him and his rigid personality. But she'd put up walls to save herself too.

Because she was self-aware enough to know he could emotionally crush her if she didn't. She didn't think *he* knew that, and that was all that mattered.

"Just my brother. Needs me to come check something out. Typical." She slid out of bed, pulled on some sweats and put her smartwatch on her wrist. But Jack didn't leave.

She shoved her phone in her pocket. Keys and shoes were out in her living room. So she moved for the door, but Jack still stood there. Blocking her exit.

"You should head home," she told him. "A bit late for you."

He didn't say anything for a few moments as he studied her in nothing more than the glow of her smoke detector. They were shadows to each other, and yet it felt like—per usual—Jack Hudson could see *everything.*

"I'm coming with," he finally said.

Not *Would you like me to? Can I? Should I?* Not for Jack Hudson. "Not necessary, Sheriff." She threw that one at him when she wanted him to back off. Usually, it worked.

He didn't budge.

"It's two in the morning."

"Yeah."

"It's your brother."

"Yeah."

"I'm going with. We can either drive together or I can follow you, but I'm going."

"And be seen together at this hour?"

He didn't say anything. But he didn't move. Because no, Jack Hudson didn't relent. He was who he was.

Sometimes she thought she was as bad as her brother. Jack was her drug, and she couldn't give him up. Because he wasn't good for her—the secrecy; the way she couldn't get past that impenetrable, taciturn wall. But the way he made her feel when he put his hands on her was worth it.

She sighed, and she didn't relent, but Jack seemed to read the surrender in that sigh.

"I'll drive," he said, turning toward her front door.

"Of course you will," she muttered, and didn't bother to argue. She just made sure Tiger didn't bolt out the door with them in a shameless effort to follow Jack.

Chloe might be a mess, but she knew better than to throw herself against a brick wall that wasn't budging.

JACK HUDSON WAS well aware of his reputation. He knew what just about everyone thought of him. It varied a bit. To some people—particularly the law-abiding citizens of Sunrise, Wyoming—he was a saint. That was how he'd won the election for sheriff time and time again. To others—usually criminals and people related to him—he was an uptight ass.

Jack knew he was no saint, but he didn't quite agree with his siblings. Maybe he was a little strict, a little more controlled than *completely* necessary. But hey, they'd all some-how made it into adulthood in one piece and were mostly successful, and that was because of *him*.

He'd held the family together after his parents' disap-pearance when he was eighteen. He'd created Hudson Sib-ling Solutions to ensure his siblings always had jobs and to help other people with unsolved cold cases—solving quite a few, thank you.

Though never his own.

His parents—good, upstanding ranchers not involved in anything shady, that anyone had ever found—had disap-peared on a camping "date weekend" one night seventeen years ago. Just vanished.

All these years later, hours and hours of police work, private investigator work, research from every single mem-ber of his family, no one had ever discovered even a shred of evidence of what had happened to Dean and Laura Hud-son.

He told himself, day in and day out, that it was over. There would never be answers, and sometimes a man just had to accept the hard facts of life.

He was also an expert in denial.

The woman in his passenger seat, case in point. Chloe Brink hadn't *always* been a problem. Or maybe she had been and he'd just been younger and delusional. Hard to say now.

They'd been engaging in this whole *thing* for a year now, and he didn't relish the secrecy. It was an irritating neces-sity. But one of the short list of positives was that this was something his siblings had no idea about and, therefore, no say in, no opinions.

Everything that happened with Chloe was *all* his.

"Don't worry," Chloe said in the dark cab of his truck as he slowed down to take the turn into the Brink Ranch entrance. "Even if Ry said something about us arriving together in the middle of the night, no one would believe him. Or at least, not believe the real reasons."

Jack didn't respond, though it required him to grind his teeth together.

He knew she didn't understand his determination to keep this a secret. He'd never tried to explain it to her because she wouldn't believe it. In her mind, he was embarrassed, and he knew her well enough—whether *she* wanted to admit it or not—that it stemmed from her own issues. It took a lot to be a cop in the same place where your last name was pretty much synonymous with *criminal*.

Hell, wasn't that part of why he liked her so much? He wouldn't say they were too alike outside their profession. Chloe was fun and friendly. No one had ever accused him of being either. Not since he was a teenager anyway.

But they both shared a dogged determination to see through whatever they thought was right.

What she would never understand—partly because of that dogged determination and a thick skull—was that people knowing about their...relationship...would cause problems for both of them.

He'd been around enough to know she'd bear the brunt of any negative reaction to their...relationship. It wasn't fair, it wasn't right, but it wouldn't matter what she did. Or what *he* did to try to protect her.

She was a woman, and she'd get the short end of the stick when it came to their work reputations. Right or not, police work—especially police work out here in rural Wyoming—

was still male dominated. Jack dealt with the public enough to know a lot of people were still stuck in the Dark Ages.

He wouldn't let Chloe get a bad rap all because he... He was weak when it came to her, and that was *his* fault. He'd be damned if he let her take the fall for that.

So it had to be a secret, but that didn't mean he didn't care or was *embarrassed* of her.

It also didn't mean he had to like it.

Jack Hudson was well-versed in all the things he didn't like but dealt with anyway.

He pulled through the open gate to the old Brink place. It was open at a crooked angle and clearly had been that way for a while, as grass and vines had grown up and twined around it.

He didn't say anything about that either. Chloe's family was her business, and *maybe* he'd on *occasion* mentioned something about her brother, this ranch and so on, but she always put him in his place.

When he pulled up to the house, Ry was standing out in front of it, pacing back and forth. Jack could see the look on his face in the harsh light of the porch—just a light bulb screwed into the wall, no cover.

Ry was all nerves. Worry. Concern. But something was missing, and he'd dealt with Ry enough in a professional capacity to find it interesting. Chloe's little brother, for once, didn't look guilty.

Yeah, interesting.

"Why'd you bring him?" Ry asked on a whisper when they got out of the truck. Not quiet enough for Jack to miss it, but he pretended he had.

"What's the emergency, Ry?" Chloe asked, sounding

less like a sister and more like a cop—but if she was thinking with her cop brain, she wouldn't be here.

"It wasn't anything to do with me. I just found it," Ry
said, louder this time, making sure Jack heard it.

Jack studied Ry Brink. No doubt he'd been high at some
point today, but whatever he'd been on was wearing off. He
was jittery, gray faced. Scared.

Chloe's expression was blank. "Show us," she said. She
switched on a flashlight Jack hadn't realized she'd grabbed
on their way out, so he figured he could turn on the one
he'd gotten out of his truck as well.

Ry leaned close; this time whatever he whispered to
Chloe was lost in the sound of insects buzzing and breezes
sliding through the dilapidated buildings.

"Show us," she repeated, whatever Ry had said clearly
not winning her over.

Ry led them away from the house, which had seen better decades. They quietly moved toward a caved-in barn.
Ry. Chloe. Jack.

It was his desire to take over, to lead the way, but he
tamped it down. Because this was Chloe's deal, no matter
how little he liked it, and he'd only come along to ensure
her brother wasn't laying some kind of trap.

Chloe might not think Ry capable, but Jack had spent his
entire adult life seeing what drugs did to seemingly reasonable people. Part and parcel with a life in law enforcement.

They walked for a while in silence, and Jack noticed
as they came around the side of the barn that there was
a battery-powered lantern sitting in the dirt, tipped over,
like it had been dropped there.

"I had this idea that I'd dig out a new entrance to the cellar," Ry said. And if he was telling the truth, it was clear

he'd been high when he'd had that idea, because that wasn't going to work.

"The first one I hit, I figured it was animal. Dad used to bury the dogs out here. You remember, Chloe?"

She didn't say anything. She pointed her flashlight beam on the unearthed dirt. A shovel lay haphazardly next to the pile.

"Then I got a few more and… It's not animal bones. I know animals. It ain't animals."

Jack didn't believe that. Lots of people mistook bigger bones for human. He approached the hole with Chloe, shined his light at the ground as well.

He sucked in a breath. Heard Chloe do the same.

Human. Definitely. A full skeleton, almost. Jack swept his flashlight beam down the bones, his mind already turning with next steps. They'd have to notify Bent County. The Brink Ranch was a little outside Sunrise's jurisdiction— and besides that, they didn't have the labs or professional capacity to deal with dead bodies.

It might not be nefarious. Ranchers back in the day buried their kin on property. There were laws against such things now, but it didn't mean people always abided by them. This could be anything. It didn't have to be criminal.

Still, Jack studied the skeletal remains with an eye toward foul play. Hard not to. He swept his beam back up and noticed that something glittered. He didn't want to touch anything, destroy the scene any more than Ry already had, but he trained his light on that glitter and crouched so he could study it closer.

And it felt like the earth turned upside down, like every atom of oxygen in his body evaporated. He saw dark spots for a moment.

Chloe crouched next to him, put her hand on his back. "Jack? Are you okay? What is it?"

He had to breathe, but it was hard to suck in air. When he spoke, he heard how strangled he sounded. But he said what needed saying: "I recognize that ring."

Chloe peered closer. "How?"

"It was my mother's."

Chapter Two

Chloe figured she'd heard him wrong. She had to have heard him wrong. But he stood abruptly and took hard strides away from the remains. She was frozen, looking down at the skeleton in the beam of her flashlight. She tried to process what he was saying.

Because it couldn't be. Of all the crazy, impossible, terrible things this *might* be, it couldn't be that.

But she saw the ring, and Jack Hudson was not a jump-to-conclusions guy. He didn't say any random thought he had. The man plotted out his life to the millisecond. Even in crisis.

If he said that the little glitter of gold and diamond there in the dirt was his mother's, she believed him.

Oh God.

She stood up about as abruptly as he had. Crossed to him. There were so many…so many horrible revolving pieces to this. And she somehow had to find a path through.

For him. "Jack."

"I'll call it in," he said roughly.

"Jack—"

But he shook her off and lifted his cell to his ear. He'd have to call in Bent County. To get a dig team, the coroner. Who'd likely have to call in a forensics team from somewhere farther afield.

Chloe's mind was whirling. Too many things at once. She had to focus. Tap into cop brain. She'd been through a million crises in the past six years of being a cop. She knew how to compartmentalize.

A seventeen-year-old cold case's first huge lead being your boss slash hookup buddy's mother's bones on your family's property?

Okay, the situation was new.

"They'll send out the detectives, a few deputies to zone it off. Get in touch with the coroner," Jack said.

"Gracie Cooper. We know her. She's good." Which, it wouldn't matter if she wasn't. She was the Bent County coroner. But it seemed a tangible thing to hold on to.

"There'll be a lot of questions for Ry."

"He'll hold up," Chloe said, with far more confidence than she felt when it came to her brother. But she'd make sure she kept him in her sight, and as long as she did that, she could make certain he held up.

Right now he was pacing from Jack's truck to some point just beyond, then back again. He raked his hands through his hair. He muttered to himself.

But he didn't run. She'd give him that in this moment. While keeping an eye on him to make sure it stayed that way.

Chloe didn't let her mind go to all the things this could mean. She didn't ask herself why—why now, why here, why anything. She focused on the next steps.

Jack would need to go tell his family. He could wait for some clearer confirmation. After all, that ring—even if it had been his mother's—wasn't irrefutable proof the skeleton belonged to Laura Hudson.

Chloe had to suck in a careful breath. She could still picture the woman all these years later. Because Mrs. Hudson had been the kindergarten-room mom since Chloe had been in class with Mary, Jack's little sister. Laura had embodied everything a mother *should* be, and nothing Chloe had ever seen a mother be, so she'd been fascinated.

But worse than that memory was the fact that this discovery affected not just Jack but also Mary, one of her closest friends. Anna, their other sister. All those Hudsons.

They'd worked so hard, but the answers had always eluded them. And Chloe had never considered what it might mean—good and horrendously awful—if they finally got them.

She looked at Jack in the shadowy dark. No matter what it meant, he shouldn't be here. He needed to be with his family.

"I'll oversee this, then have Ry drive me back to my place. You go home."

"We both know your brother's license is suspended. You're not having him drive you anywhere."

"Fine. I'll have someone appropriately licensed drive me home."

Jack shook his head. Stubborn no matter what. "I don't like that."

"You've got bigger things to deal with." He'd want to tell his family before anyone got word of this. He *needed* to.

He swallowed, looked hard into the dark—the opposite direction from where that set of bones lay in the ground.

The ground of *her* family's ranch.

Would he be okay driving home on his own? Even if it wasn't confirmed, it was *possible* that this was his mother. He probably shouldn't be driving anywhere by himself.

This is Jack Hudson you're talking about. Still, the idea

of him driving by himself back to the Hudson Ranch after this… It didn't settle right.

"Maybe one of your brothers—"

"I can handle a two-mile drive." He snapped it out like an order. Boss to subordinate. But that wasn't really him, even when they *were* working, so she just nodded.

He needed to feel in control. She wasn't going to take that away from him in this moment. This horrible, awful, impossible moment.

"Then go," she told him. Because he didn't need to see the whole production once Bent County got out here. He didn't need to *see* any of this.

Still, he hesitated. She couldn't begin to imagine all the reasons he might have, but she reached out and put her hand on his shoulder. Friend to friend. Coworker to coworker. And, okay, whatever else they were when no one was around.

"Go. I've got this. You trust Deputy Brink to do her job. That's who I am right now."

His gaze finally met hers, dark. She couldn't read whatever lurked there—because he knew how to hide. Right in plain sight. Wasn't that the crux of so many of her problems with this man?

"I trust *you*, Chloe. Period," he muttered. Then he sighed, big and deep. "Promise me."

She could have pretended to misunderstand, but she knew him all too well. "I promise I won't let Ry drive me anywhere. Go. Be with your family. I'll get you an update once I have one."

She thought he might argue some more, but there was one indisputable fact about Jack Hudson. No matter how uptight, no matter how controlling, no matter how *everything*, his family came first.

So he walked back to his truck and went to them.

JACK WELCOMED THE numb feeling that settled over him. Numbness was better than pain, and pain was pointless until he had real answers. Even then…

If he thought he could hide this situation from his siblings until he had confirmation, he would have. But with Bent County involved, there were just too many ways the whispers would start.

And come knocking on the door of the Hudson Ranch.

So he drove home in the middle of the night, not sure how everything had just flipped on him. His entire adult life, suddenly different.

If that skeleton was his mother…

It wasn't a shock in that she was dead. He'd known both his parents had to be. There was no way they had disappeared on purpose. They'd been good parents, good people. They never would have left their six kids alone and defenseless.

Not on purpose.

So Jack and his siblings had known for a very long time that even if they ever found answers, there was no happy ending to this story.

But Jack had never fully realized, in all these years, how there had still been this awful bubble of hope inside him. A stray thought that they might be alive. That there might be a reason that wasn't terrible.

This strange little dream he might see them again someday.

And now that hope was gone.

It would take time to match the bones to his mother. It

would take more time to filter through all the evidence. So they were dealing in unknowns for a while yet, and Jack was no fan of dealing with those.

But in a place the size of Sunrise, with a cold case that still lingered in the town's entire identity—in the Hudson family's entire identity—he couldn't hold off going to his siblings with the facts.

He had to tell them the possibilities.

He didn't drive his truck to the outbuilding where they parked their vehicles. He parked right out front of the main house and was greeted by a couple of Cash's dogs. He didn't crouch to pet them like he usually did. He went straight for the front door, punched in the security code and then stepped inside.

The house was dark and quiet, but only for a moment. He heard a stair creak, and then the hall light came on, illuminating Mary. She was the oldest of his two younger sisters but still eight years younger than him. He'd been an adult when their parents disappeared. Well, eighteen. She'd been ten.

And still she'd stepped up. She'd helped with meals, with keeping school paperwork organized. As she'd gotten older, she'd taken on most of the administrative tasks of running Hudson Sibling Solutions *and* the Hudson Ranch.

"What are you doing up?" he asked.

She put a hand over her ever-growing stomach. Pretty soon there'd be another baby around here. Such a strange twist and turn of fate these past few years. Marriages and babies and *adulthood* for his younger siblings, far beyond what Jack had ever found for himself.

He'd been keeping as busy as possible lately to keep from thinking too much about that.

"I was up using the bathroom for the hundredth time and heard the alarm disengage and the door open. It's four in the morning. Did something come up?"

It would be easy to lie to Mary. Being sheriff gave him the perfect alibi for everything, but Mary tended to see right through him. And really, there was no point in putting her off. This had to be done.

"Yes, something came up that we all need to discuss."

He watched her hand tighten on the banister, but no sense of foreboding showed on her face. "What is it?" she asked calmly.

He couldn't tell her it wasn't serious like he wanted to. This was incredibly serious. "No one's in danger. But this is important. For all of us. Once everyone wakes up—"

"It seems like this is something that requires waking everyone up."

"It won't change anything. To wait."

Mary studied him for a few seconds. "Then it won't change anything to wake everyone up." She turned then, not waiting for him to agree or disagree.

Jack didn't follow, but slowly and quietly—no doubt for the sake of the still-sleeping kids, since his family usually didn't do anything quietly—his siblings began to arrange themselves in the living room.

Once everyone had settled, Mary nodded at him. She stood leaning against her husband, and Anna stood next to hers as well. Grant and Dahlia sat on the couch next to Cash. Carlyle stood behind Cash, clasping his hand at his shoulder. Palmer and Louisa settled themselves on an armchair.

Jack had gotten used to being a solitary figure long before his siblings had all coupled up. He'd been the man of the house. In charge. He'd needed that separation. To not be their brother anymore but to be the adult. To be in charge so he could keep everyone together until they were old enough to go on their own.

No one had. Oh, Grant had gone off to war; Mary to college; Palmer and Anna, the rodeo for a bit—but they'd all come back home. They'd all come back.

And now, in this moment, he was the only one who knew this terrible thing, and it killed him because he wanted to keep it that way. So his siblings would never have to feel this.

But it just wasn't possible. So he jumped right in. "There was a body uncovered on the Brink Ranch. It had been there for some time. Bent County will take on the investigation and attempt to identify the body, determine a cause of death."

"Why'd you wake us all up to tell us this, Jack?" Anna asked. With the kind of gravity like she knew exactly why.

"There was a ring with the remains. I recognized it right away. Mom's wedding ring."

There was a moment of complete and utter silence, everyone absorbing those words. Then Jack watched as every single member of his family turned to each other. Mary buried her head in her husband Walker's chest. Anna turned away, but Hawk pulled her back into an embrace. Louisa wound her arms around Palmer's waist, Cash's grip on Carlyle's hand tightened, and Dahlia rested her head on Grant's shoulder.

Jack tried to swallow the obstruction in his throat to ensure his voice was calm and clear. It came out rusty. "This is not incontrovertible proof, but it's—"

"What about Dad?" Anna demanded. Her voice was harsh, but there were tears in her eyes.

"I don't have any answers, Anna. All I have is a ring." He thought that admission might break him in two, but when his heart kept beating and his breath kept filling his lungs, he figured he'd survive. "Deputy Brink is handling it. We all know we can trust her to handle it."

"Except this was found on her family's ranch?" Palmer said, no doubt echoing some people's thoughts on the matter.

But Jack didn't need to defend Chloe. Mary did it first.

"That doesn't mean anything," she said, standing up for her friend. "I trust Chloe. No matter what."

"The Brinks—"

Carlyle cut off whatever Palmer was going to say. No doubt something about the Brinks and their connection to crime, drugs and a hell of a lot of trouble.

"The Bent County detectives will be the ones handling it, right?" Carlyle asked. "Hart and Laurel? They'll be doing the investigation, and we all know they're damn good at their jobs."

Thomas Hart and Laurel Delaney-Carson had worked with Cash and Carlyle a few months back, and their hard work had helped keep Cash from being blamed for his ex-wife's murder. Hart had also been involved in helping to solve a case last year when someone had tried to kill Anna.

They were both good detectives, and Jack trusted them. He had to.

"We'll be investigating too," Anna said.

"No," Jack said firmly, looking at his baby sister and the stubborn set of her chin. "We're staying out of this."

All eyes turned to him, surprise slackening every single person's features.

"Jack. You can't be serious," Grant said in his quiet way.

But Jack was very serious. He'd made this decision the minute he'd driven off the Brink Ranch. "This is a Bent County investigation. We will stay out of their way and let them investigate. There's nothing for us to do here."

"Do you have a head injury?" Anna demanded. "This is our parents we're talking about. *Our* seventeen-year-old cold case. Why the hell would we stay out of the way now that we actually have a lead?"

"Maybe once we have all the facts, we can decide to pursue it. But for now, we wait. Because none of us need to be involved in the details of our parents' remains." No one in this room needed to see what he'd seen tonight, needed to have that haunting them for the rest of their days.

For years, they'd tried to come up with clues to follow when it came to their parents' disappearance. For years, they'd gone over the campsite. Their parents' pasts. Anything and everything. That had seemed innocent enough. Important enough that they could all be in on the investigating.

But nothing had involved bodies. Nothing had involved the reality of their parents being dead. Not just dead—*bones.*

No. None of them needed to see it. "We'll give Bent County the space to handle the investigation. There's going to be talk around town. People will want to know what we think. I want us to be as quiet about it as we can until we know for sure what we're dealing with. Because we don't know yet. All we know is, we've uncovered a ring that used to be our mother's."

For a moment, that old hope tried to grow back, but he ruthlessly plucked that weed of a thought.

His parents were dead, and it was someone else's job to figure out how. And why.

Chapter Three

Chloe was bone tired, but a text or a phone call wasn't going to cut it. Not for this.

She hadn't been back home. When the police had arrived at the ranch, she'd stayed through everything. Even when it became clear what they were dealing with, and someone pointed out that Chloe was one of the landowners.

The detectives hadn't liked that, but she knew enough to avoid anyone hauling her off the property. Just like she knew enough to keep Ry from being hauled off too. Once she'd gotten as much out of Bent County officers as she knew she was going to get, she'd driven Ry back to her cabin and insisted he stay put.

She didn't know if he'd listen, but it didn't matter. She had to drive back out to the Hudson Ranch and update the family.

Eventually, Bent County would get around to filling them in, but they were likely still organizing information. Chloe had to get in and tell the Hudsons some things before Bent County did so the Hudsons could organize.

Jack probably had a plan in place already, but he didn't know...

Chloe pulled up to the main house on the Hudson Ranch with nothing but dread in her stomach. She was used to delivering bad news. It went hand in hand with the job. And in a town like Sunrise, she was often delivering bad news to people she knew and liked.

But this was different. On so many levels. Complicated levels. And she just didn't know how to arrange it all behind her usual cop facade.

She got out of her car and trudged toward the porch. She'd been to the Hudson house for a variety of reasons over the years, but never for the reason Jack came to her place. Set lines. Set boundaries. Ones she'd helped enact because she'd thought it would somehow keep her safe from all her soft feelings.

It hadn't, and she didn't like to be reminded of that. She straightened her shoulders, knocked on the door. She'd changed into her Sunrise SD polo and put on her badge in an attempt to *feel* official on the outside since she didn't feel it on the inside.

Mary answered. She was dressed for the day, prim and proper as usual, even with her big pregnant belly. She was clearly tired, though, but Chloe wasn't about to tell her that.

"Aren't you pretty."

Mary's smile was faint, and she rolled her eyes. "I'm puffy and exhausted and ready to be done. I'm guessing this isn't a social call," she said, nodding at Chloe's badge.

Chloe tried to keep her smile in place as she shook her head. "No, I thought I'd update you all before Bent County swoops in."

Mary nodded. "Come on. We're all in the dining room." Mary led her deep into the house. Normally, there would have been lots of conversation, arguing, shouts and dogs barking echoing through the house before Chloe even got close to the dining room.

This morning it was silent. When she entered the room, the only sound was the scraping of forks on plates, though she wasn't sure anyone was eating a lot.

The table was full, everyone—and there was a *lot* of *everyone* at this house—taking a seat. Paired up with their significant others. Cash's twelve-year-old flanked between him and Carlyle. Anna's baby tucked into her husband's arm.

And Jack, sitting at the head of the table. Surrounded by his family, and yet he looked so alone.

There was a chorus of unsure greetings from the table when Mary announced her arrival. Chloe refused a seat and a plate. "I just came to give you all a few updates. I'll be out of your hair in a few minutes."

It wasn't pure cowardice. She wanted to get out before Bent County showed up and asked why she was here. Besides, she had a shift to work.

"Izzy and I are going to go handle the dog chores," Carlyle said, her hand on Cash's twelve-year-old daughter's shoulder.

Chloe half expected the girl to argue. Even she knew Izzy didn't like to be shuffled off, but it seemed there'd already been discussion and agreement since she disappeared with Carlyle to take care of Cash's dogs without argument.

"Go on, then," Jack said, not unkindly but with that stoic detachment of his firmly in place.

"Another set of remains was found next to the first." Chloe had to resist the urge to clear her throat, but she couldn't resist the urge to look at Jack, to try to see what he was really feeling under that mask of stoicism.

Mostly, she figured no one would see that lost look to his

dark eyes. They'd see the grim expression, the hard line of his mouth, and think he had it under control.

He didn't. Chloe knew he didn't, and she knew he'd die before admitting it to anyone. Even himself.

"Any identifying information?" he asked.

"They wouldn't tell me anything, but I took a slightly illegal and unauthorized picture of some evidence they gathered. I can show whoever is willing to bend the rules a little bit what I've got."

Immediately, most of the Hudsons crowded around her as she took out her phone. She pulled the picture up on the screen and tried not to betray her surprise when Jack stepped close enough in front of her to see it as well.

"You already saw one ring, Jack, but there was a ring with the other remains as well. They're both in this evidence bag." She zoomed in on the picture so they could see the rings.

Then she looked up at Jack. He didn't have to say anything. Chloe could see it in his eyes.

He nodded.

Chloe knew it would be Dean Hudson's wedding band, but maybe she'd hoped... Oh, she didn't know. There was very little possibility the two skeletal remains weren't the missing Hudson parents.

She had to remind herself to look away from Jack, to focus on her job. "The detectives will be by to fill you guys in. To ask questions, I'm sure. I...tried to convince them to let me, but it was a no go."

"It's best if it's a third party," Jack said. "We're all staying out of it, letting Bent County do their job."

Chloe opened her mouth to say something, but she forgot what because that didn't make *any* sense. "I'm sorry. What?"

"See?" Anna muttered. "Staying out of it doesn't make any sense."

But Jack's expression remained firm, and he didn't look at Anna. "Thanks for the update, Deputy Brink, but we think—"

"*You* think," Palmer interjected.

"—it's best if we let police handle this."

"Oh. Well, sure." She had just been resoundingly dismissed. She was so shocked by it, so confused by Jack's unusual response, she just stood there for a moment, not quite sure what to do.

"Are you sure you don't want any breakfast, Chloe?" Mary asked.

Chloe shook her head. No. She needed to leave. She needed... She glanced at Jack. He was calmly sipping from his coffee mug. But she recognized those careful, mild movements.

They were very deliberate. Very *careful*, like he was holding himself braced for a blow. He'd looked like that when Louisa had been kidnapped last year, when Anna had been in the hospital—basically any time a member of his family was in trouble, it was like there was a ticking time bomb inside he was doing everything he could not to detonate.

And it was *none* of her business. "Well, I'm heading into my shift. I'll..." She didn't know what to say if they didn't want insider updates on the whole thing. Well, not *they*. Jack.

But Jack ran the show. This time she had to clear her throat in order to speak. "I'll see you all later."

She turned on a heel, and she had no idea why she felt

emotional. And just so very, very alone. But she walked out of the house having to work way too hard to fight back tears.

She just needed rest. After she worked her shift, she'd sleep. Of course, first she'd have to deal with what she was going to do with her brother. Which was a whole other headache she didn't have any answers for.

Before she could reach the bottom of the porch stairs, she heard Jack say her name.

She closed her eyes and sucked in a breath. Repeated her *Be strong* mantra a few times before she turned to face him.

"Thank you for coming out," he said, a little stiffly. "We appreciate the update."

She couldn't help but be amused despite everything churning inside her. She knew them all a little too well. "Mary made you come say that."

One side of his mouth *almost* curved. "My siblings can't *make* me do anything."

"But she did. Because she's Mary, and *she* can make you do things. Especially when she's that pregnant."

He shrugged, not refuting it. He squinted out at the mountains, the pretty Hudson Ranch, and didn't say anything. But he didn't leave either.

And she knew he *shouldn't* since he had all that family under his very own roof, but she could see the loneliness on him. Because like recognized like.

"They'll run tests," she said reassuringly. Maybe she didn't understand the hands-off stance he was taking, but she wanted him to know it was handled. "They'll do what they can to determine when. How."

"I know how it works, Chloe."

It was ridiculous the little thrill she got out of this man calling her by her first name when he damn well *should*.

It wasn't like they were at work. "Sometimes it's good to hear someone else say what you already know."

He didn't say anything to that, and she knew she should go. *Had* to get out of here soon. But she just couldn't step away from him when he seemed so alone.

"They're not going to let me within a hundred feet of this case since my name is on the deed of the land. They've already questioned Ry. I'll be next."

"What about your parents?"

She shrugged, trying not to go on the defensive. He had every right to ask that question. Hell, *she'd* asked that question. "I imagine they'll do that too. But they'll have to get down to Texas to visit Dad in prison—and if they have better luck tracking down my mother than I ever have, more power to them. I'll be first because I'm here. Because I was there."

"I was there with you."

"I didn't mention it."

"Chloe. I called it in."

She shrugged. "You can always say I called you first and then you called it in."

"Why would I lie about that?"

"You know why, Jack."

"I know why *you* think I should lie, but I don't think you have any clue what *I* think."

She had no business getting pissed at him over relationship stuff. Mostly because she was just as much to blame for *everything* involved in this, but also because now so clearly wasn't the time.

But she was tired, and she was feeling all emotional over too many things to count, and *he* was the one who'd brought it up. So she snapped. "Oh, really? Then enlighten me. What does the almighty Jack Hudson think?"

"You think it's because I'm embarrassed. Because of your family or because I'm your boss."

"That's not embarrassing, Jack. It's unethical. Something you are historically very opposed to." She looked up at him to give him a kind of *so there* smirk, but his expression was serious, his gaze steady, and when he spoke, he spoke with all the gravity of the truth.

"I'm not embarrassed of you, Chloe. Not in the least."

Her foolish heart felt as though it actually skipped a beat. Was she really this pathetic?

Yes, yes you are. When it comes to him, you always have been.

She swallowed, trying to find some retort that would settle all this terrible longing inside her, but she heard the sound of a car approaching and turned toward it.

Not just any car. A Bent County cruiser was driving up the gravel road when Chloe had been planning to get out of here before they showed up. Because no doubt the detectives were inside.

"Damn," she muttered.

"Don't worry. I'm going to protect you, Chloe," Jack said, like that made any sense. But before she could ask him what on earth he was talking about, he was striding forward to meet the detectives.

JACK DEALT WITH the detectives. He didn't lie to them about being with Chloe when her brother called, but he didn't explain either. Since the detectives were more concerned with identifying the remains, keeping Sunrise SD out of the proceedings and the Brink family connection to the

Hudson family, they didn't prod for answers. It wasn't relevant to the case.

He wouldn't let it be. He'd protect her reputation. No matter what.

The detectives didn't share any breaking new information. Next steps were with the forensic anthropologist and the assurance that all the Brinks would be questioned.

He might have balked at that, but at the end of the day, it was clear the remains had been in the ground for some time. Long enough that Chloe and Ry would have been kids when it happened. Maybe the detectives thought they'd seen something, heard something, would remember something from back then, but Jack doubted it.

First, Chloe would have said long ago. And even Ry didn't seem like the type who could keep his mouth shut about much. That's half of why he got in so much trouble. No criminal mastermind, there. Just a kid with no direction who'd gotten mixed up with drugs.

It amazed him, regularly, that Chloe had somehow come out of all that to be the good cop and good person she was.

She'd left pretty quickly after the detectives had arrived, having to get to her shift, and Jack had taken the detectives inside, working with Mary to gather all the information they had on their parents' case. He handed over years' worth of files.

"You don't want to make copies?" Laurel asked with a raised eyebrow.

"We have most of this stuff digitized, but we're happy to hand over anything that might help you get to the bottom of this." He ignored the disapproving look on Mary's face.

Hart looked from Mary to Jack, a handful of files now

in his grasp. "It's going to be best if you guys stay out of it for now."

Jack nodded. "We plan to."

"You forget I've had to deal with your family before, Sheriff," Laurel offered with a smile, as if to put some kind of friendly spin on things. Jack didn't particularly feel like being friendly.

"I've made it clear to my family our best course of action is to step back and let you all do your job. I can't promise they'll listen, but I'll do my best to control the situation." That was what he'd done for the past seventeen years. No reason to stop now.

Hart and Laurel shared a look, clearly not believing him. But they didn't press the matter.

"We'll keep you as informed as we can. We're going to be looking into the disappearance again, but no real answers can come until the forensic anthropologist gives us a report. We don't have a timetable on that."

Jack nodded. He'd never dealt with a case like this, so he wasn't fully abreast of the procedure, but he knew the general proceedings when anyone had to call in outside agencies for help. No doubt it would be a long, drawn-out process. Even more reason for his family to stay out of it. Focus on the lives they were building, cases that needed their attention, the ranch.

Mary showed the detectives back out, and Jack tried not to think about how long this was going to drag out. How much he was going to have to deal with the speculation at work. How difficult it was going to be to keep his family reined in.

But difficult was the name of the game, wasn't it? It wasn't like things had been particularly easy lately. Sure, his siblings had paired off, some of them starting families, but there had been danger and threat at every turn.

No rest for the wicked.

And still, he just stood in the office where they kept their paper files and stared blankly at the now-empty drawer. Sixteen years of work. Research. Investigation. And he was just handing it over to two people who'd never met his parents.

Who'd never been hugged by his mother or listened to one of his father's corny jokes. People who'd never been surrounded by the love that Laura and Dean Hudson had imbued every last interaction with.

They hadn't been perfect people. He knew that. But they'd been good.

And he thought he'd grieved over it a long, long time ago.

He knew, mired in all this old grief, he was absolutely doing the right thing for his family. Maybe he couldn't save them from going through this all over again, but if he could make a buffer, a wall between them and all this old hurt, he would consider it a success.

"For the record, I may not agree fully, but I understand what you're doing."

Jack turned toward Mary, who was standing in the doorway, arms across her chest and resting on her pregnant belly. Expression disapproving even if her words were about understanding.

"What's that?"

"Trying to protect us from the harsh reality that our parents were murdered, put in a shallow grave some seventeen years ago, and we never would have found the answers if not for Ry Brink's random and likely drug-fueled decision to dig a hole."

Jack felt something inside him constrict at the tidy, emotionless way Mary laid out the truth.

"You saw something you don't want us to have to see," she continued.

He tried to block the image of that ring and bones from his mind, but he couldn't quite manage it.

"I think if you were honest about that, you'd have more of us supporting you. Even Anna might relent a little if she knew—"

"Hawk will keep her in line."

"I can't believe you just said that. Out loud. And no bolt of lightning came to strike you down like it very well should."

"I didn't mean it like that. I just mean he loves her. He'll protect her, and that means keeping her from diving head-first into all this." Not that Jack was sure he'd succeed, but Hawk was the only chance of Anna actually listening. So Jack would depend on it.

Mary was silent for a long while. "Sometimes love isn't about protecting people, Jack. Sometimes it's just about loving them." She didn't wait for him to have any answer to that. She just left.

Jack refused to engage with that sentiment. It was his normal weekend off from the sheriff's department anyway, so he went out and did some ranch chores. He went through his *normal* day, trying to shut everything off.

But it only seemed to settle deeper, tying tight, heavy knots in his gut, in his chest. Every step, every breath became harder. Every minute that ticked by seemed to be leading somewhere terrible.

Only nothing out of the ordinary happened. He had a normal dinner with his family. Well, not *normal*. There was a heavy quiet that had taken over the house today. Even baby Caroline appeared to have gotten the memo and wasn't overly fussy or energetic. No one could seem to muster a conversation that didn't immediately lull into silence.

People excused themselves earlier than usual. No one ate dessert. Jack had cleanup duty with Carlyle, whose nervous energy seemed to suck all his own energy away. Or maybe it was the fact that he hadn't really slept.

Once she'd brought all the dishes into the kitchen, she paused, staring at him. Since he'd never known her to hesitate over just about anything, he raised an eyebrow. "Something you wanted to say?"

"Cash wanted me to run it by you first, but I figure I'd tell Zeke," she said, referring to her brother *not* mixed up in the Hudson household. "He's got all those crazy connections to underground spy people. I know you want Bent County handling it, but Zeke might have a line on a good... What did they call it? Forensic person or whatever? He knows some people who could poke around, and they wouldn't get in Bent County's way."

Jack wanted to dismiss it out of hand. He wanted to dismiss everything out of hand, but the more people looking into this who weren't his family, the quicker this could move. "That'd be fine, Carlyle. Thank you for asking."

They worked in silence for a while; then, just about when they were finished and he thought he could escape to the isolation of his bedroom, Carlyle said something that stopped him in his tracks.

"Chloe's a good listener."

Jack turned his head slowly to stare at her. Her blue-gray eyes held his, but she didn't look accusatory or like she was holding some secret over his head.

She shrugged. "I just know, from experience, sometimes you don't want to, like…be a burden to your family. And I could sit here and lecture you for a million days how you're not, but it doesn't change the feeling you don't want to unload on the people also going through what you're going through."

"What does that have to do with Deputy Brink?"

Carlyle rolled her eyes. "*Chloe's* a good listener. That's all I'm saying." Then she shrugged and left the kitchen.

Leaving Jack standing there, breathing a little too hard. It wasn't concern that Carlyle knew he had a more-than-working relationship with Chloe. He'd had a bad feeling for a while that Carlyle had some inkling of what was going on between them. But she'd never come out and said anything, and Carlyle wasn't exactly *subtle*.

It was Mary's words about love. Carlyle's words about unloading on people. It was the oppressive silence in the house, like grief had tightened its ugly chains around the whole ranch once again.

He didn't want it to. That first year after losing his parents had been the hardest damn year of his life—all their lives—and he didn't want it touching any of his siblings again. Ever again.

But here it was, and he couldn't seem to breathe. Couldn't seem to find a solution. No amount of keeping them separate from the realities seemed to change what they were all feeling internally.

Sad and shaken and quiet.

Except there was something else inside him. A tightening in his chest, a struggle to breathe. The pressure of seventeen years beating down on him, like someone pounding a stake into the ground, and he was the stake.

He was half-afraid he was having some kind of cardiac event, but there was no shooting pain in his arm. No losing consciousness. Just this overwhelming *pressure*—worse but not all that different from when things went off-plan.

Panic attack.

To hell with that. Just to hell with it. He strode out of the kitchen, out the back door and toward his truck. Normally, he'd make sure someone knew where he was, but he couldn't. He just couldn't.

He had to get out, and even though he wouldn't admit to himself where he was going, it didn't surprise him to pull off onto the shoulder of the road that led up to Chloe's cabin fifteen minutes later.

He didn't turn into the driveway. He idled on the shoulder, staring at the front door. She likely had Ry in there. She wouldn't want her brother staying out at the ranch when he was unpredictable, and likely there was some police presence still. So this was a pointless endeavor. He wasn't going inside. He wasn't going to use her like some kind of crutch.

He did just fine on his own. Had for sixteen years. He'd finished raising a family. He'd built a business, been a cop, become sheriff. There wasn't anything he couldn't control. All on his own.

And still he fished his phone out of his pocket. Still he brought up a text message to Chloe.

He shouldn't do this. He knew he shouldn't. That was the wildest part of everything that had happened with Chloe since he'd let his guard down at that ridiculous party last year. She had touched him, wearing that excuse for a dress, and it had upended something inside.

Every finely tuned, rule-following, controlled, upstanding rule he'd set for himself, killed himself to follow…

He'd break, every time, when it came to her. Just like he was doing right now, typing out the text.

You want to go for a drive?

She didn't respond, but not two minutes later the door to the cabin opened, and she stepped outside. Her hair was wet, and she was wearing sweatpants and a sweatshirt, but she smiled at him and walked toward his truck, her cat in her arms.

And weirdly, he could breathe again.

Chapter Four

Chloe hopped into the passenger side of Jack's truck, Tiger in her grasp. The minute she was settled, the cat immediately escaped and made a beeline for Jack's lap.

He looked rough. Oh, he hid it well. The stoic expression. The way, somehow, even though he likely hadn't slept at all, he looked as alert and in control as he always did.

But she saw the little things. The way his hand gripped the steering wheel. The impossibly tense clench of his jaw.

She wanted to reach across and rub her palm against it until he relaxed. But she didn't. Not yet. She wasn't quite sure what this was yet. Truth be told, she was always waiting for him to drop the hammer. End this. Just because he hadn't yet didn't mean he never would.

But he had a lot more than *her* on his mind right now, and she doubted he had the mental capacity to finally come to his senses when it came to whatever they were doing.

"So, where we driving to?" She didn't explain Ry was staying at her cabin. If he hadn't already known it, he would have come up to her door.

"I… I'm not sure," he said.

Worry slithered through her. She wondered if she'd ever once heard Jack say those three words. She tried to sound cheerful and unbothered, though. An anchor to how lost he seemed. "How about up around the scenic viewpoint?"

He nodded. "Yeah, that sounds good." He started driving, never once looking over at her. He drove with one hand on the wheel and one hand on Tiger, down the highway toward the turnoff that would lead up and around one of the smaller peaks, with pretty views out over the larger mountain range as a whole.

But not long after they'd passed the main entrance to the Hudson Ranch, he took a sharp and unexpected turn off the highway. Chloe had to grab on to the dash to keep from slamming into the door.

"Uh, where are we going?"

"Just a different place I know." His expression was grim, and even though he was making her a little nervous, she didn't say anything or ask any more questions. She just sat back and tried to figure it out herself.

It was a side road, but she was pretty sure they were on Hudson property. Confirmed when they drove past Palmer's new house that he and Louisa had finished about the time they'd gotten married.

Then the road changed from gravel to dirt and started going…up. Chloe's grip on whatever she could find tightened. She looked over at Tiger, whose eyes were half-closed as if it was naptime.

Meanwhile, Chloe's throat constricted, and her entire body tensed as it began to feel like they were driving straight up. Up the mountain. Chloe didn't consider herself squeamish about much, but narrow mountain roads weren't her favorite. That was why she'd suggested the overlook—the road up to it was paved and well maintained.

When he came to a stop and shoved his truck into Park,

at such an angle gravity had her practically pressed to her door, she realized she'd been holding her breath. She let it out shakily, and Jack looked over at her.

For the first time today, she saw that grave, expression in his eyes turn to humor, which made her entire being *flutter*.

"Sorry. Forgot you get panicky about heights."

"Not panicky. Just not keen on tumbling to my death in a truck."

"Yeah, that's not panicky at all. Come on." He got out of the truck, Tiger in his arms like it was normal to carry a cat around. But for some reason, that cat looked content as could be wrapped up in Jack's arms.

Yeah, you know the feeling, don't you?

He grabbed a blanket from the back of his truck, tucked it under his free arm and then began marching toward some unknown point. He never said a word. She scurried after his long strides. She didn't mind heights when she was on her own two feet—or at least, that's what she tried to tell herself. Especially when Jack kept walking right up to the edge of what looked a hell of a lot like a cliff.

Chloe stepped very carefully behind him, but once she looked up from her feet, she stopped short.

"Jack," she breathed.

She'd seen a lot of pretty views. Sunrise and Bent County were full of them. She'd spent summers enjoying everything the Tetons and Yellowstone had to offer. She'd even gone up to Glacier with a friend from the police academy one summer. All those places had been awe-inspiring, gorgeous. It was amazing what the natural world could be.

But this was… She couldn't explain it. Not just the natural beauty of mountain and sky and land stretched out as far as the eye could see. There was something like a peaceful settling inside her. Like all her life, she'd been looking for this exact view, and now she'd finally found it.

The sun was sinking in the sky, but it wasn't sunset just yet. The world had taken on a softer, pinker hue, though. And Jack Hudson stood there, at the edge of this little out-cropping, holding her *cat*, and she knew she'd just…never get over him. Not in a million years.

One-handed, he spread out the blanket until she crouched to help him. Then they both sat down on it. The cat stayed curled in Jack's lap, definitely not about to give up comfort for the wild world around them.

This time she didn't resist the urge. She smoothed her hand down his jaw. He didn't relax, but he did turn to her. And when she wrapped her arms around him, all comfort, he accepted.

And finally, *some* of that tension left him.

Maybe when all was said and done, it wasn't the fantastic sex; it wasn't that he was so handsome or so good. It was this.

She seemed to be the only one who could comfort Jack Hudson. To ease that tension, to release some of those burdens he'd been perfecting carrying for so long. *She* had that power, and for all the ways this relationship was messed up and messy, she couldn't walk away from that.

When she pulled away, she didn't pull far. She leaned her head against his shoulder, and he rested his head atop hers while they both looked out at the sun's slow descent.

JACK DIDN'T REALLY know what he was doing. In so many different ways. He couldn't keep getting more and more mixed up with Chloe when he couldn't offer her anything except complications He didn't have time to just be *sitting* here, enjoying the feel of her head on his shoulder. There were things to do—ranch things, sheriff things, family things.

And still he sat, soaking in this moment in one of his favorite places on the ranch. The terms of his parents' will had been that he inherited the main house. The other kids had their pick of equal parcels of land once they reached eighteen, and Palmer had already staked out his. Grant was looking at one closer to the main road since Dahlia worked in town as the librarian. Mary and Anna seemed content to stay put in the main house and have their portions of land dedicated to the ranch, and Jack hoped they would always. Cash was still deciding what to do next after his cabin had been destroyed.

Jack had been in the main-floor bedroom since his parents had disappeared, and part of him figured he'd stay there till he croaked.

But he'd always secretly wanted to build a little house right here and wake up to that view every morning.

He shouldn't have brought Chloe here. She'd be part of that fantasy now too. And it was a fantasy neither of them could really afford.

Speaking of fantasies. "They're not going to listen to me, are they?"

She was quiet for a long while, and he wondered if he'd have to explain. He didn't want to. He already wished he hadn't said anything.

"I think you'd be surprised how much they'd listen to you if you were honest with them."

It made him think of Mary's little speech about love and protection. He didn't fully agree with her, but he understood a certain level of detachment in trying to hold everyone together, in trying to raise his siblings, had led to them thinking he was something of a benevolent dictator.

He didn't mind that. Maybe he even relished it a little bit since it made things easier. But it meant he'd lost the ability to know how to explain to them this was important. That his *protection* did come from love, no matter what Mary said.

"Then again, once they think about it, they'll probably figure out what you're actually doing."

"What's that?"

"Protecting them. It's what you're always doing. Everyone knows it. Sometimes you just irritate them enough with it, they can't see the forest through the trees."

"And what's the forest?"

"Love, Jack."

The word landed hard, right there at the center of his chest. He even tensed against it, and wished he hadn't because she'd no doubt feel it. But she didn't lift her head or scoot away. They sat there together. That silence wrapping around him like a cocoon, like a soft place to land.

Like the one place he could let his guard down enough to speak the truth. "I didn't realize that I still had this ridiculous hope they were still alive."

She rubbed a hand up and down his back, and he thought maybe he'd survive all this crushing weight if she kept doing that.

"Hope is the human condition," she said, a little too philosophically for his taste. But she shrugged and kept going. "No matter how many times he proves me wrong, I hope *this* time will be the time Ry gets clean, gets his life together. Sometimes I have this awful daydream that my mother comes back and wants to bake Christmas cookies together."

"Ouch."

"Yeah. Life's kind of an ouch."

"That's why I keep trying to turn into a robot."

Which made her laugh. A rare thing. Oh, she laughed with Mary, with Anna, with just about everyone. But not as much with him as he would've liked.

She lifted her head from his shoulder, stretched forward and squinted out at the sunset. Then she turned back and met his gaze.

"You're not much of an avoider, Jack. So why'd you come out here?" She didn't ask the other question that hung in the air: *Why'd you come get me?*

Which he didn't have an answer for. Not one that did them any good anyway. So he answered the one she'd voiced. "It's like all those years I did my best to clean the ghosts out of that house, and now they're all back."

"Maybe they aren't so much ghosts as…legacy."

"Is that different?"

"Sort of. You loved your parents. They loved you. You guys had—*have*—a great family because they built it on a legacy of love. That was always going to hurt when a piece of it was lost, but it's also like this…really cool thing. Because you've got Izzy and Caroline—and whatever Mary's going to name the baby, which she *refuses* to tell me even though I know they've decided. They're all getting raised in that same legacy even though they'll never get to meet the people who started it. Not everyone gets that, Jack. Which doesn't mean it's not sad or doesn't hurt, especially losing them the way you did, especially having to relive it now. It just means…sad isn't all bad. Sometimes ghosts can be a comfort instead of something to run from."

He knew a lot of people saw him as brave, strong. That

whole saint thing again. No one seemed to understand he always felt like he was running from something.

Except Chloe.

He wanted her. To come home with him, to share his bed. Not just because of sexual chemistry but also because of this. The moments where it felt like she was the only one he could lean on when he'd spent so many years refusing to lean on anyone.

She managed to find just the right access point to crack him open. He'd never understand how or why; he just knew that she did. And when he leaned on her, he didn't feel guilty or ashamed. She never let him.

Somehow it figured it'd be one of the few women in his life who was completely off-limits.

"We should get back."

She nodded, and that was that. She collected Tiger, against the cat's protests. Jack shook out the blanket, and then they walked back to his truck and drove all the way to Chloe's cabin without saying a single word.

He pulled into the drive this time, idling. She let Tiger out of the vehicle and then got out herself, but she leaned in.

"You don't have to wait for me to get in the door, Jack. I'm a big girl."

He nodded.

But he waited all the same.

Chapter Five

Chloe knew he wouldn't drive away just because she'd told him to. He'd wait until she got inside. She supposed it should irritate or frustrate her, but considering her parents hadn't cared that much about her when she'd been a *child*, she couldn't muster up taking offense to Jack's tendency to overprotect.

Hell, she didn't just not take offense—she downright loved it. She'd been taking care of herself and everyone else for as long as she could remember. She'd even dedicated her life to a job that protected other people, best she could.

Yeah, she didn't mind someone out there caring enough to protect *her* for once.

And that is why you find yourself in a dysfunctional, secret relationship.

So lost in her own thoughts, she nearly stepped on something on her porch, but she pulled her foot back in the nick of time.

A snake. Maybe two. Except not *full* snakes. Chunks. Mutilated. Chopped into pieces strewn about her pretty porch. She might have been able to convince herself it was the work of an animal except for the fact that the head of one was sticking out from one of her planters of cheerful pansies. *That* was pointed, and it made her stomach turn over a little bit.

"Call it in."

She nearly jumped a foot. She'd been caught so off guard by the snake, she hadn't heard Jack come up to see what had made her stop.

"Jack, it's a sick prank."

"Fine. I'll call it in."

She looked away from the gruesome sight and scowled at him. "Jack Hudson, you will not waste Sunrise's resources on something so pointless."

"Okay. You've called it in to me. I'll take the report. And the pictures." He patted his pockets, pulled out his phone and started taking pictures of the splattered remains.

"You're not on duty."

"I'm the sheriff. I'm always on duty."

Chloe rolled her eyes, but there was, per usual, no arguing with him. He took the pictures. He noted the time, looked around the house for footprints or tire prints that didn't belong to him or her cruiser.

Chloe went to the garage to figure out what she could use to clean it all up. Part of her wanted to make Ry do it, because God knew this probably had to do with him, but then he'd be out here with Jack, and she tried to keep them from being in the same orbit as much as she could.

Embarrassed of your own brother. What a great sister you are.

She strode into her garage, pushing away those old thoughts. Because Ry *was* embarrassing. He made bad choices she didn't approve of, and while that might not reflect on who *she* was as a person, while she might not be able to take over and stop him from those bad decisions, they *did* still affect her, and she got to have feelings about that.

She was a *damn* good sister, considering what her baby brother had put her through.

She blew out a long breath, attempting to get her rioting feelings under control. How ridiculous that they were more about Jack and her brother than chunks of mutilated snake all over her porch.

Maybe Jack was right, and this was connected to last night. If she removed all feeling from the situation, it was plausible. But there were a *lot* of plausible explanations. Especially since her brother was staying with her right now and he was a beacon for trouble.

She got a shovel, then trudged back to the front porch. For all the ways she was used to Jack taking over, it still surprised her when he tried to grab the shovel out of her hand.

"I've got it."

"I'll do it," he replied. "You just want it buried out back, right?"

There was that forever internal fight. Let someone else handle it versus handle it herself. Jack was the only one in her acquaintance whose stubbornness ever matched her own, and it had made her complacent. She didn't want to be that.

Except she didn't want to fight him. She let him take the shovel, scoop up the snake remains—he'd even gotten some gloves from his truck and picked out the one in her flowerpot. Then he buried it all while she stood there... internally arguing with herself.

And still, per usual, she came to no answers. Because Jack was...

A problem.

Once he was finished, he put the shovel away himself, not even asking her where it went. Still, she knew he'd put it in the exact right place. And there was something about the current situation—the potential that his parents had been murdered and buried on her family's ranch—that made her fully realize just what had made him this way.

She liked to think *Oh, that's just Jack Hudson*, but it was more, wasn't it? Trauma. Through and through. He'd been forced to take care of five siblings and a ranch at *eighteen*. And instead of faltering, instead of losing himself in drugs or bad behavior as her brother had with all their trauma, Jack Hudson had built himself into *this*.

It was amazing. But more than that, for the first time, she really just felt sorry for him. The pressure he must have put on himself. The sheer weight he carried on those broad shoulders and probably didn't even realize it. Probably didn't even think to share it.

Because he'd always had to do it on his own.

It made a lump form in her throat because she knew all too well what that felt like, and still she knew he'd taken on more.

When he returned to her on the porch, his expression was grim. "I want you to come stay at the ranch."

Okay, *that* was a step too far, even with all this emotion swirling around inside her. "Honestly, Jack, what do you think this is besides some bad joke? Either by one of Ry's friends or some kids whose beer I poured out last week or maybe the guy I arrested for domestic assault last month or—"

"Two skeletal remains were found on property you partially own last night, then it just so happens you get a threatening prank at your cabin today? That's enough cause. Go on inside and get Ry."

She blinked, so taken aback by all this that she felt like she'd forgotten how to fight when her whole life had been about the fight. "For what?"

"He's coming too. I'll call Mary. We'll have two rooms ready."

For a long time she could only stare at him. Ry at the Hudson Ranch? Ry with *all* the Hudsons. And her. No. "Jack, Ry isn't…"

"I know what Ry is and what he isn't," Jack returned. "You're both going to be looked after until we get to the bottom of this."

Chloe felt like she couldn't breathe. *Looked after.* It was one thing in secret. It was another thing if he was *looking after* things in front of his family. Another thing if Ry was involved.

"Jack, we can't…"

"I understand your reticence, Chloe, I do," he said, his voice low and less cop-Jack and more the Jack he only ever was when they were alone together. "But this is concerning. I can't just ignore it, and I can't just let you handle it on your own when you've got Ry and a job to contend with and this could be… We don't have the first clue what happened here or with my parents. Until we do, we have to act with all the caution in the world so no one else gets hurt."

He tried to hide it, but she could easily see all that grief he'd talked about up at the overlook there in his dark eyes, and she didn't know how to argue with that. So she went inside to tell her brother they were going to stay at the Hudson Ranch.

JACK LET CHLOE drive Ry and Tiger over to the ranch in her personal car, though it pained him. They both had a shift tomorrow, so he could drive her to her cabin on the way into Sunrise headquarters and pick up her patrol car.

Maybe this whole thing was an overreaction. He could admit that he did that sometimes when it came to people's safety. But the saying *Better safe than sorry* was his own personal mantra. Maybe it *was* someone who was ticked off Chloe had arrested them, and she was as trained and capable of handling it as anyone, but it could just as easily be a threat that pertained to last night's discovery. And that made everything more tenuous.

Either way, someone had laid a threat at her door. The real shock was, she hadn't really fought him on it. She'd gone inside, collected her things and her brother—maintaining a clear barrier between him and Ry.

Jack wasn't sure which one of them she didn't trust, truth be told. He was pretty sure she had a clear head when it came to her brother, but Jack also understood—even though his siblings tended to stay on the right side of the law—how easily someone you felt responsible for could blind you to the reality of a situation.

Jack pulled up to the main house, Chloe parking her car next to his truck. It was dark now, but the external house lights were on, along with a few internal.

Ry looked up at the house with wide eyes as he got out of Chloe's car. Jack understood the mind of an addict a little too well. He was likely adding up how many hits he could get for the different things he saw. Jack hoped for Chloe's sake that Ry could keep it together for this.

Ry didn't say anything. Chloe seemed pretty determined

to keep him and Jack from speaking at all, and Jack had no problem with that. He led them inside to where Mary was pacing the living room, Walker looking on disapprovingly from one of the armchairs.

"What happened?" Mary demanded. Not of Jack but of Chloe.

"Your brother overreacting?" She crouched and let Tiger go. The cat went all of three steps to lean against his leg.

"A mutilated snake was very purposefully strewn all over Chloe's porch sometime this evening," Jack said, trying to keep any and all inflection out of his voice.

Mary's expression pinched. "Then I have to agree with Jack about you guys coming here. That timing... When you've never had anything like that happen—and then all of the sudden, bones and snakes. I don't like it."

"Well, you've got us in your clutches now. The magical Hudson Ranch, where nothing bad happens," Chloe said, irreverently, of course.

Jack's scowl deepened, but he didn't have to defend his position. Mary did it for him, and Jack was well aware Mary's very pregnant belly helped soften the message, and Chloe's belligerence.

"We have an extensive security system. You won't even get one of those doorbell cameras at your cabin."

Chloe wrinkled her nose. "Those can't protect you. All they can do is potentially identify whoever might be engaging in criminal behavior in their view."

Jack narrowly resisted rolling his eyes.

"Well, we've got some rooms made up. Follow me and I'll show you where to put your things. Are you hungry? We'll get you all set up." Mary was ushering them out of the room and up the stairs before anyone had a chance to answer any of her questions.

Walker was standing now, frowning at the stairs after his wife. "I tried to tell her to relax and let someone else handle it."

"Yeah, how'd that work out for you?"

Walker grinned. "Yeah, well, I know she's exhausted, because she let me help make the beds."

"Are you sure you shouldn't take her to a hospital right now?"

"That's not funny. I tried."

Jack chuckled. If there was anything that gave him *some* level of comfort, it was the fact that his siblings had all ended up with people who tried to take care of them and ran into the same roadblocks he always did.

"This whole snake thing seems pretty personal. Meant to make her scared," Walker said, growing serious.

Jack nodded because he agreed with the assessment, but he didn't say anything else because he could also tell Walker was fishing.

"The thing is, stuff like that only scares you if you know why you're being threatened."

Jack tried not to tense. Failed. "First of all, she wasn't scared. Not nearly scared enough for the situation. Second, I've known Chloe a long time. She's one of my best deputies. She doesn't know anything, or she would have said."

"What about the brother?"

Jack's mouth firmed. He wasn't any fan of defending Ry Brink. The guy had given Chloe a lot of grief over the years, and Jack figured he'd earned all the negative talk aimed his way. But… "I'm not saying Ry couldn't be involved in *something*, but those bones were buried on the

Brink property a long, long time ago. Chloe *and* Ry would have been kids when it happened."

"Kids know things, too, Jack."

Unfortunately, Jack couldn't argue with that.

Chapter Six

Chloe didn't sleep well. When she caught snatches, she
had dreams of skeletons and snakes. Her subconscious was
real subtle.

The sun was only a faint glow in her window when she
gave up and got out of bed. She'd check on Ry, go for a run
and then figure out a way to sneak some coffee without
having to sit down to a whole Hudson breakfast.

She considered tracking down her traitorous cat, but she
had a feeling she knew exactly where Tiger would be this
morning, and it was best if Chloe stayed away.

Satisfied with her plan, she got dressed in her running
clothes, then quietly left the bedroom Mary had put her in
last night. She knocked on the door next to hers—no answer. She eased the door open, but the room was empty.
Dread curled in her stomach.

She thought she'd scared Ry enough into staying put,
into not causing trouble, but when had that ever been the
case?

She berated herself as she did her best to *silently* hurry
down the stairs. She needed to make sure he'd left and
wasn't wreaking havoc somewhere on Hudson property. Or
sneaking around this house trying to sniff out some booze.

But when she reached the bottom of the stairs, she

breathed a small sigh of relief. Ry was there, creeping toward the front door. Maybe he'd slept and was only now considering his escape. She certainly hoped so.

"What the hell are you doing?" she hissed at him.

He jumped and whirled. Then his shoulders slumped in relief when his eyes landed on her. "I wasn't doing nothing," he whispered right back.

She didn't bother to correct his grammar like she might have ten years ago. Back then she'd been so sure she could change him, mold him, at least get him to graduate high school so he'd stop hanging out with their father and *his* no-good crew.

No such luck there. Now she just hoped she could keep him sober for however long she put up with the Hudsons trying to protect them from whatever was being threatened. Then go back to the hands-off life her therapist had suggested was best.

How on earth had she gotten twisted up in this very complicated situation? She should have known all those years ago, when her father had been adamant about transferring his assets to them before he'd been arrested, that having her name on the ownership of Brink land was only ever going to bring her trouble.

So much trouble.

She got close to Ry and waved her finger at him. "You promise me, *promise me*, you don't know what that snake thing was about?" She'd already had this conversation with him in the car last night, but he'd been a little drunk after finding her secret stash while she'd been out watching the sunset with Jack.

Because that was what a girl got for doing something she wanted to do.

But anyway, she wanted to make sure he'd still promise when he was sober.

"Nobody knew I was staying at your place, Chlo. Even if they did, they're gonna steer clear of a cop's house. Why would my friends want to mess with you?"

She believed him, mostly because for all the trouble she'd had with Ry before, it was nothing like this. Nothing that targeted her directly. He'd only ever asked her to get him *out* of trouble. Or for money. No petty dead-animal games with her brother's equally useless addict friends.

It really bugged her that the most reasonable explanation for the snakes was connecting it to the skeletal remains on the ranch. Bugged her because it meant she agreed with Jack, and it meant it would make sense for them to keep staying here.

But boy, was her brother the biggest liability.

"Morning."

Ry let out a little yelp of surprise, and Chloe reached for the gun she was not wearing, thank goodness. But when she turned to face the source of the voice—Jack, of course—she noted his raised eyebrow like he knew exactly what she'd been doing.

"Going somewhere?" he asked casually.

But there was nothing casual about the way he looked at Ry. Cop to criminal. Looking for signs that he'd done something wrong. Just like Chloe herself had done.

But when Jack did it, she had to fight the urge to stand between them. To defend her brother.

"A run," Chloe said, offering him her best sunny smile. "I was trying to convince Ry to go with me, but he's not much into exercise."

Jack nodded as if he believed her story. She knew he didn't.

"Chloe tells me you're good with animals," Jack said. Directly to Ry.

Ry stared at Jack, unblinking for a full minute. "Er, yes, sir."

Chloe wanted to laugh, even with her insides all twisted up. She wasn't sure she'd ever heard her brother call anyone *sir*, but Jack was the kind of guy who brought it out in people, she supposed.

"I've got a job for you, if you're wanting to avoid running."

"Uh." Ry looked at Chloe, clearly hoping for her to make an excuse for him.

"He'll take it," Chloe supplied instead. She didn't relish the idea of Jack and Ry hanging out, but she'd seen that look on her brother's face when she'd caught him trying to creep out of here. He'd been ready to go stir up some trouble, and the only thing that ever kept him out of trouble was work. Work with animals was even better. He *was* good with them. Much better than he was with people, that was for sure.

"Cash could always use a set of hands. I'll take you over." Jack tilted his head away from the front door and toward the back of the house. "Follow me."

"Uh. Okay," Ry said, clearly uncomfortable, but it was hard to argue with Jack when he was in Mr. Ruler of the World mode. Which was most of the time, she supposed.

Ry took a few hesitant steps forward before Jack began to lead him out of the room.

"You wait right here, Chloe," Jack said firmly, his back to her as he led Ry away. "We'll take that run together."

She scowled after his retreating form. She *hated* when he bossed her around. Well, in this kind of context, anyway. But since she was a guest in this house, she felt like she had to listen to him.

Which was really, really annoying.

JACK LED RY toward Cash's dog barns without saying anything. It was a bit early yet, even for the ranch, but Jack hadn't been able to sleep. He'd laid in his bed, staring at the ceiling, knowing Chloe was right above him. Talking himself out of going up there over and over again.

He felt terrible from lack of sleep, but he was damn proud of himself for having *some* restraint when it came to Chloe.

The morning was cool—a little overcast, so the dawn seemed to hang on longer than usual. Cash and Carlyle wouldn't be out at the barns just yet since it was so early, but it gave Jack a chance to have a one-on-one conversation with Ry Brink.

He studied the man. Slight and fidgety, but not angry. Uncertain and nervous, sure, but he didn't look like he was going to bolt or be defiant.

Jack didn't know what Chloe and Ry had been discussing this morning at the front door, but it definitely wasn't a *run*. A lecture about behavior, maybe, but Jack doubted Ry was up at the crack of dawn for *good* reasons.

Jack pointed to the dog barn in the distance. "You know about my brother Cash, right?"

"Sorta. He's got lots of dogs or something?" Ry looked around the barn like he was expecting them all to come running. "I do like dogs."

"He trains them, for all sorts of things. Carlyle Daniels

works for him helping train them, but they can always use another body. It's a lot of work, training them and making sure they're in good shape. If you like dogs, it's a good way to spend a day. And you can spend as many days as you like doing it, as long as you follow instructions."

Ry pulled a face at that. Jack sighed inwardly. He dealt with people all the time who didn't like to be told what to do—his family, people he pulled over, flat-out criminals— so he knew he had to lay this out in the simplest terms lest Ry be rebellious just for the sake of not following someone else's rules.

So he stopped, leaned on the fence and studied Ry with his most detached cop look. No emotion, no reaction. Just reason and sense. "I know you don't like cops—or me. And that's fine, I don't need you to."

Ry fidgeted, not meeting Jack's gaze.

"I know a lot of things about you, Ry. But first and foremost, I know this—your sister feels responsible for you. You mess this up, you mess her up."

Ry chewed on his bottom lip, looked around at the dusky dawn of morning across the ranch. "I know." Then he shrugged. "I don't do it on purpose. I don't like messing her up, but I can't seem to help it."

"Try. For as long as it takes to figure this out, give it your best shot. We can keep you busy. We can help in whatever ways you might need that don't include substance abuse. But I need to know you want to try."

Ry's frown was frustrated but not belligerent exactly. "I just like to have a little fun and get carried away sometimes."

"You're an addict, Ry. First step in helping your sister would be admitting that to yourself."

Cold Case Discovery

The frown turned into a scowl, with some pointed anger thrown in. "I didn't have anything to do with those bones, man."

"I don't think you did."

Ry looked up at him suspiciously. "Really?"

"It takes time for bodies to decompose, Ry. I can't imagine you were more than seven when those bodies were put in the ground. Even if they were newer, you don't strike me as mean enough to kill anybody."

"I'm not."

He did not say those words proudly. He said them almost as if he was ashamed of it. Jack couldn't say he liked that take on the matter. It gave him a different kind of worry— that Ry might *want* to be capable of murder.

But he could only handle one problem at a time. "Your dad, on the other hand…"

"It does sound like something my dad would do," Ry agreed. "I mean, I never heard about him killing anybody, but he sure liked to beat people up."

Jack knew this. He'd arrested Mark Brink for a domestic assault his first year working as a county deputy. But the girlfriend he'd beaten up had refused to press charges. And Jack never liked to think about what that might have meant for the childhood Chloe endured, even if her parents had divorced early on. But she'd bounced between the two— neither one upstanding, reliable or good parents, clearly.

"You ever see him get close?"

Ry sighed, not nervous or fidgety so much now. Bored. Craving a hit. Who knew. "The cops already asked me all about Dad. I don't have like some secret memory of him killing someone and burying them at the ranch, man. And there isn't anything in it for me if I protect him, so I ain't lying."

Jack nodded. Fair enough. And he'd told himself he'd stay out of it. He could hardly ask his siblings to do what he told them if he was investigating.

He had to let Bent County take care of it.

He squinted across the yard, saw Cash and Carlyle making their way from the main house. When they reached the fence where Jack and Ry were, Jack made introductions, even though Ry and Cash knew of each other.

Jack knew Cash and Carlyle could handle this, but still he hesitated leaving them with Ry. It felt a little bit too much like foisting his responsibilities off on someone else.

But he and Chloe had work, and this was the best-case scenario in keeping Ry out of trouble.

"You do as you're told, or I kick your ass. Got it?" Carlyle was saying to Ry after she'd explained their opening procedures with letting the dogs out.

Ry's eyes were wide, but he nodded. Carlyle flashed Jack a grin.

It did a lot to assuage his worries about leaving Ry here with them. Enough so that he headed back to the main house and Chloe. He wouldn't be surprised if she didn't wait for him, but he stopped by his bedroom and changed into clothes he could run in.

If it was a bluff, he'd call it. But when he returned to the living room, she was there—bending over, touching her toes, stretching out before her run, he assumed. And she was wearing skin-tight running gear, which did support her previous story. Yet he was having trouble thinking about anything but getting his hands on her.

He didn't know what it was about her that tested all that

hard-won control he'd always been so proud of. He'd been attracted to other women before, had *liked* other women before, but something about the package of Chloe Brink made him feel like an entirely different person than the one he'd so ruthlessly crafted over the years.

She stopped stretching, looked over her shoulder at him. She didn't say anything, didn't voice her concerns, but he saw them in her eyes.

"Carlyle's in charge of keeping him in line," he said. "I think he's afraid of her."

Her mouth quirked. "Well, that does ease my concerns about going to work later. Carlyle *can* handle him. For a while, anyway."

"He'll be okay."

Chloe shrugged. "Maybe. Maybe not. But I can't twist my life around him. Learned that one the hard way." She blew out a breath. "Thought my cat would be trailing after you, per usual."

"Tiger found someone he likes better than even me." When she raised an eyebrow, he couldn't stop himself from smiling. "Izzy."

Chloe smiled at that too, as he'd been hoping she would. "Well, he's in good hands, then."

"So, run?"

Her smile died and she sighed. "You hate running, Jack."

"I don't hate it."

"You *hate* it, and I think your family would find it a little weird you're doing something you hate with me at the butt crack of dawn. I don't need a bodyguard."

Which was probably true, and maybe he should just let this go. But he didn't. "I didn't realize you were an expert on the layout of the Hudson Ranch."

She rolled her eyes. "Jack."

"Chloe."

Something in her expression hardened. "I think you're supposed to call me Deputy Brink here."

He didn't know what this was about, but he could admit that something about being *here* made him a whole lot less interested in ignoring any tension there was between them. "Do you want to have a fight about it?"

She huffed out a breath. "No."

"Then let's go run."

"Fine," she muttered.

He led her outside, pointed to the fence line. "We can follow this out toward the highway, then turn back. Should be about two and a half miles."

"I usually do five."

Jack tried not to pull a face. "We can do it twice, then." What a waste of time.

But then she laughed and slapped him gently in the chest. "Messing with you. One round is fine. Think you can beat me?"

"My legs are longer."

"Is that a yes?" she returned, eyebrows raised.

But he only shrugged. She shook her head. "All right, buddy. Ready, set, go." Then she took off. Too fast to start a two-and-a-half-mile run. Or so he thought in the beginning. He assumed he'd catch up to her, but she always maintained a distance. It got slimmer the longer they ran, but even when he began to pour it on, she kept ahead of him.

When the house came back into view, he ran as hard as he could manage. He made it close, but she still beat him. And they both ended in the front yard, bent over hands on their knees, panting.

And laughing. He didn't know why she was laughing. Maybe because she'd won. He was laughing because it was ridiculous, when he very rarely got prodded into the ridiculous. He was laughing because it didn't seem to matter what they did or why—just being around her lifted all those weights on his shoulders he'd thought were permanent.

The way she laughed, smiled, enjoyed the smallest things.

"You're going to have to run with me all the time now," she said, wiping her forehead with her forearm. "Beating you is my best time in a while."

All the time. He tried not to think about it, because their jobs made it impossible, but he wondered if she knew how little he'd mind *all the time*. Forever.

When she looked over at him, gave him a little chest pat he figured was supposed to be a friendly, *good game*-type gesture, he couldn't help himself. He held her by the wrist, pulled her in.

She didn't resist, but she did look up at him warily. "Anyone could see us, Jack."

"Yeah." But he didn't move, and neither did she.

Chapter Seven

Chloe did not understand what was happening between them. For an entire *year*, the lines had been very clear, and both of them had been dedicated to keeping it that way.

But the past few days were getting all muddled, blurry, when it was the last thing that should be happening, what with skeletal remains and mutilated snakes and her own damn family. It was turning her soft.

Because she should have pushed him away, but she let him kiss her here. In broad daylight. In front of the Hudson house, which housed like a hundred people. People who would have questions, who would tell other people, who would erase all the lines they'd carefully drawn.

And still she drowned in the kiss. They weren't supposed to *do* this, but she couldn't stop herself because he kissed her with a gentleness that undid all her paltry walls. These were the ones that really got to her. He didn't pull this out often. Usually, there wasn't time for soft, leisurely. But his hands were on her face, his grip gentle as the kiss spun out into something that reached deeper than anything else ever had, until she felt like gravity simply ceased to exist.

He eased back, his dark eyes studying her face, his mouth still just a breath from hers. She wasn't quite sure how, after a year of sneaking around, something could change, but something had.

Maybe this place was magic. *Or a curse.*

She had to shake her head to get both ridiculous thoughts out. Step away from him to find some anchor in this storm. "We have to get to work." Her voice shook.

"Yeah." His voice didn't, but his exhale did.

Well, at least there was that.

She should break it off. Stop this right now. Before it got more complicated.

It was already way too complicated.

But she walked back into his home, shoulder to shoulder to him, and didn't say a word. They went their separate ways in the house, and she ran through the shower upstairs, got dressed for work and then ignored Mary's insisting she eat something. She knew Jack expected to drive her over to her cabin and drop her off at her cruiser, but she needed some space.

She didn't even get halfway to her car before she heard him call her name. She turned. He'd also showered, changed into work clothes. He looked put together as always, in his perfectly pressed khakis and Sunrise Sheriff's Department polo.

His expression was very grim, which wasn't all that unusual for work, but there was something about him that had her tensing.

"We have to get to the hospital," he said, striding toward his cruiser.

"The hospital. Why?"

"Suzanne just called me," he said, referring to the Sunrise administrative assistant. "Kinsey was at your place when—"

"You had someone watch my cabin overnight?" she demanded, surprised by this brand-new information, which he had neither shared with her nor asked permission to *do*.

"No, I had someone drive by a few times overnight and—"

"Without telling me?"

"Yeah, without telling you. Now, would you let me finish?" He jerked open the driver's-side door. "Kinsey was shot at. Suzanne says it was just a graze, but he's at the hospital getting it looked at, and we need to go down there and get his story."

Chloe's heart slammed against her chest, enough to get over the frustration with Jack doing all that without telling her. She hopped into the passenger seat. "You sure he's okay? Should I call Julie?" Steve's wife would no doubt be worried sick.

Steve Kinsey had been with Sunrise since its inception, moving with Jack over from Bent County. He was in his late forties and had three teenagers at home, who he liked to bemoan even though he did everything he could to take time off to make all their many birthdays, holidays and sporting events.

"He called Julie himself. He's fine," Jack said, pulling out of the Hudson Ranch and onto the main highway, which would take them into Hardy and to the hospital.

But his hands were so tight on the wheel that his knuckles were white. Back to a perfectly capable outer shell and nothing inside but ticking time bombs.

Chloe blew out a slow breath, trying to focus on the important things. Steve had been shot. At her cabin? "Was someone trying to break in?"

"Suzanne didn't have the details. We'll get them from him ourselves."

They drove for a while in silence. Sometimes she wished

she couldn't read him so easily. She tried—so hard—to keep her mouth shut. To let him deal with his stuff without trying to offer some kind of comfort.

This was work. This was that line they had *both* agreed on. And it was a line that had worked for a *year*.

But as they approached the hospital, she couldn't keep it in any longer. "It could have been anything, Jack. Not just the thing you asked him to do. That's the job."

"But it wasn't anything, was it?" Jack pulled the cruiser in front of the hospital, and they got out at the same time.

Jack took the lead, a sheriff down to the bone as he talked to the front desk and a nurse, before they were finally led into a room.

Steve sat on an exam table and even smiled at them—if ruefully—when they entered.

"I'm fine, boss. Just grazed me." He wiggled his bandaged arm. "Not even keeping me." He nodded at Chloe, then looked back at Jack. "I didn't see anything, though, that's the kicker."

"As long as you're okay, that doesn't matter."

Steve clearly didn't agree, but he didn't argue with the sheriff. He launched into an explanation. "I was driving by Brink's house on my way back to the station. Thought *maybe* I saw a light. Figured she'd just left one on, but since there'd been some trouble, I got out to check it out."

"You radioed that in?"

Steve nodded. "I parked in the driveway, turned the flashlight on and started to walk toward the side of the house. Told myself I was overreacting—but then, out of nowhere, I just heard *pop*. And felt it." He gestured at the bandage. "That was it, though. Must have run off. If they'd wanted real trouble, they would have *really* shot me. Would have been easy pickings," he said disgustedly.

Chloe felt sick at the thought.

"I called it in to Suzanne. I was ready to go check out the backyard, but Suzanne's fussing about ambulances and blah, blah, blah. I think Bent County is out there looking at it now."

"Bent County? But it's our jurisdiction," Chloe said.

Steve's expression was unreadable. "Sort of."

"What does 'sort of' mean?" Chloe demanded as Steve's gaze moved to Jack. "Jack, what does that mean?"

If Steve thought it was weird that she'd used his first name instead of *Sheriff*, he didn't act like it.

"I reported the snake to Bent County."

She didn't know exactly why that made her so angry except that he was…taking over while keeping her out of it. Something that involved *her* ranch, *her* brother, *her* house, her *life*. "I live in Sunrise."

"Yes, and I happen to think all of this connects to what was found on the ranch. And that's Bent County's case. Besides, it's a conflict of interest for Sunrise to investigate."

"That's *if* it has something to do with *me*. And I wasn't home. Either time. Maybe they thought I would be, should be, but it seems strange that if this was about *me*, they wouldn't make sure they knew exactly where I was."

"Unless they didn't want you there," Steve suggested. "Seems to me, creeping around your cabin is looking for something. Maybe they were looking for your brother."

Chloe didn't glare at Steve. She didn't even look at him. She kept her ire focused on Jack. Even if none of this was his fault, either, he was an easier target.

But his eyebrows were drawn together as though he was

thinking. "Maybe it's not *you*. Not Ry. Maybe they *wanted* you out of the way. Maybe there's something *in* the cabin they want."

"What could I have in the ca…" She trailed off, a horrible thought occurring to her. "Some of my father's things. I have them in my garage."

JACK DROVE TO Chloe's cabin. She said nothing, and he didn't know what to say either, so the ride was in absolute silence. Seeing Steve had eased some of the tension about the situation—he really was fine and thinking clearly, but Jack still didn't like any of his deputies being hurt on the job.

But it *was* the job. And he had to focus on the next step of it: trying to figure out why someone suddenly had Chloe—or Ry, or her cabin—in their sights.

He pulled his truck into the driveway. Jack frowned at the fact that there wasn't anyone here. "I should call someone at County."

Chloe shook her head, already getting out of the truck. "If there was something to say, they'd be here or they'd have called me."

Jack sighed and followed her. She went right for the garage, that determined focus stamped into the expression on her face.

"He did all this stuff before he got arrested," she was saying, opening the garage, striding toward a bunch of boxes. "Wanted us to spend time on the ranch with him. Told us it was our *legacy*."

She started moving boxes, and Jack wanted to help, but he didn't know what she was looking for, and it seemed like maybe she just had to do this herself.

"He tells me he wants us on the deed. I've done all right for myself, if being a government patsy is all right. But he's worried about Ry. Wants Ry to run it, even though it's not profitable—but hey, it's a house. It's *something*, I figured." She tossed a tub out of the way. "Used all my guilt, all my worry about Ry to get my name on there too." She shook her head, clearly disgusted with herself.

"My first year at Sunrise. I know I was green, but I also knew *him*. I should have seen it for what it was. A criminal who knew his time was up. He tells me he's getting rid of stuff so he can be 'free' and all this other nonsense. Asks me if I want some family heirlooms. I should have said no. I *know* I should have said no, but I—"

"Nothing wrong with wanting family heirlooms, Chloe."

"Oh, come on, Jack. I know who my family is. Criminals begetting criminals. Sure, maybe I hoped somewhere along the line, the Brinks had this ranch because *someone* wasn't totally worthless. Maybe there was some immature fantasy about inheriting a sense of right and wrong from *someone*, but I know better. I should have known better."

She finally stopped moving things, her breath coming in pants from the physical exertion. There was an old antique-looking chest pressed back in the corner of the garage.

She glared at it. "I never looked through it. He used to do this thing. I couldn't quite believe it *wasn't* heirlooms, but I knew. I knew it was just the usual way he liked to mess with me."

"And how was that?"

She shrugged jerkily. "Once my parents really split, he was in and out of our lives. Sometimes he'd come around and Mom was tired of us, and we'd have to go spend a week or two at the ranch with him. He'd always have presents. For me. But they were just…joke gifts."

Jack doubted he'd agree with the word *joke*, but he didn't press. He had to bite the inside of his cheek to keep his mouth shut, but he did it.

"I should have looked through it and gotten rid of it." She swallowed, clearly emotional about the whole thing. "I was a coward."

"You're human, Chloe."

She didn't look at him, just kept staring at the chest.

And this was work. They weren't Chloe and Jack here. He was the sheriff. She was a deputy. There was a case to untangle. One they were both way too close to. He should call in Bent County for this, but…

She needed to handle this first step herself. She undid the latch, but paused before she lifted the lid and took a deep breath. She looked up at him.

"Whatever this is, Jack, I need you to keep in mind that if those remains are your parents, the chances my family had *nothing* to do with it are slim to none."

He knew she was right. That all the ways this was twisting was likely leading to a very clear place. Maybe that should matter to him, but with her staring at him like that, all emotionally wounded, it just didn't.

"Maybe."

She shook her head, and her eyes were a little shiny, enough to make his heart twist. When she spoke, though, she was firm.

"Not maybe. Basic reason."

"You're not your family, Chloe." He wished he could make her believe that. Wished there were some magical words he could find to erase all that pain for her.

"But they're mine all the same," she muttered, then lifted the lid.

She jumped back with a little shriek he'd never once heard come out of her. He moved, with half a thought to protect her from whatever was inside, but the scene in the chest had him recoiling as well.

Dolls. A lot of them. Mutilated and smeared in what Jack could only assume had been blood.

Chapter Eight

Chloe should not have been surprised. She certainly shouldn't have shrieked. Another joke gift. She should have known—she *had* known, but she'd wanted to live in hope that somewhere along the line, the name Brink hadn't been garbage. As long as this chest had remained closed, she could pretend there were nice family heirlooms inside. Artifacts of a family line that wasn't just waste.

She should have sucked it up, been a realist and dealt with this a million years ago. Because *now* she had to deal with it in front of Jack. Served her right, she guessed.

"It was a dumb thought," she managed to say, though her voice was rough. She moved forward, tried to keep her arms from shaking and failed as she flipped the lid closed. "No one's after this. Just his usual stunts. Probably laughed himself all the way to jail on this one."

Jack took her by the arm, started steering her out of the garage. Away from the chest, thank God. What was she going to do now? She needed to haul it out of here. She needed...

"You go on inside," Jack said. His voice was gentle, but *cop* gentle. Devoid of real emotion. Just getting the job done. "I'm going to call in Bent County. I'll put on gloves and look through it while we wait for Hart or Delaney-Carson to get here."

Panic spurted through her. No one needed to see this. No one needed to start sorting through all the gross, messed-up pointlessness of a childhood with Mark Brink as a father.

Worse than that, the idea of Jack sorting through all those horrible, gruesome dolls when she knew something worse might be lurking.

Dear old Dad had made sure to be clear that it could always, *always* be worse.

She didn't pull out of Jack's grasp, but she did move in front of him and plant her feet so he couldn't keep ushering her out. "Don't do that, Jack. Not alone. Not…" She couldn't articulate how little she wanted Jack wading through this. "He did this kind of thing. It's not—"

"Someone was sneaking around your place, willing to shoot at an officer. There are dead bodies buried on a ranch with your name on the deed. A mutilated snake was purposefully left on your porch. All in the span of forty-eight hours. We need to look into everything. No matter how off the wall it feels. No matter how little you want to."

"You think he did it. Murdered your parents. Buried them on his ranch. You think this is a clue, but—"

"*You* think he did it, Chloe," Jack said gently, and the grasp on her arm softened, his palm sliding down to her hand. He covered it with his, squeezed. "I don't know what to think. So we'll take it a step at a time. I don't want you seeing this. I'll go through it. You go inside."

She swallowed the lump in her throat that just kept growing. "There could be worse in there. I don't want *you* going through it. What if there's something…"

"Something?"

"He's an abusive, violet criminal. Those dolls could be just a scare tactic he thought was funny, or they could be hiding something worse."

Jack studied her face, something grim and...looking a lot like fury seeming to darken his gaze. Emotionless cop gone, just like that. "Were the joke gifts he gave you when you were a kid *usually* hiding something worse?"

She held herself very still, purposefully blocking out old memories she didn't want to show on her face. Her father's had never stuck around long. She liked to pretend he hadn't been there at all.

But he'd done damage in what little spaces he'd had. It didn't take a *lot* of bad experiences to know he was capable of awful things. Only one, and the threat of a repeat.

She did not want Jack knowing that, but she couldn't seem to come up with a lie to get that protective look off his face. Like he could go back in time and make it all right.

"It doesn't matter," she managed.

"Chl—"

"I said, it doesn't matter, and it doesn't. This isn't about... It was a mistake to think this is connected. It's a mistake to start digging into..." But she couldn't finish that sentence because if her father was responsible for the dead bodies on the Brink Ranch—and God knew that was looking more and more likely—everything he'd done back then would be examined under a microscope to determine motive, means and opportunity.

She wanted to throw up.

"What happened to you when you were a kid isn't—"

She couldn't take his pity. She wouldn't. "I've had therapy, Jack. I've dealt with my garbage bin of a childhood. I don't need you and your perfect one psychoanalyzing me."

She sucked in a breath, immediately regretting everything she'd just said. She could have punched herself for how insensitive it was. Sure, he'd had a great childhood—but then, he'd also spent every second of his adulthood stepping into his missing parents' shoes. "I'm sorry."

He shook his head like it didn't matter. But it did. This all mattered, and she *hated* it.

She moved her hand so she was grasping his instead of the other way around. She looked into those dark, fathomless eyes, and she didn't care if she was begging. She just needed this to not explode on her. "Please. I wouldn't ask this of you if it didn't matter. Please. Don't." She wouldn't cry. "Let the detectives handle it. With the right gear, the right warning." She *wouldn't* cry. Not in front of Jack—her *boss*. Because that's what he was right now.

Not the guy who'd kissed her this morning like she was special. It didn't do any good to think about that completely separate moment.

"Okay." His free arm came around her, pulled her close. Even though they both wore their uniforms. Their gun belts. Their radios. He shouldn't do this. She shouldn't let him.

But she didn't pull away, because she was shaking, and if he held her, maybe she could find some anchor in the midst of all this mess.

JACK COULDN'T CONVINCE Chloe to go inside, but he did get her to sit down on the stoop of her cabin porch—where he'd just cleaned up snake remains yesterday.

Only forty-eight hours. No, he didn't like this, or that it pointed to something more *current* happening around a very old potential murder.

He glanced back at her. She'd been startled by the snake,

but it hadn't really affected her. This? It had shaken her. He'd never seen her quite so affected by *anything*, not that he couldn't blame her for it. The dolls were creepy enough on their own—add the fact that it was clearly and purposefully done to mess with her by her own father...

Jack supposed it was a good thing Mark Brink was in prison over a thousand miles away, because the way all this information settled inside him was testing his usually impeccable control.

As it was, he focused on the present. He didn't sit next to her on the stoop. It seemed to agitate her more. So he stood just out of reach, waiting for Bent County to arrive.

When they did, Jack handled everything. He wasn't sure that was what she wanted, and he knew he could be overbearing—his siblings made sure he knew. He didn't mind it when it came to them, but it bothered him with Chloe.

She had a say too, but this was... Like anything else, he couldn't protect her from *everything*. But he would protect her from what he could.

Besides, he was the sheriff.

So he instructed the deputies to take the chest away and search it with the utmost caution and keep everything as potential evidence for the time being. When the detectives arrived, Jack explained the situation, and they did what they were supposed to do.

Hart separated Jack from Chloe and asked *him* questions about what had happened while Laurel no doubt did the same with Chloe. Jack didn't like it, but he understood they were doing their job. A job complicated by the fact that the people involved were also cops.

Jack could see Laurel and Chloe on the porch, but Hart

had pulled him out by his cruiser close to the street, so he had no idea what Laurel was asking or how Chloe was answering. But he had to focus on the questioning *he* was part of.

He explained what had led them to look at the chest, what he'd seen, what Chloe had said about it. Hart noted down his answers, and once he was satisfied, he switched gears to all their other issues.

"Since Mark Brink would have lived on the land at the time of your parents' disappearance, we've already been looking into him," Hart explained, "in regards to the remains. Just to get an idea of the players if the ID is positive. We called the correctional facility in Texas, and they got back to us this morning."

Jack could tell by the way Hart said it that the news wasn't going to be good.

"He got out on parole last week."

Jack swore.

"So far he's cooperated with his parole officer. It'd be quite the feat for him to get up here, wait around until the cabin was empty, do all that with the mutilated snake and then get back for his check-in."

"A feat, but not impossible."

"No, not impossible," Hart agreed. "We're arranging to have an interview with him. It might be another day or two. Lots of red tape to wade through."

"Isn't there always," Jack muttered. He really had no idea what to do with this information. It was such a strange thing, to have all these answers visible but out of reach. There was still the off chance those remains weren't even his parents'—though he didn't hold out any hope for that.

Maybe he hadn't given up on hope, on answers, but he

hadn't thought they'd land on his doorstep one random day with Chloe in tow. Surrounded by all these seemingly disparate events.

"Speaking of red tape," Hart continued. "Zeke got us hooked up with a forensic anthropologist. She got here this morning. We've got to get through some paperwork to make sure everything goes smoothly from a legal standpoint, but she should be able to get to work tomorrow. Once she can examine the remains, she'll have an ETA on identification. We'll keep moving forward with the investigation, but it's going to take time to narrow down time frames."

Jack nodded stiffly.

"We're sorry we don't have more clear-cut answers for you just yet, but we're working on it."

"Luckily, I know how it all works."

"Not sure how lucky that is."

Jack tried to force a smile but knew he didn't manage. He glanced back at the porch, where Laurel and Chloe were still talking. Chloe had definitely put her cop mask back on. She didn't look upset or rattled.

But it was lurking underneath. How could it not?

"Look, I know Brink is one of your deputies," Hart said, lowering his voice to almost a whisper even though Chloe wouldn't be able to hear them from this distance. "But this is bound to get messy. It might be better if you kept some distance. I'm not sure her and Ry Brink being in the Hudson Ranch-Hudson Sibling Solutions circle is the best move here."

Jack let Hart have his say, and he didn't bother to argue or defend himself. He just said his response in the simplest terms there were. "It's the only move here."

Because he'd be damned if he was going to keep his

distance from Chloe when she might be in some kind of danger. He walked away from Hart, not about to wait for the man's permission.

He was a sheriff. Head of the Hudson clan. And damn if he was going to be scared of *messy* when Chloe might have to pay the cost of that fear.

Laurel moved away from Chloe before Jack reached the porch, and she nodded at him. "I'll keep you updated on what we find. We'll treat it like a joint Sunrise-Bent County venture for as long as that makes sense. Unless you want to be kept out of this part too?"

Jack shook his head. "I want to know everything about that chest."

Laurel didn't say anything, but she didn't hide the fact she was studying him either. Then she shrugged and walked over to Hart, and the two took their leave.

Chloe approached Jack, chin up, eyes fierce and a little bright. He could already tell there was a storm brewing deep underneath.

"Whatever you're about to say, don't," he said. His temper was already on edge due to a million things, and he didn't need whatever she was gearing herself up to say to send him over.

"Why not?" she replied.

"Because I can tell it's going to tick me off."

She shook her head. "It's better if we don't stay with you, Jack."

"Better for who?" he returned, just barely holding on to that thread of calm.

"Everyone involved," Chloe said, and her expression was set, her voice firm, but there was something hiding underneath that cop mask. "Certainly better for you guys getting the answers you deserve."

"Did Laurel put that in your head, or is it your own wrongheaded thinking?"

She scowled at him, but he wasn't about to relent.

"Jack—"

"You and Ry are guests of the Hudson Ranch until we have some answers on the threats against you. I don't care what anyone, including you, has to say about it. That's what's happening."

"There aren't any threats against me. That snake *could* have been for Ry. Whatever my dad was pulling with those dolls happened *six* years ago. I'm not in any danger."

"I'm glad you feel that way. I don't."

"And Jack Hudson's feelings trump all else?" she demanded, but the heat wasn't there. She was just trying to pick a fight.

He was feeling a bit like letting her, but he took a deep breath. Reminded himself that whatever that chest of dolls was or wasn't, it had hurt her. Deeply enough that he'd seen all her usual masks fall.

He didn't want to add to that hurt. He never wanted to be even a contributing factor to her hurt.

But he had been. Not like this. Not deep, childhood wounds. But the nature of everything they'd been for the past year had not always been easy, and he knew…no matter how careful he tried to be, that she'd been hurt by the secret nature of what they did together outside of work.

And he knew she still believed it was for all the reasons *she* saw when that wasn't it at all. Maybe he'd have liked her to have given him more credit, to admit to herself that wasn't *him*, but… That wasn't very fair of him. He saw it more and more clearly as time went on, as little things about the way she'd grown up came out.

How she trusted anyone or anything, saw the good in anyone, *laughed* with people was beyond him. He was in *awe* of her.

Even as she kept going, determined to have that fight he couldn't muster up the anger for.

"Did it ever occur to you that I can handle me? And I can handle Ry? And I can handle *this*?" she demanded, working up to mad so she didn't have to be sad, scared, hurt. *Clearly.*

It killed him how easy it was to see through it, even as she kept on.

"Did it ever occur to you that I don't need this Jack Hudson, king of the world, 'I'll protect everyone and everything the sun touches just because I slept with you'?"

It was the strangest out-of-body thing. To watch her get mad as hell, to watch her gear it toward him, and not find himself being reactive at all. No, it was like all those walls he'd carefully erected for so long just crumbled to dust. Not even dramatically. Just slowly and silently to ash that flew away on the breeze.

"Well?" she demanded, her cheeks pink with anger, her hands on her hips and everything about her combative.

But he saw that little kernel of vulnerability she was trying so hard to protect, and for the first time in his life, he found himself handing over his own without even thinking about it.

"Did it ever occur to you that I'm in love with you?"

Chapter Nine

Chloe knew what he'd just said. She'd heard it. He'd sounded out that word, spoken it. Right here.

But she couldn't *understand* it. She couldn't put together the *knowledge* with the reality of Jack Hudson standing there saying...

No. *No*. He was...

No.

This was the weirdest time to tell someone they...

No, he was just trying to trick her. To get what he wanted. Which was protecting everyone and everything. And yeah, it wasn't like he *hated* her, but it was... It was...?

Why was her heart doing this terrible, hopeful dance in her chest? She knew better. She knew so much better. Chloe didn't trust love. How could she?

"Jack..." She tried to say more, but her throat was so tight, she couldn't seem to get words out. And he was standing in her yard, looking so good and strong and perfect.

God knew she wasn't meant for *that*.

"I think somewhere deep down, you have to know that. You know me, Chloe. Why else would I break any rule?"

She couldn't come up with an answer for that, and she tried. She tried so hard.

"So yeah, I have some issues when it comes to protecting people. I wonder why," he said, so dryly she might have laughed in another context.

But he'd said he *loved* her, and there was absolutely nothing funny about this horror show.

It had to be horror coursing through her. What else could it be?

"I'm overbearing. I think I'm right pretty much all the time." He took a few steps forward, and she had no choice but to scramble back. Away. Until he stopped moving toward her.

He couldn't touch her right now. She'd...she'd crumble.

"But I don't cross lines," he continued. "I don't break rules. I don't do *gray area*. Except when it comes to you. And if that was about fun or sex or whatever, I would have resisted. I would have put a stop to it. I would not have engaged in this whole thing for a *year*."

"Secretly," Chloe whispered, because it was the only thing she had to hold on to right now. The last line of defense against whatever he was doing to her.

"Yes, secretly. Because no matter how or when this comes out, I know how it shakes down, Chloe. I know how people will treat you. How they'll treat me. There will be whispers for sure, at a minimum."

She couldn't breathe. He'd *thought* about an "after everyone found out"? He'd considered the *consequences*? When all she'd ever done was...be sure he wouldn't want them without thinking what they might be.

"I can take it. At worst, I suffer a few comments and lose a few votes during my next sheriff election, but I still win. I won't be a party to having people question you, though. Your character or anything else. I know that most of our department won't have a problem with this, but there's a wider world, and I won't listen to people at Bent County pretend to know who you are or what you stand for because of your relationship with me. No number of speeches or interventions or *loving you* can change what people will say when I'm not there to stop it, and I never want you to have to deal with that."

She could only stare at him. All this time... All this *time*, and she'd been so sure she understood what they were doing. She'd known part of it was about work, about not breaking his precious rules, but she hadn't thought about...

And he had. What it would really look like if people knew about them. He'd thought it through. And he cared, deeply, that it would affect *her*.

She wanted so badly to protect her heart. Everyone who'd ever had it had bashed it into a million pieces.

But Jack laid out the reality of their situation, and she could see it. He laid it out and she *knew* him.

Of course the secrecy was about protecting *her*. *Of course* it wasn't superficial, about her family reputation—poor Jack didn't have an ounce of superficial in him.

Which only left one thing.

"Jack, I can't..."

"You don't have to do anything, Chloe. That's not why I said it. I said it so you'd understand. So you'd stop fighting me on this because you think... I don't know. That it doesn't matter to me? I need you to be careful. I need you to *care* that something dangerous is going on, one way or another."

This time when he moved for her, she let him. Let him take her hands in his. Let him look at her like...

Like he loved her. Because Jack Hudson, somehow and very inexplicably, was in love with her. And Jack didn't lie, except maybe sometimes to himself. But this wasn't that.

"I care that you are safe, Chloe. That you are…*happy* isn't the right word, but that you're okay. I have no feelings one way or another on your brother. I know you love him. I know how hard and complicated that is for you, and I respect it. And because I love *you*, I'm going to honor it. For as long as it takes, I need to protect you and Ry. And I need you to let me. That's all I need from you right now."

The fact that he was including Ry, that he understood just how complicated and frustrating her love for her brother was, made the tears she'd so desperately been battling all afternoon fall over.

I need you to let me. She'd give him so much—anything, really. He had to know it. "You're not playing fair," she managed to say, even as tears trailed down her cheeks.

He reached out and wiped them away. "I might play by the rules, but that doesn't mean I have to play fair."

She managed a watery laugh, but it died quickly because maybe she could believe he loved her. Maybe she would give him that thing he needed—the chance to protect her and Ry. But he was ignoring something very important.

"You have to look at the very real possibility that my father killed or had something to do with the murder of your parents. You can't just brush it away. Because when this is all figured out, it's going to matter. You have to really think about what that's going to be like."

Jack nodded. "I have."

"But—"

"No. No buts. I understand. If it's true, if we finally have the answers my family has wanted for seventeen years, it'll be a relief. But it won't bring them back, and it won't change anything. Not really."

"I'll be a reminder."

"No. You're not an extension of your father, Chloe. Any more than you're an extension of your mother or Ry. You're you, and I love you."

He said it so earnestly, holding her hands, looking at her tearstained face. Coming up with an answer for every one of her arguments. Taking away all the excuses she'd held herself up on for the past year.

It was scary—the scariest thing, really, because this had the potential to go so very wrong. But when he looked at her like that, she wanted to be someone else, just for a little bit. Someone who could just enjoy the fact that the man she'd been pining after for far too long had feelings for her too.

No, not just feelings. *Loved* her.

"You know, I've been in love with you for longer," she managed to say, not quite sounding like her usual self, but closer. More in charge.

His mouth quirked up at one side. "Is it a contest?"

She nodded emphatically. "Absolutely."

"Okay, how about this?" He pulled her close, brought his mouth next to hers. "I'll love you best," he murmured. Then sealed that promise with a kiss.

JACK HUDSON WAS a planner. He had emergency backup plans to the emergency backup plans. And yet it had never served him. He'd focused for the past seventeen years on wielding more and more control, and still…he'd never actually gotten it.

Grant had gone to war. Palmer and Anna had gone to the rodeo. Cash had gotten his high school girlfriend pregnant at sixteen. Not exactly a great parental track record to his way of thinking, certainly not if he compared himself to what his parents might have been able to do.

Then, over the past two years, Grant had been hurt on Dahlia's case; Palmer had been hurt and Louisa had been kidnapped; Anna had gotten pregnant, almost burned alive; and Mary had been kidnapped by a madman. And that didn't even get into everything that had happened with Cash when his ex-wife had tried to frame him for murder.

And every time something terrible had happened, Jack had tried to hold on tighter and tighter only to be reminded it never really mattered.

Bad things happened.

Loving Chloe wasn't a bad thing, but it was a complicated thing, and for all the ways he planned for twists and turns of fate—the inevitable *bad*—he had not ever once come up with a plan for what happened on the other side of *I'm in love with you.*

They drove to the station in silence, the weight of it sitting there between them. Because now they had to go into work.

Maybe next time he could plan love confessions around their work schedule.

"You should have let me drive my own cruiser," she muttered as he pulled up to the building that housed the Sunrise Sheriff's Department.

"Everyone will understand why I want you riding two-man right now. In fact, they'll probably be surprised I'm not making you take some leave."

She glared at him. "I'll take leave over *your* dead body."

"I know, that's why I'm not going to make you." He'd certainly considered it, but he wasn't about to tell her that.

She grunted and pushed out of the car, and he realized this wasn't so much her real frustration as it was her trying to build that wall back. So they could walk into their place of work and not have what they'd just laid out between each other broadcast to the world.

Jack had long ago given up on the world being fair. He never expected it. But it struck him in a way it hadn't in a long time what a bad hand they'd been dealt with this.

Still, he let Chloe blaze her way in first, and he took his time following. When he walked into the office, Suzanne immediately got to her feet. "Sheriff, is it true?"

For a second, Jack was distracted enough to think she was talking about everything that had just happened with Chloe. Which was ridiculous. The look on Suzanne's face was clear. Anguish.

Suzanne Smithfield, Sunrise's administrative assistant, had known both his parents. Well, everyone in town had. People loved to tell him stories about how one of his parents had helped them out of a bad situation. But Suzanne had been close personal friends with them. She'd gone to school with his dad, and his mother had babysat Suzanne's kids sometimes.

He managed a reassuring smile for Suzanne. "We don't have ID confirmation yet. It's probably going to take a while. Don't let the gossip mill upset you."

Suzanne sighed heavily. "The news hasn't made its way through town yet, but it will. And soon enough."

Jack nodded. "That's all right. I'll handle it."

"You handle too much, Sheriff."

"So they say."

She leaned in close. "All this stuff with Chloe's cabin… Is it related?"

Most people asking that question would put his back up, but he knew Suzanne cared about each and every Sunrise deputy like one of her own kids. She was worried about

Chloe, nothing else. "We don't know yet, but Deputy Brink and her brother are going to be staying out at the ranch until we get it sorted. I also want her riding two-man for the time being, so keep an eye out if she tries to dance around that."

Suzanne nodded. "Good. That's good." Then she nodded to his office. "Messages are on your desk."

Jack nodded, then focused on being Sheriff Jack Hudson and nothing else. He returned messages, worked on some paperwork, did what needed to be done. And if he occasionally took a walk around the office to get more coffee than necessary to check on Chloe, well…

Who knew that was what he was doing besides himself?

But she had calls to respond to and work, too, so their paths didn't cross, and that was fine. Great, even. Best all the way around.

If it settled in him like frustration, he was just going to have to get used to that.

Toward the end of the day, he got a call from Bent County. When he heard Hart on the other end, Jack doubted they had good news coming.

"We haven't got a hold of Mark Brink yet, but we did get a report he was spotted in Denver. Morning after the remains were found."

Denver. Pretty much halfway between Texas and them. "Going to ask around and see if anyone saw him here?"

"Already got a deputy on it. Laurel's also going to head out to the ranch and question Ry again."

"Why?"

"That's a pretty quick turnaround, Jack. Being in Denver the morning after a middle-of-the-night discovery? If it's connected, he had warning."

Jack closed his eyes and tried not to groan. He wanted to

argue with Hart, but how could he? If he was in charge of the investigation, he'd been drilling Ry for information too.

"Phone records?" Jack asked, though it squeezed his heart to do it. Chloe was a realist when it came to her brother, but that didn't mean she was going to be okay with any of this.

"Working on a search warrant, but Laurel's going to see if he'll hand it over of his own free will. Ry doesn't strike me as a hardened criminal despite his rap sheet, but I don't know what kind of relationship he has with his father."

Jack didn't, either, and Chloe clearly didn't think Ry had one. Which was maybe true. Maybe not. Either way, Chloe wasn't going to be too happy with this turn of events. She'd want to head over to the ranch right now, intervene.

"I also wanted to talk to Brink about what we found in the chest," Hart said. "Can you transfer me? She can call me back later if she's out on a call."

"Are you going to tell her about Mark?"

"No, Sheriff. I'm only even telling you as a courtesy. It's an active investigation into her father. The less she knows, the better off we'll be."

"She doesn't have a relationship with her father."

Hart was quiet for a few humming seconds. "Regard-less. She'll be kept in the loop in what directly affects her."

It was a clear-enough warning. Jack wasn't supposed to tell her either. He didn't like how that settled in him like betrayal instead of just the nature of the job.

"It's almost shift change. She should be available. Stay on hold for a second." Jack got up and stepped out of his office and peeked into the main lobby, where his deputies met for shift change.

Chloe was at the front desk, smiling over something on

Suzanne's phone—probably the insane pictures Suzanne took of her cats dressed up like old Hollywood stars.

He hated to wipe that smile off her face, but when both Suzanne and Chloe looked over at him, he saw any enjoyment melt away. Because she knew it wasn't good news.

"Chloe, Detective Hart's on line one for you."

Chapter Ten

Jack shouldn't have called her Chloe in front of Suzanne. It was a dead giveaway. Maybe not to *everyone*, but Suzanne was not everyone. She had a keen eye, an even keener ear and a nose for things other people didn't want to share.

Jack had never once slipped up in front of anyone in all this time, and dread swept through her because she had a terrible feeling that Jack had used her first name because something really bad was just about to fall in her lap. Courtesy of Detective Hart.

Chloe wanted to ignore the call, run in the other direction, ask Jack to handle it. A million things that she wouldn't do, because whatever this was, it was all hers. Just like always.

She moved stiffly into one of the offices the deputies all shared, closed the door and gave herself a second to breathe before she lifted the phone receiver. Whatever it was, she could weather it. She'd gotten this far, hadn't she? "This is Brink."

"Hey. Detective Hart here. I just wanted to give you an update on what we found in that chest of yours."

Chloe swallowed, found a spot on the wall to stare at and made sure she sounded strong and firm. "Go ahead."

"Mostly, it was just the dolls. We're going to run some

tests on the smears—determine fake or real blood and go from there. Some weapons were hidden inside some of the dolls. We'll have to keep and run tests on those too. See if they were used in any of your father's known crimes."

"Great." She hoped she didn't sound *too* sarcastic.

"There was also an old scrapbook. Delaney-Carson and I both looked through it, and we don't see any reason for Bent County to keep it. It seems more family heirloom than anything else. Whenever you have a chance to stop by County, you can feel free to pick it up."

She didn't know whether she wanted to laugh or cry or just rage. All that—dolls and weapons—and her father hadn't even been fully lying. There *was* a family heirloom hidden in there.

She should tell Hart to throw it in the incinerator. "I'll be by tonight."

"Okay. It'll be up with Administration. You know the drill."

"Yeah, thanks." She returned the phone to its receiver. Then she just stood there, still staring at the same spot. She didn't have her cruiser here; that was at her cabin. Her personal car was at the Hudson Ranch. She did *not* want Jack driving her over there. She didn't know what kind of reaction she was going to have to this scrapbook, and she didn't want him witnessing it.

She didn't want anyone with her when she picked it up, when she inevitably went through it even knowing it was pointless. Whatever she wanted to find wasn't going to be in some old, dusty book that may or may not even actually be a Brink family scrapbook.

But regardless, she wanted to handle all that alone. Where

she didn't have to worry about how her reactions might affect how anyone viewed her.

She blew out a breath, closed her eyes and tried to find her lifelong inner toughness. That thing she'd been building up since she was a kid. She had known, always, that life was nothing more than a series of blows to dodge and absorb as needed. Any good, you carved out yourself with hard work and fierce grit.

Why was she having such a hard time with these blows?

A knock sounded at the door. Chloe didn't have to be psychic to know who it was. She twisted the knob and pulled it open.

Jack stepped in, closed the door behind him and studied her.

Here was the answer to the question. Where was her grit? Well, this man had somehow washed it away. By taking care. By *loving* her.

And what was it going to get her, this love? Ridicule? Pain? Guilt? And so much fear that it would all disappear, she didn't know how anyone lived with the weight of *love* you chose.

"Everything okay?" Jack asked carefully.

"Yeah." She realized that Jack had been the one to tell her Hart was on the phone, which meant he'd talked to Hart first. "I'm sure Hart filled you in on everything."

Jack shook his head. "No. Just that he wanted to talk to you about the contents of the chest."

She shrugged, still not ready to look at him. "Running tests. Found some weapons. Mostly called because they found some old family scrapbook, I guess. I can go pick it up sometime."

"I'll drive you."

She forced herself to look at him, to be *strong*. She had not gotten this far in life by being an emotional weakling or coward. She would *not* be cut down at the knees just because he loved her. "Look—"

But this was Jack. Did she think there'd be some way to get around that bullheaded need to control and protect?

I need you to let me. He'd said that to her like…like she had any say. Like he had wants or needs he couldn't expressly make happen in the Jack Hudson world of control and determination.

Like *she* had that kind of hold over him.

"Two-man until we have answers, Chloe," he said firmly. "And I don't just mean at work. If it's not me, you're going to have to ask Baker or Clinton to drive you over. Or we'll head back to the ranch, and you can take Ry with you later tonight. Or Mary."

She wanted to do just that—pick someone else—to prove to him she could. No. To prove to *herself* she could. To put some space between them when she had to do something she knew would be emotionally painful.

But he'd said he *loved* her.

She couldn't wrap her head around why that put her more on edge than when she'd believed the whole thing had been about sex and nothing else. When she had convinced herself he was *embarrassed* of her family connections. That had been easy because it had been anger, she supposed. Indignation. Hard feelings that kept her silly heart guarded.

Now it was just soft feelings and too much outside stuff poking at her to bear.

"I need space on this, Jack." She wasn't going to cry again. Once was enough, but she could feel emotion mounting. So she needed to set a boundary. Or five hundred.

"I can give you space," he said, nodding like he was agreeing with her even though she knew better. "You want to look through it alone? Your choice, Chloe. But *someone* is going to be with you at all times when you're off the ranch until we can rule out a threat to you."

I need you to let me. I need you to let me. It kept ringing in her head, over and over. Like it was something she could count on.

When she hadn't been able to count on anything aside from herself in her entire life.

"Let's just go get it over with," she managed to say, not crying but sounding raspy nonetheless.

He nodded again; then he reached out. Just a quick, friendly squeeze of the shoulder. "I need to grab a few things. I'll meet you at my truck."

She gave him a sharp nod, refusing to react to the hand on her shoulder, the softness in his gaze or anything else.

Just had to get through the day. She could fall apart—alone—tonight. Then maybe tomorrow she'd have answers for how to deal with everything life had thrown at her today.

She collected her own things, met Jack at his truck. They didn't speak. She didn't even look at him. She watched out the window as he drove away from Sunrise and toward...

She frowned and sat a little straighter. "This isn't the way to County," she said with a frown. She glanced over at him. He was gripping the wheel, scowling ahead.

"We're going to need to stop by the ranch first."

"Why?" she asked because he seemed so serious, so determined, and she didn't understand why.

His scowl deepened if that was possible. "Delaney-Carson is interviewing Ry again. I figured you'd want to be there."

"Why is she doing that?" Chloe leaned forward, nearly screeching out the demand.

"There are some concerns he has a relationship with your father." Jack let out a long breath. "Mark Brink was spotted in Denver the morning after the remains were found."

"He's in prison."

"He's on parole." Jack looked over at her then. "Hart made it very clear I wasn't supposed to share any of this with you, but I don't want you finding it out from anyone else."

Another rule broken, a line crossed for *her*, and Chloe couldn't handle that. Not right now. She had to handle the actual information. "So, he was in Denver? What does that..." But she was a cop. She understood how you built a case. If her father had been halfway between Texas and Wyoming the *morning* the remains had been found, they were thinking someone had warned him the remains were going to be found. *If* he was involved, *if* he'd been on his way to Wyoming.

Was it even an *if* anymore?

"Ry doesn't have any connection to our father." Her father had loved to play mind games with her, but he'd actually knocked Ry around some. Ry wouldn't...

But with drugs involved, there weren't a whole lot of things she could count on Ry *never* doing. Including this. He could have called their father before he'd called her. Her father could have told Ry to dig there, and Ry didn't mention it because he knew how she felt about Mark Brink.

There were a lot of *could*s. Too many.

When Jack pulled up to the ranch, she once again didn't want to face what awaited her, but she didn't have time to wish for different. The detective's car was parked out front. She was already inside, talking to Ry.

Chloe knew she should let her. Let Ry handle himself. But...

"Can you not come in with me? I don't want the detective to think we're like marching in as Sunrise Sheriff's Department, trying to take over—or worse, make a mess of her investigation. I just want to be there if Ry needs me. I'm not stopping anything." She said that last bit more for herself than Jack.

Jack nodded. "I'll go around back."

She swallowed what was beginning to feel like a perpetual lump in her throat. "Thanks." But before she could push out of the truck, Jack took her hand, held it in his and pressed their joined hands against his chest until she met his gaze.

Serious. So damn serious. "I know Ry's your responsibility, but he's not under your control, Chloe. Trust me, as a man who has spent the past seventeen years trying to control Anna's mouth, sometimes you just have to be there to catch them when they fall, not try to stop it from happening."

She wanted to be angry that he was trying to tell her what to do, but she saw it too clearly for what it was. Commiseration. She managed a nod, then to get her hand free. She got out of the truck, didn't look back at Jack. Just marched onto the porch and to the door, which was unlocked, so Chloe let herself in. It felt a little weird, but worry over Ry superseded any awkwardness she felt. She followed the sound of voices—Ry's agitated one—and found them in the living room.

Ry was pacing the room like a caged animal while Detective Delaney-Carson sat relaxed as could be on the couch. When Ry heard her enter, his chin snapped up.

"Chloe, why won't they leave me alone?" He pointed at the detective. "Isn't this harassment? I didn't do anything *wrong.*"

"Okay," Chloe agreed, because there was no arguing with her brother when he was this agitated. She turned to the detective, tried to smile. "I thought you'd already questioned us, Detective."

She nodded. "Yes, but you know as well as I do when new information comes to light, a second, third or even fourth questioning might be necessary."

"What new information?"

The detective's expression bordered on disdainful now. "Deputy Brink, I'm not going to share—"

"She said Dad's out on parole and is acting like I know something about it or, like I'm hiding him or I don't know. But I didn't do anything wrong!"

Chloe wanted to melt into a puddle of embarrassment, but she kept her placid expression on her face as she faced the detective. "Are you charging my brother with anything?"

"No, Deputy. We're just asking when the last time he had contact with Mark Brink was, and answers have not been forthcoming."

Chloe tried to ignore her stomach sinking. If he wasn't answering… But she turned to her brother. No blame, no embarrassment, no frustration on her face. Just blank. "Ry," she said calmly, "it's a simple question. Even if you don't know the exact date, you have an idea. How long has it been?"

"You know Dad. He's not consistent. In one day, out the next. I don't remember talking to him since he went to prison, and I don't know why that's anyone's business, what it's got to do with those bones. I'm only twenty-four! You think I was a kid burying skeletons?"

"I don't think anything, Mr. Brink," the detective said, her voice on the chilly side. "And at the moment, you're hardly a murder suspect. What I am trying to do is gather information to solve a case. It would help if you could be cooperative instead of combative."

"You're accusing me of doing something wrong! You don't think I know how you people think? All your female-cop bull—"

"Rylan Jonas Brink," Chloe said sharply. Sharp enough that he was surprised into clamping his mouth shut. "That's enough. Now, are you saying you haven't had any contact with Dad since he went to prison?"

"I don't remember talking to him *once*," Ry grumbled.

Chloe turned to the detective, so tense it was a miracle her bones didn't simply shatter from the force of it all. "Do you have any more questions, Detective?" She expected to see fury or affront on the detective's face.

What Chloe saw was worse: pity.

"No. Not right now. Thank you, Deputy Brink. If I have any more questions, I'll let you know." She stood, but as she passed Chloe on the way out, she said something quietly enough so Ry couldn't hear. "If he changes his story, or if you find out something you think might help this investigation, I'd really appreciate it if you let me know. We all want the same thing here. Answers."

Chloe nodded jerkily. Because it was true. They all needed answers.

She stood in silence, watching her brother pace. She had no words. She had *nothing*. So she just watched him until he stopped pacing. Until he looked at her, all sheepish and sullen.

He was good at being angry, at blaming everyone around him, but he always broke in the face of her anger. Well, if he was sober.

"I'm sorry, Chloe," he said, crossing the room to her. "I didn't mean it. She just got me so riled up, poking at me with the same questions."

This was the problem with Ry. She believed he *was* sorry. In the moment. She just also believed he'd do it again and again because he wasn't sorry enough to change, to grow, to learn. He was determined to stay stuck in this everyone-else-is-to-blame place.

And she couldn't fix him.

She'd spent so many years trying to accept that. She wondered if she ever fully would be able to.

"How was working with Cash and Carlyle?" she asked, because she needed to make sure he hadn't ruined anything else today before she went back to the subject at hand.

He gave her a jerky shrug that reminded her of the little boy he'd been. She'd tried so hard to save him from everything, and she'd failed. "They have like a hundred of them."

"Of what?"

"Dogs." His mouth curved ever so slightly. "They didn't give us that speech in high school when they were telling us we had to think about our futures. Maybe if someone had told me, 'Hey, dog training is a thing people do,' I would have tried harder."

She didn't say anything to that, even though *she* had told him. *She* had tried to find any way of getting him to *care*, to put forth an effort. Vet school. Owning his own kennel or working on someone else's ranch. *Anything.*

But Ry had to blame someone else for where his life was. Always.

Which brought them right back to the subject at hand. "Ry, have you had *any* contact with Dad in the past year?"

"You heard what I told the detective."

"I did. And now I want you to look me in the eye and tell me that for an entire year, you haven't had a phone call, an email, a certified letter, nothing."

"I didn't do anything wrong," he said. Which was the third or fourth time she'd heard that in the last ten minutes. And didn't answer the question.

"Then what *did* you do?"

He stood there. Then slowly, his dark eyes filled with tears. "I'm sorry, Chloe. I really am."

Chapter Eleven

"He lied."

Jack looked up from the computer screen that had been giving him a hell of a headache. With Steve out and Chloe needing to ride two-man, adjusting the Sunrise SD work schedule was a hell of a puzzle he hadn't fully figured out yet. Even with him stepping in to cover daily shifts. So he didn't quite follow Chloe's dramatic statement. He only knew she was standing in the doorway, looking like a storm ready to break. "Who lied about what?"

"Ry lied to the detective."

Jack tried not to swear, tried to maintain a detached kind of calm that she no doubt needed, but he wasn't perfect. "Lied how?"

"All she wanted to know, allegedly, was if he'd had contact with Dad lately. He told her he hadn't talked to Dad since he went to prison, but he refused to hand over his phone, of course. And he kept saying he hadn't done anything wrong, and that's always when I know he has."

She looked up at Jack then. Tears swam in her eyes, but they didn't fall. "He's had contact with Dad over the past year. Text messages and emails." She raked her hands through her hair, loosening more strands from the once-tight braid she'd had at the beginning of the day.

"He said it didn't have anything to do with anything. Just father-son stuff. I can't believe he…" She was pacing the tiny office room. There was no room to pace, but she clearly couldn't sit still. Anger and frustration pumped off her, but underneath all that was the impossible pull of wanting to do the right thing for her family and needing to do the right thing for the law.

"I should have handled it better. I should have found a way to get him to admit it to the detective. He always lies when he's backed into a corner, and if I had—"

"You're not blaming yourself, are you? Because I know you know you're not to blame for Ry lying."

She took a breath and finally stopped pacing. She looked at him with heartbreak in her eyes. Then shook her head. "Bad habit."

"I know. So, let's work through this. He told the detective he hasn't had contact with your dad?"

She shook her head. "Oh, no, of course not. He said *I haven't talked to him* since he went to prison, so he's convinced it wasn't a *lie* because he only communicated in texts and emails. God, I'd like to strangle him."

"And he says these conversations were just generic. Did he let you see any of them?"

She shook her head. "He claims he left his phone at my cabin, and he'll show them to me later. I know he didn't, and I know he won't."

"So he is hiding something." Jack sighed. It just didn't add up. What would Ry be hiding? He'd been too young to really be involved in any kind of murder or coverup. Besides, if Mark Brink killed those people…

"He's protecting our father, for whatever godforsaken reason," Chloe said, clearly trying so hard to be strong. For what, he didn't know. Neither her father nor her brother really deserved that kind of dedication.

But even if they didn't, their behavior connecting to cold case murders didn't make sense either. "If Mark knew about the remains *before* Ry dug, how did Ry warn him before he dug? And if Ry knew your father committed those murders and is trying to cover for him, why would he dig there or anywhere? It doesn't make sense."

"I'm not sure what my father or brother does always adds up."

"Sure, but... We're missing something here. The timing doesn't work out for them to be purposefully covering up something Mark did that Ry knew about."

Chloe sucked in a breath. "We should let the detectives handle it. I'll tell them... I'll tell them..." She couldn't seem to get out the words. He hated why, but he understood it all the same.

"You don't want to tell Laurel what you know."

She looked up at him, her eyes still shiny, but clearly she had determined she wasn't going to cry over this. "Ry needs to be maneuvered. You can't just get answers out of him. And if there are answers to be had, I'm the best chance we have of getting them. If I involve the detectives, I just don't think it'll give us answers. Not without someone getting hurt."

She shoved her hands in her pockets, looked at some place on the wall just behind him, as if it'd give him the illusion she was making eye contact.

"I know it's wrong. I know I shouldn't still want to protect him. But he's not a murderer. Maybe Dad's wrapped him up in this but only because he knows how to manipulate him. Not because Ry did anything wrong. I mean, he did. He lied. I just…" She seemed to run out of words, or maybe they were lodged in her throat. Because she just stood there, looking miserable.

So he moved over to her. He pulled her close, rubbed his hand up and down her spine until *some* of that tension in her loosened. "Take a breath, Chloe. We'll work through it. One step at a time."

"I've got to stop laying this stuff at your feet. You're the real victim here. You and your family."

"Sounds like we're all victims."

She shook her head against his chest, but she didn't pull away from him. She let him hold her.

He figured if anything made sense about the two of them, it was this. They both felt they had to do it all, hold it all together, and because they did, the other was the only person they knew how to lean on.

"You shouldn't be comforting me. You've got your own awful stuff to deal with."

"Yeah, but mine is old, and while it's not *dealt* with, you went with me on that drive the other night. You hate heights, and you sat next to me and listened to me talk. Things I can't seem to admit to anyone else." He held her closer.

"But—"

He pulled her back so he could look into her gaze. He hadn't fully realized until all this had gone down how much she'd hidden from him in the past year. Old childhood hurts, insecurities. Trauma.

He'd had his own trauma, but he'd had a foundation to deal with it on. She'd had nothing but herself.

"All this bad stuff? It's not math. There's not a chart. You get to be upset. I get to be upset. And we'll comfort each other however we can. Love isn't a contest or a trans-action, Chloe. It doesn't work that way."

Her chin wobbled, but she firmed it on an exhale. "I don't know how love works."

"Well, I guess you'll figure it out as we go."

She rolled her eyes, but not disdainfully. And she didn't pull fully away. But the misery was still in every line of her face.

"We need to get to the bottom of this, Jack. I don't want to go to Laurel, but you need answers. We all need answers."

"So we'll find them. Together."

"How?"

Maybe he'd been avoiding it, but he'd known, since this morning, since Chloe's safety had come into question, he couldn't play hands-off anymore. Not and live with himself.

"By making this a Hudson Siblings Solutions case."

CHLOE HAD HELPED the Hudson clan with cold cases before, but mostly in a very supplementary way: getting them information they couldn't get themselves, responding to active threats connected to their cold cases. But she'd never been involved in a full-fledged Hudson Sibling Solutions meeting.

It wasn't all that different from a family dinner. Everyone shoved together in the living room instead of the dining room. The low buzz of conversations, bickering and the most recent addition of a baby occasionally fussing while everyone arrived and got settled.

Carlyle was missing because she'd made up an excuse to use Ry to do some evening chores with her and Izzy out at the dog barns. Jack had offered to let Ry be part of the meeting, but Chloe had nixed that idea.

She loved her brother, wanted to protect him with all she was, even to the point of risking things she shouldn't risk, but she couldn't trust him with *anything*. Especially this. She might want to protect him from the repercussions of what he'd potentially done, but she wouldn't do it at the expense of finding the truth.

She didn't really think Ry had done anything wrong when it came to the skeletal remains, but she could see how any involvement with their father could mean he was mixed up in *something* wrong.

"This meeting better be about what I think it's about," Anna said, with baby Caroline situated on her lap.

The fringe conversations began to die out, and all eyes turned to Jack. Chloe had always known he'd taken on too much here with his family, felt a responsibility that was maybe bigger than necessary.

But she'd never so clearly seen it in action—everyone he loved turning their attention to him, looking to *him* for answers. Since he'd been eighteen years old. Her heart ached for the young man he'd been.

"The case regarding the skeletal remains—that, I'll point out, have not been positively IDed yet—has changed on us, gotten more complicated, and now it includes a potentially current threat."

"No one is threatening me," Chloe muttered, because for all that was mixed up and wrong, some mutilated snake on her porch with absolutely no information didn't lend itself to her being worried. The dolls in the chest were an old "joke" from her father. She didn't have any actual *fear* of a threat, but she was *letting* Jack take care of her.

Or trying to anyway.

"I think a mutilated snake on your porch is threat enough,

whether we know what it's threatening or not," Mary said primly.

"Maybe it doesn't connect. The snake. Mark Brink. The remains. But the timing feels like too much of a coincidence," Jack continued. "I still want us supporting Bent County detectives in all facets we can, but things have changed enough, I think we should launch our own investigation."

Chloe expected there to be *some* reaction from the Hudson siblings. A grim kind of excitement or relief that Jack was okaying what he'd previously forbidden.

But there was silence. Dahlia snuck a look at Grant. Palmer suddenly found the ceiling *very* interesting. Anna studied Caroline's socks as if they had the answers to the mysteries of the world on them.

Jack sighed. "So go on and get everything you've been gathering in secret and against my wishes. We're looking into it now. As a team."

"Thank God," Anna muttered. She looked over at Hawk, who got up and left the room. One person from every couple did the same, slowly returning with arms full of things. One by one, they dropped files, notebooks and printouts onto the table in the center of the room in front of Jack. Chloe's eyes widened as it became a tower of papers that nearly toppled over. She snuck a glance at Jack.

He didn't look the least bit surprised. Resigned, a little disapproving, but maybe even just a *hint* of pride.

Chloe realized then that he'd known they were doing it. Behind his back. Even though he didn't want them to. And he wasn't angry about it.

Something about him knowing and just…letting them, even when he didn't want them to. It settled in her like warmth. Everyone painted him as so rigid, and he *could* be on the outside, but on the inside...

He was someone else entirely. And she loved him so much, it turned into *anxiety* inside her. Because love could so easily be taken away. Especially with a last name like hers.

"I haven't put it in my notes yet, but I *may* have eavesdropped when Detective Delaney-Carson interviewed Ry again," Anna said. She looked over at Chloe. "He's lying."

Chloe nodded. "I know." She swallowed. She didn't want to share with *all* of them what she'd found out, because she wasn't sure they would agree with Jack that they should *all* work together.

And she wanted to protect Ry, but in the audience of everyone whose parents might be buried on her family ranch, she felt the need to be honest. Even at Ry's expense.

"He admitted to me he's had written contact with our father. I haven't figured out what they talked about yet, but I'm going to." She took a deep breath. "And I'll make sure to share it with you as it pertains to the skeletal remains, but I also understand this is complicated. Well, that *I* make it complicated. Threats or no, we're looking at my father and a ranch my name is on. I understand if there's a thread of mistrust here, and I don't have to stay."

Jack gave her a sharp look, but it was nothing on Mary's.

"Chloe Brink, I have known you since we were in kindergarten. And not once, in all that time, all those different phases of our lives, have I ever thought you were *anything* like your father or your brother."

Before Chloe could respond to that, Palmer spoke. Because Chloe knew that for all Jack and Mary were on her side, it wasn't unanimous. Palmer had made it quite clear he had his doubts about her.

"It doesn't matter if she's like them if she's more worried about protecting them than getting to the truth," Palmer said. He didn't budge when both Jack and Mary glared at him. He sat where he was, looking right at Chloe. "I don't have anything against you as a person, Chloe, but your involvement is complicated."

"I agree. That's why I'm saying I don't have to be here."

Mary and Jack immediately began to argue with her. Anna looked to be on the fence, while Cash and Grant said nothing. The significant others didn't add anything at first, but eventually, when the arguing was clearly going nowhere, Louisa cut through all the chatter.

Chloe looked over at her. She was gripping Palmer's hand. Clearly they'd had a few discussions about this.

"The real question is this," Louisa said once everyone looked over at her. "If you found something implicating your brother, would you turn him in?"

Chloe turned her gaze from Louisa to Palmer. He looked so much like Jack, was *nothing* like his older brother. Except in this. That stoic, stern expression.

She could lie. She could be a good liar when she wanted to be. Hell, she lied to herself on a daily basis. But she shrugged. "I really don't know. It would depend on the situation."

Palmer leaned back in his seat, flung his arm over Louisa's shoulders. "Then my vote is that you stay."

Chloe had already started standing up to leave before the words penetrated. "Wait, what?"

"You were honest. That's all that really matters. We can't have secrets in an investigation, but siblings… I wouldn't believe you if you'd said yes. But an *I don't know*? That, I get. God knows I thought I'd have to cover up for Anna committing a crime at some point in our lives."

"You mean, you haven't?" Hawk murmured.

Anna put her hands over Caroline's ears. "Not in front of the *baby*," she said with mock seriousness. "She's going to grow up thinking her mother is a saint."

This elicited a laugh from just about everyone in the room. A laugh. While they were sitting around talking about their parents' disappearance and potential murder. Her family's involvement in such a tragedy.

But, Chloe realized, here in a room where all the Hudsons were gathered—but not just Hudsons. Significant others and offspring too. Seventeen years of unknowns while life marched on had meant probably figuring out... you couldn't live your life constantly mired in that old tragedy.

So maybe she should stop living mired in the reputation other people had given her last name.

Chapter Twelve

They went over it all. The old information the police had gathered when their parents had disappeared, what his siblings had gathered in the past few days. Nothing new, nothing groundbreaking, but it was good to talk it through.

Jack was trying to convince himself it was good. He knew it wasn't true, but he *felt* like the only one struggling with the weight of what they were discussing. Not just anyone's skeletal remains—his parents.

Not positively IDed yet, he reminded himself. Or tried to.

Though they'd all done some of their own investigating over the years, there wasn't anything really new so far. Anna and Palmer had both been looking into any connection Mark Brink might have had to their parents. Mary had been looking through old ranch records to see if something jumped out connecting anything Hudson to the Brink Ranch. Cash had been working with Zeke and Zeke's connections to see if he could get more information on the crime scene as it was right now.

"So, we did all this and we're still in the same exact spot?" Anna groused.

"It's not the same exact spot," Mary said, clearly trying to sound optimistic. "Just like any cold case. We don't know which corner might lead us to a new thread. So we keep going. I still have old ranch records to look through, and we don't know what the forensic anthropologist might have to say. It's a step."

"It's a foolish step," Anna muttered.

"I think that's a sign someone is tired," Hawk said, earning a scowl from his wife. "Mary's right. We've got next steps. Let's call this a night. Caroline's conked out anyway," he said, gesturing to the sleeping baby in Anna's arms.

She sighed and got to her feet, and everyone else began to disperse, couple by couple.

Chloe stood. "I better go check on Ry. Make sure Carlyle hasn't scarred him for life." She tried to smile. It faltered.

"Did you want to go get that scrapbook?" Jack asked.

She waved it off, already heading out of the room. "Tomorrow morning is soon enough," she muttered. Then she disappeared. Jack wanted to follow her, but Mary started tidying up, so both he and Grant stepped in to stop her.

"Go to bed, Mary. We can clean up."

She frowned at them both, hands on her hips, but Walker urged her out of the room so that it was just Jack and Grant collecting debris. Jack figured they'd work in quiet. Grant usually did.

"So, how long has your thing with Chloe been going on?"

If it had been anyone else standing there asking him that question, Jack would have had a quick answer. An easy lie. He expected things like that from just about everyone.

But never Grant.

Grant, who most people would never guess was *married* to his wife, because he and Dahlia were so private they almost never engaged in even *hand holding* in front of people. Grant, who'd taken *eons* to propose to Dahlia, if compared to Mary, Anna and Palmer's quick jumps into commitment. Who'd had a wedding so small, it had only been immediate family because they hadn't wanted an audience.

"What?" was all Jack managed.

But Grant didn't relent. *Grant.* The man who'd returned from war and kept every last effect of that to himself. No matter how obvious they'd been.

"I can repeat myself if you really need me to, but I think you know what I asked." He calmly stacked papers together.

"Who are you, and what have you done with my brother?" Grant, who was closest in age to Jack, who'd been his kind of right-hand man in keeping everything together that first year. Because he'd been the only one old enough to also drive. He'd helped with school runs and sports practices. If it hadn't been for Grant, who'd been *sixteen*, Jack would have fumbled the whole thing.

Grant's mouth curved ever so slightly. "It's a simple question, Jack. I know a lot about all the things a person tells themself that doesn't serve them. We'd hate to think you have to keep yourself some isolated paragon for the rest of us."

Jack wanted to be touched that Grant was concerned about him, but... "'We'?"

Grant's expression went *almost* sheepish. "It's been a topic of conversation."

"With *who*?"

"Well, I think it started with Carlyle, then it kind of spread from there. Not everyone believed it at first. Dahlia was an early believer though, and it's hard to argue with her. She observes things. Cash and Walker weren't so easily swayed, but recently..." Grant shrugged. "I think the lone holdout on that score is Palmer. He's convinced you'd *never* cross a line at work."

Jack wasn't sure what was worse: all the people who thought it was true or the fact Palmer was wrong about him.

"So you guys have been sitting around debating whether or not I have a relationship with Chloe?"

"You do know your family, right? And Carlyle? She brings it up every chance she gets. She's determined to be right. She is, isn't she?"

"Are you going to take my answer back to the collective?" Jack returned, a little bitterly even to his own ears.

"I don't have to. I can keep a secret." He shrugged as if it was that simple. And Jack wasn't sure if it was just who Grant was or because they were the closest that Grant was probably the only one he'd believe that from.

"I just didn't want you laboring under the assumption you weren't allowed to have a life too. Taking care of everyone has been your life for so long. I'm sure it's hard to realize we're all grown up and let that go. But we are. And we're all here. We're all good."

"It isn't that," Jack managed, though it wasn't so fully off the mark, he realized. "Maybe it was a little in the beginning, but… Working together complicates things. For Chloe."

"Life is complicated. You can't protect everyone, Jack."

He was a little tired of that getting thrown in his face at every turn, but… "I can try."

Grant shook his head, but he didn't argue. "Look, asking you about Chloe isn't the only thing I wanted to talk to you alone about."

"You want to probe deeper into my sex life for the past decade?"

Grant pulled a face, as Jack had hoped. He hadn't learned *nothing* from being Anna's older brother.

"No," Grant said stoutly. "We're not really telling everyone yet, but I figured you should be the first to know."

"Know what?" Maybe he should have seen it coming. Grant wasn't the first, but Jack was really taken off guard by Grant's next words.

"Dahlia's pregnant."

It shouldn't be a shock. Kids were going to follow marriage more often than not, but maybe Jack thought Grant would feel a little like he did. Like he'd already raised a family.

But Grant's mouth was curved, as wide as Grant ever smiled. Happy. Grant Hudson, war hero, married and starting a family.

Jack really didn't know how to absorb it, but what he tried to do in these kinds of moments was think back to their father. What would he have done?

But in this case, Jack didn't know. Because his father had never had the chance to parent *adults*. The idea of being a grandfather had probably never been one he'd entertained for too long, too busy getting his six kids grown first.

So Jack just had to rely on himself. He reached out, gave Grant's shoulder a squeeze. "You'll make a hell of a father, Grant. You've had some hands-on practice."

He shrugged. "Had some good role models to follow too." He patted Jack on the shoulder, like *he* was one of them. "You don't have to pretend with Chloe around us. No one's going to cause a problem here. Seems to me you guys should have *somewhere* you don't have to pretend."

"I'll, uh, talk to Chloe about it. Not sure how comfortable she'd be."

"Sure. I'll keep my mouth shut."

"Even to Dahlia?"

"Well, maybe not that shut. But she won't tell anyone. You have my word."

And Grant's word was good as gold. Always had been.

Jack didn't think he'd had much to do with that, but maybe…maybe some. A tiny, little bit. And it made him feel pretty damn good that he had.

CHLOE FOUND RY laughing with the dogs. Carlyle was watching them with an eagle eye, but from a distance. Giving Ry the illusion of being in charge.

It made her heart twist that it looked like he was handling it just fine. Why hadn't *she* been able to keep him out of trouble?

Well, didn't do to think about now. She walked over to Carlyle first. "Hey. How's it going?"

"As long as the animals are around? He's fine. Not irritating at all. Might have wanted to pound him on the walk over while he was whining about his tough lot in life— please, buddy, I win. Still, I think we'll be able to keep him busy and out of trouble without a pounding."

"I can't tell you how much I—"

Carlyle held up a hand. "Don't thank me. It's rude."

"How is thanking you rude?"

"Because it is," Carlyle replied. Then she gave Chloe a kind of sideways look. "So, is this whole protect-you-on-the-Hudson-Ranch thing Jack Hudson's version of trying to get in your pants?"

Chloe choked on a sharp inhale. "What? No!"

"Is that because he's already in your pants?"

"Carlyle!"

"So *that's* a yes." Carlyle looked back at Ry, who was getting the dogs into the barn one by one. "I *knew* it."

Chloe knew if there was anyone she'd slipped up around when it came to *maybe* hinting she had a thing for Jack, it was Carlyle and only Carlyle. But… "You did not."

"I totally knew it. I just couldn't figure out why all the secrecy about it."

Chloe could hedge, lie, make up a story, but she was tired and emotionally wrung out, and hell, Carlyle was her friend. "He didn't want to tell anyone because he didn't want to see me get needled at work over it."

"Aw. That's actually sweet. You know, at first I thought he was kind of a cold fish, but he's grown on me. He's just like all uptight goody-two-shoes because he's always trying to make everything right. It's annoying as all get out, but it's kind of sweet when it doesn't tick me off."

Chloe shrugged jerkily. Sure, it was. That's why it was so damn unnerving. "Well, anyway. We still work together, so—"

"Weren't you applying for that K-9 job at Bent County?"

Chloe pulled a face. She hadn't told anyone about that… except Carlyle after a few too many at the Lariat one night.

"I'm not going to apply for some job just to… Whatever."

"No, you were going to apply for it because you love dogs and were getting tired of the same old same old in Sunrise."

Chloe hadn't hit Submit on the application because as much as she wanted to try her hand at the K-9 unit in Bent County, she hadn't wanted Jack or anyone else to read into her switching jobs. One way or another. Because she'd needed to prove to herself she was strong enough not to go switch jobs in the hopes she'd have a future with *some guy*.

"No one will think that I'm moving jobs because I want a different job when my relationship with Jack gets out. They'll think I'm weak and lovesick," she muttered.

Carlyle looked at her like she'd grown a second head. "What does it matter what anyone else thinks? You *do* want a different job. And you're about as weak as a boulder."

Yes, but that's not what this was about. It was... It was... something. Carlyle just didn't... "You don't understand what it's like to grow up in a small town."

"No, but I do understand what it's like to be a grown up, Chloe. What other people think only matters if you let it."

It frustrated her because she didn't know how to argue with it. And with everything else going on, she wasn't handling that as well as she should. "Well, thanks for that after-school special, Car, but I've still got to drive over to Bent County and pick some of my confiscated belongings up." She didn't want to wait until morning now. She wanted to get out and away. From everyone. "I'll deliver Ry back to his room."

Carlyle shook her head. "Leave him. Cash is going to have him pick out a dog to keep him company inside once he's got Izzy to bed. We'll handle it."

"You don't need—"

"Chloe."

"What?"

"Scram."

"Carlyle, he's my brother and my—"

"Burden? Cool. We'll handle it for a while. And if you keep arguing with me, I'm literally going to fight you."

Chloe glared at Carlyle, but also wouldn't put it past the woman. And she was feeling so...so...twisted up, she couldn't find any words to get through to Carlyle. So she left. Left her brother as someone else's responsibility.

The Hudsons and their extended little network wanted to take over her life? Fine. They wanted to take care of her lying, unpredictable brother? Great. They wanted to watch her every move because of some nonsense threat that *Jack* perceived there to be? Let them.

She didn't know why it was getting harder and harder to breathe. Like there was a pressure in her chest, so heavy that she couldn't even fill up her lungs. It was all too much like impending doom.

Because they couldn't handle *everything* for her. *Something* was going to crash and burn, and then it'd be all up to her again—and then what?

She was going to leave. Right now. Just get in her car and go. Get the scrapbook and then head home. *Her* home. She didn't want to be protected. She didn't want to be helped. She wanted…

She started to change her route. Walk for the front, where her car was parked, instead of the side door that would lead her back into the house. To Jack.

Jack. Who *loved* her for some reason. Who'd asked her to let him take care of her. Because *he* needed that.

She swore and stopped walking, right there in the middle of the yard, starlight sparkling all around her. She couldn't be that woman who just took off. Oh, she wanted to be. *God*, she wanted to be. But it would hurt him if she went off by herself, and even if she didn't think she was in any danger, all it would take is for one little thing to go off course for her to feel like she'd been wrong.

She turned back toward the house, and then there he

was. Stepping out of the side door, the porch light shining a little halo around his head.

She loved him so much, it made her want to run away. Because what he didn't understand was that for all the ways she presented herself, for all the ways she thought therapy had helped her deal with her childhood trauma, deep down she saw—clearly, for the first time—how scared she was that it all just made her as unlovable as she'd always been treated.

But she *had* gone to therapy. She *had* faced a garbage fest of a childhood and worked on healing from those wounds. Maybe she wasn't all the way there, but it was about progress. Not perfection.

She walked over to him, not sure what to say or even who to be. It was like Ry unearthing all those bodies hadn't just caused a major issue. It was like it had turned her life inside out and nothing made sense anymore.

Least of all the man on the porch. No, least of all *herself.*

"Were you going somewhere?" he asked. Not with accusation. Not with anger. He likely felt a little bit of those things, but he didn't use them on her. That wasn't him.

So she told him the truth. No lie would form. "Thought about taking off."

"What changed your mind?"

She took the stairs, got close enough to him that she could see the way he watched her. Maybe there was a little flare of irritation lurking in his dark eyes, but mostly the only thing on his face was worry.

She leaned forward against him, wrapped her arms around him. "You."

He ran a hand over her hair. A sweet, protective gesture as he pressed a kiss to her temple. "Good."

That simple response almost made her laugh. But this whole *day* also revealed a truth that she was going to have to accept.

Everything was going to feel off-kilter and wrong until they got to the bottom of this mystery that connected to both their pasts. "Let's go get that scrapbook. I think I need to not have it hanging over my head."

He nodded. "Keys in my pocket. Let's head out."

He drove out to Bent County. They didn't really talk, just listened to the low strains of the old-fashioned country music he preferred. It suited the mood. Sad, mournful, a little weird.

When he parked and turned off the engine, he got out with her. It wasn't a surprise, exactly, but she had to fight the knee-jerk desire to tell him to stay in his truck.

They walked in together, smiled at the administrative assistant behind the desk. Sunrise worked with Bent County enough for Chloe to know everyone here by name.

"Hey, Linda. I'm here to pick up the relinquished property Hart left for me."

Linda tilted her head. "I'm sorry, Deputy Brink. Hart hasn't told me about any relinquished property. I don't think he's here, but Laurel is. Let me call her down." She lifted a phone to her ear.

Something didn't set right with that. Chloe looked up at Jack. He was frowning. But they didn't say anything, just waited for Detective Delaney-Carson.

A few minutes later, she strode into the lobby area. She stopped short and looked at both of them like she was surprised to see them there. "What are you two doing here?"

"Picking up the scrapbook Hart called me about this afternoon."

The detective's eyebrows drew together. "He told me he was going to drive it out to you before he went home."

Chloe exchanged a look with Jack. "That's not what he told us. He said I could pick it up whenever."

She nodded. "That was our original plan, but when you didn't show up, he was going to drop it by the ranch."

"Maybe take a pass at questioning Ry if he got the opportunity?" Jack offered, *sounding* casual.

Laurel studied Jack as if deciding what to say. Then she gave a little nod. "Yeah. Did he?"

"He never came by. Scrapbook or no."

Laurel's expression went from a puzzled kind of professionalism to flat-out worry. "I'll call him."

She took the phone Linda handed her, dialed the number and then waited. Her expression went from worry to cool, cop professionalism. But Chloe knew that meant something was *wrong*.

"He's not answering."

Chapter Thirteen

"Linda, can you get Hart's location? I'll take my cruiser and see if he stopped at home." The detective spoke calmly, smiled at the woman behind the desk. She gave no outward signs of distress or worry, but Jack could read it on her all the same.

Because this was out of the norm, and he knew *he* didn't like it, and he wasn't even Hart's partner.

"What can we do?" he asked her.

"Go home, Sheriff," Laurel said sharply, but when she turned to walk back into the station, Jack followed and so did Chloe.

"You've got two Sunrise deputies right here. Let us help."

"Sheriff, you know as well as I do you're both too involved in whatever this is to help in a professional capacity."

"I actually don't know that," Jack replied.

"Besides, I'm sure there's a reasonable explanation for all this," she continued, clearly ignoring him. But she didn't stop them from following her out the back exit of the station into the parking lot, which had personal cars and cruisers littered throughout.

Laurel strode toward some point only she knew, but then she came to an abrupt halt. In the dark, under the parking lot lights, one cruiser sat with its driver's-side door wide open. For a strange moment, they all stood there in stunned silence, looking at it.

"One of you go inside and tell Linda to get security footage of the parking lot up," Laurel said, her voice dead calm though she'd gone a little pale.

Chloe immediately turned and jogged back inside. Jack stayed with Laurel.

"How long would that have been like that without anyone noticing? Not long, right?"

Laurel shook her head as she approached the car. "Hard to say. Hart told me he was leaving about an hour ago. There hasn't been a shift change, so it's possible no one's been out here, but it's also possible he didn't leave right after he told me."

Jack peered into the open door of the car. There didn't seem to be signs of a struggle, but it was shadowy and dark in the car. Jack pulled out his phone and switched on the flashlight mode at the same time Laurel did.

Nothing appeared amiss, really, aside from the wide-open door. "Maybe he just forgot something?" It seemed like a leap—but then again, so did immediately jumping to conclusions about an open car door.

"No reason to leave the door open and kill the battery. Unless it was some kind of emergency." Laurel did a slow turn, eyeing the entire parking lot illuminated only by a few light towers. "It was still light out when he told me he was leaving. He's not... Whatever this is, it's not like him. *Something* happened."

Jack did his own looking around the parking lot. Bent County was hardly a bustling metropolis. Even though there was a police station right there, it wouldn't be impossible for something to happen out here and no one would see. Even if it was light out.

"He didn't get taken out of the police station's parking lot in broad daylight without someone seeing," Laurel said disgustedly, clearly more to herself than to Jack. "Without some kind of struggle. I don't know what this is, but it's not that."

Jack could hear what she was really doing: trying to talk herself out of thinking the worst. All while the worst was sitting right there in front of them.

"The footage is going to give us the answers we need. Let's go watch it."

"I don't like this," she muttered. "I told him we should have kept that scrapbook. It's all part of the Brink case. Not that I should be telling you this. Why are you even here?"

"Chloe might be a deputy at my department, but—"

"Come on, Sheriff. She's a lot more than your deputy. Anyone with eyes can see that."

Before Jack could react to *that*, Laurel was striding inside. Chloe met them halfway down the hall. "Linda says they're getting the footage up on the second floor."

Laurel looked at Chloe, then at Jack, then sighed. "All right, follow me." She took them up a set of stairs and then into a larger room clearly used for meetings. A man Jack recognized, though couldn't quite come up with a name, sat at a laptop.

He eyed Chloe and Jack, then Laurel. "Want me to put it up on the screen?"

Laurel nodded. In a few seconds, security footage of the police station parking lot showed up on the screen.

"What time you want?" he asked Laurel.

"Let's start at six. That's a little before when he told me he was leaving."

The footage sped up, people coming and going in quick time. When the man hit Play, the parking lot was empty aside from cars. Then Hart appeared. He had a box tucked under his arm.

"That's the scrapbook," Laurel explained, pointing to the box.

Hart opened his cruiser door, leaned in and put the box down, presumably on the passenger seat, though that wasn't fully visible from the camera angle. Then, before he slid into the driver's seat, he stopped, straightened and looked off into the distance with a puzzled frown.

Everyone held their breath as he turned and immediately began to jog off to the right—and quickly off-screen.

"We need footage of that side of the building," Laurel instructed the man at the computer.

"That side's a dead zone, Detective. We've only got cameras at entrances and exits—there aren't any in that corner."

Laurel swore.

"Does he see something, or does someone call out to him?" Chloe said, pointing to the screen. "Because he was getting in, but something stopped him. So someone had to have seen him. Something had to have gotten his attention."

"It's got to be a noise, right?" Jack returned. "He's getting ready to get *in* the car. Head down, then he looks over."

"But he leaves the scrapbook," Laurel added. "Keep rolling the footage," she told the man. "Because that scrapbook isn't there anymore."

Which meant sometime between when Hart went out of the parking lot and Jack and Laurel went out to the car, someone took it.

They watched. No one suggested they fast-forward the footage. They'd all investigated too many cases to let impatience get in the way of good police work. Seconds seemed to drag by, and tension settled into the air like a lead weight, wrapping around each of them as *nothing* happened on the screen. Minutes of just the trees blowing in the breeze and the sun slowly setting.

And then, *finally*, something showed up on the screen. A small figure, shrouded in a dark hoodie, moved quietly and stealthily up to the car, scooped up the scrapbook, and walked off the opposite side of the screen.

Laurel swore again. "I knew we should have kept it." She glared at Chloe. "What's in it?"

"How the hell should I know? I didn't even know it was in that chest."

"It's been in her garage, undisturbed for years. Anyone who wanted it could have gotten it easily. For years."

"Not if the person who wanted it was in prison," Laurel returned.

"If my father wanted it, he knew where it was and how to get to it. He could have sent Ry, and I wouldn't have thought twice about my brother hanging around my place. Detective, you can look into my father for anything you want, but it doesn't make sense to bark up that tree right now."

Laurel was still scowling, but she didn't argue with Chloe. "Here's what's going to happen: you're going to go back home and let me do my job."

"Who else is briefed on the case besides you?" Jack demanded.

Laurel's expression was stern. "I'll catch them up."

"We're going to look for him, Detective. With or without your permission or cooperation."

"I could have you arrested for tampering with an ongoing investigation."

Jack didn't take offense to the threat. He understood all too well what it was like to have no answers and someone you cared about in the middle of confusing danger. But he didn't bend either. "Or you could just let us help."

THEY WERE GIVEN the grunt job. They had trailed after Laurel as she'd gone from department to department, barking out orders. Then, when she'd finally stopped and turned to them, she'd told them to go search Hart's house.

Which was the grunt job because clearly Hart wasn't likely to have been there since before his shift today. Still, it was a necessary job, and Chloe and Jack drove from the police station over to Bent proper.

She couldn't blame the detective for keeping her out of most of it. Someone was going to call that parole officer in Texas and see where her father was, and if he wasn't verifiably in Texas tonight, he would be a top suspect.

But it didn't add up. Not to Chloe. Her father was shady as all get out, but he could have gotten that scrapbook whenever he wanted.

"There's something off here, Jack," she said, scanning the quiet street where Thomas Hart lived. She didn't know much about Thomas Hart's personal life, but according to Laurel, he lived alone in the little house they pulled up to.

A neat yard with no frills. A well-kept house with a porch light on in the dark.

Jack stopped the truck, and they both got out and studied the house from the front in what little light the porch and streetlamp offered.

"There's a lot of things off here, I think," Jack replied. "You don't have your gun on you. I want you to—"

"Follow behind. I know," she muttered, following him up to the porch. They'd knock on the front, then check around back. But Chloe didn't think they'd find anything here.

"The only person who knew about that scrapbook, far as I know, is my father. Nothing happened to it when it was only my father knowing. So what happened? Who got wind of it being with the cops?"

"Maybe that was the problem," Jack replied, rapping on the door. "Your father didn't want it with the police."

"I *am* the police."

Jack just shook his head as they waited. Chloe peered in the sidelight while Jack studied the front window, looking for a glimpse of anything. No one answered the door, no flicker of light or movement of curtains. Just stillness and silence.

Jack jerked his head, and Chloe nodded. They'd move around the east side of the house now. The street was quiet, the night heavy. As they moved around the side of the house, Chloe's nerves began to hum. In the front, the quiet had seemed like a comfortable small-town evening, but things were darker around back. Chloe kept even closer to Jack.

There were no lights on back here, so the postage stamp backyards all ran together like one big shadow. Some houses had lights on inside, shining in little cracks around curtains, but not many.

Jack pulled out a flashlight he must have grabbed from his truck. The beam shone across the grass, to a nice patio equipped with a ridiculously complicated-looking grill and then to a sliding glass door on the back of the house. Another curtain pulled tight. No lights here either.

"He's not here," Chloe said in a whisper. Not because they really needed to whisper, but because the night seemed to call for it.

"No."

But before they could discuss it further, something beeped, and it was so incongruous to the quiet night around them that Chloe nearly screamed.

Funny how she could almost always put her cop hat on, put the fear of danger to the side, but something about this case involving her father in *any* way made her feel more like the little girl who'd been terrified of him and less like the woman she'd built herself into.

He wasn't even *here*.

Jack pulled his phone out of his pocket. Someone was *calling* him, because little pinging noises were hardly her father jumping out of the shadows to be her own personal bogeyman.

Jack answered, and Chloe could hear the faint hum of a female voice on the other line but not the actual words. And still, something about the way Jack held himself told her it was bad news.

"Thanks, Mary. Keep me updated."

He turned to her in the dark. She couldn't make out the expression on his face, but he touched her shoulder.

Bad, *bad* news.

"Ry's missing."

She didn't know what she'd been expecting. But not that. She *should* have expected it, but somehow it took the wind right out of her. "But…" No *but*s. That's what Ry did.

She always screwed it all up, no matter how hard she tried.

"I'm sorry, Chloe."

She shook her head, not that he could see it in the dark. Maybe it took her off guard in *this* moment, but she'd also been ready for this in the long run. "I can track his phone. Maybe." She pulled her own phone out of her pocket, ignoring the way her hand shook. "I wasn't about to leave it up to chance. It's something I used to do when he was in high school, and I was trying to keep him in school. I haven't done it for years, so I was hoping he wouldn't notice and turn it off." She clicked the screen on her phone, brought up the location tracker and hoped.

The map moved around, zooming into a spot. Chloe would have felt immense relief, but he was in the middle of a campground by the mountains.

Not just any campground.

"That's where my parents were camping the night they disappeared," Jack said, his voice devoid of any and all emotion.

Chloe felt like her chest was caving in, but she didn't let it show. Couldn't. "If you don't want to go there, we can—"

"I'm going," Jack said sharply. But his voice softened on the next words. "This might connect, Chloe. Ry. The scrapbook. Hart missing. We can let someone else lead this. One of our guys. One of theirs. I can take you back to the ranch, but—"

Chloe shook her head. She had always protected her brother, would always want to, but now, in this moment, she realized if he was really involved in this… She wouldn't be able to stomach getting him out of it.

She took Jack's arm and pulled him back toward the truck. "Let's go."

Chapter Fourteen

Jack drove out to the campground he hadn't been at in a very long time. For the first few years after his parents' disappearance, he'd scoured every inch. Over and over again, with any free moment he had—which weren't many, when he'd essentially been raising five kids. But he'd found time.

He'd always found time. No doubt his siblings had as well. Always so sure there had to be an answer here. But that answer had never been found. Even now, knowing those skeletal remains were likely his parents, it didn't feel like answers were really within reach. Just farther and farther away.

It didn't bother him as much as he'd thought it would. He hadn't been fully cognizant of how the past few years had changed him. Even if now he could pinpoint it back to a moment.

Grant had finally left the military and come home for good a few years ago. That had been such a relief, not just for him but for the entire family. Tragedy hadn't struck again. Someone else in their family hadn't been here one day and gone the next.

Jack hadn't done more than glance at his parents' case since. He hadn't even driven down the road that led to the forest preserve. Maybe not consciously, but he'd avoided poking at that old wound in the same ways he'd been doing up to that point.

He didn't know if anyone else had felt that way. He wasn't even sure he'd fully realized it until this moment, driving into the forest preserve, realizing how much of his parents' case he'd put away.

Because somehow all the Hudson kids had made it into adulthood, not unscathed but alive. Building lives and families all their own. Digging into old tragedies felt like begging for trouble.

Yes, someone deserved to pay for what had happened to his parents. He still hoped someone *would*.

But what would be the cost?

It didn't matter. Answers or no. Trouble was here, in the shape of skeletal remains, missing detectives, the woman he loved and her runaway brother. So he had to see it through.

They didn't call Bent County. Jack knew they should. They were possibly going into something dangerous, and doing so without backup and without every local law enforcement agency having the information was risky. A risk neither of them should be taking. A risk he'd never take.

If it wasn't for her.

He drove, and neither of them suggested calling it in. Neither of them suggested anything. Chloe was as silent as he was. She was no doubt dealing with her own demons. Because Ry taking off *around* the same time Hart disappeared into presumably thin air felt ominous—connected, even if he couldn't see how. And there was no doubt in Jack's mind that Ry's disappearance was why neither of them were calling it in.

Bringing in other people would make it harder to protect Ry, no matter how little he deserved protecting.

When Chloe finally spoke, it was to give him directions to follow different twists and turns in the dirt road to find Ry's location somewhere within the preserve. Not too deep in it, or they'd be losing reception, and they wouldn't be able to track Ry's location if he didn't have service either, so that was good.

"Maybe we should approach on foot," Jack suggested when Chloe said they were getting close. "Gives us the element of surprise to really figure out what's going on here before Ry or whoever knows someone is coming."

"Yeah," Chloe agreed. Jack pulled off the road on the dirt shoulder. He turned off the car. "Grab the flashlight. I've got the only gun, so I want—"

"Me to stay behind. I know, Jack."

She didn't snap it. She sounded so defeated, it was like a little stab to his heart. That so many people in her life had failed her and lead her to all *this* mess, and she'd held up so well to all of it, but when did it get to be too much?

Jack knew there was nothing he could say about Ry, about her father, about *her* that could make this better. He hated that he couldn't do something to make this okay.

But there was no way to fix it, so they got out of the truck. Quietly, she came around to his side. She had her phone on, and the screen illuminated her face. She didn't look *affected* by what was going on, but her usual cop face had an air of exhaustion to it.

She switched on the flashlight from his truck and moved the beam around in front of them. "I think if we follow this road, then take the first right we come across, it'll lead us to him."

She didn't mention the possibility it wasn't Ry himself. That they could stumble upon just his phone and nothing else. So Jack didn't either. Why verbalize what they both knew?

"Got it," he replied instead. He followed the beam of light she held, making sure she stayed behind him enough that he felt reasonably sure he could stop anything unexpected from hurting her.

They moved in quiet precision. Jack was sure they were both trying to keep their minds blank, pretend like it was any Sunrise Sheriff Department case. Nothing that involved his parents or her brother.

When the flashlight beam illuminated a turn in the dirt road, Jack took it. They quickly found it wasn't actually a road, just a path to a parking area. Chloe came up next to him, sweeping her light around the dirt in front of them. Stopping when it landed on the lone car parked in the lot.

A car Jack recognized. Chloe's car.

Jack lifted his gun, looking around what little of the parking lot he could see in just the flashlight beam. It seemed to be deserted aside from the car. He glanced over at Chloe, who would be hurt by this. No matter what it was. Her brother had left the Hudson Ranch—likely hot-wired her car, since Jack doubted she'd left her keys behind—and was quite clearly up to no good.

Jack could tell she was looking straight ahead, staring hard at her car parked there. Jack couldn't make out her expression in just the glow of the flashlight, but he could feel the hurt radiating off her.

She audibly swallowed. "I'm calling Detective Delaney-Carson," she whispered, reaching for her pocket.

Jack put his hand over hers before she could grab her phone. "We can handle this, Chloe. You don't have to call it in if you don't want to."

She finally turned to look at him. He couldn't make out her features in the dark. She was just a shadow, but her voice was convincing enough. Firm and determined. "Yes. Yes, I do."

CHLOE'S HAND SHOOK as she held the phone to her ear, but she didn't think Jack saw the tremor. He was busy watching all around them, making sure they weren't sitting ducks.

For what, she didn't know. Whatever was going on... nothing added up or made any sense. But she could feel danger in the air like an impending storm.

There wasn't any movement from the car. No sounds but the rustles and chirps of an evening in the wilderness. Wherever Ry was, it wasn't right here. Chloe refused to let her mind bound ahead to worst-case scenarios. Most likely, he was out here scoring a hit from some drug dealer.

Funny how she *hoped* that was all it was.

The phone rang and when the detective answered, it was with a terse, "Yes."

"It's Deputy Brink. We haven't found any sign of Hart, but my brother took off from the Hudson Ranch. We've tracked him to a parking lot in the Franklin Forest. I don't know if it connects to Hart, to the scrapbook, but I think you should send someone over. We've found my car that he used, abandoned in a lot."

There was a pause. "I'm coming myself," she replied. "We got word from Texas. Mark Brink didn't show up for his last parole meeting. He's missing."

Chloe didn't swear. She couldn't even muster up surprise. Maybe she didn't think her father was behind stealing that scrapbook because it didn't make any sense, but maybe she was giving him too much credit to think he *had* to make sense.

"I'll send you our exact location," Chloe said.

"Good. I'll be there soon."

The call ended, and Chloe sent the location to Delaney-Carson. She took a deep breath, staring at her car. Parked. Ry's phone must be in the car, but Ry wasn't.

Unless…

She swallowed down a bubble of fear. If he was hurt, well, she'd deal with it. "Let's look at the car but not touch anything. I don't want anyone accusing us of tampering." Because if she stood here waiting for Laurel without doing anything, she'd think of a million terrible situations that involved Ry bloody and dead somewhere and she couldn't…

She was so angry at him, but she knew herself well enough to know she'd make a wrong choice if she let herself get too worked up about the possibilities of him being hurt. And she… She'd made too many bad choices when it came to her brother.

That ended now.

"Chloe—"

"If I say we should look at it, we should look at it. If you want to go first and keep me behind you, I'd start moving." She knew she was being a jerk when Jack was trying to be protective and sweet, in his way, but she was holding on by a thread.

She needed to do everything she could to treat this like a crime scene that had nothing to do with her. To treat Jack like a fellow cop, not the man she loved.

They moved forward in tandem, Chloe training the flashlight on the car. They were quiet, watching for movement, listening for sound. But there was nothing as they got close enough to the car to look inside.

Chloe swept the beam over the entire car and in each window, heart in her throat, *praying* it would be empty.

And it was. There was nothing amiss inside. It looked almost exactly like it had when she'd left it on the Hudson Ranch, with the one exception of Ry's phone lying in the console.

That made her nervous, of course, but at least it wasn't a body.

At this point, Ry had made bad choices. She could accept that. She had given him every opportunity to make different, better choices. He'd refused. She could mourn that, but she couldn't keep blaming herself for it.

But she could never stop hoping he was alive. Hoping he'd find some way to get himself out of all the choices he'd made. Maybe it hurt her heart, but that was the bottom line now.

Meanwhile, Jack Hudson stood beside her, offering *not* to call the authorities they needed to call, wanting to protect her—and if that meant bending his very strict moral code, apparently he was willing to do it.

Chloe couldn't let him. It would just about kill her.

"I want to know who he talked to, but we better wait for Bent County to open the door with gloves. There might be prints that give us a hint as to what's going on. If he was here with someone else." She looked out into the darkness around them. "Meeting someone? I don't know. But it's going to be Bent County's job to figure it out."

Jack nodded. "Okay, but if he drove your car here, left it here, we should be able to pick up his trail for a little while." Jack reached for the flashlight. He didn't take it from her but pushed it down a little so the light illuminated their footprints. Nothing super clear, but enough of an indentation to tell that someone had been walking across the makeshift lot. "Or we can stay here and wait."

It was up to her. A lump formed in her throat. Funny how she wouldn't mind him sweeping in and making the decisions for her right now. But that was because these were the kind of decisions she had to make for herself, even if she didn't want to.

Chloe used the beam, searching out footprints that weren't hers or Jack's. Eventually she zeroed in on a pair that was either Ry's or some other random person's. Jack walked ahead, gun drawn and at the ready, as her beam led them away from the parking lot and into the low grasses that made up the field in front of them. There was a path, it looked like, though it was hard to tell in only the beam of the flashlight if it was just from animals trampling through or an actual marked hiking trail in the forest.

She didn't want to follow his footsteps too far with Bent County coming, but it was hard to hold herself back knowing Ry could be out there. Doing who knew what.

"Chloe."

Jack had that tone in his voice. Like something bad was coming, but she didn't see what it could be. She looked around, she listened, but nothing.

Then his hand came over her wrist, he pulled her a little forward and he moved the light beam to something on the ground.

It was just a small little circle, but Chloe had been a cop too long not to know what blood dropped onto dirt looked like.

Her hand shook for a second, but only a second. The

light trembling was enough for her to ground herself. To remind herself she was strong, capable. A *cop*, not a big sister who'd failed.

She moved the beam up the trail. Not much farther up, there was another spot, about the same size as the first.

She took a few steps forward, and Jack never released her hand, but he didn't stop her. He moved with her.

The third circle was bigger. Noticeably so. She inhaled, knowing it was shaky. Knowing she couldn't quite make herself immune to this.

Someone was bleeding, and the chances it *wasn't* Ry felt really, really low.

"What do you want to do?" Jack asked her quietly. "Wait or follow?"

They should wait. That would be the safe thing to do. But as much as she was ready for her brother to face the consequences of his actions, she wasn't ready for him to be hurt. Or worse, dead.

"Follow."

Chapter Fifteen

Jack walked in front of Chloe, following the lead of the flashlight she held. Every few steps, there was a splotch of blood. Sometimes they got smaller, but then they'd get bigger again.

Jack gripped his gun. He occasionally looked out into the dark around them but never caught sight of anything, never heard anything that seemed out of place. Even though he was on edge, there wasn't that feeling of impending danger to him and Chloe.

But there had been danger here, that was for sure. The blood splotches along the trail no longer got smaller, only bigger, until they became almost a continuous trickle of blood.

Every so often, Jack glanced back at Chloe holding the flashlight. He could feel the tension pouring off her. She was worried it was Ry doing the bleeding, and so was Jack. The other option wasn't much better—that Ry had been the person to cause the bleeding in someone else. Both were going to be hard pills to swallow for Chloe. But there was no pill to swallow until they figured out what was going on here.

Jack wondered how long they could walk before they found something, before Bent County arrived at the parking lot and wondered where they were. He wondered a lot of things on this slow, nerve-racking walk that never seemed to end.

The trail narrowed, and the trickle of blood seemed to disappear. Though, more likely, whatever had been bleeding was now bleeding in the grass rather than the dirt.

Jack paused, not sure whether to press on or study the grassy sides of the trail for the blood. No doubt it didn't just miraculously stop bleeding.

"Jack." Her voice trembled on just the single syllable of his name.

He heard it then. The rustle and clicking sounds. Not a human threat, but animal. Still, he wasn't sure why that would scare Chloe, who'd grown up around wildlife and the potential threat and danger of them just as much as he had.

Until he turned to where the beam was pointed. Two pairs of eyes glowed back at them. But it wasn't the animals— coyotes—that had caused that reaction in Chloe. It was what they were standing next to.

A human body.

Jack moved without fully thinking. Just placed himself between her and the body. Just made sure his body stopped the beam of light from reaching that far. He hadn't seen the details, just the body—the very still body—being studied and perhaps other things by the coyotes.

"It's Ry, isn't it? It's… He… Someone…"

Jack moved forward and pulled her into him. "We don't know that, Chloe."

Her breathing hitched on a little sob. "It's *someone*."

He wanted to give her his gun and tell her to follow the trail back to the parking lot. Wait for the cops. He wanted her to let him handle whatever this was. But it would leave him with only his phone for a light and with no other form of protection. He didn't think the coyotes would be much of a problem if he didn't approach, but he'd have to approach to identify the body.

Chloe needed to know. For sure. So he couldn't send her back yet. He had to…

"Stay here. Put your phone flashlight on, and give me this one." He pried the flashlight from her fingers. He didn't think she was holding it so tight because she didn't want to relinquish control, but because she was in shock.

"Chloe," he said sharply. She jerked her gaze to him. "Pull out your phone. I'm going to get closer and see if I can get an ID."

She shook her head. "Jack, they'll… You can't approach wild animals feeding."

"I'll be careful. You stand right here."

"Jack."

But he ignored her protests and moved forward. Luckily, she stayed put, or he would have had to stop. He didn't want her seeing whatever this was, but he knew she needed answers.

He'd get her those answers.

He pointed the beam back at the animals. They didn't move, but they watched him approach. Then they started to move a little nervously. Low growls began to emanate from where they stood.

Jack made a few ridiculous noises, loud and sudden, hoping to scare the coyotes off as he approached. They were clearly reluctant to leave the body, and reluctant to deal with Jack. They backed off a *little*, though not as far away as Jack would have preferred.

He moved the beam from the coyotes to the body. An

arm was bloody and mangled, no doubt some from the coyotes, but perhaps some from whatever injury had caused the trail of blood, because most of the body looked to be intact.

Jack circled, hoping to get closer to the head and face. As he did, he saw hair, and immediately knew it wasn't Ry because the brown was too long and peppered with gray.

"Chloe, it's not Ry," he called out to her, still trying to creep close enough to get a glimpse of the face without upsetting the coyotes too much. He kept making noises and flashing the beam of the flashlight at the animals, hoping to keep them back.

They did keep inching away, but they didn't stop their warning growls or take off like he might have preferred. Still, he got to a better angle, slightly closer, and was able to point the light at the face of the body.

Not Ry. Familiar, but Jack wasn't sure… Until it dawned on him just who it was.

He let out a slow breath, then began to back away from the body, from the coyotes, back toward Chloe.

When he reached her, he realized she was shaking. She hadn't turned the light on her phone on, but she held it in her hands.

"Chloe."

"It's Ry, isn't it? It has to be. It's the only thing that makes sense." She was crying. Panicking, clearly.

He had his hands full and wasn't quite sure whether to put down the light or the gun. In the end, he placed the flashlight on the ground and gripped her arm with his free one. "Chloe, listen to me, sweetheart. It's not Ry."

She nodded, like him touching her finally got it through to her. When she finally spoke, her words were choked. "Then who is it, Jack?"

He took a deep breath. He didn't want to draw it out, and still… It was hard to say. "It's your father."

CHLOE DIDN'T BREAK DOWN. Or at least, she didn't lose it over the fact her father was dead. That information kind of helped her pull herself together. Breathe again, wipe her cheeks. In those first few moments, she couldn't have cared less about her dead father. She had just been so damn relieved her brother hadn't ended up that way.

So far.

Then the chaos had started, which was kind of a nice distraction. It was this strange, buzzing foundation to whatever was going on inside her. Jack took her back to the parking lot, where Detective Delaney-Carson had arrived and was investigating the car.

Jack told the detective everything—or at least, Chloe thought he had. The panic that it had been Ry lying in a bloody, dead heap had been hard to fully come out of. And the fact of the matter was, even knowing it *wasn't* Ry didn't ease her worry. Because Ry was still out there somewhere since this was her car in the parking lot.

Maybe Ry was the aggressor, but more likely to Chloe's way of thinking, he was another victim to whatever their father had dragged him into.

Detective Delaney-Carson called in more backup, and pretty soon there were cops everywhere. Dealing with the coyotes and the body, and determining what their next steps were going to be.

Jack had tried to convince Chloe to go back to the Hudson Ranch multiple times, and even the detective had suggested it, but Chloe couldn't budge. Not until they found Ry.

She kept expecting to feel something when they brought

her father's body out of that field in a body bag. Some sort of…not grief, obviously, when he'd been nothing to her, really, besides a tormenter. But she'd expected to feel *something*.

Instead, there was nothing but an odd sort of numbness when it came to her father's death. Murder. Whatever it was. The only feeling she really recognized was worry over Ry, over whatever was going on with Hart missing, about what this all meant for Jack's family. Really, about what this all *meant*.

Because as much as she'd felt her father didn't have anything to do with stealing that scrapbook, there were no leads here. No answers. Just a dead man. So it was more questions and no leads.

"Deputy Brink, I'd like to ask you a few questions."

"I think any questions can wait," Jack said, stepping in between the detective and Chloe herself.

It was funny how she could appreciate the gesture but not want it all the same. "No, I'd like to answer all the questions I can right now. I want my brother found. No matter what."

Jack moved to the side, still standing beside her but no longer blocking the detective, and it was the combination of sticking up for her and being able to stand aside that gave her the ability to lean on him, when she usually didn't want to lean on anyone.

"Do you have any reason to believe your brother could have killed your father?" the detective asked.

Chloe let that question settle over her. It was the natural one to ask, and it was one she'd been asking herself since Jack had broken the news to her. "My father was a cruel man. He was verbally, emotionally and physically abusive toward Ry. But in the way of abusers, Ry might have spoken badly about him, he might have even hated him, but he did what my father told him to do. Is it *possible* Ry had a moment of snapping? Of finally refusing and that resulted in some kind of altercation that left my father dead? Sure, it's possible. Is it plausible? No. Because he's still an immature boy seeking the wrong people's approval."

And he was out there. Somewhere. Probably in this forest preserve. And maybe her brother was capable of murder. Maybe that was in him, and she was blind to it. Maybe her father had pushed and pushed, threatened, started it. Maybe Ry had finished it and panicked. Possible. So possible.

And yet she just couldn't visualize it. She couldn't buy into it. Not with Hart and that scrapbook missing. There was some thread they were missing. Eventually, the detectives would find it, and normally she would step back and let them.

But she couldn't do that with Ry missing.

"Deputy Brink, I'm going to ask you to go home," the detective said. "Or to the Hudson Ranch. I'm going to ask you to leave this up to Bent County to investigate."

"Are you going to expect me to listen?"

There was a pause. The detective looked at the scene around them. Flashlights and cops and a vast wilderness that could hide so many answers. Then her gaze returned to Chloe, and she shook her head. "No, I'm not."

"Good."

"Just try to stay out of my guys' way. And keep me in the loop. I think the timing is too coincidental. I don't know how it doesn't connect, but if Hart and that scrapbook have nothing to do with your brother and father, that means we've got two cases to solve instead of one. I need your cooperation."

Before, Chloe might have hesitated, being worried about Ry and trouble. But they were in the same position, really. The detective's partner was missing, someone she probably cared about from years of working together. Someone she was responsible for due to the nature of their jobs. Chloe's brother was missing, and she loved the little rat bastard.

Connected or not, they were problems that needed solving no matter what. So they'd have to work together. "You've got it."

Someone hailed the detective, and she excused herself. Chloe turned to Jack and took a deep breath. She met his gaze—not cop-blank but worried. About her.

"I'm going to ask you to go home, Jack."

"Chloe—"

"Hear me out. This is… This place has meaning to you. Bad meaning. You shouldn't have to scour it and be re-minded. You can send Baker or Clinton out to help me. I can ask Carlyle to come out—she's got the skills to help me look for Ry. Or even Zeke would probably help. It doesn't have to be you *here*."

"It doesn't have to be, no. But it's going to be."

She'd known that was going to be his answer. She'd known she wouldn't be able to talk him into leaving. And still, she'd needed to hear him say it. To get that stern, irrita-ble look from him at her even suggesting he left her to this.

"I love you, Jack." And who the hell cared if there were cops all around them. She loved him, and no matter what horrible things were happening, they were going to make this one thing work.

She was determined.

Chapter Sixteen

Jack didn't bother to try to convince Chloe to go home and rest and eat first, though he wanted to. It would be the smart thing to do. He knew this rationally.

But he'd also been in her position before. He knew too well what it felt like to have a family member in danger. There'd be no rest, no taking care of herself, until they'd exhausted every resource in finding Ry.

Because it was one thing for Ry to be missing, running off on his own volition, but to be missing with one body already found was something else. Something urgent.

But where to begin? The cops were crawling all over the parking lot and crime scene, gathering clues, compiling evidence. Of course, their focus was on a dead Mark Brink and a missing detective, not Ry. Not yet. Not when they had one of their own missing.

"What if we follow that trail past where my father was found?" Chloe suggested. "Ry didn't come back to the car, and I'm not sure I buy that he and my father were out here if they weren't together. Especially with *my* car. Ry had to go somewhere. Somewhere in the preserve."

Jack didn't want to burst her bubble, but they had to analyze all the facts. "Your father might have had a vehicle. Ry could have taken that." Or been taken *in* that, though

Jack didn't point it out. Maybe they didn't need to analyze *every* possibility. "Whoever killed your father could have had a vehicle."

"Did you see evidence of anyone else?" Chloe returned.

He hadn't, though, in fairness, it was hard to determine what was wind mark and what was made by car and human in the dirt of the parking area. It wasn't an often-visited area since the campground was on the other side of the preserve. You'd have to be a pretty intrepid hiker to be on this side. So a lack of evidence of other people *could* point to something.

He supposed it was just as possible Ry was still in the preserve as not. But it was a *vast* preserve. "I'm not sure even with Laurel's okay they're going to let us walk down that trail again."

"Let's go around and meet it up a ways after." Chloe looked down at her phone screen and the map of the forest preserve she'd pulled up. "If we walk back to the road, then take it a while, we can cut over. Should be light by then, and we'll have an easier time of meeting up with the trail from the road."

Jack wasn't sure it was the best idea, but he knew Chloe needed to feel like she had a handle on something. Besides, even if it was the wrong avenue to go down, the entire Bent County Sheriff's Department was also looking into this whole thing. They could stumble into finding Ry as well.

Hopefully alive. Hopefully not a murderer.

But first, he had to be found, so Jack nodded at Chloe, and they started walking back out to the road. There was a hint of a sunrise to the east. She was right: it wouldn't take long for the light to catch up with them.

That would be good. That would help. Jack told himself

this over and over again. That he was the sheriff, that this was his *job*. Not a painful tightrope walk with the woman he loved, trying to unearth secrets that would hurt them both.

"Losing service," Chloe muttered, holding her phone up to the sky as if that might help. "I don't think we should cross over to the trail just yet. We need to go at least another half mile." She lifted her hand, poked at something on one of those high-tech watches Jack couldn't begin to understand.

"You know, you should get one, Jack," she said, as if she'd read his mind.

"I don't even like my cell phone. Why would I want it on my wrist?"

She shook her head, her mouth curving ever so slightly. The old, familiar argument was something like a comfort in the middle of all this unfamiliar.

"Do you know where it was?" she asked, not looking at him as they walked.

He didn't have to be a mind reader to understand what she was asking. "The campground on the north side was the last place anyone saw them. I've been up and down every inch of it, and this preserve. We're pretty far away."

She nodded. "Ry was too young to have been involved in that, but… Maybe we should head that way after we follow the trail for a bit. I don't think any of these things make sense enough to connect, except for the timing. I want to ignore the timing, I really do, because it feels so circumstantial. But…"

"Timing is part of it. I agree. We'll head out that way if the trail doesn't offer anything."

This time, she did look over at him. "Another thing you don't have to be here for."

"I'll be here," he said, and realized she had said the same exact thing, at the same exact time, mimicking his deep voice while she did it.

He frowned at her, but there was no heat behind it. In truth, he was glad she could still make fun of him in the midst of this mess.

Still, he wanted to make sure she understood. "Not leaving your side, Chloe."

She reached out with her free hand, laced her fingers with his. "Thanks."

They walked, hand in hand, in silence for the rest of the way until her watch beeped, signaling they'd walked far enough to cut through the low-level brush and find the trail.

The world was all alight now, still pearly and dim, but they wouldn't be risking twisting an ankle or stepping on something that didn't want to be stepped on by heading off-road to cut toward the trail.

They'd taken only a step or two off the road when they both paused. Jack thought he'd heard something from behind them. Likely from the parking lot, where even now a couple of Bent County deputies were working; though that wasn't the direction the sound had *seemed* to come from.

But in their stillness, Jack heard it again. A noise. A human noise. From the opposite direction of the parking lot. It had to have been.

Because it was someone's voice. And whatever they'd said sounded a lot like *help*. The cops certainly wouldn't be yelling for help.

"Is that someone calling for help?" Chloe asked, her hand squeezing tight in his. Too hopeful, too desperate for it to be Ry.

So he held her still to keep her from immediately running toward it and hated having to be the voice of reason. "Sounds like it—but we need to be careful, Chloe. We don't know what we're dealing with. Calls for help are just as likely tricks to—"

"I know, Jack," she said, but she was already moving toward the noise. Though she didn't pull out of his grasp, just pulled him along with her. Back onto the road and farther up.

He could have stopped her, but he didn't have the heart. They'd approach carefully. Together. They'd protect each other.

Jack realized they were close to the edge of the preserve that backed up to the highway. It could have been a trick of noise carrying. It could have been...

But as they walked around a curve in the road, they both spotted someone. Jack put his free hand on the butt of his weapon as he scanned the area. One solitary figure. Stumbling.

Too tall to be Ry, but there didn't appear to be a weapon, a threat. Still, Jack didn't take his hand off his gun until...

Both he and Chloe seemed to recognize the man at the same time, because they said his name and moved forward at a jog in unison.

When they reached Hart, he stumbled a little when he lifted his head to look at them. It was clear he'd been hurt. Blood crusted over the side of his face. But he was alive, and that was better than Mark Brink.

It wasn't Ry, and that was a shame for Chloe, but maybe it was a lead. If all these disparate things connected.

"Hart, what the hell happened?" Jack asked, dropping his hand off his gun and offering an arm for the man to lean against him. The fact that Hart did gave way to just how hurt he was.

"It was a woman," he rasped. Jack couldn't make sense of the words right away.

"A woman?" Chloe repeated gently. She stood on the other side of him, ready to take any other needed weight.

"I was getting into my car at the sheriff's department, and I heard a woman scream for help," Hart said, clearly trying to find the strength to stand on his own two feet as he recounted what had happened. "I looked over and I saw her. So I jogged over. I think I did…? I don't know. It's a little fuzzy. The next thing I really remember is waking up. Which I did, because I fell." He gestured with one arm, hissed out a breath, clearly in pain. "Not sure where I was. I think I might have been dumped out of the back of a truck. Once I could, I got up and started walking, hoping to find someone."

That would make sense, as they were close to the highway out here. Jack surveyed the distance between where they were and the parking lot where the other Bent County deputies were. Too far.

"We'll call you an ambulance," Jack said.

"Call Laurel. She'll get it sorted and know I'm okay all in one fell swoop, and she can pass it around to my family."

Chloe nodded and pulled her phone out of her pocket, taking a few steps away—in search of service, no doubt.

"I don't know what the hell's going on, Sheriff," Hart said in a quiet tone Chloe wouldn't be able to hear. "But I do know whatever it is ties to the Brink family. There's just no way it doesn't."

CHLOE JOGGED AWAY in search of service. Jack and Hart followed at a slower pace, and when she finally had a bar, she lifted her phone to her ear and called Detective Delaney-Carson.

She tried to feel relief as they moved through the next steps. A sense of happiness that even though Hart was hurt, he hadn't ended up like her father.

But Ry was somewhere out there, and she wasn't sure she'd feel anything good until she knew where. Until she knew he was okay.

With the phone call made, Chloe fell back into step with Jack and Hart. Chloe wondered if they should have him sit and rest, but if he'd suffered any kind of concussion, he probably needed to stay alert.

"What did this woman who called for help look like?" Jack asked Hart.

Hart licked cracked lips. He needed water. Probably some stitches for that gash on his head. They should really let him take it easy, but Chloe wanted answers, so she didn't stop Jack's questions.

"I don't really remember. It happened so fast. I heard it more than anything. 'Help.' Someone needed help." He said it as if trying to convince himself when it was clear that it had been a ploy. A ploy to get him away from the scrapbook, and that had to have been perpetrated by more than one person.

And none of those people could have been her dead father. He hadn't had the scrapbook on his corpse.

Ry also couldn't be involved in that. Because Hart had disappeared *before* Ry had taken off from the ranch. So he wasn't involved. She tried to comfort herself with that knowledge.

But she was too much of a cop not to accept that while he hadn't been part of the ploy to distract or hurt Hart, that still didn't mean he couldn't be involved in other things that connected.

Some comfort.

"I didn't have my full belt on me, but I did have my gun. They took it," Hart said with disgust. He stumbled a little, even with Jack holding him up, so they stopped their progress.

Chloe knew she shouldn't keep poking at him. He was hurt. But… "They also took the scrapbook. Out of your car. From the security footage, it seems like that's what they were after. Them letting you go seems to add credence to that theory."

Hart scowled. His gaze lifted briefly to Chloe, but then he looked back at Jack. He didn't say anything to that, so Chloe continued.

"You guys looked through the scrapbook when you had it. Right? You looked through it and couldn't find any evidence of note. But Delaney-Carson said she thought you should keep it, and you were the one who wanted to give it back."

"She wanted your take on it," Hart confirmed.

"So, what was in it?" Jack asked.

"It was black-and-white pictures. Old people. Ranches. Homesteader stuff with plat maps. Boring. Pointless." He glanced at Chloe again. And even though she could see suspicion in his gaze, she couldn't get mad at a man with a bloody face who couldn't even walk without help right now.

"I figured if it connected to what's going on, you'd lead us to whatever connection once you had it."

Then she realized what Hart's plan had *really* been. "You were going to follow me." It shouldn't make her angry. It was decent enough police work.

But it was barking up the wrong tree, so she couldn't quite ignore the feelings of frustration bubbling up inside her.

"I was going to investigate," Hart said coolly.

By following me. But she supposed she didn't need to argue with an injured man. It didn't change anything. He'd been hurt, the scrapbook had been taken and she didn't have the first clue as to *why.*

"Did you ever see the woman who called for help? Stranger? Maybe someone familiar?" Jack pressed.

Hart took some time to think about it. "I'm not really sure. I think… There had to have been two of them, right? If I went to help the woman, someone had to jump me from behind." He gestured at the bloody portion of his head.

True. And either one could have been the person in the hoodie who'd come back and taken the scrapbook. But there also could have been a third. Too many people involved now. What kind of sense did that make?

The ambulance finally came and so did Detective Delaney-Carson, relief etched in every line of her face. She explained that she'd called his family, asked him a few questions and then instructed the ambulance to take him away.

Laurel watched the ambulance go, then turned to face them both. Her expression was grim, her words all warning.

"We're dealing with two attackers—that we know of, there could have been more. These could be our murderers, or there could be more. I'm going to go to the hospital in a bit so I can ask him some more questions once he's been fully checked out. I know you guys want answers just as much as I do, but I wouldn't recommend heading out into this isolated place just the two of you. That's begging for trouble."

When neither Jack nor Chloe said anything, she sighed. Then she opened the bag she was carrying. She pulled out a couple of granola bars and two water bottles.

"This won't do much, and I'd recommend a full meal and some sleep, but you're not going to listen, so..." she said as they took the offered sustenance. "I have to focus on my investigation, my guys. Understand the risks before you go wading into it."

Chloe nodded and glanced at Jack, who was doing the same.

"I'll leave you to it then. Watch your backs. I'll try to contact you when we get some answers, but if you go out there, it'll be hard to reach you."

Again, silence seemed to be the best response, so Chloe kept her mouth shut and so did Jack.

Laurel shook her head. "It's a bad idea, guys."

But she turned and left them to it without any further warnings.

Chloe wasn't sure what their next move was going to be, but she'd search every inch of this forest preserve to find Ry. And she couldn't possibly go home and rest or eat before she did.

"She's right," Jack said once Laurel was gone.

Chloe turned to face him, her stomach sinking. Because she couldn't go back to the ranch and just wait. She *couldn't*. She knew he wouldn't leave her to handle this alone, but she couldn't possibly let him bulldoze her into going back to the ranch. "Jack—"

"Just the two of us *is* begging for trouble," he said firmly. Then his gaze moved from the horizon to meet hers. "So let's call in reinforcements."

Chapter Seventeen

A little over an hour later, they had a group of Hudsons and Daniels huddled together in the morning sun at the center of the forest preserve. Zeke, Carlyle, Grant, Hawk, Anna and Palmer had all come out. Louisa would join them later, after she was done working at her parents' orchard, if it took that long.

Because this was what family did. Jack had spent a lot of years considering himself the solitary, lone leader. The person who had to keep it all together without leaning too hard on anyone else for help. He'd spent a lot of time and energy trying to protect his siblings from pain, danger, risk.

Of course, he'd always had help, particularly from Mary and Grant in those early years, but he'd also made sure most of the responsibility lay on his shoulders. Or tried to.

If there was anything the past few years had taught him, it was that he didn't need to do that anymore. It had been hard to let go of all the responsibility he felt had defined him, but he thought he was finally really getting there. His siblings' lives the past few years certainly hadn't given him much choice.

Still, he hated asking for help. But for Chloe? He'd ask anyone. Because she was part of it too. She'd given him some hope for a future, even if he worried how well he'd be able to give her what she deserved.

But for right now, they had to find her brother.

He explained the entire situation to everyone who'd come, and Carlyle and Anna flanked Chloe like two sentries ready and willing to fight for her.

Because she wasn't alone, and she wasn't going to be. None of them would let her be. He hoped she was beginning to understand she didn't have to take it all on her shoulders herself too.

Grant had had the presence of mind to bring a paper map they could spread out and all look at to determine how they'd approach the search.

"Chloe and I will take the campground," Jack said, pointing to it on the map. He met Chloe's gaze because she'd opened her mouth to argue, but one sharp look from him and she closed it. He wasn't going to repeat himself about being by her side. It was a done deal.

"We'll approach from the south end. Zeke and Carlyle, I'd like you guys to come at it from the north." Because Zeke and Carlyle hadn't come into the Hudson orbit until long after their parents were gone, so they shouldn't have any emotional connection to the campsite. He'd send his siblings off into other corners and hope that it wasn't a mistake.

"Can I beat him up if I find him first?" Carlyle asked darkly, holding a grudge against Ry for sneaking away on her watch.

"With my permission," Chloe returned vehemently.

Jack could see she was trying to hold on to a kind of tough outer demeanor, and maybe it would have been better for Chloe if he'd paired her up with Carlyle. Maybe it was selfish to want to keep her in his sight, by his side.

Well, so be it.

As for his siblings, he paired them up and gave them their assignments. Anna argued with him about a few minor details, because of course she did, but when Chloe took his side, Anna backed off.

"Most of us won't have cell service as we move deeper into the preserve, but everybody has a flare, right?" Everyone nodded. Palmer had brought packs that would keep them going for a while, provided everyone with water and a weapon as well as a flare. They could feasibly spend the rest of daylight hours out here searching.

Jack hoped it wouldn't come to that.

"No matter what, everyone meets back here at four. No exceptions."

Everyone murmured their assent, then began to pair off into vehicles that would lead them to their different corners. They'd go to their assigned areas, canvass on foot for a few hours, then meet back here in the middle of the preserve.

Hopefully, with a safe-and-sound Ry Brink in tow.

Jack climbed into the driver's seat of his truck, waited for Chloe to get into the passenger side. They said nothing. Jack just drove through the twists and turns of paved roads, then gravel ones, until they approached the campground.

Tension seeped into him. If those skeletal remains on the Brink Ranch were his parents, there was nothing about this place that should make him tense, that should make dread and grief settle deep in his gut. Because if they'd been buried elsewhere, there was likely no remnants of what had happened to them *here*.

And yet no matter what he *thought*, what he knew, the

feelings were twisting around inside him as they got out of the truck at the entrance to the campground. He shouldered the pack Palmer had brought for him and tried to shake away his unease as he scanned the area.

On this side of the preserve, spruce trees towered and reached for a bright blue sky. It dappled the campground in dark shadows in direct contrast to the sunny day. At the front of the truck, Chloe reached out and took his hand.

None of his inner scolding had settled the anxiety he felt, but her hand in his did. It didn't take it all away, but it soothed some of those jagged feelings. They were in this together, whatever the answers might be.

They moved forward in unison, not quite sure what they were looking for. Signs of life. Signs of Ry. *Signs.*

The campground had some tents and some campers. Definitely not as deserted as other areas of the park. So he and Chloe walked down the little campground road, eyeing each campsite for anything that might stand out.

There was an older couple huddled around a campfire, putting together some kind of lunch. Jack didn't realize he'd stopped walking until Chloe gently tugged at his hand. He looked away from the couple and toward the road. He couldn't bear to look at Chloe and see sympathy on her face.

It didn't do him any good to think that his parents might be doing just that if they'd lived. They hadn't, and he had to focus on the living. But Chloe let go of his hand, tucked her arm around his waist so they were walking hip to hip.

He managed a slow, big breath that loosened the tightness in his chest. Focus on the living, on the future. On the task at hand. Which all centered on her.

They reached the end of the campsite road. Carlyle and Zeke would be catching up to them soon unless something had happened. Both Jack and Chloe looked around. Then Chloe pointed at a little outhouse. "There's a trail there. Are there more campsites that way?"

"Usually not when the campgrounds have empty sites closer to the facilities, but let's go check."

They moved past the outhouse, onto a trail that led to overflow campsites. Jack didn't see any tents set up along the trail, but as he and Chloe began to move, he heard someone. Just the whisper of a word, like a curse under someone's breath. And then the heavy, pounding footsteps of someone running.

Away.

Jack swore himself, turning to see someone's quickly retreating form.

Not just *someone*. Ry.

So Jack took off after him.

CHLOE WANTED TO cry with relief, and at the very same time, she wanted to beat her brother up. Tears threatened, but luckily, running as hard as she could through the forest helped keep them from leaking out.

If Ry was running, it was bad in that he was probably mixed up in a hell of a lot of trouble. Because he had to have seen it was them, so he wasn't in the kind of trouble he wanted help with.

But he was *running.* So he was alive and whole, and no matter how angry she was at him, relief lightened all her harsher emotions.

She was going to *figuratively* kill the little bastard. Right after she hugged him so tight, she was sure he was okay.

Jack had longer legs and could move faster for short-term distances, but Chloe had a better stride for longer distances

176 of Cold Case Discovery

and, because of her smaller size, was able to dodge trees with more agility, so after a bit of running, she bypassed Jack and was quickly gaining on her brother.

"Rylan Jonas Brink, stop running right now!"

He didn't listen, though he looked back over his shoulder. Tactical mistake, because after a couple more steps, he tripped and then went sprawling. Giving Chloe just enough time to catch up to him and pounce.

He struggled under her tackle, trying to buck her off. "I didn't do anything!"

She got her knee in his back, managed to wrench one arm behind him even as her breath sawed in and out. "Then why are you running?" She resisted punching him though she itched to, even as she was desperate to hug him and hold him tight. Alive, *alive*.

And in so much damn trouble.

"Let me," Jack said beside her. She realized he was holding handcuffs, and she sighed. She adjusted her hold so Jack could do the honors.

Though she wouldn't have minded cuffing her brother herself in this moment.

Jack secured Ry's hands behind his back and dragged him back a few feet so that he was in a sitting position and could lean against a tree trunk.

Ry's gaze moved back and forth, from Jack to Chloe, then beyond them as if he was looking for someone to come rescue him. Or maybe take him away.

"What are you guys doing here?" Ry demanded, falling back on being surly and accusatory. Because why wouldn't he, cuffed and outnumbered?

She really hoped whatever he'd gotten himself mixed up with, whatever punishments ended up being doled out, would get through his thick skull and make him realize he could be so much more than he allowed himself to be.

"What are *we* doing here?" Chloe said, barely resisting a sneer. "You snuck away from the Hudsons. You *stole* my car. What the hell do you think we're doing here?"

"I'm just borrowing it! Why do you always have to over-react?"

Chloe had often wondered if her brother would give her an aneurysm, but this really took the cake. She took a deep breath, trying to resist the urge to scream at him.

"Why did you take my car to that parking lot, leave your phone in it and end up all the way over here?" Jack asked, his voice low and calm. Clearly trying to de-escalate the situation.

Chloe didn't know if that was possible. "And how?" she added darkly.

"I don't—"

"Don't lie to me." She pointed her finger at him, narrowly resisted poking him. Hard. "Do you know what kind of trouble you're in right now? Tell the damn truth, Ry."

Ry rolled his eyes, and she would have reached out and punched him, probably, but Jack put a hand on her arm. She swallowed down the suddenly swirling anger. Or tried to.

She didn't know how to get through Ry's thick head, and he was making it impossible to feel any kind of sorry for him.

"You'll just get ticked off, but there's nothing to get mad about," Ry said, in his usual defiant, oh-so-victimized way. "Dad wanted to meet up. He's on parole, so it'd have to be quick so he could get back to Texas. I knew it'd get back to you if I did it anywhere where people could see, so we agreed to meet here. I drove over and I waited for him, and

he didn't show. I knew you'd start looking for me, so I figured I'd just walk around for a bit."

It was a lie—or at least, partly a lie. She doubted very
much Ry had walked all the way from the parking lot to
this campground. Maybe it was *possible* in the hours that
had passed, but he didn't look like he'd done any major
walking or hiking.

Granted, it didn't look like he'd killed anyone, either,
but she didn't know what to think about his ability to do
that anymore. So she told him. Flat out.

She knelt next to him, looked him straight in the eye.
Not because she wanted to soften the blow, whatever blow
it would be, but because she wanted to watch every last
inch of his reaction. "Dad's dead, Ry."

She watched as Ry's expression drooped and his entire
face blanched. There was no shifty discomfort, no guilt,
just straight-up shock. "Dead? He shouldn't be…" Ry swallowed. "You saw him? Dead? You're sure he's dead?"

"Yes."

"But…" Ry shook his head. He looked up at Jack, then
back at Chloe right in front of him. Some little war played
out over his expression, but she had seen Ry guilty enough
times to know none of it was guilt. She'd seen him lie
enough times to know what he was working through wasn't
a lie.

"Chloe, you have to get out of here." He said it seriously,
urgently, leaning forward. "I've got it handled, okay? But
you've got to go. She'll…"

She? It made Chloe think of what Hart had said: a
woman had called for help. A woman was involved. Did
this connect to Hart more than their father? But Ry didn't
say anything, just trailed off.

So she leaned forward too, got in his face. "Who, Ry?"

He shook his head vehemently, his eyes wide and worried. "I can't tell you, Chlo. Please. *Please*. Save yourself. Just let me go. There's no way it works out if you don't get out of here. Fast." He was so earnest, and yes, Ry was a good liar when he wanted to be, but she saw something like genuine fear in his gaze.

Like he actually was trying to protect her. She leaned back a little, his fear sparking her own. Ry trying to be noble felt more worrisome than anything else that had happened today.

She reached out, gripped his shoulder tightly. Hoping some kind of connection would get through all…whatever this was. There was always this wall between them, and she needed to scale it. His attitude, his refusals. Hurdles he refused to acknowledge. But she had to get through to him somehow. "You need to be straight with me. For once. Damn it, Ry. For once, tell me what the hell is going on."

He leaned forward, so close that their noses were almost touching while she held on to his shoulder. When he spoke, he enunciated each word clearly, his eyes a maze of fear and determination she'd never seen in him before.

"I can't tell you, Chloe."

"Good boy," a female voice said, and Chloe dropped Ry's shoulder, whirling as best she could on her knees. Jack had also turned and had his gun out and pointed at the voice—but there was more than one woman standing around them. And they all had their own guns, trained at each of them.

Chloe stared at the trio in utter disbelief. It had been so long since she'd seen the woman with a gun pointed at Jack, she only recognized her because she saw so much of her own face in the woman.

Her mother.

The one with a gun trained on Chloe herself was also familiar. She'd had an off-again, on-again relationship with her father when Chloe was a teen. Sarah, if Chloe remembered correctly. It had been a volatile enough relationship that Chloe had once had to mop up the woman's bloody nose. She'd been fifteen at the time, maybe? The third woman, with a gun pointed square at Ry, looked vaguely familiar, but Chloe couldn't place her. Maybe another one of her father's girlfriend's? She was on the young side, so maybe one of Ry's?

Either way, Chloe didn't know what on earth to make of any of it. She looked at Jack. He had his sheriff's face on and was unreadable, gun held calmly and relaxed, pointed at Chloe's mother. But it was three guns to one.

"I'd put the gun down, Deputy," Jen Rogers said, smirking at Jack. "Or it's going to get real bloody, real quick."

"It's *Sheriff* these days, Jen." Because of course Jack had had dealings with her mother when he'd been a deputy for the county years ago. Why wouldn't he have?

"Well, *Sheriff*, put the gun down, or I start shooting."

Chapter Eighteen

Jack didn't immediately drop the weapon. If any of the women really wanted to shoot, they could have done it before drawing anyone's attention. They could have killed them all, then and there, because he and Chloe had been so intent on Ry.

A mistake. His own. But he couldn't worry about how he'd failed just yet. He had to get them out of this first.

"Sarah?" Jen—Chloe's mother—said, her gaze never leaving Jack's. "If he doesn't put the gun on the ground by the time I count to three, shoot her," she said, clearly referring to Chloe. "To kill."

Jack knew it wasn't a bluff. Part experience, part the look in Jen's eyes. He held his hands up in mock surrender, or maybe *temporary surrender* was a better term. Slowly, he crouched and gently laid the gun in front of him.

Just as slowly, he straightened.

"Courtney? Collect his gun."

The third gunman—someone Jack felt like he vaguely recognized, probably from run-ins with the law—scurried over and picked up his gun. Jack could have stopped her, but he was afraid it would prompt Jen or Sarah to start shooting.

Maybe they didn't want to take them all out, but he wouldn't put it past Jen.

Jen's attention turned from Jack to Chloe. "Didn't I always tell you to listen to your brother?"

"Yes, because you shared all his worst impulses," Chloe returned, her voice cool, calm and collected even as fury shone in her eyes.

But Jack was relieved she looked more mad than emotionally hurt, more determined than scared. They could get out of this if they kept their wits about them.

Or so he'd keep telling himself.

"Mom, make them let me go," Ry groused from where he sat on the ground, still handcuffed. "This hurts."

Jen looked at Ry sitting on the ground, eyes narrowed. "Do you think I'm *brainless*?"

Ry didn't meet his mother's gaze. He looked down at the ground. "No, ma'am."

"Get up, then. Your feet aren't cuffed, and your legs aren't broken. And stop whining."

Ry struggled to get up on his own. Jack didn't feel the need to help him, though Chloe was clearly fighting the impulse.

Jack considered the interaction between Ry and his mother. What Ry had said before Jen had shown up made him rethink…everything. Ry had clearly been working with these women, not with Mark Brink. But what did that mean for the murder? For the scrapbook that connected to the *Brink* family, not Jen Rogers? Why would she have hurt Hart, taken the scrapbook? Was it really all disparate parts that didn't connect? Or was there something bigger he couldn't fathom?

Jack wasn't sure which would be worse.

"Why'd you try to kidnap a cop, Mom?" Chloe asked, sounding bored.

"I didn't *try*. I succeeded," Jen snapped.

Jack wasn't sure it was smart to rile Jen up, considering she was clearly a violent criminal, but Chloe probably had a good sense of her own mother no matter how little they'd communicated recently. So he followed Chloe's lead.

"Why didn't you kill him, then?" he asked, keeping his voice and demeanor conversational. "Because we found him, and he'll survive. Probably ID you pretty quick, and then what?"

Jen barked out a laugh. "They'd have to *find* me. What do I care if they ID me? I could have killed him. Don't for a second think I couldn't have—or that I won't kill you." She waved the firearm in the air like she was swatting at an irritating gnat. "We didn't need a missing cop. That always makes your kind crawl out of your holes. Can't have one of your own disappearing, can you? Honestly, we would have left him bleeding in the parking lot, but we needed a little bit more time to create confusion."

She sighed heavily, surveying Jack and Chloe. "Cops. Always causing problems." She shook her head, then looked at the two women she was with. "We'll have to do this one special, girls."

The two women with her nodded like they knew what that meant. Jack did not think *special* was going to be good.

"What about him?" Courtney asked, gesturing her gun at Ry.

"Good question. Not sure yet. Let's get everyone home and go from there. Courtney, you take the lead. You three will follow. Sarah and I will handle the rear."

"Where are we going?" Chloe asked.

"On a fun little hike, sweetie. You just used to *love* those, didn't you? Anything to escape me, right?" Jen demanded, bitterness and something akin to hysteria tinging her tone.

Courtney started off down where Ry had initially run. There was no clear trail, but it was easy enough to follow the woman. Chloe walked stiffly at Jack's side, and Ry stumbled behind them. Unnecessarily, in Jack's estimation.

But Ry was in handcuffs. Chloe and he were free. They didn't have their weapons anymore, but they had training. Jack still had his pack on. Play their cards right, they could take down all three women without anyone getting too hurt, set off a flare, and end this here and now.

But the guns made it riskier than he liked. He'd have to bide his time.

Jack considered it his good fortune that he'd been over every last yard of the forest preserve, especially this area around the campground. Wherever the women took them, he'd have a general idea of where they were and where they'd need to go to get out.

He thought about the flare in his pack. The women hadn't searched it yet—clearly not quite the thorough criminals they fancied themselves. Not that he could currently use the flare, so maybe he shouldn't pat himself on the back just yet.

"Have they found him yet?" Jen asked. When the question was met with silence, she reached forward and tugged Chloe's ponytail. Hard.

Before he thought the move through, Jack reached forward and grabbed Jen's wrist to stop her from hurting Chloe. Which earned him a gun shoved into his chest.

He dropped Jen's wrist immediately, then held up his arms slowly. "Let's everyone keep their hands to themselves."

"Yeah, *let's*." She studied him through narrowed eyes, then Chloe.

"Have they found who?" Chloe asked, her voice devoid of any emotion. But when Jack slid a glance at her, her hands were curled into fists. Fury flickered in the depths of her dark eyes. And she was purposefully drawing her mother's attention away from *him*.

And it worked. "Your father, of course." Then Jen's mouth spread into a wide smile.

Jack was stunned silent. He hadn't known what to expect, but this was…

"You killed Dad?" Chloe said, sounding as shocked as he felt.

Jen laughed. "Of *course* I killed him. That's what this is about. That's what it's *always* been about."

There was something about the way she said *always* that settled in Jack all wrong. *Always*. Here in this campground. Where his parents had last been seen.

Always. Like *all* the way back. Like skeletal remains on a ranch Jen might not have owned but would have had access to at the time. Would have known where to bury bodies without them being found. "You killed my parents."

Jen flashed a grin at him. Mean and with a frantic kind of glee in her eyes. "You're finally catching on, *Sheriff*. Good for you."

CHLOE THOUGHT SHE was going to be sick. Of all the things she was prepared for, all the worst-case scenarios she'd considered, her mother's involvement in any of this had never once crossed her mind.

And it should have. Dad and Ry had always had a contentious relationship. Abusive, yes. Ry had been somewhat submissive to Dad on occasion. But they'd *fought*.

It was their mother who had true control over Ry. Always had. Chloe had just been under the impression Mom had taken off and was as no-contact with Ry as she was with Chloe.

Chloe tried to wrap her mind around it all. Years of… her mother being a cold-blooded killer from way back? Even if she couldn't put murder past her volatile mother, her killing Jack's parents just didn't make any sense that she could come up with.

So she asked the simplest, most concise question she couldn't swallow down. *"Why?"*

"You should learn a lesson, Chloe, from his bitch of a mother." She jerked her chin at Jack. "Sticking your nose where it doesn't belong is always going to come back to bite you in the ass."

She heard Jack's intake of breath, but she couldn't look at him just yet. She would crumble if she did. And if she reached out for him, comforted him in any way, her mother would see. And pounce on it like it was a weakness.

Chloe wouldn't be a weakness. She wouldn't risk Jack. Not now. They had to save each other. And she couldn't think about what this revelation meant to him if she was going to accomplish that.

"Move along now. Not much farther." Jen gestured with her gun, so Chloe felt she had no choice but to swallow and follow Courtney once more. Courtney led them through thick trees, over a tiny trickle of a creek and to the craggy rock face of a mountain.

Jen and Sarah came around to the front of them, stopping at a small crevice in the rock. Jen pointed at it. "In you go."

"Mom, you can't make me go in there with them!" Ry said, sounding like a petulant teenager. When he was a *grown* man. Would he ever get over himself? After this, if they survived, Chloe was finally going to have to accept the answer was no.

Jen stepped forward, up to Ry. Chloe recognized the expression on her face. It *looked* sympathetic, but that was how you knew something awful was coming.

Before Chloe could step in front of Ry—because old impulses die hard—their mother whipped her gun back and slammed it across Ry's face so he fell backward and onto his butt. Chloe tried to catch him, but she hadn't been fast enough.

"Get in the cave. Now," Jen said.

Chloe grabbed Ry by the elbow, and Jack grabbed his other. Pulling him toward the crevice, still cuffed. All while Ry moaned and sniveled.

Chloe hesitated at the opening of the crevice. All dark. All black. A small, little opening. Chloe wasn't even sure Jack would be able to fit through if he tried. She tried to swallow an old panic fluttering around in her stomach. She didn't like heights and she didn't like enclosed spaces.

She had learned to keep her fear of heights hidden from her parents, but only because her fear of enclosed spaces had been something she hadn't known she should hide until her parents had used it against her when she was a little girl. Mom especially. She'd loved to lock her in the little closet in their apartment in town.

Chloe had to focus very hard on not remembering, on not going back to those old feelings of being a helpless little girl. She was an adult. She was a cop. She could handle this. She could survive it—just like she had then.

"Go on, Chloe. Get in there," Mom said in a little sing-songy voice, clearly reading her panic and enjoying it.

Chloe took a deep, steadying breath. She wouldn't give her mother the satisfaction of panic. Not when she had to somehow protect Ry and Jack from whatever this turned out to be.

Because if she'd confessed to essentially three murders, Jen had no plans to let them go. Maybe she wasn't ready to kill them yet for some unknown reason, but that had to be the plan.

"I'll go first," Jack murmured as they approached the rock. "Push Ry in after me, and I'll pull. Then you." He looked at her, right in the eye. "Got it?"

He was trying to be her anchor, and she appreciated it. Because she needed one, and if anyone could be one, it was him. Jack Hudson.

Who is in this mess because of you. Whose parents are gone because of yours.

And who loved her anyway, she reminded herself. Because he did. She saw it in his eyes, in his move to protect her *and* Ry. So she would be strong for him as much as for herself.

Jack flattened himself against one side of the rock and shuffled in through the crevice, just barely making it. Chloe couldn't see him, but she pictured his dark, steady gaze and helped Ry maneuver himself inside as well.

She glanced back at the trio of women with guns. She knew she shouldn't do it, shouldn't give her mother a chance to see her fear. But it was her mother she studied now.

"What are you doing, Mom?"

Mom's mouth curved into a vicious smile. "Ruining as many lives as I can. Just like how your father and high-and-mighty Laura Hudson tried to ruin mine."

It made no sense. It had never made any sense. Her mother's unending well of anger, of blame, of needing to hurt anyone and everyone she could reach.

"Get inside, Chloe. Or I start shooting."

Chloe nodded and then pushed herself through the crevice. Inside, it was so dark. Damp and cold and dark and—

A hand clasped around her forearm and gently pulled her inside.

Jack.

She wanted to lean into him, but she was afraid to allow herself the weakness. Afraid of what her mother might see and use against her.

So she held herself upright and tried to allow her eyes to adjust to the dark. But not long after they'd all gotten inside, a light clicked on. A lantern, some battery-powered thing hanging from a hook dug into the rock face. The cave was much bigger than the crevice had let on and was full of things. Makeshift beds, a table, a whole little outdoor-kitchen setup. Like people lived here.

Mom had said *home*. Was this... Was *this* where she'd been living all these years? It didn't make any sense, except that it explained why no one had been able to find her. A cave in a remote forest preserve.

But...why?

Chloe watched as Sarah settled herself in a chair at the entrance of the cave, gun pointed in their direction. Had the three of them been together all this time? She understood them conspiring to kill her father. And they'd clearly spent years planning it, as Mark had been in prison for six years now.

But Jack's parents... So many years ago. It just made no sense.

"Make yourselves comfortable," Sarah said with a mean smile.

Mom entered, standing next to Sarah, scowling. "For the love of God, shut him up," she said, referring to Ry.

Chloe looked down at her brother. His mouth was bleeding, and he was making little whimpering noises. Chloe felt a mix of worry and sympathy and bone-deep anger that he'd been part of this at all. "Come on, Ry, buck up," she told him. Just like she had when they were kids and she had to be the strong one. The one to protect them both.

He glared up at her, anger in his gaze. Anger when he was half the reason they were here. For so many years, she'd given him a pass. Because their childhood had been rough. She'd blamed herself for not being strong enough, smart enough, *good* enough to save him from all the trouble *he* caused.

But she'd had no one, and she'd turned out okay. Better than okay. She'd cobbled together a damn good life for herself, and Ry had complained and blamed and worn his victimhood like a second skin.

Chloe just wished she'd realized all this sooner.

"I thought you didn't want the hassle of cops trying to find other cops," Jack said, sounding so calm and in control. He couldn't be, though. Not knowing the woman standing in front of him had killed his parents. He was holding on to their training. He was dealing with the crisis at hand.

Chloe felt like everything she'd ever learned about being a cop, about de-escalating a situation, about self-preservation, had deserted her. Her entire world twisted inside out.

Except Jack.

Jen smirked at him. "Sure, it's a hassle when you don't have time to do it right. When there's too many witnesses. Now I have all the time in the world to make sure you all end up just like your parents, Sheriff. Because that's what happens to people who butt their noses in where they don't belong. They *disappear* without a trace."

Chapter Nineteen

Without a trace. Those words landed like blows because it was true. His parents had disappeared without a trace. Jen had committed a crime that she'd escaped for seventeen years, and Jack still wasn't sure what had prompted Ry to find those remains—accident, on purpose, it didn't matter.

Jen Rogers knew how to get away with murder, and he had to put that knowledge away. Set it aside so they could figure out how not to be her next victims.

Jack wondered if Jen knew they had a group of people already on-site. People who, come four o'clock, would start looking for them. And knew exactly where they'd been. Had she been watching them all this time, or had she stumbled upon them in the campground simply because of Ry?

He considered bringing it up to see if it would prompt Jen to panic, to make a mistake. That's all he needed. One little mistake.

"Now, I want both your cell phones," Jen said, holding out her free hand.

"What are you going to do with those? We don't have service in a cave. Can't ping us in here."

"It's called *distraction*, Sheriff. Now, hand them over."

Jack reached into his pocket. He considered "accidentally" dropping the phone. Destroying it rather than have it be used against him. But Chloe was taking hers out. She looked back at him and held her hand out like she'd take his too. So he tried to give it to her.

But she didn't take it. She put hers in *his* hand and gave him a look. A meaningful look.

Then he realized what she was trying to tell him. She had that damn smartwatch on her wrist. No one would be able to track them in this *cave*, but it was something. A potential lifeline. Without reacting, he took the two phones and walked them over to Jen. He handed them out to her.

She took them. Then she smiled at him. "You look like your dad."

Even knowing it was meant to hurt, meant to elicit a reaction, he couldn't stop it from landing. He *did* look like a carbon copy of Dean Hudson. He was reminded every time he looked in the mirror of the father he lost all too soon.

"Your mother could have survived, you know."

Jack held Jen's mean gaze. Inside, he was a riot of pain, but he kept his expression bland. And he said nothing.

"It could have just been your worthless father. Trying to tell me how to parent my children. Trying to get me into trouble with all those nosy family-service agents." Jen's self-satisfied smirk faded into an angry scowl, like she was reliving it. "I would have settled for just taking him out. She could have escaped. But she had to try and save your father."

"It's what people with souls do, Jen," Jack returned, ignoring how rough his voice sounded. "Help each other. Save each other. Love each other."

"No one's ever done that for me!" she shouted, stomping her foot like a child. And Jack could see where Ry had gotten some of his self-victimization. It stemmed from right here. He could almost feel bad for the guy. Almost.

Jen kept on shrieking. "No one did anything for me, ever!"

Jack shrugged. "Sounds like you deserved it."

Even in the orangish glow of the lantern light, he could see her face mottled red with rage. Her hands had curled into fists. Sarah murmured something softly to her, and Jen inhaled sharply, then let it out slowly. Calming herself, minute by minute, until she aimed one of her nasty smiles at him again.

"I want you to know, they died begging for mercy."

He should let it go—God knew, he should let it go. But when it came to his parents, their memory, he couldn't let her have the last word. "Sounds like they died fighting for it."

She let out a cry of rage then, guttural and furious. She wrenched back her arm. Jack went with instinct and blocked the blow by grabbing her arm before she could slam the gun across his face like she'd done to Ry.

It was a mistake—he knew that the minute his hand had come into contact with her arm. But it was just instinct, self-preservation.

It was pure stubbornness and anger that kept his grip on her arm. Until she lifted her left hand, and there was a gun in that one too. Pointed right at his head. *Then* he thought better of his fury and hurt.

"No!" It was, shockingly, Sarah's voice. She leaped off the chair, grabbed Jen's left arm. Jack still hadn't let go of her right. So she was now being held—on one side by her partner and on one side by her victim.

"You can't shoot him," Sarah said, seeming afraid. Desperate. "It's not the plan. You said it yourself. We can't deviate from the plan. We've already messed up once. We can't mess up again. It all goes to hell. You *know* that."

Jack was so surprised by the unexpected save that when Jen ripped her arm out of his grasp, he didn't even try to hold on. He stepped back, giving the women the space for their argument, and hopefully the distraction was enough so that Jen's anger was pointed to the woman she worked with.

Maybe that was a weakness that would allow them to escape.

"They're *my* plans," Jen said, her entire body turning toward Sarah. Her back to Jack and Chloe and Ry behind them. Like none of them even mattered. Like they couldn't be a threat.

Could he tackle her now, Jack considered? Would Chloe be able to get to Sarah's gun in time to take her out before retaliation? But that still left Courtney, who was presumably outside the cave.

But what if she wasn't? Was it worth the risk? Jack kept himself ready, watching, waiting for just the right moment—and he knew Chloe beside him was doing the same exact thing. Poised and ready to lunge.

He wanted it to be now, but it wasn't. But they would know when it was. They'd be ready. He believed that.

He had to.

"Any mistakes today have been *your* fault. I think you know that," Jen was yelling at Sarah.

Sarah's eyes widened, a mix of fear and offense. Panic, maybe. But she stood up to Jen. "I do *not* know that! It was your plan that was faulty. We did everything you said! Courtney got Ry to lure Mark here. *I* took the first shot and didn't kill him. *Just* like you said. I—"

"You hesitated! You know you hesitated! If you'd taken that shot when you were supposed to, I could trust you. But now? I can't. So I think we need to retool our plan."

Sarah was shaking her head. "We have to stick to the plan, or we'll get caught! I'm not getting caught!" She pointed her finger in Jen's face, panic mounting. "I'll tell the cops *everything*. I'll tell them it was your idea, your plan. Lure Mark here. Get Chloe away from the scrapbook. I'll tell them—"

The sound of a bullet exploding out of a gun erupted around them. Instinct had Jack jumping back toward Chloe, who'd hit the deck with her hands over her ears.

When he looked up, he saw Jen holding a gun in each hand while Sarah lay on the ground, still and lifeless. A pool of blood slowly growing bigger around her.

"You won't be able to tell them anything now, will you?" Jen said to Sarah's lifeless form. She blew out a breath, shrugged her shoulders a few times like she was shrugging away tension. "Man, I feel better." She turned to face them, evil smile back in place. "Now. It's time for a new plan."

THE GUNSHOT WAS still echoing in Chloe's ears. She didn't let herself look at the dead woman on the ground. She looked up from the defensive position she'd fallen into and focused on the woman who might kill them all.

Chloe couldn't remember ever loving her mother. Even when she was a little girl, too young to understand her childhood was a dangerous disaster, she'd wondered why her mother had bothered to have one child, let alone two.

And still, this was all such a shock. Bits and pieces she could make sense of, but the whole of what was happening, what had happened, was just too bizarre to fully fathom.

Clearly Mom's plan had been to kill Mark and get away with it. She was teaming up with Mark's other victims to do it. She'd killed Jack's parents because they'd called family services on her.

But what did it have to do with the scrapbook?

There were no answers to that yet. No answers could come if they didn't survive.

So she focused on the one most important thing to her.

She would find a way to get Jack out of this. She certainly wasn't about to let her mother make another Hudson a victim of her sociopathic ways. No matter what. Chloe would do anything and everything to get him out.

"Now you have more bodies to clean up," Chloe pointed out. Her voice was steady, her tone cool. She kept her expression blank when her mother turned to sneer at her.

"It's not about the bodies. That's easy." She gestured at the cave. Like…there were bodies back there, deeper in the cavern. A shudder chased down Chloe's spine, though she ignored it.

"And some bodies, like your father's, don't matter. No one will care that Mark Brink was murdered in cold blood. They'll do some cursory due diligence, then mark it down to his past." Her lips curled back even farther. "*Hudsons* and *cops* are different, though. We've got to make sure there's no trace. It's not about *bodies*, it's about trails."

"Forensic investigations have come a long way in seventeen years. You'd be surprised how easy it is to pin you to Mark Brink's murder," Jack said blandly.

Every time she poked at her mother, he did too. He took her lead and ran with it. It gave her hope that somehow they could outsmart her mother. They were good cops, a good team. They could do it. They just needed a chance.

Jen took a threatening step toward Jack, those guns in her hands making Chloe have to fight the need to step between Jack and her mother. To protect him.

It would be a death sentence for him. Chloe knew that.

"Even if they could pin it on me, even if they bothered, they couldn't find me. Do you know how long I've been here? Right here. Living, loving and laughing my ass off while no one could find *anything* about your do-gooder parents."

The whole time. Ever since Mom had just not come home one day and Chloe had spent the next few years struggling to keep Ry on the straight and narrow, trying to keep Dad from ruining their lives. Mom hadn't been running away, chasing a score or a guy or whatever.

She'd been living in a *cave*? "But why hide if no one knew you'd murdered the Hudsons?"

"Your *father* was meant to stumble over those remains and get himself into a heap of trouble. Your *father* was supposed to take the fall. But he never did listen, did he? He never followed through or did what he should. So I had to adjust my plans. You see, Chloe, one thing you never could understand was the beauty of *patience*. Always had to be going, moving, doing. Sometimes sitting and waiting is the best thing in the world. Because no one will ever know. And Mark Brink is dead. Finally."

Chloe didn't see how sitting and waiting had been best for her mother. Jen had always been mean, cruel, narcissistic and rotten to the core. But she had never been quite this unhinged, or so it had seemed to Chloe at the time. Chloe supposed she should be grateful because *unhinged* left room for error. One little mistake and Chloe or Jack would take advantage of it and get out of this.

Chloe was sure of it.

Courtney stepped through the cave entrance. She nearly stumbled when she saw the body on the floor, but aside from a wide-eyed expression, she didn't voice any surprise. She blinked once, then turned toward Jen.

"A couple saw them running after Ry and called the police." Her voice betrayed her a little. It shook.

"Damn interfering busybodies," Jen said grimly. "They'll be crawling all over now."

"I don't think we should do it here," Courtney said, eyeing Chloe, Jack and Ry before turning her attention back to Jen. "We need to move."

Chloe didn't know what *do it here* meant for sure, but she had a bad feeling it meant *kill them.*

Jen shook her head. "Moving is too dangerous with cops crawling around. We need a distraction. Time and a distraction." She turned to face them. "Ry, get over here."

Chloe looked over her shoulder and watched as her brother struggled to his feet, keeping his eyes downcast and refusing to meet her gaze as he shuffled over to their mother.

"You're going to go out to that campground. You're going to let a cop find you—don't you go searching them out, just let them find you. You're going to hedge, lie a little bit, take your time, but eventually you'll confess you saw your sister and the sheriff, and you told them where the scrapbook is."

"They'll arrest me if they think I had anything to do with the scrapbook!"

Jen laughed. Low and mean. "Yeah, so what? A lot worse happens if you don't." She jerked her gaze to Jack. "Uncuff him. And give him that backpack you've got on. That'll prove he saw you guys."

Jack didn't respond right away. He looked at Chloe. She couldn't think of a way to get out of this—and as much as it pained her to be thinking about Ry's well-being after all this, Ry would be safer in jail than he was here. So she gave Jack a little nod.

He pulled the key out of his pocket and tossed it toward Jen. She didn't catch it, but she did scowl at him. "I can't *wait* to make your death slow and painful."

"I've never known a drawn-out murder to work out for the murderer," Jack replied.

Jen's smile was pure *evil*. "Remind me to give you a step-by-step of how I took my sweet time with your parents." She picked up the key he'd thrown. "But first things first." Roughly, she jammed the key into the cuffs and released Ry.

"You tell them you sent them off to find the scrapbook. You tell them Mark told you he left it in a hotel room in Hardy. You don't know the specifics, but that's what he told you, so that's what you told them. Do you understand?"

Ry nodded.

"If you don't do exactly as I say, what happens?"

"The pit," he said, sounding like the little boy Chloe remembered all too well. Not always sweet, but always trusting.

Chloe didn't know what *the pit* was—no doubt some kind of torture. Mom was always good at that.

"You didn't like your last stint in the pit, did you?"

Ry shook his head vehemently.

"What's better, Rylan? The pit or getting arrested?"

"Arrested," Ry muttered.

"That's right. Go get the backpack off him," she said, pointing to Jack.

Ry trudged over. He didn't meet Chloe's gaze or Jack's,

just kept his eyes on the ground and held out his hand. When Jack didn't immediately hand it over, Ry slowly looked up.

Even slower, Jack shrugged the backpack off. With careful, precise movements, he held it out to Ry. When he spoke, it was low and quiet. Maybe Jen heard over by the entrance, maybe she didn't, but Chloe figured it didn't matter. It was only the truth.

"She deserved better, Ry."

Ry didn't say anything, didn't even give her a glance. He just took the bag and scurried back over to their mother.

"Not one wrong move, Rylan. Not *one*," Jen said menacingly.

He gave a little nod. He took a step toward the cave entrance but then looked back at her and Jack. "Sorry, Chlo," he said, before Jen pushed him out the crevice of the entrance.

It was funny. She almost believed he was.

But what she didn't believe was that he'd help.

Chapter Twenty

Jack knew better than to count on Ry going against his mother's wishes and helping them out of this mess, but he hoped for Chloe's sake Ry might mess up his assignment somehow. If he ran into Zeke or Carlyle back at that campground, they'd surely see through him. They'd retrace his steps.

Or, if he had even an ounce of intelligence, he'd use the flare in the pack and really help them.

But Jack wouldn't depend on Ry to fix this for them. He and Chloe would have to devise a plan. One that took into account that his family was out there and would start looking for them. All they had to do was stay alive past four o'clock.

"Do you think he's actually going to listen?" Courtney asked Jen in a low voice, but in the cave, it carried over to him and Chloe.

"He knows what happens to him if he doesn't," Jen replied darkly.

"What if—"

"That boy is a *coward*. Always has been. Always will be. Besides, we have secret weapons. So *many* secrets. Let's go show them one." She turned her attention from Courtney to Jack and Chloe. "You're going to turn around. You're going to start walking. And you're not going to stop until I tell you to."

Jack shared a look with Chloe. It was two against two now, and going deeper in the cave was only asking for trouble when it was clear Jen's plan was to kill them. Why keep giving her easier and easier ways to get away with it?

"I don't think we will, Jen."

Chloe inhaled sharply, but she nodded. She moved so that they stood shoulder to shoulder, facing Jen and Court-ney and eyeing the cave exit behind them. All they had to do was get past them without getting shot.

Without getting *fatally* shot, really. He knew Chloe wouldn't appreciate it, but if *he* drew both their gunfire, she could get past them. Get out. Maybe there'd be a chance. Oh, she wouldn't thank him for that. She'd end up beating herself up for it, especially if he did get fatally wounded.

But she'd be alive.

"You will because if you recall, *I've* got the upper hand. *All* of the upper hands. You do what I say."

"So we can die the way you want us to?" Chloe shook her head. "Pass."

"Pass?" Jen replied, then she laughed. High-pitched and out of control. "*Pass*, she says. Oh, Chloe, you did not inherit *any* of the Rogers family smarts, did you?"

"I hope to God not."

Jen was aiming her gun at Chloe now, and Jack knew he needed to do something. Intervene before she ended up dead here in this dark damn cave. Not on his watch.

"It seems to me this only works out for you if we follow what you say. I don't think we have much interest in this working out for you, so I guess we're at an impasse. I guess you'll have to shoot us." He tried to angle his body so he was in front of Chloe, but she was doing the same thing to him.

He wanted to tell her to quit it, wanted to shove her out of the way, which distracted him enough that he wasn't giving Jen the attention he should have been.

"As you wish," Jen replied with a shrug. Then he didn't have a chance to so much as blink. Jen must have pulled the trigger as she lifted the gun. The pain that blasted through his shoulder was more shock than the sound of the gun going off.

CHLOE FORGOT EVERYTHING in that moment. Every minute of training, every potential threat around them. She only saw Jack stumble back and blood bloom on his shoulder, and she leaped for him.

She looked around wildly for something to stop the bleeding and came up with nothing. *Nothing.*

"I'm okay. It's okay," he said, but he did not sound like himself. He was in pain. He had been *shot*.

"It's not okay," she returned, pulling the hem of her shirt into as much of a ball as she could and pressing it to his shoulder.

His hissed out a pained breath. "Trying to convince myself here, Chloe." He swore once, twice. He didn't sit still, moving around as if trying to find some comfortable position, even though a *bullet* had passed through his shoulder.

"Stop moving. I have to put pressure on it. I have to—" The yank at her hair took her by surprise because she'd let panic and worry and *love* blind her to the imminent threat. She fell back as Jen stepped forward.

"Am I clear now? You can either fight and die right here or you can get on your feet and move."

Chloe held Jack's pained gaze. She couldn't let him die here. She couldn't. But they couldn't go deeper into this cave. Not with his wound, not with her mother's plans clear. Jen wanted it too much, when it would be so easy to just shoot them right now.

Clearly she had something deeper in the cave where she thought she could kill them and get away with it. Chloe would die before she gave her mother that.

It had to end right now. "Sounds like it's easier for you if we move. So maybe we choose to die right here."

"Do you think I won't shoot you both?"

Chloe knew she would. Knew this wasn't looking good. But if they walked any farther, it would be over. And maybe no one would ever find them. Another Hudson mystery.

No. She wouldn't let that happen. "If you're going to kill us, I'd much prefer you get caught."

Fury stamped all over her mother's features. It reminded Chloe too much of a childhood she'd spent a lot of time blocking out. Her therapist had told her not remembering a lot was a *bad sign*, and now Chloe fully understood what she meant by that. She'd blocked out *this*. That violence. That total lack of empathy for another human being.

Chloe didn't want to leave Jack's side, but she forced herself to stand. To face her mother. "And if you're going to kill us anyway, I might as well *fight*." She took a few steps forward, bracing herself for pain, for a gunshot wound to stop her in her tracks.

But instead, there was a voice.

"Drop your weapons."

Chloe whirled around, and nearly wept right then. Carlyle stood next to her brother, Zeke, both with guns trained on Jen and Courtney.

But Chloe also knew her mother. So she dove immediately into her mother's legs, hoping to knock her off her feet so she wouldn't have a chance to shoot *anyone*. It worked. Jen tumbled down on top of Chloe, but not before another gunshot went off.

Hopefully Carlyle's or Zeke's. *Please, God*. She scrambled out from her mother's weight. Jen kicked, clawed, pulled, but Chloe could fight too. She managed to get the gun from her mother, to wrestle her into submission.

Zeke came over to her and knelt on the other side of Jen, pulling out a zip-tie and using it to bind her hands together. Chloe looked over at Courtney. She was in the same position as Jen now, so Zeke must have gotten her first.

Chloe pushed to her feet. They needed to get Jack to the hospital. A gunshot wound to his shoulder wasn't good, but if they could get him…

He was lying completely prone on the floor now. More blood. Not just on his shoulder, but lower. Carlyle had something pressed to his abdomen. He'd been shot again. *No, no, no*.

She scrambled over to him. Repeating his name. Maybe crying. She didn't know. But he was pale, and he wasn't moving or responding to her in any way and *oh God*.

"He's breathing, Chloe," Carlyle said sharply. "So put something on that shoulder."

Chloe looked around for something, even as tears clouded her vision. But then chaos erupted around them. Just absolute chaos. Screaming. Yelling. Pounding footsteps. But she just concentrated on Jack's breathing. Because he was breathing. She felt like as long as she stayed here, her hand on his chest, his heart, she could *will* him to keep breathing. As long as he was breathing…

Someone pulled her off, and she fought them. If they pulled her away... If...

"Let the medics help," Zeke said, firm and authoritative in her ear as he banded her arms at her sides to stop her from fighting him.

Carlyle stepped in front of her, blocking her view of Jack. Jack. Who'd been shot twice. *Twice.* Because of her.

"They're going to take him to the hospital. He's going to be okay," Carlyle said.

"How do you know?" Chloe demanded.

And Carlyle didn't answer. Because the truth was, he might not be. And she would always have to live with that.

Zeke's grip on her loosened. She would have crumpled then and there, but Carlyle held her up by an arm. Medics were working to find a way to get Jack out of the small crevice of the entrance.

A couple of cops had Jen and Courtney cuffed, face down on the cave ground. They screamed and argued and fought, but they weren't going to be a problem anymore. They were going to go to prison. For murder. Multiple murders.

It should have been a relief, but nothing would feel like relief until she knew Jack would be okay.

They had to stand in this awful cave while the medics got Jack out, while the police got Jen and Courtney out. Chloe would have hyperventilated if not for Carlyle rubbing a supportive hand up and down her back.

When they were finally given the go-ahead to leave, Chloe knew there'd be questions. So many questions. But she wouldn't be able to answer any of them until Jack was okay.

When she emerged from the cave, she saw her brother.

He was cuffed, sitting on the ground, a deputy talking down at him.

She could only stare. He'd betrayed her. He was part of *all* this. When he looked up and saw her glaring at him, his eyes got big and shiny.

"I know I messed up, Chlo, but I fixed it. Didn't I?" he called across the distance between them. Cops looked at her; Hudsons looked at her.

She stared at her brother.

"He found Zeke and I," Carlyle said quietly, standing next to her. But Chloe could hear the disgust in Carlyle's voice. "We were pretty close, but we hadn't found the entrance to the cave. He is why we found you in the nick of time, and we didn't have to shake it out of him."

She wanted to feel good. She wanted to feel relief. Her brother wasn't all bad. He'd helped. Even with Mom threatening him the way she had, he had asked Carlyle and Zeke for help. He'd done the right thing.

She wanted to believe that, but she saw him sitting there and knew he'd just done the *easiest* thing. Because he always did. So she just felt *angry*. Because Jack was hurt. And sometimes doing the right thing was too little, too late.

She walked over to him. He wanted reassurance. He wanted to know he'd done okay. After being such a huge part of how this had all gone so badly. Years ago, she would have reassured him. Forgiven him.

Today, she had nothing left. "If he dies, I'll never, ever speak to you again," she said. "I will never lay eyes on you again. I will never, ever have anything to do with you. Ever."

Ry's eyes widened, and the hope in them died. "You're choosing him over me?"

"No, Ry. I'm choosing *me* over you. I will always love

you, but I can't be part of your life anymore. Not until you can take some responsibility for it. Maybe jail will teach you that. Maybe it won't. I won't know because I won't be in contact. I won't be helping. I'm done." She should have said all those things years ago. Now, just like him, it was too little, too late.

But she'd done it.

"That isn't fair!" he yelled. After all he'd done, he thought anything should be *fair*.

She shook her head and walked away from her brother. She hoped someday he'd find some better version of himself. But until he did…she was done.

Chapter Twenty-One

Jack thought he heard a baby crying. Where had a baby come from? It was nighttime. Somewhere. Where was he?

Cave. Cave? The cave and— *Chloe*. He tried to say her name, but nothing came out of his mouth except a raspy kind of noise. He couldn't seem to open his eyes. Heavy, too heavy. After the spurt of panic, he told himself to breathe, to count, to settle. He couldn't protect anyone if he couldn't open his eyes.

He started to become aware of things. The beep of machines, the feel of something on his arm. The sound of people shuffling. He managed to open his eyes to bright, blinding white. Hospital.

Well, he was here, so he had to be alive, he supposed. But then he caught sight of a woman. A woman with dark hair and soft eyes. Maybe he was dead after all. "Mom?"

But it only took a second or two to realize it wasn't his mother. It was Mary. "Sorry," he rasped.

Her smile was a little strange, definitely teary. He tried to get his brain to engage as he looked at her standing there next to his hospital bed. She looked different. She had a little bundle in her arms. Even with his brain fuzzy, that all made sense to him. "Mary."

"Sorry Walker couldn't help you guys. We were a little busy."

"You had the baby." A baby. He'd been fighting for his life, and she'd been giving birth. What a strange, strange life.

Both his sisters had *babies*. He remembered *them* being babies, and now they were mothers. His brain was too fuzzy to fully comprehend all this. He wanted to sit up. He wanted to ask a million questions.

"You're going to have to hurry up and get better so you can hold him," she said. She didn't cry, but he could hear the pain and fear in her voice.

"I'm okay." Of course, he had no idea if that was true. He'd been shot. Twice, if he remembered correctly. He tried to move, but he couldn't quite manage and the pain was starting to flutter above the fuzzy feeling.

"You will be. We'll all baby you till you are."

"I can't sit up. Let me see him, huh?"

She tilted the bundle until he could see the scrunched up little face of a sleeping newborn with a shock of dark hair.

"The problem is, I married a man whose last name is Daniels."

Jack didn't quite follow. "Why is that a problem?"

"I could hardly name my son Jack Daniels," Mary replied, looking lovingly down at the newborn in her arms.

"Why would..." He wanted to shift uncomfortably. "You don't have to name anyone after me."

Her eyes were full of tears. "Of course I don't have to. But I wanted to—Walker and I wanted to name our son after the best men we knew. You're at the top of that list, for both of us. I want that legacy for my son. I wanted him to have someone he knew, someone he'd spend his life looking up to. So he always knew what was right. Because his namesake would be right there, showing him."

Jack was completely and utterly speechless. "Well." But he remembered Chloe talking about legacies, and ghosts and how being sad is not all that bad. It felt like a million years ago.

"So, we did the best we could, all things considered," Mary said with a little sniff. She used her shoulder to wipe a tear off her cheek. "This is Jackson Dean Daniels. If we end up shortening it, he can go by JD. But it's after you, it's because of you. His name. Who we all are." She started crying again, tears rolling down her cheeks. "I'm so glad you're okay."

Okay. That cave. Today. This whole thing. "Chloe? Ry? I… I don't remember exactly…" Chloe had been okay. She had been. Had to be.

"They're both fine. Carlyle and Zeke got to you guys just in time. Jen Rogers and her two accomplices have been charged with the murder of Mark Brink and our parents. I knew you'd want the details, and they're still wading through them all. But everything with the bones, with the snake and Detective Hart, it was all part of planning to murder Mark without Chloe getting any wind of it."

Jack closed his eyes. His mind was whirling in too many directions. He wanted to see Chloe. Wanted to see for himself she was okay, but she wasn't here. Mary was and…

And after sixteen years, they finally knew. "We've got answers now, Mary. Who killed Mom and Dad. Why… If you can call it a why. Everything we tried to find all these years."

"It's so strange," she said, her voice a creaky whisper. "I just don't care."

He managed to open his eyes, and she was gazing down at her son, those tears still on her cheeks. She kept talking. "You're okay, and I have him. We all have...so much. It's a tragedy to have lost them. It'll always be a tragedy. But answers didn't change anything. Us all living our lives on the foundations they gave us. That's the only thing that matters."

It was such a strange thing, to agree. After years of thinking having answers would change something in his life, he now had those answers and nothing changed. Not really.

"Mary, where's Chloe?"

"She's fine."

"That isn't what I asked."

"She... We aren't sure where she went. She got checked out by doctors, answered all the police's questions, but we kind of lost her in the fray. It's okay. Carlyle and Anna are out trying to track her down, but we know she's okay."

He tried to sit up, but he couldn't. He cursed his own weaknesses. Cursed everything. "She's going to blame herself. She can't seem to help it. I just—"

"Don't worry, Jack. We'll find her, and we're all going to make sure she knows just where she belongs."

Here. She belonged right *here*.

CHLOE KNEW SHE couldn't just sit in the hospital parking lot forever. She had to act. She had to... She didn't want to see him, and she didn't think she'd ever be able to breathe again if she didn't see with her own two eyes that he was okay.

He wouldn't blame her. He'd be irritated she blamed herself. She understood all these things rationally, but she could not seem to move past all the swirling things she knew about Jack and who he was and the horrible things she felt about herself.

Hey, this is why we go to therapy. Well, she'd have a doozy of a session at her next appointment.

"What the hell are you doing here?"

Chloe looked up to see Carlyle stalking up to her, Anna not far behind.

"We've been looking all over for you," Anna said.

Chloe shook her head. "You should be with Jack. You should—"

"And who do you think Jack wants to see?" Anna returned. "Come on. Get up. Let's go."

They stood on either side of her, taking her by the arms and hauling her to her feet. But she didn't let them pull her to the door.

"I can't go in. I wanted to. I just…"

They didn't let her go, but they did stop trying to pull her.

"Chloe, you've had a day," Anna said, as gently as Chloe had ever heard her say anything. "But neither you nor Jack are going to rest until you see each other. Trust me. I know." Because her husband had been shot last year, and she'd been hurt too. So maybe she was right, but…

"My mother killed your parents, Anna."

"Yeah. Hell of a thing."

Like it was that simple. "My brother made it worse. Everything…it all connects to *me*."

"Self-centered much?" Carlyle said under her breath, making Anna snort out a laugh.

"I just want to curl up and die." Which was not something she would have ever admitted to out loud if she wasn't having a *day*, she supposed. And she didn't really want to die. She just wanted…

"Wow, that's super melodramatic," Carlyle said, and she was gently tugging her forward.

"I'm impressed. I didn't think you had it in you," Anna added, also applying pressure to move her forward.

"You guys…"

"Chloe, we know you. All of us. I get it, better than most, how having a parent with that kind of evil in them can mess you up, but you're too well loved to let what other people have chosen ruin your life."

Too well loved. Ouch.

"*And* Jack loves you. He needs to see you. And since you love him, you're going to get over yourself and go see him." Anna gave her yet another tug.

Chloe didn't know how to argue with that, so she was somehow being pulled down hospital corridors and to a hospital-room door. Anna shoved it open. "Go on, now." Then Anna and Carlyle stood shoulder to shoulder like they were blocking any potential exit.

So Chloe *had* to step in. Had to look.

Jack was in a hospital bed. Hooked up to all sorts of awful things. But his eyes were open, and he was talking to Mary.

Chloe must have made a noise, because Mary turned, and Jack looked over at her. She would have kept looking at Jack, but Mary was holding something. She was… "Mary… You… You had the baby."

In the middle of all this *awful*, a baby had been born.

Mary smiled at her and took a few steps closer, holding the baby so Chloe could see his face. "Meet Jackson Dean Daniels."

Chloe looked at the little newborn. She'd never been

around babies much. The little bundle seemed like an alien lifeform to her. And still…

"He's perfect." She couldn't help but smile down at the baby, especially when he blinked open his deep blue eyes and seemed to be squinting at her in suspicion. "Perfect." *Jackson.* After Jack, no doubt.

It made her want to cry all over again.

"I think so," Mary agreed. Then she looked at the doorway. Chloe looked over her shoulder to see Walker standing there.

"Good to see you both in one piece," he offered, presumably to Chloe and Jack. But he didn't tear his gaze away from Mary or the bundle in her arms. "Time's up, honey. You need to rest."

Mary nodded, but as she passed Chloe, she leaned close. "Stay with him until someone else comes, okay? I don't want him alone."

Chloe wanted to argue. She wanted to run away. But that was just childish and probably her exhaustion talking. She nodded at Mary, then hesitantly moved closer to Jack in the bed.

He looked too big for it. Too vital. He'd been shot twice. Gone through surgery. And still he seemed just like himself. When she felt like a bag of broken, rusty, disparate parts.

"Hi," she offered.

"Hi," he returned. And said nothing else. Just kept that steady gaze on hers.

Everything inside her felt bruised. He didn't say anything, just looked at her with dark eyes. But she had seen that expression on his face for a while now. In every smile, in every secret goodbye in the dark, in the way he protected her. In the way he let her in when he let no one else in.

And still, all the ways today connected to her felt like a wall she couldn't cross. So she fell back on what she usually used as a shield. That cop persona she'd developed.

"The police arrested everyone, including Ry. They're all turning on each other, so sentencing should be straightforward once they get that far. There are still some questions. The scrapbook is missing, and no one will spill on why it's so important. So there's work to be done. Bent County will handle it, though."

He gave a little nod but still didn't speak.

"Jack, I—"

"I need you to do me a favor," he said, cutting her off, even though his voice was weak and raspy.

And because it was, she immediately swallowed the apology. She'd do anything for him. Always. "Okay."

"I need you to never, ever, for the rest of our lives, say you're sorry to me about this."

She should have known. "Jack—"

"Listen to me. It hurts. It hurts to watch you blame yourself when you dug your way out of all that trauma, all that awful, and made yourself into a smart, *honorable*, wonderful person. I don't look at you and see them. Never did. Never will. And I know you can't magically wipe away any feelings you have on the matter. I get that they're complicated and messy, but I love you no matter what. So I can't take any apologies when *you* have nothing to apologize for. Okay?"

She *knew* he was right, but she hadn't felt it. Until he said it. Then it was like… God, she could breathe again, even as tears filled her eyes. She took the rest of the steps so she stood next to the bed now. She wiped at her eyes with the backs of her hands. She wanted to touch him, hold him, but... "I don't want to hurt you."

"Then stop crying, Chloe." He held out his hand at kind of an awkward angle, she supposed because that was the only way he could manage it. She took his hand, and he squeezed.

Him, lying in a hospital bed, trying to make *her* feel better. She grabbed the chair that was situated a ways away from the bed and drew it closer so she could sit next to him. So she could press her forehead to his hand. She couldn't quite stop crying, but she tried.

"I'm not sure I would have... I'm glad you're okay. I'm..." She looked up. Met his gaze. Pain was in his expression. Physical. Emotional. The whole gamut. "How about we leave it at, I love you and I'm glad you're here."

He smiled a little, but he didn't say anything at first. Just kept looking at her in a way that made her want to fidget.

"What do you say we get married?"

Her mouth dropped open because *what*? "What?"

"We've been together for about a year now. Why not?"

"Because a million reasons. And we have *not* been together. Sneaking around to have sex is *not* being together. What kind of meds are you on?"

"Okay." He yawned, winced a little. "We can wait."

She didn't know why that made her feel deflated. She clearly just needed sleep. But he just lay there in the bed, holding her hand, starting to look sleepy and...

"I put in an application to Bent County." She hadn't been going to tell him. Not until she got the job—*if* she got the job. But it just seemed right, somehow.

It was his turn to be surprised. "What?"

"They're starting a K-9 unit, and I wanted to be a part of it."

"I thought the applications on that closed a few months back?"

"They did, but one of the people fell through, so they've got one position. I... I didn't do it originally because I didn't want anyone to think I was doing it for you. To have you." She swallowed, looked down at their entwined hands. "I didn't want *you* to think that, or maybe I was afraid that... I don't know. Afraid. Period. Always. I just... The past few days have been a mess, but it was a mess you were there through. No matter what. You didn't leave my side. Even when it hurt. Even when it got you shot. You were there and..."

She looked up at him.

"Chloe, marry me. Please. Because no matter what, I'm always going to be there."

She wanted to laugh. And cry. And...agree. Most of all, agree. Not try to think it through, not try to worry it out. She just wanted him. "Okay," she managed.

"What changed your mind?"

"Seemed wrong to say no twice to a guy who was shot twice by my own mother," she said, sniffling as tears kept falling over her cheeks.

"Yeah, that is a bit much."

But it wasn't the truth. There were so many truths, but the main one had hit her over the head when she'd first come in. "You look at me the way Walker looks at Mary."

"I believe that's called *lovesick*."

"I'll take it. Because I've never had... No one's ever cared. Not the way you do. And you're not perfect. I want to punch you half the time, but you are the best man I know, Jack Hudson."

"That's mighty handy, because I happen to believe you deserve some best, Chloe Brink. And I plan on giving it to you."

And Jack Hudson always came through on plans.

* * * * *

Don't miss the stories in this mini series!

HUDSON SIBLING SOLUTIONS

Cold Case Discovery
NICOLE HELM
January 2025

Cold Case Murder Mystery
NICOLE HELM
February 2025

MILLS & BOON

Shadowing Her Stalker

Maggie Wells

MILLS & BOON

By day, **Maggie Wells** is buried in spreadsheets. At night, she pens tales of intrigue and people tangling up the sheets. She has a weakness for hot heroes and happy endings. She is the product of a charming rogue and a shameless flirt, and you only have to scratch the surface of this mild-mannered married lady to find a naughty streak a mile wide.

To my adopted home state and all the Arkansans who have made me one of their own—even if I still sound like I'm "not from around here." Thank you for sharing the beauty of the Natural State with me.

CAST OF CHARACTERS

Cara Beckett—Millionaire lifestyle guru. Face, voice and cofounder of the LYYF app, a tech company poised to go public. She has recently been doxed, and the harassment she's faced as a woman in tech has morphed into real-life threats and attempts to harm her.

Wyatt Dawson—Special agent with the Arkansas State Police Cyber Crime Division. Wyatt is tasked with protecting Cara and tracking down whoever is terrorizing her while she takes refuge in her home state.

Elizabeth (Betsy) and James Beckett—Cara's parents. Owners of a successful family cattle farm in the foothills of the Ozark Mountains.

Chris Sharpe and Tom Wasinski—Cara's partners and the tech geniuses behind the LYYF app. When the stock goes public, all three partners stand to make a fortune beyond their wildest dreams.

Zarah Parvich—Cara's virtual assistant. Based in California, Zarah is a key resource for both Cara and Wyatt, since she has access to almost every facet of Cara's personal and professional life.

Chapter One

Most of her life Cara Beckett dreamed of being one of those actors who had to wear a disguise to get through an airport undetected. Yet, here she was—rich, famous in a way she never imagined and completely incognito as she walked through Little Rock's Bill and Hillary Clinton National Airport dressed in soft, faded jeans and a flowing white tunic.

When she booked her flight, it hadn't even registered she'd be traveling on October 31. She'd been too wrapped up in thoughts of getting out of California to notice anything different at LAX. Then, when she changed planes in Dallas, a woman who was either dressed as a witch or channeling her inner sorceress sat down across the aisle from her in the first-class cabin. As the other passengers boarded, she noted at least three men dressed as a high-profile European soccer coach, a couple teenagers in full pop star mode and multiple women wearing sweaters or appliquéd sweatshirts with pumpkin or fall motifs. She'd forgotten all about Halloween.

For the first time in a week, she breathed easy. She was definitely not in LA anymore.

The young woman working the rental counter was wearing a wedding dress with strategically placed rips and tears and a smattering of bright red paint Cara supposed was meant to be blood. Her heart lodged in her throat as she inched closer to the counter. She was glad the girl didn't know actual blood was darker. Thicker. And definitely didn't smell like craft paint.

One week ago, Cara found out her personal information—full name, address and mobile phone number—had been posted on a forum favored by self-proclaimed tech wizards. Not being a techie herself, she'd never heard of the message board, nor had she thought the breach of privacy would turn out to be a real threat. She'd thought the doxing was puzzling. At first, she was annoyed. She couldn't figure out why anyone would care who she was or where she lived. She wasn't truly a big shot in the tech sector.

But her lack of industry credibility was exactly what angered the people coming after her. And in the last week they'd gone beyond angry to terrifying.

Someone attacked her neighbor Nancy as she walked her dog two nights ago. Nancy had paused to let her Pomeranian, Buster, use the tiny patch of meticulously maintained lawn in front of Cara's Los Feliz property as his toilet, though Cara had expressly asked her not to. Cara found Nancy sprawled on the grass bleeding from stab wounds to her abdomen and side with her ever-faithful Buster barking his head off.

Nancy would recover, thank goodness, but the incident had left Cara shaken. She didn't become truly terrified until detectives looking into the stabbing showed up at Cara's door the night before asking if she had reason to believe someone would wish to harm her. They believed she had been the intended target. According to Nancy's statements to the police, her assailant had called the name "Cara" when he jumped from the passenger seat of a nondescript gray sedan. He'd also repeatedly said, "Breathe in life," while stabbing poor Nancy.

"Now, go out there and breathe in LYYF," was the tagline

Cara said at the end of each lesson or meditation offered by the app she'd helped create.

To some in the tech world, she was an actress who lucked into doing free voice-over work. They believed Chris Sharpe and Tom Wasinski were the geniuses behind LYYF, the lifestyle and social application downloaded on over seven hundred million mobile devices each year. She was simply the face. And the voice. Few would call her the key to the app's success, though the truth was, the business hadn't been going anywhere until she'd stepped in.

At times she wished she never had.

Curling her lips in, she bit down, breathing deep and evenly through her nose. She needed to keep her anxiety at bay for now. In ninety minutes, give or take, she'd be safe at home with her parents. All she had to do was get in a car and drive. Soon she'd be about as far from Los Angeles as a person could be—mentally, if not geographically. Far from a world where people measured every success against their own failures. In a place where internet and cellular service were both still spotty and the residents had more important things to worry about than whether they had Wi-Fi available 24-7.

Ahead of her, a man argued with the rental agent. Apparently the largest vehicle available was a midsize sedan and they'd reserved an SUV. She glanced over and saw a harried woman trying to keep track of three kids under the age of ten. Cara smiled sympathetically. It was clear both mother and father were fighting a losing battle.

When he finally stepped aside, resigned to shoehorning his family into the available Hyundai, she took her place at the counter with a wan smile. Holding up her phone so the agent could scan her reservation, she said, "I'll take whatever you have."

The young woman pulled up the reservation, asked Cara to answer the rental agreement questions on the tablet mounted to the counter and, with a relieved smile, offered her a map of the area.

Cara waved it away. "No, thank you. I know where I'm headed."

"You can choose whichever car you like from section 104," the agent said as she slipped a printed ticket into a sleeve and wrote "104" across the front in black marker. "Thank you and Happy Halloween."

Cara took the paperwork from her. "Thanks," she replied tiredly.

Making sure her massive leather tote was still riding securely atop her roller bag, she wheeled out of the line. The man behind her stepped up, peering closely at his phone, thumb scrolling frantically. "Hang on," she heard him say to the clerk. "I can't find my reservation email."

Should have used the app, Cara thought as she strode toward the exit.

She spotted a ladies' room and decided to stop. She had a long drive ahead and too much coffee in her system. After washing her hands, she flicked a few drops of cold water at her face in hopes of freshening up. By the time she exited, she saw a brown-haired man dressed in the Midwestern male uniform of khaki pants and a polo shirt making a beeline for section 104. There were only two cars parked there—identical silver subcompacts.

She smiled as he slowed to a halt behind her. "Should we flip a coin?" she asked.

He shook his head, but barely glanced in her direction as he held out a hand. "Ladies first."

"Thanks."

Too worn out to do anything but keep moving, Cara approached the vehicle on the left. Not bothering with the trunk, she stowed her roller bag in the back seat, then tossed her tote into the wheel well on the passenger side. The fob for the ignition was in the cup holder. She put her foot on the brake and pressed the button and the engine purred to life.

She saw the man move to the driver's side of the rental beside hers as she pulled her door shut. Mentally mapping her route out of Little Rock, she was fastening her seat belt when the passenger door opened and the khaki-clad man dropped into the seat beside her.

"Don't scream, no one's around anyhow," he said in a gruff whisper.

Wide-eyed, she stared at the gleaming weapon pointed at her. *Gunmetal gray*, her brain supplied unhelpfully. She looked up to find her new passenger had pulled a safety-orange balaclava down over his head and topped it with a leaf-and-twig-printed cap.

A flash of a long-forgotten trip to the feed store with her father came to mind. Home from California for Thanksgiving, she'd been about the only person in town not dressed in forest browns and bright orange. Her father had cracked himself up musing about how camouflage was never more effective than in the fall in Arkansas.

It was true. Too true.

"What do you want?" She pointed a trembling finger at the tote half-crushed under his feet. "There's cash in my wallet. Take it. Take what you need."

The man gave a derisive snort. "I am taking what I need. Now drive, or I'll shoot you right here."

In the moment, the notion of being left for dead in a sub-compact rental parked in section 104 of a nearly deserted parking deck sounded like the worst possible fate. So she shifted into gear, and pulled out of the space.

"Where do you want me to go?"

"Get us out of here," he ordered.

She chanced a glance at her passenger as she pointed the car toward the exit. No, she hadn't imagined the gun. Or the khakis. Or the polo shirt. But even if she could describe them down to the weave of the cotton of his shirt, the police would still be looking for a needle in a haystack.

There was absolutely nothing notable about the man beside her.

Cara eased out of the parking deck and into the lane leading to the airport exit. There'd be a gate to clear. Someone would see them. She'd be able to get help.

Consoling herself with the knowledge they were in a well-populated area, she headed for the parking attendant. But as they rolled to a stop behind another car, she saw none of the white booths with their sliding glass windows were manned.

To her horror, she saw the velvet-cloaked arm of the wizard family patriarch wave his rental agreement at a scanner attached to the side of the booth. The electronic gate lifted, and the overstuffed sedan rolled away.

When Cara pulled up to the booth, she gazed up into its emptiness in bewilderment. The man beside her bumped her elbow. She jumped and looked down. Had he nudged her with the gun? No. His hand. He shoved the rental envelope she'd tucked into her tote at her.

"Stop messing around," he growled.

She blinked back a hot rush of frustrated tears as she took the sleeve bearing the printed barcode and held it up to the scanner.

The barrier lifted, but she couldn't seem to take her foot off the brake.

"Drive," her abductor ordered.

"Drive where?"

He turned in his seat to square up with her, the gun clutched in his right hand. "Go. Now."

He uttered the commands through clenched teeth, and Cara's brain engaged. She hit the gas and the small car lurched forward, engine revving. The road leading away from the single-terminal airport was nearly deserted. As she approached the entrance to the major arteries surrounding the capital city, she instinctively lifted her foot from the gas.

"Take the ramp," he ordered.

She put on her signal, but took the right turn at a high rate of speed. Cara chanced a glance at her passenger. He gripped the console between the seats to keep his equilibrium, but kept his weapon pointed in her direction.

The bypass ended a few miles from the airport, one lane leading to downtown Little Rock and Interstate 40. She gravitated toward it, intent on following the route to her parents' ranch in a snug valley of the Ozark Mountains, but the man beside her had a different plan.

"Stay in the middle lane," he instructed.

"But—" she began to protest.

"Middle lane," he repeated, cutting her off as an eighteen-wheeler forced its way out of the merge lane, neatly boxing her in.

She followed the flow of traffic onto Interstate 30 South. The other lane circled the south side of the city on its way to Texas. Cara's mind raced across the miles ahead. She wasn't overly familiar with the southwest corner of the state. She'd never been to Texarkana or any of the other towns between Little Rock and Dallas. And the only times she'd been to Dallas, she'd flown.

"Where are we going?" she asked, speaking only to fill the silence. Perhaps, if she got him talking—

"We're going to drive until I tell you to stop."

She gripped the steering wheel tighter, her knuckles glowing white against her skin. "You can take the car. I don't care," she offered. "Take it."

"I am," he said, a note of smug amusement in his tone. "And I'm taking you with it."

His insouciance annoyed her, but she kept her eyes glued to the traffic ahead of her. The last thing she needed was to tick off the man with the gun. Traffic was light as they raced past the small bedroom communities flanking the highway on the other side of the county line.

They flew past strip malls and chain restaurants, budget hotels and car dealerships. Logic told her the thriving commercial areas denoted miles of civilization beyond. They were driving through what passed for urban sprawl in a sparsely populated state. But it wouldn't last long. Soon, there wouldn't be anything but large tracts of forest dotted with tiny towns. Sleepy, slightly run-down communities with a post office, possibly a diner or barbecue joint and, if they were lucky, a gas station.

Sure enough, shopping centers gave way to a few edge-of-town motels. A billboard advertised a travel plaza at the next exit. Green highway signs listed the mileage to Hot Springs, Arkadelphia and Texarkana.

As the highway narrowed to two lanes in each direction, Cara forced herself to take three deep, deliberate breaths, counting in her head as she cycled through each one.

"There you go, breathe in life," the man beside her said, his voice faintly mocking.

Cara's blood ran ice-cold.

Breathe in life. Breathe in LYYF. She'd ended every recording she'd ever done for the LYYF app with those soothing words.

Now they terrified her.

The guy who'd pointed a gun at her in an airport parking deck had twisted them. Taunted her with words meant to reassure. He knew who she was. This wasn't some random carjacking. Had he been waiting for her. Why? This could not be happening.

Clutching the steering wheel, she turned to look at him, wide-eyed. "What did you say?"

"You heard me," he answered, waving her disbelief away.

"You know who I am?"

She cringed as the words came out of her mouth, but her brain was blown and she wasn't feeling up to playing cat and mouse. What was the use when the cat was holding her at gunpoint.

"Do you buy into all the woo-woo meditation stuff, or do you do it because they pay you to say it?"

He sat there pointing a gun at her and he expected her to answer questions about her job?

She clenched her jaw as one of the three semis boxing her in decided he wanted to work his way into the right lane. She slowed to avoid being clipped as the big rig edged over. A sign advertising a gas station with a fast-food franchise flashed past her window. The truck ahead of her slowed. Cara looked to her right and spotted the brightly lit station.

The driver ahead of her sped up as they approached the ramp. Cara accelerated too, but when she checked her mirror, she saw the semi on her rear bumper was signaling his intent to exit.

They were almost past the ramp when Cara jerked the wheel hard to the right, throwing her passenger against the door.

The tires kicked up loose gravel from the shoulder.

The man beside her cursed a blue streak.

The driver behind them indicated his displeasure by blowing his horn at her.

A trailer hauling wood chips sat stationary at the bottom of the ramp, right turn signal flashing. Cross traffic on the county road at the bottom of the ramp did not let up.

"What do you think you're doing?" the man holding the gun yelled, reaching across to grab the steering wheel.

Cara jammed on the brakes, her arms locked against the steering wheel to counteract the laws of physics. Her passenger boomeranged into the dash. Behind them, brakes screamed in protest and the driver laid on his horn.

The moment they jerked to a halt, she thrust the gearshift into Park, popped the latch on her seat belt and rolled out the driver's door onto the gritty berm.

The man shouted, but she didn't look back.

She ran.

Cara ran flat out, streaking down along the side of the trailer filled with fragrant wood shavings. Oblivious to the drama playing out behind him, the driver let off his brakes enough to make the hydraulics sigh with anticipation. Cara skidded into the ditch running alongside the ramp, thanking the stars above she'd had sense enough to wear sneakers for the plane ride.

She watched as the truck crept forward a few feet, then jerked to a stop again. Glancing behind her, she saw a battered pickup hurtling down the county road. She heard another shout, followed by a terrifying pop.

Cara didn't wait for the man to get a second round off. Using the pickup as cover, she darted across the ramp in front of the semi, praying the driver wasn't tempted to inch any farther into the intersection.

Breathless, she slid down the slope on the other side of the ramp. Peeking over tall grass, she saw her passenger sliding behind the wheel.

Flattening herself in the damp grass, she held her breath as she heard the rev of engines. Another blast of impatient honking told her the driver stuck behind her abandoned rental had had enough shenanigans for one day. Seconds later, she heard the rumble and sigh of air brakes again.

Cara raised her head enough to peer over the edge of the culvert. Beyond the beams of a tractor hauling a flatbed filled with spooled steel, she saw the taillights of a silver subcompact flash as it sped up the entrance ramp on the opposite side of the country road.

He was taking off without her.

Relief pulsed through her veins.

He was gone.

Panting, Cara lowered her head to rest on the backs of her trembling hands. Cold dampness seeped into the knees of her jeans. Her palms throbbed. She had no doubt she'd find them speckled with glass and gravel from her dive for safety, but she didn't care.

He was gone.

She was alive.

She was safe.

"Breathe in life," she murmured. And she did. She drank in the cool, damp air until her lungs were full to bursting, and held it there.

Then, a pair of battered boots tramped down the grass right in front of her. Every oxygen molecule she'd ingested exploded out of her when a man spoke.

"Do you have some kind of death wish or something, lady?"

Chapter Two

Wyatt Dawson didn't mind working late. Truthfully, he preferred the office after hours. Because they were a small team, most of the members of the cybercrime division took work home with them, but he liked the time in the office alone. He wasn't antisocial, though some would say he was; it was more that he liked the idea of keeping his work at work.

And he was so close to zeroing in on a solid lead.

Sitting at his desk with his feet up, he was scanning lines of data, looking for the IP address needed to confirm his suspicions. If he could connect the dots, all the extra hours would pay off. The spot on the multiagency task force investigating the sale and movement of illegally produced distilled spirits through northwest Arkansas would be his. He was close. He could taste it. So close he was tempted to ignore the ringing desk phone.

But he couldn't. The cybercrime division was still in its infancy. He and his tiny group of talented colleagues were on a mission to prove their worth to the Department of Public Safety. And because they were worthy, he would take the call. Even though it was after hours.

Even though it meant shifting mental gears at the precise moment he needed them locked on target.

He frowned as the desk phone continued to pester him.

The short two-tone ring indicated an intraoffice phone call. The last thing he needed was for someone on the inside to insinuate they weren't pulling their weight. Dropping his feet to the floor, he reached for the receiver of the desk phone and wedged it between his ear and shoulder.

"CCD, Dawson here," he said as he typed a note into his spreadsheet to mark where he'd left off.

"Agent Dawson? This is Trooper Chad Masterson," the caller said with brisk efficiency. "I have a sort of unusual circumstance unfolding here, and I'm wondering if you might be able to help me."

Wyatt shook his mouse to keep the computer from transitioning into sleep mode then sat up straighter in his chair and took hold of the receiver. "Happy to. How can I help?"

"Have you ever heard of a woman called Cara Beckett?" the trooper asked.

Scowling, Wyatt picked up a pen and jotted the name on a pad of sticky notes he kept beside the phone. The name did ring a bell, but he found the man's coy approach annoying. He wasn't a big fan of fishing expeditions whether they employed a line and hook, or clumsily delivered yes or no questions.

"I'm gonna need a little more than a name," he informed his colleague.

"Cara Beckett," the trooper repeated. "Says she works for a company called LYYF. Spelled with two *Y*'s. *L-Y-Y-F*." Masterson was unable to mask the disdain in his voice as he spelled out the company name. "I believe it's some kind of phone application."

Wyatt sighed. The number of electronic troglodytes he encountered within the ranks of law enforcement never failed to amaze him. Sure, they were all for DNA matches and advanced ballistics, but tie a computer, tablet or smartphone to a crime and they bragged about how they were still using AOL as their email provider. Or pretended they hadn't heard of one of the tech world's biggest sensations.

"Yes, I'm familiar with the application," he said briskly.

Truthfully, he was more than familiar. He was a daily user. He reached for his own phone and swiped through a couple of screens, stopping when he spotted the bright orange icon with the stylized *L* at its center. The home page loaded and he stared at the photo of a woman seated in the lotus position, her eyes closed and her lips curved into a serene smile.

All the puzzle pieces fell into place.

"Cara Beckett is one of the founding partners of LYYF. It's a lifestyle and wellness application." He tapped his pen on the desk a couple of times then opened the app, anxious to put the name and face together. "You probably have it on your phone too," he informed Trooper Masterson. "Our health insurance provider gave everybody a free subscription to the service for a year as part of our benefits package a couple years ago."

"Hmm, I'm not familiar," Masterson said, unable to mask the hint of derision in his tone. "I'll have to ask my wife if she tried it. She likes all those lifestyle things." He guffawed. "I pay for the whole dang cable package, but all she ever watches is the home-makeover channel. If I come home to one more set of paint swatches I'm going to spit."

Wyatt clenched his jaw. He had to take one of the calming breaths he learned from using LYYF before posing the obvious question. "Why are you asking me about Cara Beckett?"

"From what I gather, she's some kind of celebrity."

Wyatt frowned at the descriptor. Celebrity? Maybe in some circles, but not in the way Masterson would recognize.

"Not a Hollywood celebrity, but in other circles, yeah, maybe," he conceded. "Again, why do you ask?"

"Because I got her sitting in an office down here. A trucker said she practically leaped out of a moving vehicle to get away from the guy she was ridin' with."

"Leaped out of a moving car?"

"Says she was abducted. Man with a gun jacked her rental car at the airport. The woman is pretty shaken up. No purse or phone or ID of any kind. No money. The guy who found her took her up to the truck stop and waited with her until a patrolman arrived. They brought her back here and dropped her at my desk, but I'm not quite sure what to make of her story."

"Is there a reason why you don't believe her story?" Wyatt asked.

"No particular reason," Masterson replied cautiously. "It's not something that happens around here very often."

"Oh, I'd say we see our fair share of carjackings." Wyatt himself had a friend who was lured from her car at a fast-food restaurant and left standing by as her vehicle sped away. She'd been one of the lucky ones.

"She keeps talking about somebody docking her and I'm not sure what she means." Wyatt could hear the guy scratching his head. "She seems to think there's some connection between the docking and what happened to her today. Keeps saying it can't be a coincidence."

"Docking?" Wyatt scowled as he watched the progress bar at the bottom of his screen creep toward completion. He glanced down at the name he'd scrawled on the sticky note, then zeroed in on the blinking cursor as if it might give up the answer to what was nagging him.

"What is Cara Beckett doing in Arkansas?" he whispered, talking to himself.

But Masterson answered. "Says she's from here. Folks own a place up in Searcy County. Ranchers."

"Searcy County? That's north, isn't it? They were heading south," Wyatt noted.

"I don't think this guy with the gun was hoping to meet the folks," Masterson said dryly.

Wyatt turned the information he'd been given over in his head. "Docking? I don't know what she means."

"Makes two of us. I tried to get a better answer out of her but she kept goin' on about her home address and phone number being leaked and someone called Nancy gettin' attacked outside her house. Frankly, she's a bit…overwrought," Masterson drawled.

Wyatt sat up straighter partly because he was annoyed by the trooper's supercilious attitude but mostly because he was catching on to exactly what Cara Beckett was trying to tell them.

"Do you mean doxing?" he demanded, his tone sharp.

"Excuse me?"

"Doxing." But saying the word louder didn't help it penetrate the trooper's skull. "Doxing is when somebody on the internet, usually a hacker or some kind of troll, unearths someone's personal information and publishes it for the world to see."

He paused to let the explanation sink in, but Trooper Masterson remained quiet.

"It's slang for dropping the documents on someone."

"But why? Who is she?"

"She's a partner in a tech company."

"So shouldn't she be able to stop this, uh, doxing thing?"

Wyatt rolled his eyes at the man's naivete. "Picture some internet users as a pack of rabid dogs. There are always a few who will chase after a person at the slightest provocation."

"You think this Cara Beckett person provoked this threat against her?"

"I'm not saying anything of the sort. She could simply be guilty of nothing more than breathing oxygen on a daily basis. It doesn't take much to get a few disgruntled users to go after a high profile target."

"You think her profile is high enough people would, uh, dox her? Kidnap her?" The other man sounded dubious. "I've never even heard of her."

"You follow tech trends pretty closely, Masterson?"

"I know who Jeff Bezos and Elon Musk are," he countered.

"Congratulations," Wyatt said dryly. "Listen, the lady you have sitting in an office down there might not be Bezos or Musk, but she's far wealthier than you or I can ever dream of being." He thought back to the article he'd read about the masterminds behind LYYF. "They're about to take the company public. Soon Cara Beckett's net worth will be stratospheric."

"She doesn't look like a millionaire right now," Masterson grumbled.

"Billionaire," Wyatt interjected.

"She's wearin' jeans and a plain white shirt. All muddy and stuff from rolling in the ditch. And the trucker gave her twenty dollars because she didn't have any walking-around money." Masterson added the last bit as if it was conclusive evidence against Wyatt's claims. "She's down here right now making some calls to see if she can round up a hotel or place to stay the night using a police report as ID."

Wyatt swiped at his cell until his internet browser popped up. A quick query yielded the article he had read a few days before. In it, a slim smiling young woman with chic, close-cropped blond hair and wide blue eyes beamed out at him. She stood a half step in front of the men she claimed were her two best friends from college.

There were plenty of people who thought an out-of-work actress didn't deserve the 33-percent partnership the creators of LYYF offered her in exchange for voice-over work when they were prestart-up. But they made a deal, and Cara Beckett become the voice and later, when their popular video sessions were added, the face of LYYF.

The trolls and tech bros liked to grumble about the equal partnership Chris Sharpe and Tom Wasinski had traded for her services at the beginning of their venture. But no one could deny Cara Beckett was as much a part of LYYF's success as their clever coding and attractive graphics. No amount of superior interface could have made the app a phenomenon. Her face and voice were key. As was her willingness to step out from behind the curtain and become the public spokesperson her collaborators never wanted to be.

He scrolled through the profile he'd skimmed the week before. In the article, her cofounders weren't shy about giving her the respect she deserved. Without Cara Beckett's easy, open smile and welcoming demeanor, the application wouldn't have been half the hit it was.

Glancing back at the desk phone, he noted the extension Masterson was using and rose from his chair. "Hang tight. I'll be there in a few minutes to talk to her. If even a little bit of what you say she says happened to her is true, at best we're dealing with the situation straddling multiple jurisdictions."

"And worst-case scenario?"

"The media finds out," Wyatt said grimly.

"Exactly what I'm afraid of." Masterson heaved a sigh. "Come on down. She's got nowhere else to go and no way to get there anyhow."

MASTERSON WAS EVERYTHING Wyatt expected from their conversation. Tall and not quite barrel-chested, he wore his dark

hair in a high and tight buzz cut. As he drew closer and the
two shook hands, Wyatt could see short strands of silver
intensified the effect of the trooper's white-walled haircut.
Deep creases furrowed the man's brow, and squint lines ra-
diated from cool blue eyes. Wyatt couldn't blame the man
for his natural skepticism. No doubt, the man had seen some
strange things in his years of service.

Cara Beckett sat in one of the small offices on the perim-
eter of the bullpen. The door was closed, but the miniblinds
covering the office window were drawn up. She looked different in person. It wasn't the grass-stained clothes or the
smudge of mud dried on her jawline. Her hair looked softer.
It was an inch or two longer than in the photos on the app,
and the color was more a honey gold than beachy white-
blond streaks.

She looked tired. Small. And though he knew from her
yoga videos she was strong and almost rubber-band flex-
ible, under the fluorescent lights of the Arkansas State Police Headquarters, she came across as almost unspeakably
fragile.

"Have you gotten anything more from her?" Wyatt asked.

Masterson shook his head. "She just got off the phone."

Wyatt nodded, then gestured to the door. "Do you mind
if I have a chat?"

Sweeping an arm toward the door, Masterson said, "Have
at it. I have a call in to the rental company to try to get the
information on the stolen vehicle."

With a nod, Wyatt started for the office door. He gave it a
couple raps with the knuckle of his index finger, then cracked
it open. Cara Beckett looked up with wide, frightened eyes.

He kept the opening to little more than a crack, but made
sure to smile to show her he meant no harm. "Hello. Ms.
Beckett?" She nodded, but he made no move to enter the

small office. "I'm Special Agent Wyatt Dawson. I'm a member of our cybercrimes division. Trooper Masterson called me. May I speak with you for a few minutes?"

She eyed him warily. "Cybercrimes division? They have one of those here?"

He pushed the door open a few inches more, and allowed his smile to widen as well. "Anywhere the internet goes, so go the scammers."

"And the trolls," she said, bitterness edging her tone. "And the out-and-out criminals."

"May I come in?" He pointed to the chair opposite the small desk where she'd sat to use the telephone.

She inclined her head, and he caught the light bounce off the diamond studs she wore in her ears. They weren't ostentatious, but were certainly more than mere chips. As he settled in the chair he took in the gold bangles on her wrist. A delicate chain holding a pendant with a large multicolored stone encircled her throat. She wore rings on multiple fingers and one thumb, but the third finger on her left hand was bare. He filed the information away as he leaned back in the chair, assuming a pose more in line with casual conversation than interrogation.

"You don't believe the man who abducted you intended to rob you." He made it a statement, knowing it would draw more of an answer from her than a question.

She shook her head. "No. I offered him my wallet, the car, anything he wanted. He said he wanted me."

Wyatt pursed his lips, letting the words hang in the air for a minute as he formulated his next question. But before he could ask it, she shook her head.

"No, not wanted. Needed. I told him to take what he needed, and he said he was, then ordered me to drive."

Nodding, Wyatt resisted the urge to lean forward in

his chair. He didn't want to come across as aggressive. He wanted her comfortable enough to tell her story her way. To remember things as they actually happened without framing them through the lens of hindsight.

"He wasn't familiar to you at all." Again, a statement, not a question.

"It's been a long time since I've lived in Arkansas, Special Agent Daw—"

"Wyatt," he interrupted.

"Wyatt," she repeated with a nod, a small smile tugging at the corners of her mouth.

"Something funny," he asked.

"I don't run into too many Wyatts in LA."

He smirked. "Maybe not." Since she felt comfortable enough to mock him, he leaned forward, planting his elbows on his knees and clasping his hands. "May I call you Cara?"

"Yes."

"Cara, tell me about the doxing incident," he said, driving straight to his main point of interest. "Do you know what precipitated it? What fallout have you experienced? Did you feel you were in danger in California?"

She gaped at him for a moment, seemingly stunned by the abrupt shift in conversation. "I, uh, I don't know why," she managed to stammer. "I mean, there have always been, um, detractors, but no. I have no idea why someone decided to make my personal information public. And I don't know why anyone would be interested. I'm not a celebrity or anything." She opened her hands in a helpless shrug. "I'm not even an influencer."

Wyatt huffed, charmed by her naive assessment of her standing in the virtual community. "Aren't you?"

He pulled out his own phone and woke the screen. The welcome page of the LYYF app appeared, and front and center was a close-up video of Cara asking, "Are you ready to get the most from your LYYF?"

She didn't respond, but her expression hardened. "As for fallout. My address and phone were posted on a number of message boards. If you're at all familiar with the internet, you know there are some users who aren't always pleasant."

"Harassment?"

She nodded. "Mostly in-app and social media messages at first, but then they hacked my company email and things spiraled even more from there. The LAPD have been on the case. I can give you the information of the…" She paused, grimaced, then shook her head. "I had contact information in my phone, but now—"

Her phone was gone.

He watched her swallow hard and hoped she was gulping down her fear. It was hard to outrun internet harassment. Life outside of the app would be better if she gathered her resolve and found a way to stand her ground. Then again, the woman had jumped out of a car in the middle of nowhere when a man was holding a gun on her. If knowing when to bail wasn't the biggest part of taking control of one's life, he didn't know what was.

"You've never seen the man who abducted you?" he asked, shifting into lightning-round mode.

"No."

"Did he mention LYYF, or give any indication he knew who you were?"

She started to shake her head, then stopped. "Not directly. He only said the part about taking what he needed then ordered me to drive."

"But you believe the implication was you were what he was after," he concluded.

"Yes."

Wyatt nodded, then pressed on. "Did he make any sexual advances? Insinuations? Touch you in any way construed as intimate?"

"No. He didn't touch me at all." She let out a whoosh of breath. "No. Nothing, uh, sexual."

"So let's assume for now robbery and sexual assault weren't his motive." He sat up straight in the chair again, holding her gaze. "If he wasn't someone you knew or recognized, we might also shelve personal agenda."

"Personal agenda?"

"Old boyfriend, spurned lover, the guy who wanted to take you to the homecoming dance but never worked up the nerve to ask you," he said with an offhanded wave. "You tick anyone off on the plane?"

The question coaxed a short huff of a laugh out of her. "I don't think I talked to anyone."

"Hog the armrest?"

She shook her head. "Dozed most of the way here. I haven't been sleeping well."

"Who knew you were coming to Arkansas?"

She shook her head. "My assistant. I think she told my partners. The neighbor who shares my cat."

Lifting a brow, he asked, "You share a cat?"

"She's a stray. Huge commitment issues. The McNeils and I both feed her. Why settle, right?"

He gave her a wry smile. "Smart cat." Nodding to the desk phone, he asked, "Did you call your folks?"

She shook her head, but when she spoke her voice was barely more than a whisper. "No."

"No?"

She raised one shoulder in a shrug, and the ruined white shirt she wore nearly slid off her shoulder. She wore some sort of spaghetti strap tank top thing under it. Her skin was tanned to a shade lighter than a golden glow. He wondered if the color came from the sun or a booth. Or maybe she had one of those spray-on jobs done. Either way, it was definitely more California tan than the blistering burns the Arkansas sun doled out.

She tipped her chin up. "My parents didn't know I was coming. And now... I don't want my mom to worry."

Wyatt sensed there was more to the story there, but he didn't press. Shifting gears, he hooked an arm over the back of the chair. "There are some nice hotels downtown. New ones, or you could go with a classic and stay at the Capital Hotel." He bit the inside of his cheek. "Were you able to contact anyone who can help?"

She nodded. "Trooper Masterson let me call my assistant, Zarah. Thank goodness she had contact information on her website. She's having a phone delivered from the Tech-Mobile store and overnighting my passport, so I have official ID, and a credit card. I have a copy of my driver's license in cloud storage as well. I assume I can use it along with the police report, if needed." He nodded and she went on. "She also rented a condo here in town for a couple of nights. I'll get a rideshare from here once I get the phone and pick up a new rental tomorrow."

Wyatt pressed his lips together to keep from letting out a low whistle. "She sounds very efficient." It never ceased to amaze him how money could pave right over the biggest potholes in life. Still, he wasn't sure she'd thought her plan through. "Did she set the phone up from your previous account?"

Cara blinked twice. "I assume so. Why?"

He did his best to hide his grimace. With a single-word question, she'd proved the tech bros right about her lack of

technological savvy. "You said you've been receiving messages from strangers either through apps or email?"

"Yes."

"Texts as well?"

"Yes."

Her eyes widened as she turned toward the window.
Trooper Masterson approached the office, his expression
sour as he raised his hand for them to see. A plastic bag im-
printed with the TechMobile logo dangled from the tip of
his index finger. The man was clearly peeved to be reduced
to the role of delivery boy.

Wyatt stood and opened the door. "Thank you," he said
as he relieved the older man of the parcel. "If you want to
finish up with Ms. Beckett's statement, I'll get this set up
for her to use."

"You don't need—" she started to say as she rose from
the chair, but she stopped when Wyatt looked over to her for
permission to pull the familiar box from the bag. She nodded her assent.

"I'm happy to set this up to forward any communications
coming in to your number to a dummy we'll set up here.
Once I'm finished, I'll talk you through how best to use it
without giving too much information about your location
away," he interrupted. "Then, if you'd like, I can drop you
off at your rental." When she seemed taken aback by the
offer, he rushed to put her at ease. "Or we can get a patrol
car to take you. Rideshare apps rely on cellular signals and
GPS to triangulate location. We want to avoid anyone getting a read on where you are if we can."

"You think someone will use my phone to track me?"
She appeared both incredulous and horrified by the notion.

"It's the fastest way. With all the apps we rely on and

location-based services, we make it too easy," Wyatt said with a grim scowl. "But I can help you. Let me help you."

Cara Beckett scooted out from behind the desk to join Trooper Masterson in the doorway. She eyed the uniformed man for a long moment, then turned to Wyatt, taking in his flat-front khakis and checked button-down shirt.

"Thank you," she said quietly, then slipped past the trooper to head back to his desk.

Wyatt and Masterson exchanged a nod-shrug combo before the older man turned away.

The second they were gone, he unboxed the phone and powered it up. The greeting screen appeared, and a smirk twisted his lips as he zipped through the multistep setup, denying the palm-sized supercomputer access to any of Cara Beckett's information. As he continued to delete applications, deny access and ignore dire warnings, he murmured a steady stream of mumbles. "No. Nope. Bye now. Can't accept. Decline. Nope. Nuh-uh," he muttered to himself.

Once he'd pared the smartphone down to its minimal functions, he sat back, satisfied with his work. Reaching for his own phone, he dialed the number displayed in the settings. Cara's phone sprang to life. He declined the call, then saved his contact information in her empty contact list.

He'd have to go over a list of dos, don'ts, and never-evers with her. Surely she'd see the reasoning behind it all. She had to. He'd make her see. Somehow, he had to make Cara Beckett understand if she wanted to get her life back, she'd have to do so without the help of the LYYF app in the short term.

Chapter Three

Cara sat on the rock-hard sofa of the condo Zarah had secured for her and stared down at the phone Special Agent Wyatt Dawson had programmed for her. She couldn't recall the last time she'd held a device set up to have so little function in the modern world. Cara took him up on his offer to drive her to the short-term rental. She was still reeling from the events of the day and found she was more than willing to let someone else take over.

As if defying the man with the gun and taking a leap toward freedom had depleted all her decision-making capabilities.

Agent Dawson, Wyatt, had insisted on walking her to the door. He actually groaned when he spotted the bags waiting for her on the unit's welcome mat. "Who is this Zarah person?" he'd asked as he helped her carry the haul inside.

"Zarah Parvich is my assistant. Virtual assistant. She works out of her home in the San Fernando Valley."

"She's definitely on the ball."

"I'd be lost without her."

Wyatt set the bags on the condo's kitchen island, then launched into a lengthy spiel on smartphone safety. Then he proceeded to check and double-check the settings on her new device. By the time he was finished, she was looking at a phone she could only use as, well, a phone.

"I programmed my number in as well as the numbers for Masterson and the CCD extension," he said as she continued to stare at the unadorned wallpaper on the screen. "I've also set it to decline any unknown callers. I'd recommend you refrain from adding more contacts. Any call coming to this new number will go straight to voicemail."

No apps. No email. No turning the cellular signal on unless she intended to make a call, and then she was to remember to switch it off the minute she hung up. She had a new phone number, one she'd have to use to call Zarah and communicate verbally if she was getting the gist of Agent Dawson's instructions.

"Assume everything is compromised," he told her. "For the time being, write things down."

He gestured to the spiral-bound notebook Zarah had shipped with the bags of food, toiletries and a wardrobe of leggings, T-shirts and zippered hoodies. Zarah knew Cara well enough to include a journal. Cara was a big fan of journaling and often encouraged others to dump their concerns onto the page.

She tried not to think about the notebook tucked into her carry-on bag. All her innermost thoughts and worries were riding around with a kidnapper. Possibly fodder for ongoing stalking.

"Do you think it would be okay to connect to the Wi-Fi here?" Wyatt nodded slowly, and Cara could practically feel the tug of his reluctance. "What?"

"I downloaded a more secure browser. It's the one with the fireball icon. Use it instead of the default." He went on, rambling about how Wi-Fi connections in public spaces where log-in was not required would be best from a security standpoint. He mentioned fast-food restaurants, coffee shops or stores, but cautioned her against attempting to log into any of her social media accounts. "Oh, and be sure to clear your cache when you're done."

She nodded. "Thank you. I will."

Wyatt clapped his hands together, then rubbed his palms. "Okay, then. You'll be all right here?"

His obvious reluctance to leave her alone in this strange place touched her. "I will be."

He walked to the window and peered down into the complex's parking area. "It's a weeknight, so there shouldn't be much trouble."

"I'll call if there are any issues." Wyatt scraped his palms down his pants as he turned back. He looked...nervous. "Is there something you're not telling me?"

"Nothing. Uh—" he flashed a weak smile "—I, um, I wanted to say... You should know..."

When he petered out without actually saying a damn thing, she set the stripped-down phone aside and rose to her feet. "I should know what?"

He shook his head, holding up his hands in futile surrender. "Nothing bad. I was only... I use your app."

The words came out in such a rush it took Cara a moment to process them. "Wha— Oh. Oh... You do?"

"Yes." He wet his lips, then gave a vigorous nod. "Actually, I know a few people who do. They made a free trial part of our healthcare package a couple years ago, and well, I'm a fan." He tossed the last off with a dismissive little laugh. "Ponied up for my own subscription."

But Cara wasn't inclined to dismiss anyone who appreciated her work. "Wow. I'm flattered. And so gratified you find it helpful."

"Very helpful."

She wanted to ask what he liked best. Wanted to know if he was in it for the finance or life coaching, like most men claimed, or if he stuck around because he found some benefit in the wellness practices. Or had he—as the fouler emails and messages she'd received implied—found a more prurient solace while watching her videos or listening to her voice?

She didn't want to know.

Not only was he a competent, attractive man who looked good in his buttoned-up clothes, but also because, like the truck driver who'd coaxed her out of the ditch and made sure she was delivered into safe hands, Wyatt Dawson seemed inherently decent. He didn't seem to be infected with the sort of Southern-fried misogyny Trooper Masterson and so many of the young men she'd known growing up were steeped in. He hadn't once condescended to her, or made her feel like a nuisance. Quite the opposite. He was warm, easygoing and seemingly determined to put her mind at ease.

Fixing her most serene smile in place, she rose and offered him her hand to shake. "Thank you… Wyatt. I appreciate both your diligence and your kind words."

He bobbed his head, then backed away. "I'll get out of your hair. If I hear anything, I'll call."

"Thank you again," she said.

He stepped into the hall, but made no move toward the building's entrance.

"Is there something else?" she asked.

He didn't bother to hide his sheepish smile. "I guess I don't need to remind you to lock up."

"No, but you can stand there and listen as I do." She flashed a quick, shaky smile. "Good night, Special Agent Dawson."

He inclined his head and mimicked touching the brim of a hat. "Good night, Ms. Beckett."

She closed the heavy door between them, then made a racket of engaging the locks before moving to the electronic alarm panel. It was set up differently from the one at her home, so she took a moment to scan the printed instructions the unit's owner had framed beside it.

"Don't forget there's an alarm," he called from the other side of the door.

"I'm doing it now," she called back. "Jeez. Give a person a minute."

"Sorry."

The buttons beeped and she pressed them in the preset sequence. Three short bleats signaled her success. She glanced down to where a slit of light from the hall crept into the unit. She could see his shadow.

Cara was about to call out to him. She wanted to chastise him for hovering, but his presence was disturbingly comforting. A childish part of her wanted to chase him off for that reason alone. She could accuse him of acting like a creeper. Say he was—

"Good night." His voice seeped through the door, quiet, calm and deep. "Try to rest tonight. Tomorrow is as good a day as any to start fresh."

She listened to his footsteps as he walked down the hall. The outer door latched with a loud *ka-thunk*. Stepping back into the unit, Cara placed her hands on her hips and let her head fall forward. She drew two breaths before releasing her hands and shaking her arms until they went noodle limp.

Once she'd released some of the tension in her neck and shoulders, she made her way into the small galley-style kitchen to sort through the bags Zarah had had delivered. As she unpacked each item, she made herself pause for a moment of gratitude.

She was alive.

She was well.

She had everything she needed.

Cara truly believed her life was better than a fairy tale. She got to build a company from the ground up with her two best friends at her side. Every day, she got to do work she loved. She brought people comfort in times of anxiety and solace in moments of sadness, and helped them find peace in the beats between each breath.

On the day Chris and Tom asked her to do the voice-over work on the new application they'd created as part of their final project before graduation, she'd planned to audition for a shampoo commercial. But they were desperate, and she didn't want to let them down. She'd been so naive when they met in their freshman dormitory at the University of California, Los Angeles. Like thousands of other transplants, she planned to be a star. Chris and Tom wanted to be the next Jobs and Wozniak.

They'd been the first friends she'd made in California, and for a lonesome girl from a small town in Arkansas, their friendship meant more than the possibility of commercial residuals.

She reached into another bag and her hand closed around a tube. She pulled it out and saw Zarah had thought to buy her favorite brand of deodorant. Tears filled her eyes as she offered up heartfelt gratitude for her young assistant.

Cara knew she had people who loved and supported her.

People who knew her and understood her better than her own family.

Her folks thought the whole acting thing was a phase. They didn't mind her going out to California for college because she'd sailed out on a flotilla of scholarships and financial aid programs. Cara knew they had not so secretly hoped when she got out to LA and realized how mercurial Hollywood could be, she'd settle into a more practical degree program. They hadn't counted on her loving every bit of the hustle and grind.

They never imagined she wouldn't come home and take over the land three generations of Becketts had toiled over. A sharp pang of guilt twanged through her as she glanced over at the phone she'd abandoned on the coffee table. Should she call them? Maybe not get into the details of what happened, but let them know she was coming to stay for a little while?

Her heart rate ramped up at the very thought, but the next thing she knew, she was palming the phone. Her thumb hovered over the keypad as she checked the time. They'd be getting ready for bed. Things had been strained between her and her parents for so long. They weren't estranged, exactly, but her refusal to come home after graduation had cracked the foundation of their relationship.

Biting her lip, she punched out a 424 area code rather than the 870 attached to the landline her parents insisted on keeping.

Zarah picked up on the second ring. "Hello?"

"It's me," Cara informed her.

Her assistant let out a long breath. "Are you okay?"

"Yes. Yes, I'm fine." Cara nodded, even though she knew the younger woman couldn't see her. Maybe she was trying to reassure herself.

"Did you get the stuff I ordered? Is the place okay?" the younger woman asked, breathless. "I can't believe this happened to you. In Arkansas! I mean, I expect to hear about bad stuff out here, but I didn't know you had anything more than, uh, farmland in Arkansas."

"You're not far off. Actually, rice is the biggest crop here," Cara said, doodling the words "rice is nice" on the first page of her new notebook.

Zarah's spongelike ability to absorb random bits of information was one of her most charming quirks. The quickest way to talk her down was to load her up with tasty tidbits of trivia she could whip out at a moment's notice.

"Really?" The younger woman hummed as she filed the information away in her mind palace. "I had no idea."

"Facts are fun," Cara said, forcing a bright note into her tone. "Were you able to get into my place without any trouble?"

"Oh, yeah. No problem. I grabbed your passport for ID and found the credit card right where you said it would be. I raided petty cash for a couple hundred and put it in the envelope in case. I overnighted it all to you in care of Special Agent Dawson at the Arkansas State Police. It should arrive before 8:00 a.m."

Cara fought the urge to roll her eyes. When Wyatt Dawson found out Zarah had sent supplies from one of the superstores to the condo, he insisted she call her assistant back and route any future shipments through him. Cara thought it was overkill, but she'd been too tired to fight him on it.

"Thank you so much for all you've done."

"Oh, jeez, no problem," Zarah said, allowing her native Minnesotan to show through for a second. "I'm so relieved you're okay. So scary, you know?"

Smiling her first genuine smile of the night, Cara said, "I know."

"Are you calling me from the new phone?"

"Yes, but don't give the number to anyone yet. The police are cloning my old number. Anything sent to it will show on this one too. They're monitoring both numbers, so they can capture any calls or texts."

"Oh. Cool." She gave a little laugh. "It sounds like they're pretty cyber savvy there in Arkansas."

Cara frowned, both mildly offended on behalf of her home state and bemused by the younger woman's blunt assessment. "Yes, they are. But that also means the guy who has my phone might be checking it too, if he can get past my security code. I'm not putting anything past anyone these days."

"I totally hear you," Zarah said.

Tired, and not prepared to answer questions, Cara shifted into business mode. "Hey, so I need some contact information. If I send you a list, will you email them back to me?"

"Email? Can't I text them?"

Zarah sounded perplexed by the notion of using such antiquated means of communication. Smirking at the notebook where she started jotting names, Cara wondered if Zarah would find Special Agent Dawson nearly as cute if she passed on his suggestion regarding the pen and paper.

"We're trying to go low-tech on this," Cara informed her. "I'm staying off apps, and texts are not secure. We know my work email has been hacked, but I have an old address I use as a spam catcher. I was thinking maybe if you don't mind me sending a list to your personal email?"

"Oh! Yeah. Totally makes sense."

Zarah rattled off an email address. They ended the call and Cara tapped her pen against the pad as she racked her brain for any other contacts she wanted to add to her list. Then she opened the secure browser and attempted to access the email account she never used. It took three attempts before she recalled the correct password, and even then she had to run the gauntlet of selecting security images of cacti and bicycles before the server demanded access to send a one-time code to her phone.

Gnawing her bottom lip, she weighed the risk of exposure before typing in her digits. She figured her detractors would have to be pretty darn dedicated to watch her every move all the time. Besides, she'd done all of her travel correspondence through her work email. The odds of anyone tracking down the handle she'd barely used since college had to be slim.

She fired off the list of names along with her heartfelt thanks for going above and beyond, and the reassurance there was no hurry to reply because she'd be logging out and heading straight for the shower then bed. The message whooshed its way to California. Her inbox was full of unopened newsletters, discount codes and special offers she'd relegated to limbo. With a couple taps, she sent them all to the trash bin.

She logged out of the email server, then backed out of the secure browser, sure to wait until flames rolled up the screen as an indication the connection had been torched. Satisfied she'd done all she could to cover her tracks, she stowed the last of the food items before grabbing the clothes and toiletries and heading for the bathroom. The sooner she got to sleep, the sooner morning would come.

Standing under the hot spray, she did her level best to tap into the gratitude and positivity she touted on the app, but her mind continued to whirl. Then her ankles gave out.

Sitting on the floor of a strange tub with her legs drawn close and her head pressed to her knees, she let the tears flow. They ran down her cheeks hot and salty as the cooling water pummeled her shoulders and back. Shivering, she told herself everything would be better in the morning.

It had to be.

Because if things could get worse than being abducted at gunpoint, she didn't want to know how.

HEAVY POUNDING WOKE her from a fitful sleep. She wasn't quite ready to surface, but the dream of someone sawing her in half was every bit as disturbing as the persistent thumps.

Cracking an eyelid, Cara found herself staring at sunlight streaming through unfamiliar curtains. Another round of demanding knocks came, and the phone she'd clutched until she fell asleep buzzed insistently from under her pillow.

She sat up, her eyes gritty from too many tears and too little sleep.

Someone was calling her name through the door. She ran a hand over her hair. It was flat on one side and sticking up on the other. She'd fallen asleep while it was still damp.

"Cara? If you don't answer in the next thirty seconds, I'm busting down this door."

The person issuing the threat was a man. But it didn't sound like a threat. It sounded like a warning. Yanking the phone from its nesting spot, she swung her legs over the side of the bed as she read the name on the screen. Swiping with her thumb, she said, "Agent Dawson?"

"Why aren't you answering your door?" he demanded. His tone was edgy and sharp.

"I was sleeping," she grumbled, staggering across the living room to the door.

She started disengaging the locks, but his gravelly bark stopped her. "Peephole."

"I know it's you," she argued. "I can hear you through the door and the phone."

"Check anyway," he growled.

She obliged him with a huff. Sure enough, Special Agent Wyatt Dawson stood in the hall holding an overnight envelope and wearing a shearling-lined denim jacket. "Nice jacket," she said, matching him grump for grump. "You headed out to rope some steers this morning?"

"Disarm the alarm."

She wanted to tell him where he could get off, but she was

hoping the envelope contained the cash, cards and passport Zarah had shipped.

"Sir, yes, sir," she replied, turning away from the door. She disabled the alarm system, then twisted the locks. Stepping back to allow him entry, she muttered, "You're eager to get a jump on the day."

He stepped over the threshold, then quickly closed the door behind him. Once he had her locked in again, he turned and thrust the envelope at her. "Do you have a Webmail address?"

"What?"

"Do you have a Webmail email account?" he demanded.

"Yes, but I don't use—"

"Did you send an email to someone last night?"

Cara pushed her hand through her hair, her anger rising even as her stomach sank. "What if I did?" she challenged.

"If you did, you exposed your account and someone got hold of it," he shot back.

"How? I was barely on there for two minutes," she cried, incredulous.

"Doesn't take long if someone is tracking your every move. Did you do some kind of password recovery or two-step verification?"

She squeezed her eyes shut and blew out a long breath. Apparently, Wyatt Dawson knew a confession when he heard one, because he pressed on.

"We got a call from a sergeant with Company E this morning. A woman claiming to be Elizabeth Beckett contacted them about an email she received concerning her daughter," he said, watching her closely.

"Elizabeth Beckett? My mom?"

His lips flattened into a thin line. "I suppose so." Wyatt pulled out his phone and started tapping. Once he got what he was after, he turned his phone over to her. It was a photo of a computer screen. On the screen was an email from the account she'd used to contact Zarah the night before, but this one was addressed to her parents' email address.

It was a ransom letter from a man who claimed to have taken her from the parking deck at Clinton National Airport in Little Rock. The amount he was asking for to secure her release was absurd. Her parents were ranchers. Even if they sold every head of cattle and every acre of land, they couldn't have come up with the outrageous figure demanded.

She looked at the time stamp on the email. It was sent less than an hour after she emailed Zarah the list of contact names. "Oh, my God," she whispered. She swiped at the phone screen, desperate to make the message disappear. "I need to call them."

"They know you're okay," Wyatt assured her, gently removing his phone from her grasp. "I spoke to your mother. Your father too. I gave them a brief rundown on what's happening, but I think we should vacate in case this location is compromised."

"Compromised?" she repeated, willing her brain to catch up.

"They obviously have a thumb on your correspondence. Probably phished your work email to identify your personal accounts. I'm going to need details on everything since you were first aware someone had your information." He blew out a breath, his hands braced on his hips as he scanned the condo. "Gather your stuff. You can call your folks once we're out of here."

Her stuff? She looked down at the package he'd thrust at her. Pulling the tear strip, she peered into the envelope. An envelope she assumed held the cash Zarah had mentioned, two credit cards—though who knew if they'd be any good to her—and her passport.

"What do you mean *we*?"

"Apparently, Mrs. Elizabeth Beckett knows people," he said with a wry smile. "You related to Paul Stanton? An uncle or something?"

"Paul Stanton?" she repeated blankly. "I, uh, I don't have an uncle. There's my aunt CeCe, but she never married."

"Nope. The name doesn't ring any bells? Lieutenant Governor Paul Stanton," he repeated.

She squeezed her eyes shut as she tried to recall the bits and pieces of hometown news her mother relayed whenever they spoke. Finally, the light bulb came on. "Oh, Paul Stanton. He's not actually my uncle. A family friend. Or friend of my mother's, I should say. He and my mom went to prom together and kept in touch. My dad hates him, but I remember her telling me he's some kind of big shot now."

"Well, your mama called him, and good old Uncle Paul made a couple calls, and it looks like you've got yourself your very own special agent," he said, holding his arms out wide.

"What?"

"Come on." He made his way to the kitchen and began bagging the supplies she'd unpacked the night before. When she didn't move, he motioned to the bedroom. "I'll fill you in on the way."

"On the way to where?" she asked, standing her ground.

He dropped a box of her favorite cheese crackers into the delivery bag and looked up at her, one dark brow raised. "I am to escort you home, Ms. Beckett."

"Home?" Dread pooled in the pit of her stomach when she pictured poor Nancy bandaged up in her hospital bed. "To California?"

"Oh, no, ma'am. I'm under strict instruction to deliver you into the hands of Mrs. Elizabeth Beckett ASAP."

"My mama?"

He looked her straight in the eye. "We're headin' to Snowball. Hope you have a jacket. It can be chilly up in the hills this time of year."

Chapter Four

Forty-five minutes later, he had Cara Beckett and her meager belongings packed into a state-issued SUV heading north on US 65. They were quiet as they exited the busy metro area north of Conway and headed up into the foothills of the Ozark Mountains. The moment she'd sat down in the car, she called her mother from his phone, having surrendered the new mobile to him by way of tossing it at the condo's sofa.

Wyatt didn't call her out on her decidedly less-than-Zen attitude. Her life had been ripped out from under her feet in the past week or so. And with the LYYF company's public offering about to take off, things were only going to get more hectic.

He'd offered her coffee and a fast-food breakfast, but she'd refused, keeping her arms crossed tight over her chest. He ordered a bottle of water along with his morning dose of caffeine.

Caught by a red light in Greenbrier, Wyatt cast a sidelong glance at his passenger. She sat stoically staring through the windshield when he offered her the bottle of water. "Single-use containers are poisoning our air and killing our oceans," she said stiffly.

He stared back at her, keeping his expression neutral though he could feel his ears heating. "How did you sleep last night?"

"I didn't," she retorted.

He waggled the evil water bottle in front of her. "A lack of proper rest can lead to dehydration. Right now, my mission is to keep you alive. We'll worry about the planet tomorrow."

"Exactly the sort of attitude responsible for our current climate change crisis."

"I'm not covering the planet today. I'm tasked with taking care of you. Drink the water," he ordered, tossing the bottle into her lap as the light changed.

He accelerated, trying to swallow back his exasperation. She wasn't sulking, per se, but she was not thrilled about the arrangement. And she wasn't drinking the water. He added stubborn to his mental list of things he knew about Cara Beckett. A list not nearly long enough if he was going to be any help in figuring out who was behind the cyber and real-world attacks against her.

"So, you grew up in Snowball?"

She shook her head. "Snowball is the closest dot on the map."

"Your parents own a ranch?"

"A little over six hundred acres. My dad keeps anywhere between fifty and seventy-five head of Black Angus cattle."

Her tone was flat, but he picked up a hint of pride in her delivery. "Wow. Sounds like a lot. Is it a lot?" he asked, glancing over at her for confirmation.

She shrugged. "I'd say about average for a family ranch." Her monotone response faded into a faintly mocking tone. "Let me guess, you're a city boy? Grew up in Little Rock?"

He shook his head, his lips twitching into a smirk meant to show her exactly how wrong she was about him. "Nope. Born and raised in Stuttgart, home of Ricebirds."

He felt her appraising stare. "Were you a farm kid?"

Unable to keep up the ruse, he allowed the smirk to take over as he shook his head. "Nah. My dad sold insurance."

"Ah."

Awkward silence descended like a thick fog. Grasping for information and a conversational straw, he asked, "You get along with your parents?"

She shot him a sidelong glance. "Do you?"

"Yeah," he replied without hesitation.

"I do too, but you know what they say…"

"What?"

This time, she couldn't repress the smile. "You think you're enlightened, spend a week with your family."

He chuckled. "I get you."

They drove in silence for a while. Finally, he prompted her to tell him her version of the story. "Start at the beginning. What was the first odd thing you noticed?"

Cara's fingers curled around the edge of the console between them. She was quiet, and for a minute, he thought perhaps she would not answer. He couldn't blame her for wanting to play things close to the chest. Her personal information had been scattered across multiple forums. He'd seen at least a half-dozen entries himself. And the threats came standard with this kind of cyberattack. People talked tough when tucked safely behind a keyboard. But somebody, or some people, had taken a giant step out of the shadow of internet anonymity.

Hopefully, it would make them easier to find.

"It's hard to say," she murmured, her face turned toward the scenery whizzing past.

The fall foliage was near peak color as October gave way to November. It seemed wrong to spoil such beautiful scenery with talk of ugliness.

"There have always been messages. Even before the app

took off. You know, the usual online slime. People trying to slide into my inbox. Once LYYF started gaining traction, I got hit up for money more often than I was hit on," she said, a wry smile twisting her lips. "Tom likes to say he knew we'd made it when guys starting fishing for my account numbers rather than my phone number."

"Tom is Tom Wasinski," he clarified, shooting her a glance.

"Yes. Tom Wasinski."

"He and Chris Sharpe are your partners in LYYF," he stated.

"Yes."

"And you knew them from…college," he prompted, hoping to get her talking.

"Yes. We were suite mates our freshman year. Stayed friends through school and after."

"You did the voice-over work for them from the beginning?"

When she didn't add anything more to the story, he stole a peek at her. She stared stone-faced through the windshield, and he winced. "Sorry. I didn't mean to trample all over your story."

"Not my story," she said in a clipped tone. "But you seem pretty well-versed in the lore of LYYF, so who am I to spoil it for you?"

Biting the inside of his cheek to keep from groaning his frustration with himself, Wyatt tightened his grip on the steering wheel. "You're right. I'm sorry. I think I was trying to impress you with how much I know." He offered her a wan smile as they slowed to pass through one of the myriad small towns along the route. "I want you to feel comfortable talking to me. Safe. I'm here to help."

She shifted in her seat, turning to face him more fully. "If you want me to feel comfortable telling my story, you might try listening. I don't need you to recite the press clippings to me."

Chastened, he ducked his head to acknowledge the point scored. "I'm sorry," he repeated. The tires hummed as silence overtook them once again. He waited, but when she didn't volunteer anything more, he pressed his lips together and nodded, owning his ignorance. "Would you tell me what happened?"

She blew out a long breath, letting her head fall back against the seat. The woman beside him didn't look anything like the glossy, glowing guru on his app. She looked haunted. Hunted. When she spoke, her voice was hoarse.

"Everyone latches on to the voice work like all I did was show up and read a few cue cards one day."

For once in his life, he had sense enough to keep his lips zipped.

"They were working on a finance app." She gave a dry little laugh. "It wasn't much more than a bookkeeping tool. Like one of those account trackers my mom used to use to record each check or ATM withdrawal. You know, the little booklet with three years' worth of calendars printed on there?"

"Checkbook register," he said with a nod.

"Exactly. Anyway, they were developing it all through school. It changed and evolved as we did. People weren't tracking checks and more banks had apps where you could see your transactions real-time, so they started retooling it to be more of a finance guide for kids our age." She waved a hand dismissively. "Simple stuff. Interest calculators, a stock market widget and some how-to guides one of the business majors a couple years older than us wrote up as part of their thesis project."

"Interesting."

She scoffed. "It wasn't. It was boring. But by the time we

graduated, almost everyone we knew had made some sort of contribution." She gave him a smirk. "I recorded a few videos with tips and tricks for acing job interviews."

"And this was under the LYYF banner?"

"At the time it was Life. *L-I-F-E.* We even had some cheesy tagline about it being the only tool a person needed to win at the game of life."

"Catchy."

"Anyhow, the concept grew and evolved, and as Tom and Chris became better programmers, the possibilities kept expanding."

She propped her elbow on the door and pressed her thumb into her temple as if talking about the past gave her a headache. But he didn't give her an out. He couldn't. Her life was on the line.

"How did LYYF as we know it come about?"

She gazed out at the passing scenery. "Sometime in my sophomore year, I'd gone on a commercial audition where I met a woman who was into Transcendental Meditation. We got to talking, she told me about a retreat happening near campus. It was free, I was…searching…"

The last word trailed away, and he let it go for a few minutes. He knew sifting through memories was sometimes like reading lines of data—whatever you were looking for usually popped out the moment you let your focus go a bit fuzzy.

They were navigating one of the steep downhill stretches before she spoke again.

"Anyhow. I got into meditation and yoga as a way to deal with the constant rejection," she said quietly.

"And all this time you were in school?"

She nodded. "I booked a few local ads, but never a national campaign. I was too generic for most casting directors."

He blinked, taken aback. The woman had to know she

was a knockout, but her unflinchingly harsh assessment of her looks sounded too clinical to be false modesty.

"You're hardly a generic anything."

The words he intended as a compliment came out awkward, stilted by his desire not to cross any professional boundaries. When he chanced a peek at her, he found her wearing the serene half smile she wore on the app's welcome screen.

"Not only is he a protector, but also he's a poet," she mocked, eyes crinkling with humor.

Heat prickled his neck. Determined to brazen out his embarrassment, he shot her a quelling look. "You know what I mean."

"I do. And thank you," she said, sounding thoroughly amused. "But pretty enough by Arkansas standards means I wasn't even in the ballpark in LA." Before he could argue the point further, she continued. "I was telling Tom all about this breathing technique I was using to help deal with nerves, and he said something about how it wasn't only actors who needed coping skills. The next thing I knew, I was cooking up a short script about how I got into meditation and the practical applications." She shrugged. "We purposefully omitted as much of the new-age terminology as possible and replaced it with some of the corporate catchphrases we were hearing all around us. Soon, we had about ten sessions written up, each focusing on a particular stressor or coping technique we thought would be helpful. I recorded them on my phone sitting in my closet using an earphone mic. And now you know the real LYYF origin story."

"Why were you sitting in a closet?" he asked, perplexed by this odd little detail.

"Sound absorption," she explained. "It had this nasty beige carpet left over from the nineties. We hung blankets on the walls and pushed most of the clothes back so they wouldn't be too close around me, but yeah. It worked."

"I guess so," he said, impressed.

"By the time we graduated, the guys were off and running with the life management idea. I was still making the rounds, doing auditions and waiting tables."

"Where were they getting their money?"

"Chris had money. Trust fund kid. Tom's parents supported him too. His dad was a surgeon and did well enough, but it wasn't inherited money like the Sharpes'. But Tom's parents were the competitive type. They wanted to keep up with the Sharpes, so they pretty much gave him an unlimited line of credit."

"And your folks..." he trailed off.

"Are rich in land and not much more. You know how it is," she said with a shrug.

And he did. There were plenty of families like hers around Stuttgart. Rice farmers with large stretches of valuable farmland who scrimped, saved and relied on government subsidies to keep from selling parcels off as the modern world closed in around them.

Cara continued her story. "When those first ten sessions started getting more clicks than some of the other sessions, they asked if I wanted to do more." She shrugged. "I wrote another ten and people seemed to like those too."

"And eventually, they asked if you wanted to be their partner?"

Pressing the tip of her tongue to her upper lip, she shook her head hard. "Uh, no," she said with a sharp little laugh. "They asked me to write and record more. I had two waitressing jobs, was pulling some temp hours doing reception work and still trying to land a part, any part. I told them I didn't have time."

"I see."

"A couple weeks passed, then Chris called me back saying they would pay me."

"Did they?"

She nodded. "A thousand bucks for another ten sessions. It doesn't sound like much now, and in context, but at the time it was the difference between making rent or buying a plane ticket home." She sighed, twisting her fingers together in her lap. "But, naturally, they were always more focused on the technology than the content. When the new sessions dropped and users started asking for more, they didn't want to spend time and money on developing content to be delivered regularly. Chris was the one who suggested they cut me in as a partner."

"Sounds like a big leap. For all of you," he added.

"It was a great deal for them. Particularly if the app didn't find traction. I was responsible for writing, producing and performing all consumer-facing wellness and lifestyle content. Research, scripting, recording…everything. We used to like to joke about how they made the widgets, I made the rest."

He let out a low whistle. "I had no idea."

"Most people don't." She gave a short laugh. "At the time, I was still auditioning for my big Hollywood career, so I was happy to let them handle what little press we got for LYYF. Since the only exposure we got in the early days was on tech blogs and forums, the narrative developed from there."

"Chris and Tom went on to become tech stars and you were cast as the wannabe actress who finagled her way into a very lucrative partnership."

She nodded, but her smile was self-deprecating. "I can't complain. It's been the most celebrated role of my entire acting career."

"Made you famous."

"It made me known in certain circles," she corrected. "Anyway, my point is, there have always been people who believed I didn't deserve what I had. They let their feelings be known on forums and chat rooms, then when the app itself became geared more toward interaction, direct messages. So, you see, it's hard to pinpoint a time when the harassment started, because it's been happening all along."

Wyatt hummed his understanding. The tech world was still disproportionately male, and some quarters were openly hostile to female interlopers. "What was your first hint it was going beyond the usual?"

"I started getting more direct messages on the app and on social media."

"What kind of DMs?"

"The usual. Name-calling. People saying I'm nothing but a parasite. No talent. Ugly. Commentary on my body, my voice, the way I breathe," she said tiredly.

"The way you breathe is a lifesaver for some people." The words were out of his mouth before he could vet them. Mortified, he kept his gaze locked on the series of curves ahead of them.

"I tell myself it is," she said quietly. "But some days it's easier to believe the bad over the good."

He knew the feeling too well. "I understand."

"I didn't start to get worried until the texts began."

"I imagine those were more of the same?"

"Yes," she confirmed. "But coming directly to my phone, they felt more...menacing."

"What did you do?"

"I sent them to Tom. He's always up for solving a mystery. In this case it wasn't much of a challenge for him. A simple search showed my name popping up in various forums. The next thing I knew, we found my cell number along with my home address, as well as several personal email addresses posted." He sensed her looking at him and turned. "The one I used last night was not one of them."

"So someone is actively monitoring your internet usage," he concluded, meeting her gaze.

She heaved a weary sigh as she smoothed her eyebrows with her thumb and middle finger. "I need to text Zarah and tell her I've checked out of the rental."

He nodded. "Use my phone." As if on cue, his phone rang. The display showed the caller to be Trooper Masterson. He hesitated for a moment before answering, but at Cara's questioning look, accepted the call.

"This is Dawson. We're hands-free," he announced, wanting to give the other man fair warning.

"Dawson. Is Ms. Beckett with you?" Masterson asked.

"Yes," Wyatt said.

"I'm here," Cara answered at the same time.

"Ms. Beckett, I wanted to let you know your rental car has been recovered," the trooper informed her.

"It has?"

"Where?" Wyatt asked, stepping over her words in turn.

"It was found in section 104 of the parking deck at the airport," the older man replied.

"Section 104," Cara murmured.

"Anything recovered?" Wyatt pressed.

"We have a team going over it now, but it appears most of your belongings were left intact. There was a large leather bag with your wallet, phone and other personal items on the front floorboard, and a travel bag in the back seat."

He let off the gas and coasted toward the shoulder of the road, tires crunching on loose gravel as he slowed to a stop. A car whizzed past. Seconds passed before a speeding tanker truck left them rocking in its wake. He and Cara shared a glance.

"Any cash or credit cards in the wallet?" Wyatt asked.

"My officer on scene checked. Says it doesn't look like your passenger took anything."

Wyatt did his best to keep his expression impassive. She was searching his face for clues, and he didn't have one to give. "So no theft," he said, his tone flat.

"Other than the vehicle," Masterson supplied.

"Which was found in the exact spot where Ms. Beckett found it," Wyatt supplied.

"But I... He..." she spluttered. "This wasn't some fantasy abduction I made up to scare people," she insisted, voice rising in agitation. "The truck driver. Eustace. Mr. Stubbs. He saw us. He saw me jump out of the car. He saw a man take off with the rental car."

"We do have Mr. Stubbs, the driver who picked you up. He gave a statement and as much of a description as he could," Masterson said in a patronizingly soothing tone. "And we may get lucky with some hair or other fibers."

But it didn't sound like he was expecting much. And even if they did come up with forensic evidence, the perpetrator would have to be somewhere in the system for there to be a match.

"Okay," Wyatt said, hoping to redirect the conversation. "Let me know what the forensics team finds. I have Emma Parker with the CCD working on some data tracking for us too. I'll have her loop you in if she uncovers anything helpful to the case."

"Appreciate it," Masterson said gruffly. "I'll keep you updated."

Wyatt thanked the man, then ended the call.

A logging truck rumbled past. Two minivans and an SUV

zipped along close behind it. All three of the drivers jockeyed to be in position to overtake the larger vehicle, all too aware once they got past Clinton and started climbing into the hills, the highway would narrow to a single lane in each direction. When they hit the switchbacks, there would only be the occasional passing lane made available for traffic relief. He'd be stuck behind them all.

He was already so far behind.

Who was hacking into Cara Beckett's accounts? Who disliked a woman who swore by gratitude journals and daily meditation enough to terrorize her? Chase her from her home? Kidnap her in broad daylight?

"Why would he leave everything?"

Her tremulous question broke into his thoughts. He turned to face her, but when his eyes met hers, he could see she already knew the answer. Robbery was never the intent.

This time, she spoke in little more than a whisper. "Why does someone want to hurt me?"

"I don't know," he answered honestly. "But I promise I'm going to do my best to figure out who it is and stop them."

Understanding arced like an electric current between them. But she didn't reach for his phone. Instead, she held his gaze so long he had to jerk his attention back to the road.

"Do you mind if we stop and get a coffee before we head for my parents' house?" she asked. "I'd like a moment to… collect my thoughts."

Wyatt nodded and checked their location against the GPS. "I know exactly the place." Hitting his blinker, he craned his neck to check traffic. A rooster tail of grit and dust rose behind them as he steered the SUV back onto the highway.

Chapter Five

Cara clutched the paper cup holding her coffee close as a breeze with a biting edge to it whipped her hair from her forehead. The view from the scenic overlook touted on a billboard outside of Marshall did not disappoint. The valley stretched below them like a patchwork quilt sewn from scraps of vibrant autumn colors. Red, orange and gold specimens shone bright against a backdrop of dark evergreens and leaves already dried to crisp golden brown.

"The cemetery where my mother's grandparents are buried sits on top of a hill covered in these huge red maple trees," she murmured when Wyatt approached. "Every fall, they turn the most incredible red-gold color I've ever seen. I bet it's spectacular about now."

"We can go there if you like. It's not like we'll have to hide out in your parents' basement."

"Good to hear," she said. He half turned and flashed a wry smile. "Because they don't have a basement. Nothing but a nasty old storm cellar filled with ancient canning jars and spiders." She glanced back at the SUV where he'd been making and taking calls while she ruminated. "Anything new?"

"We have an IP address from where the email was sent. It gave us a trail to follow. There's a forum user from Hot Springs we suspect may have been your, uh, passenger."

Cara whirled to face him. She swiped at her hair ineffectually. "Is it so easy to find people?"

"If you know how and where to look. Special Agent Parker has a talent for tracking these things down. Probably because when she was younger, she used the same talent to cover her own tracks."

"What do you mean?"

He smirked. "A member of our team was once a teenage hacker."

"Like Tom." The words slipped past her lips. She raised her hand to cover her mouth, but it was too late. She could tell by his expression he'd caught them. When he didn't express any surprise or press her for additional information, her eyes narrowed. "Did you know?"

He shrugged. "It's one of those open secret things. The truth is, a lot of people who go into programming or security started out trying to break into things. It's not much different from kids who grow up to be mechanics or engineers taking stuff apart to see how it's put back together again."

"Except it's illegal."

"Right. But most don't do anything truly harmful like hack into NORAD."

She blinked twice. "Right," she echoed. Then, shaking her head in disbelief, she turned back to the view. She cradled her coffee in the crook of her arm and pulled the cuffs of her sweater down over her hands. "So, they're looking into this lead?"

He nodded. "She'll call me as soon as they can get something solid."

She drew on her bottom lip, biting down to quell the swirl of anxiety and anticipation pooling in her belly. Letting her gaze go soft and unfocused, she imagined pulling the lovely patchwork blanket of fall foliage up around her shoulders.

The visualization helped a little but not enough. She needed to let Wyatt know what he was in for on this trip.

"You should know my parents and I have a...shaky relationship."

She felt his glance but could tell by the shift in his posture he'd gone back to staring out over the vista. "Okay."

"We don't fight or anything," she felt compelled to add, waving her coffee cup in a dismissive circle. "I'm an only child and let's say we wanted different things—for me—and leave it there."

"I understand."

He shifted his weight, and Cara got the feeling he actually did.

"My dad wanted me to take over his insurance agency. They only had me and my older sister. Shelby went off to school at Ole Miss, met my brother-in-law there and never came home. When I was up at the U of A, I majored in computer science. I told my dad I could use everything I learned to bring the agency up to date, automate everything, you know..."

When he let the story trail off, she turned to face him again. "But you never went to work for him."

Wyatt shook his head. "I met a guy who worked for the Department of Public Safety. They were recruiting on campus. Looking for people with tech skills to join the state police. I imagined myself as the guy who figured out who was sneaking around the dark web and what they were doing and stopped it all before things got too out of hand," he said dryly.

"So you and Agent...Parker, was it?" He nodded. "You come at things from different angles."

He shrugged, his hands buried deep in the pockets of his jeans. "I suppose you can say we do. But we work well together. Balance each other out."

"That's nice. Balance is good." She sighed. "I suppose we should get moving." Turning on her heel, she walked off in the direction of the car. She settled her coffee into the cup holder and waited for Wyatt to join her.

He took another moment to drink in the view. Which gave her the same opportunity with him. He was tall by Hollywood standards, probably just over six foot. He was lean, but not skinny. The Henley he wore with his jeans showed off broad shoulders and toned arms, but he didn't appear to be pumped up like a gym rat. All in all, he suited the scenery. Natural and unaffected.

He dropped into the seat with a soft "Oof," and she jumped.

"Sorry," she said, laughing at her own skittishness.

"No worries," he assured her.

"I just need to take a breath," she murmured. When she inhaled deeply, he did the same.

"Okay, now let it go," he said, parroting the words she used so often in her meditations as he started the car. "Now breathe in. Breathe in LYYF."

His eyes crinkled as he said the last bit, and a laugh burbled out of her. She reached over and gave his arm a friendly swat. "Don't mock me."

"Mock you?" he repeated through a laugh. "You? The guru? Never."

They'd strapped into their seats when the phone she'd left in the console vibrated. Beside her, Wyatt tensed. They both eyed the device warily.

"Text message," he grumbled, giving the notification the stink eye. "Know the number?"

She shrugged. "Not off the top of my head, but I don't memorize many numbers anymore."

"We've been forwarding all calls from unknown numbers

to headquarters. You should only be getting messages from people who have the new number."

"I gave it to Zarah. She may have passed it along to Tom or Chris," she speculated.

He nodded, but neither of them reached for the phone despite another insistent buzz.

"I suppose you should check it," he said at last.

A chill of apprehension ran down her spine as she leaned over to grab the phone. The screen sprang to life, and Cara sucked in a sharp breath when she saw the number in the little red circle. Seven. Someone had sent seven text messages to her phone. She opened the first.

856-784-4544: Have you missed us, Cara?

773-238-5795: Did you think we wouldn't be able to tell you rerouted us?

413-648-7993: I don't think she wants to talk to us anymore. I'm hurt.

630-721-9173: Hear she's run away to Arkansas, of all places.

325-545-1899: Arkansas sounds…like Arkansas. I bet Cara has ditched her shoes, cut off her jeans, and is kissin' a cousin right now.

213-566-5487: I can't believe some hick from a flyover state thinks she can cash in on Chris and Tom's genius because she slept with one or both of them back in the day. Where is Arkansas, anyway?

565-982-1167: You breathing LYYF in, Cara? Does the air taste better in Ar-Kansas?

"Oh, my God," she whispered.

"What?" Wyatt leaned over to get a look at the screen.

"They're texting this number," she said, jerking her gaze up to meet his.

"What?"

"They know we were forwarding calls and messages," she said, eyes wide. "They must have somehow traced the forwarding back to this number."

The phone in her hand vibrated again, and she jerked so violently she squeezed it from her grip. Bobbling the device, she let out a gusty whoosh of breath when Wyatt caught and held it still in his steady hand. Then, Cara read the latest entry.

228-798-1163: It's nice here, isn't it, Cara. Warm days and cool nights. Isn't sweater weather the best?

She began to shake. "Oh, no," she murmured, shaking her head. It started out a slow denial but grew more adamant with each swing. "No. No. No. They can't come here." She turned pleading eyes on Wyatt, unable to hide behind a mask of cool any longer. "We can't go to my parents' house."

"We're going to your parents' house," he replied, pressing the button to power down the phone.

"But we can't. I can't." Her voice grew sharper with agitation. "I can't bring all this to their doorstep. They didn't want me to be a part of this from the very start. I can't show up with a passel of stalkers hot on my tail."

"Understood," he said in an annoyingly calm tone. "But there isn't a passel of stalkers following you."

"Didn't you read what they said? It is sweater weather. They know where we are going."

"They do not. Those texts were all sent through an auto-dialer. The phone numbers were too random. Someone may know you flew into Little Rock, and they may figure you know people here, but it doesn't mean they know where you were heading."

"They emailed my mother a ransom demand," she practically shouted at him.

"Because they found someone with the name Beckett in your address book on an ancient email account," he countered. "They got lucky."

"No one gets that lucky," she argued.

"Either way, it doesn't matter. When I spoke to your mother, she said the first thing she did was pick up the phone and call her friend the lieutenant governor's office. From a landline," he added. "She didn't reply to the email or forward it to anyone from her account."

"Paul Stanton," was all she could manage to mutter.

"Your mother didn't do anything but open the message. They have no way of knowing they hit a bull's-eye."

He tossed the phone back into the console. Cara wanted to snatch it back and toss it out the window. But she knew she couldn't. They would need every scrap of evidence they could gather.

He swiveled in his seat to look her straight in the eye. "All the sender could possibly know is someone opened it. They're fishing, Cara," he said, reaching over and wrapping his fingers around her forearm. "I wouldn't take you anywhere near there if I didn't believe we could keep you all safe."

The gesture surprised her. From the moment they'd met, he'd kept a respectable distance between them. But this touch didn't feel like a boundary crossed. The size of his hand was reassuring. The warmth of it, a balm. He held her gaze, sure and steady. And she believed him. He would do as he said. He'd keep her safe.

"Fishing," she repeated.

"Or phishing, with a *p-h*, if you would," he said with a self-deprecating smirk. "Don't freak out, Cara. We're on top of this, you have my word."

"I don't know you. Your word may not be good for much," she muttered sourly.

One side of his mouth kicked up. "Let me put it this way. I value my career too much to take a celebrity who has been the victim of a crime, and has friends in high places, into a situation I believe to be dangerous to her or the people around her."

She choked on a laugh. "Celebrity? Hardly. And my mother is the one with the friends in high places. I haven't lived here since I was eighteen. I doubt I could pick the actual governor out of a lineup, much less the guy my mom went to the Marshall High prom with in 1978."

"I guess we should consider you an unreliable witness, then," he teased, reversing out of the parking spot. "For all we know, good old Uncle Paul Stanton might have been the one tryin' to hitch a ride with you at the airport."

"Ha ha."

He glanced over at her before accelerating onto the highway again. "I wouldn't put you or your parents in danger. I don't want to be in danger," he added with a laugh. "I know the title special agent sounds cool and all, but I'm a desk jockey. A computer nerd, remember?"

She huffed a laugh. "I've spent most of my adult life surrounded by computer nerds. Trust me, you carry the special agent thing off much better."

His lips curved into a sly smile. "I think there may have been a compliment wrapped up in there somewhere."

"Only an observation," she disputed, willing herself not to blush. Focusing on the curving road winding its way down into the valley carved by the Buffalo National River, she steered the conversation back to the investigation. "Tell me what's happening behind the scenes. Maybe I'll feel better about everything if I know what's going on behind the curtain."

Wyatt nodded. "I get you." He paused. His mouth puckered as he considered his words. "Okay, so we start with what we know. Someone has hacked into your accounts. They likely found their way in through one of your personal accounts rather than something attached to LYYF. Corporate security, particularly in tech firms, tends to be tight. Corporate espionage and so forth."

"I think everyone at LYYF knows I'm not the one who will be swiping critical codes," she said dryly.

"Perhaps not, but I'd wager most people inside and outside the company would assume you have access to critical information."

He lifted his foot off the gas and signaled for the left turn onto AR-74. Leaving the highway behind, they crossed Bear Creek and headed deep into the rolling hills and lush valleys of Searcy County.

"I'm guessing it was through a social media platform. They tend to be the most vulnerable, and some barely even try to make it hard to cage user information. From there, they likely gained access to other platforms, and possibly your company accounts." He paused for a moment, mulling something over. "Did you receive emails at your LYYF address as well as your personal accounts?"

"Yes, but they started with PicturSpam messages. I think you're right, they messaged on various other accounts, including LYYF, before the emails started."

"And I assume you were getting direct messages and

emails long before they leaked your information and the texts started."

"I wouldn't say long before," she hedged.

"In internet terms, long can mean hours or days," he clarified. "Think wildfire speed."

The Californian in her shuddered at the comparison, but she nodded. "Right. It was probably no more than a day or so. It seemed like everything happened at once."

"I can take a good guess at what most of the messages said, but tell me someone said something to make you hop on a plane less than two weeks before your company goes public and you become a multimillionaire."

Cara stared out at the scenery, wishing she could jump out and hide behind one of the huge round bales of hay dotting an autumn-browned pasture. Heck, it wouldn't be the first time she'd leaped from a vehicle this week. But Wyatt was sailing down the county highway at a steady clip, and she knew there was no way she could outrun the madness infiltrating her life. The only way out would be through, she reminded herself sternly.

"It wasn't what they said, it was what they did," she said, unable to look directly at him.

"Okay," he replied, the very soul of patience. "What did they do?"

"Well, let's see…" Pausing to gulp down the fear clawing at her throat, she focused on her hands clasped in her lap. "There was the petty vandalism. Nasty words spray-painted on my garage door, crude graffiti on my driveway. I've gone through three mailboxes in two weeks. All this in addition to the barrage of written and verbal harassment."

"Death threats?"

He asked the question as casually as if he was curious about her favorite color. So she answered in the same offhanded way. "Of course. Who gets doxed and doesn't get their fair share of death threats?"

Wyatt cast a quelling look in her direction. "Any the police were particularly interested in?"

"I'd like to believe they found all of them interesting, but there were a couple with, uh, specifics."

"You gonna tell me, or do I need to wait until the records we requested from California come through?"

She drew a deep breath, then let it out to the count of six. "One...person...said they liked my dog, and they'd be sure to take good care of it when I died."

He glanced over at her, his brow knit. "Your dog? I thought you said you have a cat."

"Half a cat," she corrected. "JuJu is a time-share."

"A stray you and the neighbor both feed," he recalled.

"My neighbor had a dog, though. Has. She has a dog. They are both alive and well, thank God."

Wyatt shifted in his seat, and she knew he was catching on, but she wasn't quite ready to say more. Instead, she pointed to a large metal building ahead of them. "Go past the Bakers' barn, you'll want to take a right on County Road 36. The road is barely more than one lane, and Mr. Baker likes to make a point out of farm equipment having the right of way around here, so look out for cranky old men on tractors."

"Got it."

Wyatt flipped on the turn signal even though there was no other car in sight. Cara smiled. He must have been telling the truth about growing up in farm country. Only city dwellers waited until the last second to signal their intention to turn. Out in the country, one never knew who or what might be coming up behind or poking along around a bend.

The tires scrambled for purchase on the crumbling concrete roadbed. Cara was pleased to note he'd heeded her caution and accelerated at a sedate pace. He let a good mile or so pass before he asked, "What happened to your neighbor?"

"She was out walking her dog. A car pulled up and a guy jumped out and grabbed her. He had a knife," she said, her words ending in a whisper.

"He stabbed her?"

Knowing he was watching her out of the corner of his eye, she simply nodded.

"But she wasn't fatally wounded," he confirmed.

"No."

"And the dog wasn't hurt."

Cara couldn't help but release a tense little laugh. He sounded so falsely encouraging it was ridiculous. She didn't know Wyatt Dawson well at all, but she felt safe in assuming optimism didn't come naturally to him. Why would it? He was a cop. He spent his days up to his elbows in all the worst things people did to one another.

"Buster is fine. Has a new little harness with LAPD printed on the back." She nodded to a crossroad ahead of them. "Keep going, but our turn will be coming up on the left."

"Got it. So Buster is an official K-9 officer now?"

"I wouldn't say official, but he was tough enough to get one of the officers to say every department should train a pack of Pomeranians. They may not be able to take a bad guy down, but they can sure wake the neighborhood." She pointed to a narrow driveway marked with three blue reflectors on their left. "Here we are. Home sweet home."

Chapter Six

When they pulled to a stop in front of the single-story ranch house at the end of a very long lane, a lazy yellow Labrador retriever bestirred itself enough to let out a single warning bark, then lay back down. Apparently, he felt he said enough. No one would ever accuse the big yellow dog of being a Pomeranian.

Wyatt barely switched off the engine before a tall, slender woman with long gray-blond hair woven into a thick braid burst through the screen door and bounded down the stairs.

"You're here," she cried, arms flung wide.

Cara fell out of the passenger seat and into the woman's embrace. "We're here," she replied, her voice muffled by an exuberant hug.

Wyatt watched them, arrested by the sight of the two women wound tight around one another. He nearly laughed out loud when he spotted a man wearing a shearling-lined denim jacket just like his and an Arkansas Razorbacks ball cap speeding toward them on an all-terrain utility vehicle. Her father abandoned the battered old gator before it came to a complete stop and hopped the low fence separating yard from pasture.

Wyatt noted the older couple were both strikingly attractive. Looking at them, it was no stretch to see into Cara's future.

"Hey, there," Cara's father said gruffly, pulling his daughter from her mother's arms and into his own. Like his wife and daughter, he was tall, but James Beckett was anything but willowy. Barrel-chested and burly, the man was more akin to a sprawling live oak tree.

"Hi, Daddy," she murmured as he crushed her to him.

"Hi, Sugar," her father grumbled into the top of her head. Without releasing his hold on Cara, he extended a hand toward Wyatt. "You're with the state police?"

"Yes, sir. Wyatt Dawson." He supplied his name as he shook the man's hand.

"I'm Betsy and this is Jim, and in case you haven't figured it out, we're Cara's mama and daddy."

"I put the pieces together," he said as he shook hands with Elizabeth. "Pleased to meet you both. Wish it were under better circumstances."

"Oh, my stars, I know." Elizabeth Beckett threaded her hand through his arm and propelled him in the direction of the porch. "I can't even believe this is happening." She whirled and pinned Cara with an incredulous glare. "Why is this happening?"

"Because the world is a crazy place, Mama," Cara said with exasperated patience.

By the time they reached the porch the dog had roused itself enough to stand at attention. "Hello, Roscoe," Cara cooed. "Who's a very good boy?"

Betsy snorted. "Good for nothing but warming the floorboards," she said, herding them all up the steps. "Come in. Come in. I have some stew on the stove and a pan of corn bread if you're ready for lunch. I know Jim's probably ready to eat his hat."

Cara's father pulled the battered Razorbacks hat from his head the moment he crossed the threshold. "I am hungry."

Wyatt stole a glance at his watch. It was early afternoon, but the Becketts had been hard at work long before the call from his commanding officer woke him. The scent of richly spiced beef stew filled the entry. He tipped his head back appreciatively and Cara's father chuckled.

"Come on in and have a bowl while you get us all caught up," he said, gesturing for Wyatt to follow his nose.

Betsy turned to Cara, her forehead crumpled with worry. "Now, I know you don't eat meat, but I forget whether cheese is okay or not."

"I, uh, yeah, it's fine, Mama," Cara said, her cheeks turning pink. "Don't worry about me. I can sort out whatever I need."

"Born to raise beef cattle, but the minute she stepped foot in California she turned vegan on us," Jim Beckett blustered.

"It didn't happen the minute I moved to California," Cara shot back. "Like every other red-blooded college kid out there, I lived on pepperoni pizza and pad Thai for the better part of four years."

She turned toward Wyatt and rolled her eyes dramatically. He couldn't help but wonder if he was there to protect her or act as referee.

"But I'm not vegan anymore. I love dairy too much."

"I should ship you off to the Bakers. They can keep you in milk and cheese if my beef isn't good enough for you," her father grumbled as he pulled out a kitchen chair. "Have a seat, Officer Dawson. Tell me what you plan to do to catch the jerk who sent that email," he ordered.

Wyatt fought back a smirk. Jim Beckett was clearly a very focused man. He wondered what Cara and her father would say if he attributed her ability to maintain balance and stay centered to him. Before he could get himself settled, Cara jumped in, acting as his self-appointed public relations representative.

"Actually, it's Special Agent Dawson, Daddy. Wyatt is a member of the Cybercrimes Division."

"Cybercrimes?" Betsy repeated as she ladled up bowls of stew. "Sounds fascinating."

"Betsy loves watching those crime shows. The ones with all the DNA testing," Jim said with a nod. "It is amazing what they can figure out with nothin' more than a few hairs or a drop of blood."

"You like them too," his wife shot back.

"Yes, uh, technology has helped in some incredible ways." He cast a glance at Cara and found her reaching into a high cabinet to pull down a jar of peanut butter. Her sweatshirt rose as she stretched, exposing a couple centimeters of skin, and Wyatt felt compelled to shift his gaze back to her father. "I deal more with the ways it hasn't helped," he admitted with a wry smile and apologetic shrug.

"Like the email," Betsy said, juice flying from her ladle as she pointed it at him.

"Exactly." Wyatt surreptitiously wiped the droplet of scalding stew from his cheek as he debated what information to divulge. He didn't want to panic the Becketts, but he also needed them to be on their guard. "And you did exactly the right thing by not replying to or forwarding the email, Mrs. Beckett."

"Pssht. Call me Betsy," Cara's mother said as she plunked a bowl down in front of him. With a quick intake of breath she drew back as if she'd burned her hand, a worried frown bisecting her brows. "I didn't ask. Do you eat meat, Special Agent Dawson?"

"It's Wyatt, and yes, ma'am. I love stew."

"Oh, good," she gushed, clearly relieved. "I poured tea for everyone, but if you want something different—"

"Tea's great. Thank you."

He picked up the spoon Betsy placed on a paper napkin, but waited until Cara and her mother joined them at the table to dig in. Cara darted a glance in her father's direction and rolled her eyes. James had already depleted half his bowl. By his daughter's bemused expression, he gathered this was the norm in the Beckett household.

"Help yourself to some corn bread," Betsy invited, gesturing to a napkin-lined basket she'd placed at the center of the table.

Cara raised an eyebrow, smirking at the basket of warm corn bread as she slathered peanut butter on a saltine. Apparently the presentation of the corn bread was not a part of the norm. He smiled as he helped himself to a wedge of the warm bread, then crumbled some into his stew.

"Thank you. It all smells delicious."

"If you ask me, everything smells fishy," James declared, not looking up from the depths of his bowl. "Why don't you tell us what the heck is goin' on here?"

"Jim, let them eat their lunch in peace," Betsy admonished.

Wyatt met Cara's eyes across the table. She swallowed the cracker she'd been chewing, then washed the crumbs down with a gulp of sweet iced tea. When she was ready, she folded her hands in front of her and angled her body to look her father directly in the eye.

"I'm not sure if you're aware, but my partners and I have decided to take our company public. We'll make a number of shares available for the public to buy on the stock market," she began.

"I know what goin' public means," James growled. "I'm

not uneducated, and no matter what you think of this place, your mother and I don't live under a rock."

"I know, Daddy," Cara said with the wary patience of a person who has covered this ground before. "Okay, so I guess you know it means I'll make a lot of money when it happens. On paper, at least."

"I told you from the beginning, this whole thing is like a house of cards," James started. "Monopoly money. It's all paper printed up in New York City and assigned a value by some…guru who pretends to know the value of air."

Cara tensed and Betsy cringed. This obviously wasn't the first time they'd heard his opinion on Cara's business.

James waved his hand in the air like he was wielding a magic wand. "How can you build anything real without hard assets? Land, buildings, equipment, cattle—"

"Cattle you take to market and sell at a price set by demand on the commodities market," Cara interjected. "A made-up number conjured by the beef oracle of the sale barn."

"Actually, companies like LYYF and other web-based businesses do have real assets. Intellectual property, patents, trademarks and copyrighted catalog are all tangible and valuable assets," Wyatt interjected smoothly. "There's also licensing, subscription and franchising." James opened his mouth to argue, but Wyatt shook his head. "But we're not here to debate the valuation of Cara's company. We're here because your daughter has become the target of some very real threats."

Cara's father's jaw snapped shut and a hush fell over the room. Wyatt nodded to Cara. "Go on. Tell them."

"I started getting messages online. Which, to be honest, is not unusual. Women are not particularly revered in technology circles. There's a small, but vocal, faction of people out there who don't believe I should be a full partner in

LYYF because I didn't contribute to the technological side of its development."

"But it's your face out there," Betsy countered. "Your voice people want to hear."

"Thank you, Mama."

Cara sighed and reached for another saltine even though the rest of them had stopped eating. She smeared creamy peanut butter onto cracker after cracker, setting them out in a row as she detailed the threats she'd been receiving, the attack on her neighbor and finally her flight to Little Rock and the events of the past twenty-four hours.

"Oh, my Lord, Cara," Betsy said, pressing one horrified hand to her chest and covering her mouth with the other.

James Beckett sat with his fist clenched tight and his head bowed. Silent. Unmoving. And seething.

"You can rest assured we have our best people working on the case," Wyatt said, speaking up for the first time since Cara started her recitation.

"Your best people?" James lifted his head, his jaw set and his eyes alight with the need to take action. "What about the FBI? Shouldn't they be working on this? She was kidnapped, for the love of everything holy," he cried, shoving his chair back and jumping to his feet.

Wyatt didn't move. If he were to get up too, it would only stoke Cara's father's ire. What they needed now was de-escalation. Calm. Sanctuary.

In other words, they all needed to take a deep breath.

"We are liaising with agents in the FBI field office, but since Ms. Beckett has been recovered unharmed and no one crossed state lines, they are deferring to the state police as lead on the investigation. Of course, we have full access to any resources they have when it comes to the identification and apprehension of the man who abducted her."

"I have every faith in Special Agent Dawson and his associates," Cara announced.

Wyatt did his best to mask the surprise and pleasure he took from her endorsement. Still, it was good to hear.

"And I promise you, we have been taking the case quite seriously." Wyatt glanced over at Betsy and flashed his most winning smile. "Even without the nudge from the lieutenant governor's office."

"Lieuten—" James started then stopped on a grunt, shooting his wife a sidelong glare. "Naturally, you called your old pal Paul for help."

"I told you I called him," Betsy said, rising from the table. She picked up her own barely touched bowl, then snatched James's nearly empty one from his place.

"You think I couldn't have called someone?" James demanded. "Dewey Roarke is a senator, for crying out loud, and we've been buddies since we were seven. We could have called him."

"Dewey is a state senator, and he's *your* buddy," Betsy countered, dropping the bowls into the sink with a clatter. "You were out at the barn when I saw the email, and I called who I knew to call."

"Good old Paul Stanton, always ready to ride in on his white Cadillac."

"I called you first," she shot back. "It took you forty-five minutes to get back to the house."

"I was in the middle of feeding—"

"Hey," Cara shouted, cutting through their bickering like a hot knife through butter. "It doesn't matter who called who. I didn't need anybody to ride in to rescue me. I'd already rescued myself."

Mr. and Mrs. Beckett both fell silent. Betsy turned toward

the sink, gripping its edges for support. James slumped, his broad shoulders sagging and his hands falling limp to his lap.

"You must think we're awful," Betsy whispered, shaking her head side to side.

An awkward beat passed, then Cara asked, "Me or Wyatt?"

A watery laugh escaped Betsy Beckett. "Both."

"Oh, Mama." Cara slid out of her chair and went to wrap her arm around her mother. Betsy's shoulders shook until Cara pressed her cheek against her mother's back. "I love you even when you're awful. It must be nice to know Daddy's still a bit worked up over the guy who took you to a dance back when you all still had a feathered hairdo."

Betsy choked out a laugh, and James moved to them as if they were magnetized. Soon, both women were engulfed in the larger man's arms again. "I hate he drives a nicer car than me," he grumbled into his daughter's hair.

"I'd buy you whatever car you want," Cara said, her voice muffled. Gradually, their family knot loosened, and Cara swiped at her cheek. "I'd even shell out for one of those enormous pickup trucks killing the planet."

"You know I have no use for a truck too pretty to haul hay," her father answered gruffly. "Let's sit down. I need to hear more about what started all this."

Before they could resume their places, Wyatt's phone rang. He checked the caller ID and saw it was Emma Parker. She was calling instead of sending a message. He could only guess something big was happening. "Excuse me for a moment, please," he said, scooting his chair back. "I need to take this."

Wyatt didn't wait to see if the Becketts were put off by his abrupt departure from their table. Nor did he look back. "Dawson," he said in a low voice, hurrying back through the living room toward the front door. The screen door didn't squeak when he pushed it open, and old Roscoe didn't stir from the patch of sun on the porch. "What's happening?" he asked as he ran down the shallow steps.

"We know who the guy is," Emma informed him without preamble.

"What? How?" Wyatt pushed a hand through his hair, all too aware he was firing questions faster than she could field them, but unable to stop. "Are you sure it's him?"

"We got latent prints off the steering wheel and gearshift, but those could have been anyone's since it was a rental car. But we had two different prints match with some we lifted from her phone."

"Is he in the system?"

"He is. Permitted for concealed carry," she informed him.

"Seems like everyone is these days," he grumbled. "This joker have a name?"

"Yes. Gerald Griffin. Thirty-eight. Residence Garland County, outside Hot Springs."

"Okay." Wyatt gave the back of his neck a squeeze, then let his hand fall as he turned back to take in the scope of the Becketts' ranch. "I guess we need to start looking for good old Gerry."

"Found him," Parker informed him, her tone grim.

Wyatt froze, his gaze locked on the overfed dog napping on the porch. "You answered fast enough to make a guy say *uh-oh*."

"I traced a debit card Mr. Griffin used to buy gas at a station near the airport."

An incredulous laugh burst out of him. "He topped off the rental before he returned it? What kind of a criminal is this guy?"

"A dead one," Emma said bluntly. "I'm thinking he filled up his own vehicle. It was parked outside his double-wide when the sheriff's deputies got there a little while ago. They identified themselves when they knocked. Mr. Griffin responded with a single gunshot."

Grimacing, Wyatt tore his gaze from Roscoe's sweet face and focused instead on the mud-splattered utility vehicle James Beckett had left parked on the other side of the fence. "He shot himself."

It was neither a question nor a statement, so Emma's only response was to expel a long breath.

"Notice anything unusual when you were poking around in his financials?"

"Depends. If you consider a series of deposits under ten K apiece made over the past few days unusual, then yes."

"I take it Griffin hadn't been getting regular direct deposits before?" he asked, knowing the question was a mere formality.

"Only his unemployment draw," Agent Parker responded tiredly.

"So we're assuming someone paid him to take her." Wyatt nodded as he allowed the pieces of information gathered to settle into place. "Safe to assume the payments came from encrypted accounts?"

"Yep. Offshore and numbered."

"And you're digging into his online activity?"

"Yeah. Nothing directly tying him to Cara Beckett, but ugh, the dude totally suffered from main character syndrome."

She scoffed in such a derisive way, Wyatt ached to refrain from asking her meaning. He already felt like he was aging out in the cyber world as it was, but he needed to know. "Main character syndrome?"

"Thinks he's the main character in every story, you know? Reading his posts you'd never guess he was driving a rusty compact and living in a run-down trailer out in the middle of nowhere."

"Delusional?"

"I'd say more aspirational," Emma hazarded. "From what I can see, grabbing Cara at the airport wasn't the only odd job he's picked up."

"Other abductions?" Wyatt pressed the heel of his hand to his forehead, wondering if this Griffin guy was some sort of kidnapper for hire.

"Nothing I can find. Lots of other things, but nothing this big. Skimming ATM cards, robbery—both commercial and residential—random credit card scams, pretty much a jack-of-all-trades."

Behind him the screen door opened, and the dog let out a low snuffling sound. He didn't need to look to know Cara was standing on the porch waiting for him. He could feel her stare.

"Okay, well, keep digging. Thanks for the intel."

He ended the call, then did a quick search for the term *main character syndrome* on his go-to slang database. A quick scan of various entries made him wonder when they'd stopped calling people plain old narcissists. He turned and found Cara sitting on the top step, feeding the dog bits of her peanut butter crackers as he gazed at her adoringly.

"News?"

The knowing trepidation in her tone told him she'd seen or heard enough to be wary. "Yeah. We identified the man who carjacked you." He crossed back to the porch, but stopped when his foot came to rest on the bottom step. "Unfortunately, when officers went to his home to speak to him, he, uh…" He hesitated for a moment, then decided there was no good way to break the news. "He killed himself before he could be questioned."

She dropped the sandwich, and her hand flew to her mouth. Her eyes squeezed shut as she murmured, "No no no no no," against her fingertips.

Wyatt scooped up the remains of the sandwich before old Roscoe could get his paws under him, then took a seat on the step beside her. "You know it is not your fault," he said, pitching his voice low.

"I know," she whispered. But it was clear from the rigid set of her shoulders she didn't truly believe what she was saying.

"I'm not even going to go into all the ways this man's choices were not your responsibility," he continued, steamrollering whatever internal meltdown she was currently experiencing. "You need to get there yourself."

"I know," she repeated, sounding the slightest bit steadier. "Who was he?"

"A guy out of Garland County named Gerald Griffin. Sound familiar?"

She shook her head. "I'm not even sure where Garland County is."

"Hot Springs," he answered, giving her a geographic touchstone.

She shook her head some more. "No. I don't know anyone from Hot Springs. I went right from here to California for college. We only went to Little Rock to shop or catch a flight. If we vacationed, we went north to the Buffalo or sometimes Branson or Lake of the Ozarks in Missouri."

"We have to fill your parents in."

"No." The word was little more than a croak, but the stubborn set of her chin reminded him of the spat he'd witnessed at the kitchen dining table. The Becketts were fighters, it was clear. And they were tough. Resilient. Like their daughter.

"They need to know. You can't keep them in the dark.

Not only is it not fair, but also it could be dangerous. For you *and* them."

Her eyes flew open. "What do you mean?"

"Someone paid this man to take you, Cara." Gripping her upper arms, he bent until he looked her straight in the eyes. "He was paid to take you and do what with you…? We don't know."

"You think someone will come for me again," she concluded.

"We have to assume they will. And until we have the instigator in custody, I think we have to believe they are not going to be satisfied with a job half done."

Chapter Seven

Her parents' reactions to the news about the man named Gerald Griffin came as no shock to Cara, but she could tell by Wyatt's stunned expression he expected more questions than he received.

Once it was made clear the man who'd taken her was no longer a threat, her father had slapped his knees and pushed himself out of his chair, promising to be back from the south pasture before dark. Her mother murmured an insincere "Lord have mercy on his soul" before retreating to her kitchen to clear away the remnants of lunch and start preparing dinner.

For her part, she'd shown Wyatt to the guest room, told him he was welcome to set up his laptop in the seldom-used dining room and provided him with the network and password information for the Wi-Fi. Physically and emotionally drained, she retreated to her childhood bedroom, hoping some time alone would allow her to rest her mind and perhaps gain some desperately needed calm.

Gerald Griffin.

Stretched out on the twin bed she'd slept in as a girl, she tried to conjure a mental image of the man who'd turned her world upside down, and failed. How many nights had she lain in this very bed dreaming of a man sweeping her off her feet?

Too many. Then, when one actually did, he turned out to be a mercenary with a gun instead of a knight on a white horse.

Had she taken a good look at him? All she had were bits and pieces cobbled together into a jumbled composite of good and evil. Brown hair? She thought so. Polo shirt. Khaki pants. Camouflage. Safety orange.

He'd seemed so harmless. Boring. An average guy renting a boring car at a middling airport in a medium-sized city in the middle of a state most non-natives would never deign to visit.

Then he'd jumped into her car, and he was the personification of a threat, complete with a handgun and masked face. The irony of it was, he was probably less remarkable without the disguise. Maybe the addition of the disconcertingly bright safety orange made him seem more menacing.

"Breathe in," she coached herself in a whisper.

She counted to four as she inhaled, waited four more seconds, then exhaled slowly. But three rounds of box breathing later, her heart still jackhammered against her breastbone. How was it possible she managed to escape a gun-wielding maniac, but found it impossible to relax in the room where she'd spent nearly half her life?

For a moment, she missed her phone with an almost physical ache. She wished she could open up the LYYF app and disappear into dissecting and critiquing her own meditations. Or tap into someone else's reserve of Zen for a bit. She'd even go for a podcast, or a particularly juicy audiobook.

Better yet, a boring one.

A book with a narrator so monotone it lulled her to sleep.

Inspired, she rolled over to gaze at the shelves above the desk where she completed hundreds of homework assignments. She spotted the cracked spines of a teen detective series she'd devoured as a girl. On impulse, she hopped up and pulled one down. Smiling, she drank in the horrendously dated cover art as she carried it back to the bed.

Less than thirty pages in, she was sound asleep with the book spread over her chest.

A TAP ON her bedroom door startled her. She sat up, pressing her hand to her startled heart. "Come in."

The door opened a crack, but rather than her mother, Wyatt Dawson peeked in. "Sorry," he said gruffly. "I hate to disturb you, but your mother says it's almost time to eat."

Cara glanced at her watch. It was nearly six o'clock. "Wow. I sacked out."

"You needed it."

She swung her legs over the side of the bed, but before she could rise, he held up a hand to stop her. She raised surprised eyebrows as he stepped into her bedroom and closed the door. She suppressed a wholly inappropriate giggle. She'd never been allowed to have a person of the opposite sex in this room. Part of her couldn't help wondering if her mother was on the other side of the house having a complete meltdown.

"I've been on the phone with the office most of the afternoon. Listen, I'm sure you want to call your partners, but I wanted to talk to you before you speak to them."

"Okay," she prompted cautiously.

"First, I want you to return any calls from your new mobile or even mine. I don't want to take the chance of anyone tracing your parents' phone number or mine through theirs."

"Sounds reasonable."

"Second, I'd like you to, uh, obfuscate a bit about your exact location."

He looked awkward and uncomfortable, and she couldn't help wondering if it was due to his word choice or the action he was asking of her.

"Obfuscate," she repeated. "I can...but why? I assume Chris and Tom know what's happening. Zarah said she would reach out to them."

"I'm only asking you to keep things vague. How much do they know about your hometown, anyway?"

She shrugged. "They know I grew up in a rural area of a state they like to poke fun at."

He pressed. "Would they know the name of your hometown if asked?"

"No, but I've mentioned it in interviews, I'm sure. It's never been a secret. As a matter of fact, I'm sure I've referred to the peace and tranquility I've found in the Ozarks in more than a few recordings."

He bobbed his head. "You have. I guess what I'm asking is how much your partners in particular know about your folks and where they live."

She stood, suspicion blossoming into incredulity. "You suspect Chris and Tom of having a hand in this?" she asked, offended for her partners. They may not be as close as they were before success pulled them in different directions, but Cara still regarded the men as two of her closest friends.

"I have to consider it," Wyatt replied, his tone even and reasonable. "They have means and a strong motive." She must have looked as horrified as she felt because he rushed to soothe her. "I sincerely hope I am wrong because I have admired them both for some time, but as an investigator, I have to take a long, hard look in their direction. They have both the money to pay someone to terrorize you and enough followers to whip into a frenzy."

"A strong motive?" She gaped at him. "What motive? We've been friends since we were eighteen, and now all of a sudden they want to get rid of me? Have me kidnapped?"

"Someone did," he interjected. "Someone paid thousands

of dollars to a guy you've never met or heard of but happens to live in your home state to grab you at the airport. Someone who knows you well enough to know your schedule. Your movements."

"They didn't know where I was going."

"As far as you know," he shot back.

He crossed his arms over his chest, straining the shoulder seams of his shirt. Cara looked away. She knew he was speaking the truth, but for the first time in her life she was learning that the old cliché about how the truth could hurt underplayed the sensation. *Hurt* was not a harsh enough word for the searing pain a few stark facts inflicted.

"Your abduction wasn't random. It wasn't a crime of opportunity motivated by robbery, like most carjackings. Gerald Griffin was waiting for you. He took you. You said it yourself. You offered him money and the car, told him to take what he wanted. He said you were what he needed. Why? What did a man you've never met need from you?"

"I don't need you to remind me," she snapped.

"No, but you do need me to help figure out who's behind all this and make them stop," he responded.

She closed her mouth so hard her teeth clacked. Cringing, she crossed her arms over her chest and leaned her head against the door frame. "I know, but I—"

She took another big gulp of air to center herself, then did exactly what she encouraged people who used their app to do. She asked for exactly what she needed.

"Can we not tonight?" Her voice trembled, but she squared her shoulders and let her hands fall to her sides, standing her ground. "I understand time is of the essence, but for tonight, one night, can we eat my mom's pot roast and talk cows with my dad? My brain is tired. I'm on anxiety overload. I need to…be for a few hours." His broad shoulders rose as he inhaled. She rushed into the breach. "I promise we can start fresh in the morning."

Wyatt allowed his cheeks to fill before he let the oxygen seep out between parted lips. "Okay. We can wait until morning."

"Thank you," she said, clasping her hands over her heart.

He started to turn away but froze as if remembering something important. "Wait. You don't eat pot roast."

Cara inclined her head in acknowledgment. "Nor will I eat the potatoes and carrots cooked with it."

"You're going to starve here," he grumbled.

She smirked, both tickled and touched by his grudging concern. "I won't, I promise. We live in the middle of nowhere. Mom keeps the pantry well stocked and I'm sure the freezer in the cellar is filled with good stuff put up from her summer garden. I'll throw something together."

He gave another one of those slow, thoughtful nods. "I won't grill you any more tonight, but tomorrow, I need everything you can give me."

"Deal," she said with a brisk nod. "Were you able to get set up okay?"

"The connection out here must be bouncing off a satellite launched during the Ice Age."

"Slow, huh?"

"Glacial. But steady so far." He held up his crossed fingers. "I'm getting surprisingly good reception on my phone, though."

She nodded, then reached past him to open the bedroom door. "Yeah. Much faster to build cell towers than to run fiber-optic cable up here."

"If I need to speed things along, I may run into town to get a wireless router," he said as he followed her down the hall to the living area.

"I hope you realize running into town from here will likely mean going back to Conway or heading up to Harrison," she warned. "Maybe Clinton, but I doubt it."

"I figured. But I haven't reached the level of frustration where I feel the need to shop," he said with a chuckle.

Cara smiled at the attempt at levity. "Well, if the urge does overcome you, the router's on me. I keep offering to upgrade things for them, but Mom insists she only uses the computer to place supply orders and check email."

"She told me she plays a mean game of online mah-jongg," he informed her as they passed through to the kitchen.

"Does she now?"

Cara raised her eyebrows when she spotted the woman in question transferring a hunk of cooked beef onto a serving platter usually reserved for Thanksgiving. Biting back any commentary about houseware choices, she crossed to the counter and pressed a kiss to her mother's cheek. "I'm sorry I fell asleep. You should have given me a shake. I would have helped."

Her mother's mouth curved into a pleased smile and Cara stayed where she was, inhaling the familiar scents of home cooking mixed with Chanel she bought for her mother each Christmas.

"You needed rest," her mother said in her usual no-nonsense tone. "I made you a sort of stir-fry." She jerked her chin at the sauté pan brimming with a jumble of colorful garden vegetables. "Used a bit of oil, some soy sauce and some all-purpose seasoning. I also have some rice. It's the boil-in-a-bag kind, not the fancy stuff," she warned.

"Sounds great, Mama," Cara said, then gave her mother another impulsive peck on the cheek. "And I don't need rice, regular or fancy. But thank you."

Cara wasn't sure if these unexpected concessions to her

dietary choices were because Wyatt was here or if her mother was simply glad some strange man hadn't made off with her only child. Nor did it matter. She appreciated the effort.

"Your father is getting washed up," Betsy informed her. "If you'll get Wyatt whatever he'd like to drink with supper, I'll get this to the table."

"Here. Let me," Wyatt said, stepping up and extending his hands to take the platter.

To Cara's surprise, her mother acquiesced without even a token protest.

"Sweet tea okay for everyone?" she asked, turning to the fridge. It was a rhetorical question as far as she and her parents were concerned, but she didn't know Wyatt well enough to presume.

"We also have milk, water and what appears to be a lifetime supply of fruit-flavored carbonated water," she called.

"It was on special at the store. Buy two, get one free," her mother said with a sniff.

"Tea is fine for me, but—"

Wyatt trailed off as Cara pulled a pitcher filled with sweet tea from the fridge. But when she turned, she found him standing beside the round kitchen table where they'd eaten lunch looking perplexed. She quickly ascertained the cause for his concern. The table she and her parents had used for most meals had always been big enough for the three of them, but now, with the addition of a place setting for Wyatt, there was no room for the serving platter.

"I'm sorry I've taken over your dining table." He turned to her mother, a deep furrow of consternation bisecting his brows. "If you'll give me a minute, I can get things cleared—"

"Oh, for heaven's sake," Betsy interrupted, then pushed past him to remove the wooden napkin holder with its nested salt and pepper shakers to make room. "There." She gave him a brisk nod. "We never eat in there anyway." She pulled Cara's plate from her usual spot. "You can fill your plate at the stove, can't you, Sweets?"

"I can."

Cara was pouring tea over crackling cubes of ice when her father appeared, freshly showered and changed into clean clothes. With his damp hair combed and the remnants of his summer tan offsetting his blue eyes, Cara caught a glimpse of the handsome young man who'd wooed and won the heart of Elizabeth Watts. Her parents were an attractive couple. One day in an LA spa and they could easily shave twenty years off the birth dates shown on their driver's licenses.

She listened with half an ear as she filled her plate at the stove. Their conversation was so casual, so normal, it made her hands tremble. This time the day before, she'd been diving out of a moving vehicle. Now her father was naming off random items he wanted her mother to add to their supply list. Yesterday, a strange man named Gerald Griffin had been alive and well and pointing a gun at her. Today, he was dead, and her mother was pushing food on a handsome special agent from the state police.

Staring down at the kaleidoscope of vegetables on her plate, Cara focused on the vibrancy of their colors. Rounds of bright orange carrots, red pepper and yellow squash were offset by dark green zucchini and pale chunks of cauliflower. She was safe. She was home. Her mother had made this gorgeous stir-fry for her, and she was grateful. More grateful than she could say. Wetting her lips, she grasped the plate hard enough to mask her terror as she turned to join them at the table.

She wouldn't let whoever was doing this steal these precious moments from her. She would pass the few hours in peace, then tomorrow morning she and Wyatt would put their heads together and start figuring things out.

Forcing a smile, she placed her plate on the table and dropped into her chair. When she was sure she had the shaking under control, she reached for her glass and gulped the sugary sweet tea. As the cool liquid soothed her parched throat, she couldn't help thinking about how horrified her friends back in La-La Land would be if they knew she was sucking down tea brewed with leaves trapped in bags with little tags and sweetened with no less than two cups of refined white sugar.

Wyatt's phone rang and they went still.

"I'm sorry," Wyatt murmured, but they all knew the apology was both reflexive and performative. Of course he would take the call.

"It's almost as if people are aiming for our mealtimes. Go on," her mother encouraged, but her smile was nervous and forced. "We want to know everything we need to know."

But do we? Cara thought as Wyatt rose, swinging his leg over the sturdy wooden chair and pulling his phone from his pocket in a fluid motion now familiar to her. She placed her cutlery across the edge of her barely touched plate. She stared down at the brightly colored dish her mother had gone to the trouble of preparing for her, knowing she wouldn't manage another bite. Her stomach was too sour. Her throat bone-dry.

Betsy reached over and covered Cara's hand with hers. "Try to eat something. You need your strength."

Across the table, her father sat with his knife and fork clutched in each hand. "What do these people want?"

"Honestly? I don't know," Cara confessed.

"Is it money?" he persisted, jabbing his fork into his slice of roast a mite too forcefully. "They asked for ten million dollars in the email." He snorted. "Who could possibly come up with so much money?"

Cara bit her bottom lip. She didn't know how to tell her father she could. If she were to sell her portion of LYYF to Chris and Tom now, she'd be able to cover the ransom demand and still have money left over. And if she waited until after the company went public...well, according to Chris, ten million would be little more than pocket change.

As if reading her mind, her mother zeroed in on her. "Do you have that kind of money?"

Uncomfortable with the topic of money in general and feeling cornered, Cara squirmed in her seat. "I, uh," she started. Her father stopped chewing and stared at her as if he'd never laid eyes on her before. Caught in his steady blue gaze, she confessed, as always. "Not, um, you know, liquid."

Her dad gently lowered his silverware to his plate and pulled his napkin from his lap, never breaking eye contact. "But you have access to large amounts of money?"

Cara cringed inside. She'd spent most of her adult years downplaying the perceived extravagance of her California lifestyle. Particularly in the three years since the app went stratospheric. She'd sent them photos of her charming little house on Sunset Drive, but she never told them she'd paid nearly two million dollars for fifteen hundred square feet of space. It wasn't the kind of math people who clip coupons and pride themselves on canning homegrown vegetables and preserves would understand.

"I do," she replied, but added nothing more. Thankfully, Wyatt reappeared and the subject was dropped. "What's happening?"

"Not a lot. I guess Chris Sharpe has left for New York. Something about meetings with some fund managers before the stock offering. Emma says she spoke briefly with Tom Wasinski, and he says he'd like you to call him."

"Nothing more on tracing the money?" she asked as he reclaimed his seat.

Wyatt settled his napkin into his lap. "No, we've hit a dead end on the numbered accounts, but Emma is monitoring chatter on a couple forums she thinks Griffin was active on, and I have some other angles I want to track after dinner." He picked up his fork again. "I'm sorry for the interruption."

The rest of dinner passed in fits and spurts of congenial small talk. After they were through, Cara helped her mother with the dishes while her father saw to Roscoe's evening kibble and Wyatt retreated to his laptop. She was settled in the den with her parents watching a police procedural when he reappeared, looking rumpled and worried.

"Anything?" she asked, motioning for him to join them.

He skirted Roscoe's enormous orthopedic pet bed as he stepped into the room. The dog gave him a cursory snort as he passed. "Nothing we didn't already know. Countersurveillance on your accounts is running as it should," he reported, taking a seat on the opposite end of the sofa. "Nothing has popped yet."

The detective in the television show started rattling off a list of supposedly damning physical evidence they'd collected during a cursory search of the victim's sister's bedroom, and Wyatt let out a disdainful scoff.

Cara and her mother looked over at him, surprised by the interruption, but her father was the keeper of the remote. The moment the scene cut to a commercial, he muted the volume and shifted in his recliner to look directly at Wyatt.

"I take it things don't tie up so neatly in the real world," he said with a nod to the television.

"Most of the testing they mentioned doesn't exist. Or, if it does, it either produces results too unreliable to use as evidence or is so expensive most municipalities couldn't afford to implement it," Wyatt explained. "Good physical evidence is much harder to come by than fictional."

"I can't believe you dare to sit here and spoil one of our favorite shows," Cara accused.

Wyatt raised his hands in surrender. "Not another word," he promised, a smile playing at the corners of his mouth.

"I think it's far more interesting to know what's real and what isn't," her father interjected.

"Jim is hooked on those true crime documentaries they show on CineFlix." Betsy shuddered. "I prefer my crime scenes off camera and the bad guys rounded up at the end of an episode." She gave him a wan half smile. "I don't suppose it happens very often in the real world."

Cara shot him a look, hoping he'd tread carefully. Given the circumstances of their visit, the last thing she wanted to do was add to her mother's worry by piling on depressing crime statistics.

"You'd be surprised," Wyatt said, crooking his arm on the back of the sofa and angling his body in the direction of her parents' matching leather recliners. "In most cases, things are so obvious they wouldn't make for good television."

They finished out the hour and by unspoken agreement segued right into the next episode. "Tell us where they get things wrong," her father prompted as they joined the investigators on the scene of yet another grisly murder.

"I have to tell you, I've been to relatively few crime scenes," Wyatt warned. "I'm more the guy back in the office pulling the background reports or analyzing data."

"Fake it," Cara said out of the corner of her mouth. "I promise we won't know the difference."

So he did, and for the next hour, the three Becketts peppered poor Wyatt with all manner of questions, doubts and pie-in-the-sky theories as to the unraveling of the crime. By the time the case was resolved, the four of them were exhausted from poking holes in each other's theories. And Cara was able to forget she was the subject of an ongoing investigation.

For a few hours, at least.

Chapter Eight

Cara awoke to five young men dressed in an assortment of leather pants and jackets gazing down at her, each one smoldering harder than the next. She rubbed the sleep from her eyes, then rolled them as she recalled Wyatt's smirk when he saw the old poster tacked to the wall of her childhood bedroom. Fixing her gaze on her longtime favorite, she whispered, "Don't worry, guys. He's jealous of our love."

It was early. The light coming through the partially open blinds was the dusky rose of dawn. Reaching out, she switched on the milk glass lamp on her bedside table. Gold incandescent light flooded the room, and idly, Cara wondered when her parents changed the bulb. Probably not long after she'd stopped gazing longingly at her teenage crush each night before she drifted off to sleep, she figured.

Lifting her arms over her head, she indulged in an extravagant stretch. It felt so good, she laced her fingers together and pressed her open palms toward the ceiling. The next thing she knew, she'd fallen into a rhythmic four-count breathing pattern, her gaze fixed on the blooming sunrise.

She heard her parents moving around the house. The rumble of an ATV engine signaled her father's imminent departure. When it faded into the distance, she closed her eyes and listened hard for any clue as to whether her mother had gone with him to the barn. The clank of cast iron against the stovetop grate rang out with the promise of breakfast.

Cara smiled as she sank into the moment, feeling more centered than she had in weeks. It always felt good to come home, even if she hated admitting it.

The sky morphed from peachy pink to pale violet. Memories of running through the back door of a simple clapboard farmhouse that used to stand less than a quarter mile up the lane came flooding back. The slap of the screen door. The scent of fresh-baked bread. Sheets snapping in the stiff breeze whistling around the tree-covered mountains and through the valley.

She loved her grandparents' house. The old house, as it was called. There was always a pan of leftover biscuits on the stove. Whatever wasn't eaten at breakfast would be gobbled up with whatever Grandma tossed together for lunch. Or dinner, as she'd called it.

After Granddad died, Grandma moved up to the new house with Cara's parents. Her dad claimed the old house was falling down around her ears, but Cara didn't see it. When you're a kid, you don't think about drafty windows, rotting floorboards on the porch or dripping pipes.

Grandma June brought little more than her cast-iron skillet and her love of all things Hollywood with her to the new house. She slept in the room Wyatt currently occupied until the day she passed. They watched old movies together well after her parents had turned in. When she was small, Grandma June happily paid a shiny quarter for a ticket to whatever living room production Cara cooked up in her head. She'd helped Cara run lines for every school play or drama club soliloquy.

Her grandmother was the one who'd dipped into her life savings to cover Cara's airfare to California. Her gran was the first person she'd called when she'd thought she'd blown an audition or got a callback for a second look. When she passed, Cara'd spent the entire flight home sobbing into a wad of paper napkins a kindly flight attendant had provided while the businessman next to her pretended not to notice.

In her absence the old house had fallen into even more disrepair. Sitting empty, there was water damage. Rot. Termites. Black mold. When it was demolished, Cara was hurt beyond reason. She accused her parents of tearing down the best parts of her childhood. Trips home became less frequent. Phone calls were kept brief and perfunctory.

She opened her eyes, a fresh surge of anger and betrayal coursing through her veins. If they had only waited a few more years, she could have had the old house restored. But she knew such wishful thinking was fruitless. Her parents would still have been saddled with the upkeep on a house she'd visit once, maybe twice a year. She shook her head, dismissing the thought and the rush of emotion it rode in on.

Her father had done what he needed to do.

Resolved to make the most out of this unexpected time with her parents, she swung her legs over the side of the bed. The floorboards were cool underfoot. She reached for the hooded sweatshirt she'd hung on a bedpost and pulled it on over the T-shirt she'd slept in. By the time she shimmied into yoga pants and some socks, the tantalizing scent of bacon drifted down the hall.

She closed her eyes and drew from the well of inner strength, hoping it would allow her to withstand temptation. Of all the foods she'd eschewed when adopting a vegetarian diet, bacon had been the hardest habit to break. Turning the doorknob, she stepped into the hall, promising herself an enormous bowl of old-fashioned oatmeal topped with brown sugar and pecans.

The guest room door opened, and Wyatt poked his head into the corridor. She smiled when she saw one side of his hair was still artfully rumpled, while the other appeared to be suffering a near terminal case of bedhead.

"Do I smell bacon?" he asked, darting a hopeful look in her direction.

"Undoubtedly," she replied. "Dad usually only has a cup of coffee first thing. He'll come back in for breakfast once the cows are fed and turned out."

He pointed to the bathroom door. "Do I have time to shower?"

She nodded. "Yeah. I'll go help Mama and take mine after we eat."

He gave a quick nod then ducked back into the bedroom. Shoving her hands into the pockets of her sweatshirt, she shuffled through the house, her shoulders hunched against the autumn chill.

Cara found her mother fishing strips of crisp bacon from Grandma June's skillet and smiled as she listened to her hum an old Beatles song. Not for the first time, Cara thanked the heavens she'd inherited her father's ear for music. Her mother couldn't carry a tune in a paper bag.

"Mornin', Mama," she said, falling back into the easy vernacular of her youth. "Can I help?"

"Morning, Sweets," her mother said, turning from the stove with a wide, guileless smile. "I've got bacon, eggs and toast." Her smile faded and she cast a worried glance in the direction of the bedrooms. "I hope that'll be okay with Wyatt."

"I'm sure it will be," Cara assured her. She moved to the cupboard where the coffee cups were kept and pulled down the biggest one she could find. "He smelled the bacon."

Her mother wiped her hand on the crumpled dishcloth beside the stove and nodded. "I won't start the eggs until your daddy comes in, but what am I gonna feed you?"

Cara bit her bottom lip and refrained from shaking her head. Every meal, the same despairing question. "I was hoping for some oatmeal," she said as she poured the rich, black coffee into her mug. "And maybe a handful of pecans if you have some stashed somewhere?"

Her mother gave an indelicate little snort. "You can have more than a handful. Those trees your granddad planted dropped enough to feed an army of squirrels this winter."

"Then I definitely won't starve." Cara cradled the mug in both hands and took a cautious sip of the steaming brew.

Thirty minutes later, the sun was up, Wyatt had emerged fully dressed, her father had returned from the first of his morning chores and Cara was doctoring a steaming bowl of cereal. She could feel her father's gaze on her as she swirled a liberal sprinkling of brown sugar and cinnamon into the oats before dropping chopped nuts into the mixture.

"Would you like some of my oatmeal, Daddy?" she asked without looking up. Her father hated hot cereal. Always had, always would, he'd proclaimed on more than one occasion.

He picked a strip of bacon cooked shy of burnt off his plate and held it out to her. "Wanna bite, baby girl?" he taunted, his voice morning gruff.

Cara smiled. "No, thank you," she replied sweetly, looking up in time to see a puzzled expression cross Wyatt's face. "It's a thing we do," she explained.

Their customary exchange complete, her father pierced the orange-yellow yolk of his perfectly fried egg with the corner of a piece of toast, then pinned Wyatt with a stare. "So tell me, what is it you do exactly?"

She wanted to object to the blunt question, but Wyatt's

quiet chuckle assured her there was no offense taken. On the contrary, he seemed bemused.

"Do you want the big picture version or the dreary details?"

Her father took his time chewing his toast before answering. "I want to know how whatever it is you're doing applies to keeping my daughter safe. I want to know how you're going to catch whoever's doing this to her."

Wyatt paused, giving the question serious consideration. Idly, he broke off the end of a strip of bacon, popped it into his mouth and chewed, his gaze never leaving her father's face. "Do you remember me telling you the tracing technology had far exceeded what you see on the television police procedurals?"

"Yessir," her father replied, sopping up some more of the runny yolk with his toast. "Why I'm askin'. It seems like you should be getting more answers than you have."

"We do have answers. We simply don't know how they fit together yet. We know what's happening. We know how they're surveilling her. We know what's being said online and by whom in many cases. We even know where some of the communications have originated."

Her mother spoke up. "If you know who and where they are, why aren't you going after them?"

"Because most people don't use landlines anymore. We can ping whichever towers a cellular call is coming from, or trace the IP address of a message, but the technology is mobile now." He shrugged. "And even if whoever is posting these things is sitting in the parking lot of a police station, the most we can do is question them. What they say is protected under their First Amendment rights."

Wyatt said the last with an edge of rancor, but her parents responded with true outrage.

"People can't go around publicly threatening people," Betsy argued. "Isn't it some form of terrorism?"

Her father dropped his fork with a clatter. "What if there's evidence those threats are credible? Someone abducted her at gunpoint."

"We have no evidence connecting Gerald Griffin to any of the threats against Cara. From everything we've uncovered, he was hired help."

"Hired help," her mother repeated. "What a world we're living in."

Cara reached over and gave her hand a gentle squeeze. "The world is wonderful. There are some bad people in it, but there always have been." She gave them a sad smile. "The only difference is, now they have more ways to spread ugliness."

"Exactly," Wyatt said with a decisive nod. "Most online chatter is nothing more than someone using a keyboard to make themselves feel heard. They can say whatever they like about somebody, and no one can stop them. Makes the powerless feel powerful."

They fell silent for a moment, their cutlery still as they digested this unsavory bit of reality.

"I don't know about y'all, but I'm feeling pretty powerless right about now," Betsy admitted.

"Me too, Mama," Cara said softly. Then she thought about those desperate people sitting at their keyboards grasping for any opportunity to feel heard. She looked from her father to her mother, then across at Wyatt, then she smiled. "But at least we aren't alone."

CARA WAS PARKED at the dining room table pretending to write scripts for upcoming recordings, but it was hard to come across as calm and centered when her life was skidding out of control. Catching her bottom lip between her teeth, she stole another glance at Wyatt. He'd been alternating between feverish typing, glaring at his screen and muttering soft oaths under his breath for the past hour. She'd tried to engage him in conversation a couple times, but his curt answers and unwillingness to look up for more than a second telegraphed his unwillingness to engage in her procrastination efforts.

Thankfully, her phone rang.

Wyatt frowned at the name on the screen, then slid it across the table to her. "Zarah."

"Hey, Z," she said into the phone. "Hang on, let me go in the other room."

She slipped from her seat to move to the other room, but Wyatt caught her wrist as she passed, shaking his head and mouthing, "Stay."

Everything in her rebelled against his high-handed order. But the man was here because of her. He'd packed a bag, picked her up and taken up residence in her parents' house all to keep her safe. She needed to stop fighting for control. The sooner she gave herself over to the situation she was in, the sooner she'd find her way through it. Struck by her own moment of clarity, she moved back to her notebook, anxious to capture the thought. She scribbled the words "give over to get through" on the paper, then reclaimed her seat with a grin.

"What's up? Aside from you," she added, glancing at her watch. It wasn't even seven Pacific time. "You're usually still unconscious until at least nine."

"I got a call from the short-term-rental company," her assistant began, and Cara sucked in a sharp breath.

She'd completely forgotten to text Zarah to let her know she'd left the condo. "Oh! The condo." Her gaze flew to Wyatt. He widened his eyes, then grimaced. He'd clearly forgotten about checking out of the place too.

"Are you okay? What happened?" Zarah demanded. "Where are you?"

The level of panic in the younger woman's voice set alarm bells off in her head. Cara pulled the phone away from her ear, pressed a finger to her lips to indicate Wyatt should keep quiet, then put the call on speaker. "What's going on?"

"You tell me," Zarah demanded. "They called this morning saying the place was torn up and informing me they were charging the entire security deposit. Not the unit owner, but the actual company. The app," she babbled. "Little Rock police got a noise complaint. Neighbors said it sounded like there was a big fight going on. Anyway, they called the owner, but they live in Oregon. They asked the cops to check it out, and when they did, they found the door wide open and no one there. It was trashed."

She and Wyatt exchanged wide-eyed stares. Cara wet her lips, then forced a word past her suddenly dry throat. "Trashed?"

"The police sent pictures. The unit looks like someone was totally raging."

Without a word, Wyatt reached for his own phone and started typing a text.

"I left early yesterday morning and everything was fine," Cara said in a rush. "I meant to text you so you could check out, but I forgot. I'm so sorry. I didn't trash the place. You know I would never. But I packed up my stuff and left. I'm sure I locked the door after me." She darted a glance at Wyatt for confirmation. He thought for a moment, then nodded his agreement. "When did they get the noise complaint?"

"They said yesterday morning," Zarah replied. "I guess it took some time for it to get from the police back to the owner to the rental company. I freaked when I heard. I thought maybe the kidnapper was coming after you again."

"No. No one came after me," Cara said, her mind awhirl.

"Where are you?" Zarah asked again.

She opened her mouth to speak, but clamped it shut again when she caught sight of Wyatt wagging his head hard. "I, uh, I'm staying with a friend. I didn't like being alone after, um, what happened."

"What friend? Where?"

"Listen, Z, I want you to go ahead and reach out to the company and the owner and assure them I did not do this. Also let them know I'm happy to cover any damages, though. I should have let them know I was out of the unit. You have access to my cards and accounts. Do what you need to do to make this right."

"But you're okay? You're safe?" the other woman prodded.

"I'm safe."

"When are you coming home? Do you need me to book a flight for you?" Zarah persisted.

"Not yet. I'm still…decompressing. Catching up with my friend. But I'll call you as soon as I'm ready," she promised. "Would you please take care of the condo for me? I feel horrible. Maybe I didn't lock the door properly after all. Either way, at the very least, I should have let them know I was out so they could set the alarm." Wyatt made a motion for her to wrap it up. "I'll call you back later, I promise."

She ended the call before Zarah could wedge another question in and looked up at Wyatt aghast. "Someone broke in yesterday. It must have been right after we left."

His mouth pulled into a grim line. He nodded as he raised his phone to his ear. "I have a friend with the LRPD. I'm going to see what I can find out from them."

"Do you think it was this Griffin guy? I mean, could it have been?" She moved her chair a few inches closer to his, shaken and needing to feel his proximity.

"It could have," he murmured. "Need to see if the time-line fits." He held up a finger for her to hold the thought. "Yeah, this is Wyatt Dawson from the state police. Is Mark Jones in, please?" He must have been put on hold because he lowered his finger and resumed their conversation without missing a beat. "Does he return the car, gas up his truck, then go looking for you? No." He shook his head, dismissing the chain of events. "He'd go looking for you in the rental. Wouldn't want to risk anyone ID'ing his vehi— Hey, Mark," he said, his tone shifting from speculative to professional in the space of a syllable. "Wyatt Dawson. How are things?"

He listened for a minute, nodding. "I hear you. Yeah, we'll have to do that. Listen, I won't keep you, but do you think you can find out who's handling a break-in and property damage case for me? I think it's connected to an active investigation." He rattled off the address of the condo, tapping his pen against the side of his laptop. "Yeah, give them my number. Appreciate you."

Cara couldn't suppress her bemused smile.

When he looked over at her, the crease between his brows deepened. "What?"

She shook her head and wiped the smile from her face. "Nothing. I was— It's funny, is all."

"What is?"

"The weird kind of conversational shorthand guys have. If I'm interpreting your two-minute conversation correctly, you commiserated about the job, asked for what you needed, confirmed the urgency and need for response, and made some vague plan to get together—"

"Which we never will," he interrupted.

"Exactly. All wrapped up in a neat little package." She skimmed her palms together as if drying them off. "I wasn't criticizing. In fact, I was admiring your skill."

He dropped the pen to the table and leaned in to look at her. "It would have to be a wildly tight timeline for it to be Griffin," he mumbled.

She watched as he snatched up his phone and started to fire off another text.

Narrowing her eyes, she asked, "How do you know your messages are safe?" His head popped up, and for a moment he looked affronted. "I'm only asking. I mean, are they regular texts or do you have some sort of secure channel like on TV?"

"We have an encrypted network, but it's not foolproof. Some people love to crack codes," he muttered, finishing his message.

She inclined her head. "People like you and Agent Parker," she said quietly.

He studied his screen, a smile tugging at his lips as he jabbed at the trackpad. "Exactly." Then he scowled at his laptop. "I don't know how your folks can stand service this slow. Thank goodness they weren't trying to use a computer while watching CineFlix—it would crash the bandwidth. It'd get hung up right in the middle of the big forensics reveal."

His phone dinged and he glanced down at it. "Eight fifty-three a.m.," he reported. "If he trashed the place, he wouldn't have been too far behind us."

"What time did we leave?"

"Somewhere around there. I got the package with your stuff and came right to you."

"So he was doing all this in broad daylight," she murmured.

"Sometimes it's easier. People notice a commotion in the night. We're actually pretty lucky someone was home to hear it. Most people would have left for work already."

"Yeah, we're so lucky," she said with an edge of sarcasm.

He fixed her with a stern stare. "We are. We were already

gone. Now, Emma's emailing a copy of the receipt for the file." He checked his computer, then grabbed his phone. "I'm going to switch to my phone's cellular hot spot. This is driving me crazy."

A few seconds later the email with the scanned transaction from the gas station came through. He sent off two more emails before switching off his hotspot and settling back in his chair, fingers poised over the keys. "You up for running through this all again?"

Cara nodded, sitting up straighter in her chair. She spoke low and steady, keeping her breathing even as he typed a bullet-point timeline of events starting with the day she noticed an uptick in hostile messages and brought them to the attention of her partners. When they got to the attack on her neighbor Nancy and her decision to fly home to Arkansas, he slowed her down, asking her to get more granular as he added incident after incident. Her voice cracked when she recounted her decision to jump from the car, still not quite able to believe she'd done it. She hadn't realized how high and tight her voice had become until Wyatt stopped typing and reached over to cover her hand with his.

"Breathe," he encouraged. "It's okay. I've got the rest."

She nodded, dragging in a deep but shaky breath. "Okay. Okay."

"I've got you," he assured her, giving her hand a quick squeeze before releasing it to resume his typing.

Cara sagged in her seat, exhaling slow and low and feeling more confident than she had in weeks. "Yeah. We've got this," she whispered.

Chapter Nine

The rest of the day passed with agonizing slowness—on all fronts. Wyatt tried his best to refrain from grumbling about the antiquated internet service running to the house, but programs and scans he could run at high speed in Little Rock seemed to be caught in some old sci-fi movie's vision of a wormhole. Whenever he could, he switched to using his phone as a hot spot. It seemed counterintuitive to be able to get better mobile reception than satellite internet. When he mentioned as much to James Beckett on their afternoon ride around the property, the older man simply pointed to the flashing beacon on a tower poised atop the nearest hill and muttered something about Betsy's boyfriend opting for improved cell service instead.

When they returned to the house in time for Jim to fire up his propane grill, they found the fridge restocked and the two women sitting on the back deck sipping white wine.

Betsy Beckett countered her husband's raised eyebrow with a smug smirk. "I thought pork tenderloin would be nice for a change. Cara has some vegetables in there she'd like you to grill too. Oh, and I bought you boys some beer."

"Sounds good," Jim said. He leaned down and kissed his wife's cheek on his way to the door. "You pick up ice cream for dessert?"

Her lips curved into a serene smile. "You know I did."

"Perfect. I'll get things ready, then be out to get things fired up."

"I chopped and seasoned some veggies and threw them in the grill basket. Would you cook them up for me, Daddy? You're so good at grilling," Cara called after him.

Her father simply raised a hand in acknowledgment of her shameless flattery. Wyatt smiled at Cara. She looked a thousand times more relaxed than she had when he left with her father after lunch. Whether it was the wine or the nap she'd planned to take while he was out, he wasn't sure. Either way, it looked good on her. An afternoon in the fresh air had done him a world of good. Wyatt decided he was going to do his best to be sure the rest of the evening remained mellow. They all needed a bit of a breather.

"All quiet on my end," he assured her. "I'm gonna go help your dad."

She toasted him with her wine. "We expect great things from you," she called as he followed her dad into the house.

In the kitchen he found Cara's father rooting around in the back the refrigerator. When he surfaced, he held up a package of microwavable mashed potatoes and fixed him with a challenging stare. "Life lesson—there's no need to peel, chop, boil and mash when you can have these hot and tasty in less than five minutes. Don't judge me."

"I grew up eating instant rice."

"We both believe in working smarter," Jim said with a conspiratorial nod. "Let's get this going. I'm starved."

When they sat down to dinner, her mother picked up the platter of sliced tenderloin and offered it to Wyatt as she addressed the table in general.

"Did I tell you I ran into Delia Raitt in town?" He helped himself to a piece of the meat, but before anyone could answer, she pushed the platter back at him. "Take two. Y'all look famished and you know Cara isn't going to have any."

His attention caught on how Cara stiffened at the name, he did as she asked with a murmured "Thank you," then relinquished the fork. When no one commented on Betsy's conversational gambit, he asked, "Delia Raitt? Is she someone you went to school with?"

"Mrs. Raitt was the principal's secretary when I was in school," Cara answered stiffly. "Liked to stick her nose in everyone's business."

"Well, the school district has consolidated and she's working for the superintendent now. The school system is all different now, but Delia is the same."

Jim Beckett ate steadily, oblivious to his daughter's unease. "Still nosy."

Betsy didn't seem to notice Cara's discomfiture, because she continued on without further encouragement.

"So nosy I'm surprised she doesn't trip over the end of it," Betsy said with a tinkling laugh. "Anyhoo, Dee said they've been getting calls about you."

"What kind of calls?" Wyatt asked, working to keep his tone neutral.

"Reporters, mainly. She said people have been calling and asking about your big business deal in New York," she reported, blasting Cara with a wide, proud smile. "I didn't say anything before because I wanted your daddy to hear too, but she said they're all real proud of you around there. Apparently, all sorts of fancy technological magazines have been calling and asking whether you'd come home to talk to the kids about working in big tech and what it's like to build a business from the ground up and all." She waved her fork in an all-encompassing circle before using it to stab a hunk of grilled squash.

Jim Beckett dropped his fork and stared at his wife with the open disbelief Wyatt wished he could show. "Are you kiddin' me with this?"

Betsy blinked, her smile slipping as she cast a glance at Cara, then back to her husband. "No, I'm not kidding. I told her we were proud of her too." She reached over and gave Cara's hand an encouraging pat. "And we are. Even if we don't understand it all. Aren't we, James?"

Cara's father blinked, then stared at her with such naked incredulity Wyatt cringed inwardly. "Were you drinking before you went to town?" he demanded.

"What?" Betsy asked on a sharp inhale. "No. Of course not."

"Don't you get it?" Jim shook his head. "The people callin' the school might not be reporters. They could be the people behind this whole mess." He threw his hands in the air. "Criminy, Elizabeth, we're not supposed to let anyone know she's here."

"I didn't tell anyone she's here," she retorted, shoving her chair away from the table. "I'm not a fool, and I won't be spoken to like one in my own home."

"Okay, okay," Cara interjected. "Let's all…take a breath."

Her father rolled his eyes. "Take a breath," he muttered under his. "Same mumbo jumbo for the folks willin' to pay for it."

"Fine," Cara snapped. "Let's all calm down and talk rationally," she demanded, sounding about as far from calm and rational as a modern-day guru could. "Do you think we can manage to get through one meal without bickering or picking at each other?"

Wyatt held his tongue as the older man nodded then ducked his head, reapplying himself to his plate. "I'm sorry. I didn't mean to be a jerk," Jim said quietly.

"You were a jerk, but your apology is accepted," his wife responded, punctuating her largesse with a prim sniff.

"People are calling the local school asking questions about Cara?" Wyatt asked, rephrasing the gist of the conversation.

"Yes," Betsy said, her tone markedly more subdued. She twiddled her fork, routing out a divot in the mashed potatoes he'd so painstakingly nuked. "I didn't think it sounded threatening. At least, Delia Raitt didn't make it come across like it was. She was goin' on about what a big deal Cara was now, and how proud we must be, and how she never thought little Cara Beckett would turn out to be a fancy big shot." She turned to look at her daughter. "Her words, not mine."

"Did she happen to name any of the publications they said they were calling from? Did you recognize any of them?"

Betsy shrugged, then shook her head, her smile turning rueful. "She said a couple of names, but they sounded computer-y to me." Jim snorted and her eyes lit with fire. "Like you know any better, James Beckett. You tell me the name of one of those tech blog thingies," she challenged.

"Doesn't hafta be one of those. It's been all over *Forbes*, the *Wall Street Journal*, the *New York Times*," Jim said quietly. When they all turned to look at him, he glanced up from under lowered eyebrows. "What? I don't live under a rock."

Cara ducked her head, and Wyatt couldn't help but stare as a peach-pink flush crept up her neck to her cheeks. The woman practically glowed with pleasure at this small concession from a man Wyatt himself had reclassified from remote and disinterested to quiet and observant over the course of an afternoon in his company.

"There are dozens of legitimate publications interested in profiling your daughter," Wyatt said, gently breaking the spell. "I know to those of us back here at home it may seem like she has put herself out there with LYYF, but in truth,

Cara is kind of an enigma in tech circles. Aside from her work published on the app and the social media connected to it, she has stayed out of the media. If there are interviews to be given, it's usually one of her partners in the spotlight."

"Usually Chris," her mother said with a nod. "He loves to be the one doing the talking. Always was the slick one. I remember from the time we came out there to visit."

"Chris is a talker," Cara conceded.

Wyatt jumped back in before they strayed too far off track. "From everything I can find, and believe me I have looked through all accounts connected to her, Cara doesn't put much of herself out there. Which is why she found it such a shock to have people on the internet taking such an, uh, intense interest in her personal life."

"I don't even take pictures of my food," she said with a wry smile.

"And here I thought all people put on those sites were pictures of their plates," her father said gruffly.

Cara flashed him a grateful smile and Wyatt felt his shoulders drop as the tension in the room dissipated.

"I can't," Cara said, her tone turning serious again. "I learned early on. The second I post something, a yummy dinner or a pretty blue sky, people crawl all over themselves trying to interpret the hidden meaning behind my post."

"Some people can't accept the appreciation of a pretty blue sky at face value," Wyatt said, nodding his understanding.

"Exactly. People say I'm making a statement about climate change, or take the opportunity to lecture other community members about the proper use of sunscreen. I have to be very careful about everything I post online. You never know how people will interpret it, and there's always someone waiting to pounce."

Her father shook his head in disgust. "People have nothing better to do."

"Everyone has to share their opinion," Wyatt commiserated.

"My daddy used to say opinions were like belly buttons—everyone has one, but you don't need to go around flaunting it," Betsy chimed in.

"I heard it using a different body part," her husband said under his breath.

Betsy frowned. "What body part?"

Wyatt chuckled at their byplay but refused to further the conversation. Instead, he turned to Cara. "I'm assuming the company has a publicist or PR firm they work with?"

She nodded. "All official media requests are supposed to go through a woman named Amanda Pierce. She has a boutique firm out of Palo Alto. It's called APPR," she added. "But it's not unusual for people to try to work around the process. We all get requests. Zarah fields them for me every day."

"But the bigger outlets will go through the publicist," he asserted. "I can see individual vloggers trying to get around the gatekeeper, but there'd be no reason for the *Times* or the *Journal* to do an end-around. Publications like *WIRED*, *TechCrunch*, *CNET*…they'd want everything on the record, and they'd want to be able to follow up on anything newsworthy."

"You think these people calling the school district were only pretending to be reporters?" Betsy asked, fear warring with incredulity in her voice.

Wyatt flashed an apologetic smile. "It's possible. You're sure you didn't give any hint of Cara being here?"

A deep crease of concern appeared between Betsy's brows, and she bit her lip as she closed her eyes, no doubt scouring her memory for any innocuous little comment. "I'm sure," she said at last. "She asked when we were going to California to visit again, and I said something vague about maybe over the holidays."

She flashed a wince of a smile, and Cara reached over to squeeze her hand. "You know I'd love to have you out anytime you can get away."

Both women looked at Jim, who'd remained laser focused on his food through this whole exchange. Without looking up from his plate, he mumbled, "I did like fresh-squeezed orange juice in the mornings."

Judging from the radiant smiles breaking across the women's faces, his confession was as good as a promise. "My lemon tree has started producing too," Cara informed him.

"No need to gild the lily, sweetheart," Betsy admonished softly. "We'll make arrangements for one of the Ford boys to come look after things while we're gone."

The ladies spent the rest of the meal extolling the many virtues of California living, only requiring the occasional "Huh" from him and grunts of affirmation from Jim. By the time Cara jumped up to retrieve the ice cream and bowls, the mood was considerably lighter. But the supercomputer in Wyatt's head hadn't stopped running probabilities and turning over possibilities.

After they were through eating, Jim said something about needing to make some calls. Wyatt escaped to the dining room and his laptop. A few quick queries gave him the low-down on the newly consolidated school district and its administration. If he'd grown up anywhere else, he might have marveled at the odds of a cold caller actually connecting with a person who knew Cara and her family, but he was an Arkansan. He knew better. People born and raised in the Natural State either stuck close to home or ran far away.

He'd stuck close.

Cara had gone about as far as she could go, shy of buying a boat.

Grabbing his phone, he fired off a quick text to Emma to let her know about the calls to the school administrator's office. It wasn't critical information, but at this stage they were massing every bit of data they could and sifting through them like the tourists who spent days sieving dirt at Crater of Diamonds State Park. At this point they were hoping one of the bits of nothing they unearthed turned out to be a precious gem.

Next, he ran a general search on Cara's name. Scrolling past results for her website, links to LYYF, a Wikipedia entry and optimized entries for some of the more popular pages on the LYYF website and blog, he found an article in a respected tech journal about the company's upcoming stock option and the buzz surrounding one of the world's most popular apps. He skimmed nearly halfway through it before he realized her name had not appeared in the text. He hit the Control and F keys and typed "Beckett" into the pop-up search box.

One result returned.

Holding the arrow-down key, he scanned the screen until he found the highlighted name.

When he spotted it, he stared at his screen in disbelief. Cara, the face and voice of the LYYF app, and her 33 percent ownership, didn't garner a single mention in the body of the post. He'd found her tagged in the article's keywords, but nowhere in the lengthy, and somewhat fawning, narrative about the company's inception and astounding growth.

Skipping back to the top of the article, he checked the byline. The author was someone named Nate Astor.

He searched the site for other articles by the same author and discovered Astor was one of their main contributors.

Scrolling through his previous articles, he found two more related to LYYF.

One was a one-on-one interview with Chris Sharpe published the previous spring, and the other was an opinion piece in which he debated the value of creation versus content. About two-thirds of the way through the article, he spotted Cara's name. Biting the inside of his cheek, he read and re-read the man's hot take. Wyatt found it ironic the reporter, whose job it was to create content for an online magazine, dared to question Cara's contribution to the LYYF app's success.

"So much for solidarity, huh, Nate?" he muttered, clicking back to look through more of the man's work.

Not surprisingly, he found more than one post concerning GamerGate. He grimaced. He'd been in school when a band of misogynist jerks claimed to be on a quest to fight "political correctness" in the online gaming world by harassing, doxing and threatening female media critics and game developers with bodily harm.

"Finding anything good?"

He jumped, reflexively tipping the cover of his laptop down to shield her from his discoveries.

Cara blinked, then let out a bitter huff of a laugh. "Wow. I was kidding, but I guess you did. Was it about me, or were you looking at X-rated websites in front of my mother's Precious Moments?"

"What?" He glanced over his shoulder when she gestured to the collection of figurines on display in a corner curio cabinet. "Oh. No. You startled me is all."

"Reading something good?" She sank into the chair adjacent to his, her stare unflinching.

"Went down the GamerGate rabbit hole," he confessed.

She made an exaggeratedly horrified face. "I didn't peg you for a misogynist, so you must lean toward masochist."

"The guy who wrote the article has also done a couple on LYYF," he explained. Then, angling to face her, he asked, "Does it bother you when they leave you out of the press coverage?"

She opened her mouth, then closed it. He could almost see her swallowing whatever flip answer she kept on hand for this type of question. Rolling her shoulders back, she met his eyes directly. "Yes."

"Do you ever say anything about it to them?"

"No." She shook her head. "Not anymore."

"Why?"

She pointed to his laptop. "Ironically enough, Gamer-Gate." Folding her hands in front of her, she let her gaze slide down to the computer. "Whenever Chris or Tom even mentioned my name in connection to the business end of things, the trolls came swarming out. So we stopped." She dropped her eyes to her clasped hands, a rueful smile curving her lips. "I contented myself with the idea of being the face of LYYF, and for the most part, I like it better this way too. I get to be the star without the freaky hero worship Tom hides from, or the constant pandering Chris loves and loathes."

"But in serious publications where they're discussing the future of the business…" He trailed off, unsure he wanted to push too hard on a point that was glaringly obvious to him but may not have occurred to her.

"The lack of attribution may make people think my contributions have not been commensurate with full partnership," she concluded.

"Or give the impression your partners feel they are not," he said, fixing her with a pointed stare.

Cara unwound her tightly knotted fingers, splaying her

hands open wide and flat on the tabletop to stretch them. "At first, I was happy to have what I thought would be a shield from the vitriol," she said, nodding toward the laptop again. "But after things took off there were times I felt credit wasn't being given where credit was due."

"Did you speak to them about it?" he prompted again.

"I did. On more than a few occasions," she said flatly. "To be fair, most of the requests for interviews have been fielded by Chris. He enjoys the spotlight more than Tom."

"Enjoys it to the point of hogging it. In most of the articles I read, Tom is relegated to nothing more than a couple lines. Even then, he's spoken of as some kind of tech wizard hiding behind the green velvet curtain. You're barely mentioned at all."

"None of us got into this to be famous," she pointed out.

"But I have to assume the guys, at least, got into it to get rich," he retorted. "It was basically a run-of-the-mill personal finance app until your posts started taking off." He tapped on his phone to wake it, then opened the application. Within seconds, the Cara Beckett who'd calmed his anxieties and gently lulled him to sleep appeared. He turned the phone to face her. "You made this app what it is. Everything they built…it's all scaffolding for your genius, not theirs." He leaned in, his stare searching. "Are you trying to tell me it doesn't bother them?" When she didn't answer, he gentled his tone. "Why haven't they called, Cara?"

She shook her head. "You don't get it. Things are complicated—"

"No, I don't get it." He interrupted whatever excuse she was planning to employ to excuse the shortcomings of the men she still called friends. "And I don't see it as complicated. If my friend was being attacked from all sides, I'd be there. If my friend had been abducted at gunpoint, I'd do more than text her assistant for updates. But then, my friends aren't about to increase their wealth exponentially by taking a share of the money I may or may not believe to be rightfully mine."

"Now, wait a minute—" she began, but he held up a hand to halt her protest.

"I won't say anything more. They are your friends and your partners. You know them a thousand times better than I do," he conceded.

"I do."

"But I want you to know, as far as I am concerned, no one is above suspicion. Because you and I both know there's no enemy with better ammunition than a person's best friends."

"I understand."

"And you mentioned something about Zarah having access to your accounts. Do you mind if I do a deeper dive into your financials?" He didn't need to ask, really. He could probably hack his way into every account she'd ever opened without any trouble, but she was starting to trust him, and he didn't want to risk compromising her trust.

"My financials?"

"I only want to be certain there are no...anomalies. If people have accessed everything else, it wouldn't be much of a stretch."

"Oh, wow. I never thought." She cocked her head. "I hardly ever even look at bills or account balances anymore. Zarah has everything covered."

"Just a cursory glance," he assured her.

She nodded and looked to be about to say more when Betsy appeared in the dining room doorway.

"Come on, you two. Enough work for one day. Jim has time for one episode before he hits the hay and I want to see if you can solve the case before Detective Pemberton figures it out." She made a shooing motion, then declared, "I'm making popcorn."

With a sigh, Wyatt powered down his laptop and closed the lid. Cara showed no inclination to move. Placing his hands on the edge of the table, he pushed his chair back. "Come on. Your mom is right. We've done enough for one day."

Wordlessly, Cara followed him into the family room, where her father had an episode of a murder mystery cued up and ready to go.

Wyatt smirked when he saw the show they'd selected. "You remember I'm not a homicide detective, right?"

"Neither am I," Jim answered gruffly.

"But I bet you have a friend who's one," Cara said, petulance lacing her tone.

"I do, as a matter of fact." He turned to look at her, but she stared straight at the screen. He'd hit a tender spot in questioning the quality of her friendships with her partners, but he couldn't say he regretted doing so. If she spent even a few minutes thinking deep thoughts about her relationship with the men she's helped make rich, maybe she'd reach the same conclusion he had.

Internet bullies were thick on the ground, for certain. But no one had better motive for wanting her out of the picture than Chris Sharpe and Tom Wasinski. Everything she'd told him about her life and the lives of the two men would suggest their friendship had become distant. A relationship bearing a label bestowed by nostalgia, but in truth boiled down to a business arrangement forged by people who were little more than kids.

But it wasn't a real friendship.

"Hurry up. I have to be up in seven and a half hours," Jim called to his wife.

"Hold your heifers," she retorted as she bustled back into the room. She distributed bowls of microwaved popcorn to each of them.

"Isn't it supposed to be 'Hold your horses'?" Wyatt asked Cara, hoping to break the ice, but she remained silent.

"Not on a cattle ranch," her parents replied in unison.

Jim pointed the remote at the screen as Betsy claimed her seat beside him. The opening theme music played and he darted another glance at Cara. She sat stone-faced, her jaw tight as she glared at the television screen. In the dim light, he thought he caught the faint shimmer of tears in her eyes and looked away.

They were less than five minutes into the show before he and Jim pointed to a slick-looking charmer on the screen and declared, "That one," in unison.

"Oh, honestly," Betsy muttered as she rolled her eyes. "My grandma could have seen him coming." With a huff, she grabbed the remote away from her husband and clicked through the menu. "Go to bed, spoilsport."

Chuckling, Jim kicked the footrest of his recliner back into place and rose with a groan. "Maybe I should become a homicide detective. What time do y'all have to be at work most days?"

"Long after you are," Wyatt replied with a sympathetic smile.

"Night, all," Jim called as he dumped the remainder of his popcorn into Betsy's bowl. "Wire to stretch in the morning."

"I'll be along in a bit," his wife promised as she scrolled through the options. She paused on one featuring characters in elaborate costumes. "Oooh. Wyatt, do you like *Pride and Prejudice*? Cara and I love this one, don't we, hon?"

Wyatt smiled and nodded, stuffing his cheeks with popcorn to avoid having to say more. If watching people who carried parasols and walking sticks was what it took to get back on Cara Beckett's good side, he could take it. At least, he hoped he could.

Chapter Ten

Cara jerked out of a dream where she was hurling herself from a car being attacked by birds. Why she thought she'd be safer outside when they were pecking viciously at the glass, her conscious mind could not fathom, but there—

The tapping came again. Pushing up to her elbows, she glanced at the window first. No. Someone was pecking at her door. She blinked into the darkness, then figuring it was one of her parents coming to tell her they were off on their predawn errands, she croaked, "Come in."

The bedroom door swung inward, but Wyatt stayed firmly on the other side of the threshold, his phone pressed to his ear. She sat up in her single bed, the covers drawn up to her chin, waving him in. The last thing she wanted to do was wake her parents.

"Emma Parker," he mouthed to her, indicating the other agent was on the opposite end of the call as he stepped into her room. He glanced at the door and raised a brow. She nodded and he closed it behind him, sealing them both into the small bedroom. She hit the switch, and the glare of the ceiling light set them both blinking.

"You said someone called Cara's phone? Which one?"

Cara threw back the covers and sprang from the bed. The

display on her ancient clock radio showed it to be approaching 2:00 a.m.

"And what did they say, exactly?" he persisted. Cara scowled and tugged on his arm, but he held firm, his lips thinning as he listened. "I see. Any confirmation of damage?"

She tugged again, and he pulled away, then motioned for her to remain patient.

"What is happening?" Cara hissed between clenched teeth. She grabbed hold of his free wrist and squeezed. "Damage to what? Where? The condo?"

"Ah, okay. I see." He nodded, then gently removed her hand. "I'll let her know and call you back when we've had a chance to figure out next steps."

He ended the call, then lowered the phone, his brow furrowed with worry. "What? What is it?"

"A little after midnight Emma had a call come through to your original mobile number from the new one and thought it was odd, so she picked up."

Cara frowned. "After midnight? Is she working twenty-four-hour shifts?"

He shrugged. "We're a small department and most of our work can be done off-site. We often take our work home."

"You said something about damages. What happened?"

"The caller claimed there was a fire at your residence, then hung up. Emma checked the voice mailboxes for both numbers and found one where the caller said something along the lines of 'accidents happen when you play with fire.'"

"Play with fire?"

"Emma put in calls to the LAPD and fire departments, and was able to confirm an emergency services call to your address, but they wouldn't give any additional information and the detective assigned to your case has not returned her calls as of yet."

She let out a breathy snort. "Yeah, I can believe it. I know they have their plates full, but…yeah." She pushed a hand through her hair, and the corn-silk strands fell right back over her eye. "So what do we do?"

"Do you have anyone you can call who lives nearby? Zarah?"

Shivering, she tugged at the hem of her top, wishing she had long sleeves and pajama bottoms rather than the cotton T-shirt and sleep shorts Zarah had procured. Shifting to place one cold foot atop the other, she shook her head. "Zarah lives out in the Valley. We do most of our work virtually."

"A neighbor? Your cat people?"

Color flooded her cheeks. "We, uh… I don't have their phone numbers. Any of them," she added, looking down at her hands clasped in her lap in bewilderment. "It's not Arkansas. I've only lived there a few years and…"

He tried to pretend he understood, but the idea of not knowing at least some of his neighbors must have been almost incomprehensible to him. Little Rock was a good-sized city, but in many ways it was still as interconnected as a small town. The truth was, there were few degrees of separation between most Arkansans, and even the city folk tended to look out for their neighbors.

He cleared his throat, and plowed ahead. "Em has been on the forums." He gave her a sympathetic wince. "The scuttlebutt online is it wasn't an accident and the damage is pretty bad."

"You think someone set fire to my house?" She blinked up at him, not quite certain they were speaking the same language.

He reached past her, plucked a hoodie from the bedpost where she'd hung it and handed it to her. "I'm telling you there was possibly a fire at your residence in Los Angeles, and we have heard rumors it may have been the result of arson, and the damage is extensive. Nothing is confirmed, and no one has tried to reach out to you. Not the local officials, not Zarah or any neighbors. For all we know, this is a hoax."

Cara shrugged into the sweatshirt. "Someone is saying they set fire to my house," she repeated flatly.

He nodded slowly. "Yes."

"They said they'd burn it all down," she murmured as she huddled into the fleece-lined warmth.

"Who did?" he prompted, his brow furrowed. "Who said 'burn it all down'?"

Cara shook her head, her bewilderment turning to helpless fury. "They did." She practically spit the words. "The people sending me nasty messages and scaring my poor mother half to death. Whoever paid Gerald Griffin to pull a gun on me in an airport parking garage." She threw her arms out wide, as if gesturing to the wide array of invisible threats closing in on her. "They are doing this. Whoever *they* are."

"Until we can get confirmation from a trusted source, we need to assume these are simply rumors." He held her phone out to her. "Emma sent the number for the person she spoke to with LAFD. You need to be the one to call." She reached for the cell phone with a sticky note affixed to the glass, but he held firm for a beat too long. "It's possible they won't give you any information over the phone."

"They'll give me the information. If being a semipublic figure is good for anything, it's being recognized." She yanked the phone from his grasp.

She stared down at the name scrawled below a number with the familiar area code. Investigator Shanna Gleason. The moment the call connected, she introduced herself and, reading from the sticky note he'd handed her, asked to speak to Investigator Gleason.

A moment later a woman picked up. "ACTS, Gleason here."

"Um, hello. Yes," Cara stammered, her gaze darting to Wyatt. "Am I calling the Los Angeles Fire Department?"

"Yes, ma'am."

A huff of self-conscious laughter escaped her. "Sorry. I guess I expected you to say LAFD when you answered, but you said something else and I wasn't sure," she rambled.

"Who's calling?" the other woman asked.

"Oh, right. This is Cara Beckett. I'm calling about reports of a fire at my house on Sunset Drive in Los Feliz," she said, focusing on the facts. "I believe you were contacted by Special Agent Emma Parker with the Arkansas State Police trying to confirm there was a fire?" Again, her gaze found Wyatt's, and he nodded encouragingly.

"Yes, ma'am, I spoke with Agent Parker," the investigator on the other end confirmed.

When she said nothing more, Cara gestured her frustration at Wyatt. "Ask to put her on speaker," he whispered.

"Ms., uh, Investigator Gleason, I'm here with Special Agent Wyatt Dawson of the Arkansas State Police. Do you mind if we put you on speaker?"

There was a moment of hesitation on the other end, then a curt response. "Sure."

Cara pressed the speaker button, then nodded at Wyatt. "Investigator Gleason, this is Agent Dawson. I work with Agent Parker and am currently with Ms. Beckett. What can you tell us about these reports of a fire at her property?"

"Are you currently in police custody, Ms. Beckett?" Investigator Gleason asked. "Isn't it the middle of the night in, uh, Arkansas?"

"It is, but I am not," Cara answered, stiffening at the implication. "Agents Dawson and Parker are working on a case in which I was the victim."

"I see," the other woman answered in a cautious tone.

"Ms. Beckett has been the target of several credible threats to her safety," Wyatt informed her. "One of those threats turned into a reality when she landed in Little Rock. I am here with her now as both an investigative and protective partner." He caught her eye and held her gaze. "Tell me, what does ACTS stand for?"

"Arson Counter-Terrorism Section," she replied crisply.

"I see," he replied.

Cara only whispered, "Arson."

"You believe someone set the fire intentionally," Wyatt prodded.

"I'm afraid so. I'm happy to hear you were not in the structure at the time, Ms. Beckett. Can you confirm whether anyone else should have been on the premises in your absence? House or pet sitter? Guests?"

"No. No one."

Cara pressed her fingertips to her chin to keep it from trembling. She loved her house. It was the one extravagant purchase she'd made since the app took off, and she'd spent countless hours making it her sanctuary. Now, because some jerk hacker decided to post her address for all the trolls to see, someone had violated her sanctuary. Again.

"How bad is the damage?"

"Looks worse than it is," the woman on the other end assured her. "You'll need to contact your insurance company and get someone out there to start restoration. It may take a while, but in my estimation, the house should be habitable again."

"I'm assuming you found evidence the fire was set intentionally?" Wyatt asked.

"We didn't have to look very hard. They left gas cans in the yard. And before you ask, no, we weren't able to get any physical evidence from them. I'm assuming our firebug wore gloves."

"I see." At a loss for how to proceed from here, Cara sought Wyatt's steady reassurance again.

He nodded to her cell phone. "We'll ask Ms. Beckett's assistant to help with the insurance and getting the place secured. Has Agent Parker shared any information with you on the case we're working here?"

"Only to route all attempts to contact Ms. Beckett through your office for the time being."

"Thank you. I do have some information I can share. I think it may be helpful to you. If you would send me your email address, I will send you a link to the files. I warn you, it'll be encrypted and will ask for about everything but your blood type and the guarantee of your firstborn son."

He said the last in a lighter tone, but Cara couldn't even muster the weakest smile.

The other woman chuckled. "My son is acting every minute of his fifteen years these days, so if you want him, you are welcome to him." She paused to take a breath. "I'm curious to see what you have in your file, Agent Dawson. As long as it doesn't have one of those 'click on pictures of bridges' things," she added. "And Ms. Beckett?"

"Yes?" Cara responded in a reedy voice.

"I'm very good at catching firebugs," Shanna Gleason assured her.

Cara straightened her spine and inhaled through her nose as if taking in the other woman's confidence. "I'm sure you are. Thank you," she added, a small smile tugging at the corners of her mouth.

She ended the call but didn't relinquish the phone.

Wyatt looked down at her and sighed, his expression troubled. "Maybe I shouldn't have told you until I knew more."

"No." She sat down on the edge of the bed. "Don't shut me out. What I don't know *can* hurt me, Wyatt. It can hurt me badly. I don't want you withholding information from me."

He inclined his head. "I agree. So now you know." He stepped back, groping for the doorknob. "It's unlikely we're going to get more information at this hour."

"I guess not," she conceded.

Then she heard a muffled cough from down the hall. Her parents. Biting her lip, she looked up at Wyatt, her expression pleading. "Listen, can we keep this quiet for now? I don't want to worry my parents any more than I already have."

He nodded solemnly. "What happens in California stays in California." Wyatt held out his hand. "I'd like to hang on to the phone. Emma and I are still checking incoming messages and voicemails regularly."

She placed the device in his hand without protest. She was discovering how pleasant it could be to have a buffer between her and bad news. "Take it."

He ran a hand through his hair. "Try to get some rest. There's nothing we can do from here. We can come at this fresh in the morning."

She sank back onto her heels and smirked. "Are you going to sleep?"

"I'm going to try." He gave her a lopsided smile. "I know things start earlier around here than they do in Little Rock."

She glanced at the ancient clock radio on the bedside table. "My dad will be up and out in a few hours."

"Try to sleep. There's nothing we can do right now. Your house can be fixed, and we know you're safe here." He started to back out of the room. "We'll go after them again tomorrow."

"Right," she said, though she couldn't imagine how he planned to go after anyone. She felt like Don Quixote, fighting off imaginary foes. "We'll go after them again tomorrow."

"Good night, Cara." He pointed to the poster on her wall, then hit the light switch as he backed into the hall. "Try to get some sleep. Dream about boy bands," he added in a loud whisper.

Cara snorted and wondered why her mother had left the poster tacked to the wall for all these years. "Good night."

The door clicked shut behind him, and Cara climbed back into bed. Pulling the sheet and quilt up over her legs, she leaned back against the pillows, the hood of her sweatshirt pushing up against her ears. She yanked it up over her head and sank into it.

Trolling, threats, doxing, attempted assault, thwarted kidnapping and now arson. Uncrossing her arms, she stretched them wide before drawing them into her sides. The ceiling stared back at her. Closing her eyes, she reached deep into her bag of tricks.

It took three rounds of deep sleep meditation before she landed on a course of action. Decision made, her mind quieted and she finally drifted off.

WYATT WAS UP a while longer. Grumbling about the slow internet connection, he attempted to comb through the hundreds of direct messages, forum entries, social media posts and emails sent to Cara within the past month. Sure enough, he found some reference using the phrase "burn it all down" in every mode of communication. Bone tired, he created a folder titled "Fire" and added screenshots of each one to it.

When he was finished, he powered down his laptop and set it aside in favor of pen and paper. But rather than making case notes, he reached into the bag of tricks he'd picked up from the LYYF app in an attempt to clear his mind. Pen in hand, he numbered a blank page in the battered composition notebook he carried with him with numerals one through ten. Then he did his best to distill everything nagging him into a list of no more than ten bullet points to be addressed the following day.

Thoughts, hunches and random observations. He listed them all in no particular order. Everything from his suspicions about Cara's business partners to the need to talk to Jim about getting better locks installed on his doors. He noted the guest room was decorated in a trendy farmhouse scheme, but Betsy Beckett had left a poster of a boy band taped to the wall of Cara's old bedroom. He started an entry about her blue eyes, but caught himself in time to change it to a more businesslike inquiry regarding whether she wore prescription eyeglasses. Then, annoyed with himself, he re-copied the list of IP addresses he'd isolated and wanted to run the next day as punishment for getting too personal.

In the end it was a mishmash of to-do items, reminders and worries a desk jockey like himself was in over his head on a protection detail. He was forgetting something. What was it?

Tapping the end of his pen against the paper, he gnawed his lip until he tasted blood. When was the last time he'd been to the shooting range? He'd been raised in duck-hunting country and firing weapons since he was big enough to hold a pellet gun, but being responsible for the safety of a living, breathing woman was a far cry from shutting down phishing schemes and heading off malware attacks.

He set the notebook aside and rolled out of bed and padded down the hall to check the door locks. If nothing else, he could cross number three off his list straight off the bat.

Satisfied they were as secure as the flimsy lock sets would allow, he returned to the guest room. The notebook teetered on the nightstand. The inside of the waistband holster he preferred took up much of the free space. He'd found an outlet for his phone charger behind the headboard. It sat charging and silent since the call from Agent Parker. He could only assume everyone was in bed. As he should be.

But his mind would not slow.

On impulse, he grabbed his phone and scrolled through his contacts until he found the number for a guy who'd graduated from the academy not long before him. For most of his career with the Arkansas State Police, Ryan Hastings had provided personal security for politicians, visiting dignitaries, sports figures and, most recently, a very high-profile heiress before retiring to start his own agency.

Having done all he could do for now, he toed off his shoes as he tapped out a quick message for Ryan to contact him at his earliest convenience, then stretched out on the bed without bothering to undress or pull back the duvet.

Wyatt stared at the ceiling for a full fifteen minutes before his flighty thoughts landed on the thing he'd forgotten. Grabbing his pen and paper, he scrawled, "Follow the money," on his list of things to do, before tossing the pad and pen on the unused pillow.

He was asleep in seconds.

Chapter Eleven

He awakened to a light knock on the door. Wyatt cracked an eyelid and was surprised to find bright autumn sunlight streaming through the window. Judging by the angle, he guessed it was early by city standards, and likely midday in ranch time.

"Come in," he croaked.

The door opened and Cara poked her head in. "Hey. I tried to let you sleep, but I couldn't wait any longer."

He sat up and swung his legs over the side of the bed. Feet planted firmly on the floor, he scrubbed the sleep from his face with his palm. "No. I should be up." He checked the time on his phone. Seven thirty. He'd slept for a few hours, but it still didn't feel adequate. "You get any sleep?"

She smirked and shrugged. "Some here, some there. Restless."

"Fretting," he corrected.

"I think I'm entitled."

Her retort was sharp enough to jolt him fully awake. "Of course you are."

"Sorry." She glanced over her shoulder, then returned her temple to its resting spot on the door frame. "My mother always says I get snappy when I haven't had a good night's rest." She paused long enough to roll her eyes. "I hate it when she's right about me."

"Parents. They think they know everything." He pushed to his feet and stretched. "I suppose yours have been hard at work for hours?"

She nodded. "Dad said if you want, he'd take you out again later."

Wyatt nodded and scratched his stubbly cheek. "I'd like that."

"They left biscuits and sausage gravy for you."

"Great." Then he caught her wording and paused. "Left? Did your mom leave?"

Cara's eyebrows shot up. "Was she under house arrest?"

"No, I thought…" He trailed off, his ears burning.

"You thought she stayed here all day making stew and doing the mending?" she teased.

"No. I mean, I know she handles the paperwork and such, I didn't know she did, uh, work out there." He hooked a thumb over his shoulder. He clamped his mouth shut. He was digging himself deeper with every single word. "I need coffee."

Cara took mercy on him. "I'll pour you a mug. Mama went to pick up some wire fencing they need for repairs. She'll be back by noon, but I warn you it's Daddy's day to cook, so it'll be cold cuts for lunch and something grilled for supper."

Wyatt inclined his head to indicate her message was received. The Beckett Ranch was an equal opportunity operation. "I'm going to take a quick shower. Clear the cobwebs."

"Go for it," she said, pushing away from the doorjamb. "I only wanted to get my phone."

"Your phone?"

"My cellular device?" she prompted. "I don't want to take the chance of anyone tracing the landline, remember?"

"Right, but who are you going to call?"

This time, only one brow rose. "Do I have to clear it with you?"

The icy edge in the question had him straightening his shoulders. "No, but it would help things if you kept me in the loop."

"I'd like to call my assistant, if you don't mind," she returned with a sniff.

As if on cue, the phone sang out its generic ringtone. Cara raised an eyebrow at him, then let her gaze trail over to the phone lit up atop the dresser. The display showed Zarah's number. "Speak of the devil. It's Zarah," she informed him, swiping to accept the call.

"Put it on speaker?" He did his best to phrase it as a request rather than a demand, but it could have gone either way. Thankfully, Cara complied.

"Hey, Z. You're on speaker and my pal Wyatt is here," she said, darting a glance at him. They'd agreed to play their relationship to one another off as friendship in case someone was listening in.

"Cara! I can't believe it," Zarah said in a rush. "Is it true it's a total loss? Your beautiful house. It was so adorable. I'm heartbroken."

Cara's eyes darted to his and Wyatt scowled. He tapped the mute button then said, "We need to think for a minute about how much you should say to people. Can you tell her you'll call her back? Let me get a cup of coffee and kickstart my brain."

She nodded, the tip of her tongue pressed against her top lip as she blinked rapidly, clearly trying to get her emotions under control before she spoke. He squeezed her shoulder, then stepped away, giving her space. "Hey, yeah, we're actually on another call. Can I call you back? I'll fill you in as soon as I can."

"Of course. Call me if there's anything you need me to do. I don't mind driving down there," Zarah offered.

"I appreciate the offer. I'll let you know when I've wrapped my head around it all."

Wyatt waved his arm to get her attention and when she looked over at him, he mouthed, "How did she know?"

"Yeah, um, Z? Did someone call you or something? I mean, how did you find out?"

She darted a glance at Wyatt and he gave an exaggerated nod. She'd hit exactly the right note of vague but focused calm. It wasn't until he saw her take a slow, deep inhale that he realized it was because she was using the same voice she used for meditations on the app.

"Find out? The news. It's all over the news," she cried. Then she caught herself. "Oh, wait. It's probably not making the local news there, is it?"

Cara pulled a face, then shook her head as she wrapped up the conversation with promises to call back.

Wyatt pulled up the browser on his phone and typed "Cara Beckett house fire" into the search engine. Within seconds he had all the information he needed. Without a word, she took the phone from his hand, her lips parting in shock as she took in the photos of what used to be her picture-perfect home.

Wyatt stared too. Though he had been the one to deem the posts a credible threat, he hadn't truly believed someone had done the deed. But they had. Whoever they were. They set fire to her house. The house he'd looked up on a popular real estate site the night before. To a guy from the mid-South, the California cottage looked high-end. Sleek, clean lines. Solid surfaces. It looked like it was built to withstand anything Mother Nature could throw at it.

Too bad there was no way to guard against the darker side of human nature.

Beside him Cara emitted a guttural groan.

"I'm sorry," he murmured, knowing the words to be wholly inadequate.

"I have to…" She fumbled with her phone. "I'm calling Zarah back."

He reached for her hand, but he wasn't sure if he was trying to stop her or steady her. "Hang on a second."

"I can't. I can't hang on," she insisted, her voice rising with agitation. "I have to get back." Zarah must have answered because Cara snapped into planning mode. "I have to get back. Can you book me a flight?"

Wyatt had no idea what Zarah's response was, but he started shaking his head. "No. You can't."

"I'm a couple hours from Little Rock, so I'd need a flight tonight," she continued, undeterred.

"Not a good idea," Wyatt insisted. He reached for her elbow, but she spun out of his grasp.

"Maybe look at flights out of Springfield, Missouri. Or the regional airport in northwest Arkansas?" she persisted. "Or even Memphis."

"Cara, it's not safe for you to go home right now," he said, raising his voice in a vain attempt to break through her stubborn streak.

She spun on him, her eyes bright with fear and fire. "It's not safe here, either."

He stepped closer to her, hoping to force her to back off from a bad plan. "You know it's better here than there. No one knows where to find you here. And even if they did, they'd have to go through me to get to you."

Their gazes clashed and locked. She lowered the phone from her ear, and for a split second he thought maybe he'd gotten through to her. But rather than pressing the button to end the call, she switched the audio to speaker.

"I can get you out of Little Rock after seven tonight. You'd connect through Dallas and get into LAX a bit after midnight," Zarah reported.

Cara continued to drill holes into him with her laser-like focus. For a hot second, he fooled himself into thinking she was coming around to seeing things his way.

Lifting the phone close to her lips, she looked him dead in the eye and said, "Book it."

She ended the call, then stepped calmly around him and stalked back to her room.

"Cara," he called, whirling on his heel. "I know those photos are awful, but you have to think this through."

But he was speaking to an empty hallway. He skidded to a halt in his sock feet, gripping the frame of her bedroom door to slow his momentum. She was riffling through one of the plastic bags of clothes.

"You can't go to California."

"I'm not going to California," she replied in a tone so placid he wondered if he'd imagined the whole phone call.

"But you—"

"I asked Zarah to buy an airline ticket," she interrupted. She pulled a pink hooded sweatshirt from the bag and snapped the tag off with a vicious yank. "I didn't say I'd be on the plane."

He blinked twice. "You're not going?"

"I'm not a fool," she said, shrugging into the hoodie.

Narrowing his eyes, he assessed the woman in front of him. "I would never mistake you for one, but do you care to clue me in on your plan?"

She started pacing the room, phone clutched in her hand and movements jerky with pent-up frustration. "I don't have a plan. All I know is some joker posted my private information for all to see, and my neighbor got attacked in front of my house. I try to get out of town for a few days, and a random guy I've never laid eyes on tries to kidnap me. I get away from him, but then, said random guy ends up dead. Meanwhile, back on the coast, someone set fire to my house, Wyatt. I don't know if they thought I was in it, or if they even cared—"

"They know you weren't in it," he interjected.

She whirled. "How do you know?"

"We're monitoring the chatter online." He pressed the heels of his hands to his eye sockets in a vain attempt to quell the throb building in his brain. "Can I please take a shower and have some coffee before we play twenty questions? We need to talk, and I can't think," he said, exasperated.

"Fine." She waved a hand at his rumpled clothes. "Go take your shower. I'll go brew a fresh pot."

"Thank you." He exhaled the words in a gust, then turned and trudged down the hall to gather his stuff. If they were going to go multiple rounds on how best to handle this fire situation, he needed to be as clearheaded as possible.

CARA POURED STEAMING coffee into two mugs as she waited for Wyatt to shower and change. The scent of her mother's fluffy biscuits still filled the kitchen. She lifted one corner of the tea towel covering the ancient iron skillet. Her stomach rumbled like distant artillery as a battle of will raged inside her. Cara knew the heavy pan had been greased liberally with the bacon drippings collected in the can on the counter. But the biscuits themselves were made from the same self-rising flour her grandmother had used, and fresh butter and buttermilk from a neighboring farm.

Nostalgia made her chest ache. The sight of those golden brown biscuits made her mouth water. Her stomach gurgled again, and she abandoned her principles.

"Desperate times," she murmured as she pulled one from the still-warm pan.

She split the biscuit, slathered it with butter and drizzled fresh honey on top before taking an enormous bite. Closing her eyes, she hummed her appreciation as she chewed. It was a taste of her childhood. A bite of a time when things were simpler. Safer.

Absently, she licked at a drip of buttery honey oozing down the side of her hand.

Cara popped the last bit into her mouth, chewing slowly as she doctored the other half. This time, she nibbled at the edge of the biscuit, letting the butter and honey flow onto her tongue as she peered out the window over the sink. The land where the old house once stood had long since been reclaimed by Mother Nature, but it was still vivid in her mind's eye.

"What's your plan?"

She jumped at the sound of Wyatt's voice, and the remains of the biscuit crumbled in her hand. Butter and honey oozed between her fingers. She'd been so deep in her thoughts, she hadn't heard him approach. Her face flamed with embarrassment and a touch of shame as she shook the clumpy mess off into the sink.

"Sorry," he said as he approached. "I thought you'd have heard me talking to Roscoe."

"No, I was…" She turned on the tap and cool water rushed out, coagulating the goo coating her hand. She closed her eyes and drew a steadying breath as she waited for the water to warm. "I was in another world."

One filled with biscuits baked in grease-coated cast iron and dusty memories. A world where she envisioned herself being the next Meryl Streep rather than an internet-famous—or infamous—voice-over artist being terrorized by internet trolls.

He lifted the corner of the towel and eyed the leftover biscuits still nestled in the pan. "These look great. My MaMaw used to make biscuits in a cast-iron skillet too. Refused to eat the kind out of a can."

His use of the pet name for his grandmother triggered an involuntary smile. "Mine too. This was her pan."

Wyatt eyed the pan covetously. "I buy the frozen ones once in a while. They're better, but not like this."

"They're okay, but so full of preservatives."

"Californian," he muttered.

Cara chuckled as she wiped her hand on the dishcloth hanging beside the sink. "Plates are in the cupboard in front of you. Gravy is in the microwave."

She scooped the remains of her sodden biscuit from the sink with a paper napkin and deposited the wad in the trash. Then, taking one of the coffee mugs, she retreated to the kitchen table. Settling into a chair, she warmed her hands on the ceramic mug as she watched Wyatt move easily around the kitchen. His dark hair was still damp from his shower, curling slightly at his nape. He had the lean build of someone who runs, and overall, he seemed fit. She remembered him mentioning a float trip on the Buffalo River, and wondered if he was a hiker. He looked outdoorsy.

He turned toward the table, plate and mug in hand, and caught her staring. "What?"

Rather than giving in to embarrassment again, she switched into interrogation mode. "Are you the outdoorsy type?"

Wyatt eyed her warily as he took the seat across from her. "Why? You planning on dropping me out in the woods with nothing but a compass and a water bottle?" He pointed the tines of his fork at her. "I have to warn you now, I don't go anywhere without a laptop and a hot spot."

She shook her head, though the image of him trudging

through the woods using his phone as a compass and with his laptop bag strapped across his chest was amusing. "I was curious. You mentioned floating the Buffalo."

"Oh." He turned his attention and his fork on the plate of food in front of him. "Yeah, sure, I like floating. I prefer a canoe to a kayak, even though I know kayaks are cooler right now. I hike the trails at Pinnacle Mountain a couple times a year, but mainly because it's so close to Little Rock and sometimes I need to get out of the office and out of my head, you know?"

"I get you," she said before taking a sip of her coffee.

Using the side of his fork, he cut the gravy-smothered biscuit into bite-size chunks. "I'm not big on camping," he said with a shrug and sheepish smile. "I'm fond of electricity."

"Me too," she assured him. "I mean, me neither." She gave a short laugh then summed it all up. "I don't camp."

"So, why are you asking if I'm 'outdoorsy' when I ask what your plan is?"

"Oh, I wasn't planning…" She laughed at the roundabout of non sequiturs they'd been riding. "Two separate trains of thought converged. Sorry."

"Ah, okay." He shoveled a bite into his mouth and chewed, closing his eyes appreciatively. After washing it down with a sip of coffee, he pulled a pained face. "I'm never going to be able to eat another frozen biscuit again."

"Ruined, huh?"

He stabbed another gravy-slathered bite but met her eyes when he answered. "Completely and utterly."

"My mama's biscuits can have an effect on a man," she cooed in an exaggerated drawl.

Wyatt only smirked as he chewed. She watched as he demolished half the plate before she spoke. "My plan is to stay here with you. Hunker down. Does your department have enough sway with Homeland Security to make it look like I boarded a flight?"

"We have sway, and we have, uh, other ways," he answered without looking up. "You want it to look like you're headed back."

"I figure it will buy us at least a day or so, and maybe a little breathing room." She wrinkled her nose. "What do you think?"

"Sounds solid. I'll loop Emma in on the plan, she'll let the others know."

"I'm going to use my phone to make a hotel reservation."

His approving expression morphed into a frown. "A hotel reservation?"

Wrapping her hands around the mug, she leaned in. "I need to make it look like I'm coming back to take care of the fire stuff. I can't stay at my house, so a hotel reservation makes sense."

"But they'll charge you for it."

Cara caught sight of the red flush creeping up his neck and opted to make light of his needless commentary. She might have money now, but it didn't mean she lost the practical frugality of a born and bred Arkansan. "I know, but I think it's important to sell whoever's watching on the notion of my imminent arrival."

He bobbed his head, but focused on his plate. "Right. Right. Good thinking."

She watched as he methodically demolished the rest of his breakfast. The moment he placed his fork on the gravy-streaked plate, she spoke up again. "There's more."

"I figured the wheels were turning." He wiped his mouth with a paper napkin, a wary gleam in his eye as he sat back. "Hit me."

"I'm going to call Chris and Tom today." Abandoning her

grip on the coffee cup, she sat up straighter. She waited as he slotted the puzzle pieces into place.

"Okay."

She inclined her head. "I know Zarah sent texts letting them know I'm okay, but I need to talk to them. We have a lot happening in the next couple weeks and I need to be in the loop."

He studied her closely, biting the inside of his cheek as he weighed her plan. The morning light streaming through the window brought out hints of gold in dark eyes fringed by unfairly thick, dark lashes. The intensity of his stare should have made her uncomfortable. But it didn't. She felt safe with him. She could trust him. And, more important, he seemed to trust her.

"What do you plan to tell them?"

"Nothing in particular," she hedged. "I want to get their thoughts on what's been happening. They're far more involved in the tech community. Chris with the investors and entrepreneurs, and Tom with the people on the tech side of things."

Wyatt raised his arms and laced his fingers behind his head. She could see the temptation to rock her mother's kitchen chair back on two legs. Watching him wrestle it into submission was amusing and more than a little endearing. She wondered if he got away with tipping his own mother's chairs back. Something told her he didn't.

"What's their response been when you've had issues before?"

She shrugged. "Obviously, we've never had anything near what's happening now. Until now all I got was the usual mix of sour grapes and good old-fashioned misogyny." Thinking back on their cavalier dismissal of the vitriol slung at her day after day made her wonder if she shouldn't have been slotting them in with the chauvinists.

As if reading her mind, he asked, "Did they take it seriously?"

"No."

The answer slipped out of her before she could give the question more than a moment's thought. But it was the truth. They didn't take the chat room slurs and vaguely threatening messages posted by anonymous commenters to heart.

But now she couldn't stop shaking all over. Someone had tried to make good on those threats. It was time for Cara to insist her partners take her contribution to the company and the threats to her safety more seriously.

"Which is why I need to talk to them now."

Chapter Twelve

Cara pulled her phone from the pocket of her hoodie and placed it on the table between them. Wyatt glanced down at the blank screen then up at her, a question in his eyes. "You want me to listen in?"

A lump rose in her throat. Unable to trust her voice, Cara simply nodded.

He eyed the phone askance. "Do they know where you are?"

She shrugged. "Maybe." When his brows drew down, she knew the time had finally come to explain how complicated her dealings with her business partners had become. "My relationship with Chris and Tom has grown…distant over the past year or so."

"Distant as in contentious?"

She shook her head, dismissing the notion a smidge too quickly. "No, I wouldn't say so," she hedged. Wyatt lowered his arms and crossed them over his chest. He didn't speak. A tactic which proved more compelling than she cared to admit. "We've grown up. Grown apart. There hasn't been a fight or anything."

What she didn't tell him was she was almost one hundred percent certain the lack of friction could be attributed to her unwillingness to engage. The truth of the matter was, she wasn't as involved in the day-to-day running of LYYF as either Chris or Tom. Until this latest onslaught of abuse, she'd simply considered their arrangement a convenient division of labor. She handled the content. Chris kept them in capital and worked publicity like a pro. And the whole house of cards was built on a platform Tom created. The collaborative efforts of the company's early days were long gone. Now, instead of pizza, beers and brainstorms, they had conference calls.

"Tell me about them," he prompted.

She raised a shoulder and let it fall. "You've probably already read most of it."

"Give it to me from your perspective."

"Chris handles the money matters. Always has. He likes wheeling and dealing. Being in the middle of the action. He bought a place in Palo Alto the minute money started coming in and moved up there to be in the center of it all. Tom stayed down in LA for a while longer, but he hated the congestion. The only things he needs to be happy are surfing, solitude and a keyboard, so he bought himself a multimillion-dollar shack near Big Sur. I stayed put."

"You never wanted to live anywhere else?"

She gave him a rueful smile. "I was still chasing fame in Hollywood, remember?"

"Then it found you on the web," Wyatt concluded. "So the three of you live and work in completely separate areas?"

She nodded. "Yes. In both the company and geographically. Which isn't an issue. We're a digital company. There's no need for us to share office space." She shrugged. "We have operations offices for the tech side of things in Mountain View, and my content team has a small production studio near me in Silver Lake."

Wyatt took a moment to process the information. His

gaze dropped to the phone again, then he asked, "Do you like your partners?"

She should have been startled by his bluntness, but Cara was becoming adept at cop speak. He was trying to catch her off guard. He didn't realize she had no reason to have her guard up. Not here. And not with him.

"I do."

The answer was simple and mostly true. Chris had grown more than a little pompous, but he'd never been lacking in the self-esteem department. Tom was surlier and more reticent with her these days, but she'd chalked it up to a natural drift. Plus, the run-up to the stock offering was forcing him out of his happy place behind a keyboard and into the spotlight. A part of her hoped they'd both revert to the easygoing guys she'd met on dormitory move-in day, but she knew it wasn't likely. She wasn't the same starry-eyed young dreamer she'd been then, either.

"Have you ever...?" he started, then stopped. She looked up at him, all too aware of what his next question would be. She'd been asked dozens of times. Still, for some reason, it nettled to know it would be coming from Wyatt. But when he spoke, his surety surprised her. "You've never been romantically involved with either of them."

She shook her head. "No. I mean, Chris hit on me once. He'd come home from a party drunk our freshman year. I didn't take it personally, though. The minute I said no, he turned his attention to another girl on our floor." She gave him a weak smile. "As far as I know, he hasn't changed much. Chris's focus has always been money. The business. Women come and they go," she explained with a dismissive wave. "I've never known him to be serious about anyone."

"And Tom?"

"Tom was as focused as Chris, but more on the nuts and

bolts. We, uh, he liked what I was doing with the meditation stuff. Tom was the one who convinced Chris to put it out there. They were light on content, and as I told you before, I was working for takeout in the early days."

"And your relationship with him never…crossed any lines?"

Her cheeks heated, but she held his gaze as she dismissed the notion. "No. I think… There was a time when I thought maybe he had feelings for me," she admitted. Gritting her teeth to ward off the blush threatening, she pushed through. "But I didn't, um, encourage him, and he never…pushed." She looked down at her hands, then chanced a peek at him from under her lashes. "I think his feelings sort of…fizzled. You know how it is. Nothing more than a crush."

"Who do you want to call first?" he prompted.

"Tom," she answered without hesitation.

Wyatt made a sort of there-it-is motion to the phone, and Cara couldn't help feeling she'd given her growing discomfiture away. Curling her lips in, she bit down gently as she took up the phone and dialed the number she'd jotted in her spiral-bound notebook. The call went directly to voicemail. When the tone sounded, she swallowed hard and did her best to keep her tone chipper. Upbeat.

"Hey, Tom. It's me. I guess Zarah has been keeping you guys up to date with what's happening with me. I, um, well, I was only checking in. Give me a call when you can," she finished, then jabbed at the red button to end the call.

"Well. Okay. Strange," she muttered under her breath.

Wyatt tapped a finger on the table to prompt her to look up at him. "Why strange?"

She exhaled long and low, her lips curving in a sad smile. "I can't remember the last time he didn't take my call."

"It's an unknown number."

She allowed her smile to grow and the blush to come. "Right. Makes sense. Logically. Feels strange though."

"Do you want to try Chris, or wait until after Tom calls you back?"

Cara caught the corner of her lip between her teeth. Staring down at the phone with its generic background and out-of-the-box ringtone, she tried to smother the unease she felt with Wyatt's confidence the call would be returned.

"I'll call him now," she said, grabbing the phone before she lost her nerve.

Once again, her call went to voicemail. She could feel Wyatt's all-consuming stare taking in every word and each morsel of nuance as she spoke. Drawing on all her years of training, Cara left the same chipper message for him, careful to say nothing more or less than she had to Tom.

When she hung up, a heavy blanket of silence fell over the room. Unable to sit still and wait, she pushed out of her chair. "More coffee?"

Wyatt declined with a shake of his head. "Your eyeballs are going to start spinning."

"I'm going to grab some water."

When she returned with two glasses filled with tinkling ice cubes, he was speaking into his own phone.

"No, I appreciate you calling me back, man," he said to the mystery caller. Mouthing an apology, he got up from the table as she reclaimed her seat, motioning his intention to take the call outside.

Cara sat at the dining table, studying the porcelain figurines her grandmother had collected for as long as Cara could remember. Her mother had helped Cara pick a new one for every birthday and Christmas Grandma June had celebrated. She'd displayed them on nearly every open surface at the old house. Now they stayed locked in a glass case, waiting for someone to take notice of them.

At times she felt like one of those Precious Moments dolls. There were days she felt her contributions to LYYF captured something innately human and essential. Other days, she wondered if she was purely decorative. She picked up her silent phone and scowled at it. The dark screen of her phone bounced her reflection back at her and she quickly altered her expression. There had been a time when she'd spent hours looking into mirrors, trying to nail the emotions with a simple shift in facial features. She could, when necessary, inject deep feeling into her tone.

Tom and Chris used to love it when she drew on her theatrical training to place their delivery or drive-through orders. "Tacos!" she'd exclaim into the speaker, breathless with desperation. "I need six tacos and a bean burrito or they'll kill me!" But LA servers were often actors or wannabe actors themselves. They rarely rose to the bait, even when she gave a performance her best friends declared Oscar-worthy.

"I called a guy I knew from the academy," Wyatt said as he strode back into the room, jolting her from her memories.

"Yeah?" she managed.

"Ryan Hastings," he said with a nod. "Worked for years on protection duty. He left the force last year to start his own security and protection firm up in Bentonville."

"Ryan Hastings," she repeated. "Why does his name sound familiar?"

"He was involved in a pretty high-profile case last year. Some big-shot attorney and his son were killed. Ryan was assigned to protect the widow. Turns out the guy's brother, a US senator, was involved."

"Yes, I remember hearing about it." She mustered a self-effacing smile. "Probably from my mother. I'm not big on absorbing the news of the world."

"It can do a number on you." Wyatt nodded. "I limit how much I take in too and try to get information from a cross section of sources."

"Wise," she affirmed.

The default ringtone on the mobile phone in front of her rang out. Cara glanced at the screen and drew in a deep breath. "It's Tom." Without looking to him for direction, she swiped to accept the call, then activated the speaker. When Wyatt sank back in his seat, she understood he meant to listen in unnoticed.

"Tom." She exhaled her old friend's name.

"Cara, are you okay? I heard about your house," he told her, sounding genuinely upset.

"Wow. It made regional coverage?" She shot Wyatt raised eyebrows. "I wouldn't have figured more than a mention on *LA Today.*"

There was a moment of hesitation on Tom's end. "Zarah sent me a link."

"Ah. Okay. Makes sense."

"She said you weren't home?"

"I wasn't."

"Any word on the damages?"

"I haven't made it back to see for myself yet, but I'm told it's all fixable."

"Thank goodness." Tom released a gusty sigh. "Where are you? Are you coming back before New York?"

When she met Wyatt's gaze, he gave an imperceptible shake of his head, but shrugged as if to say it was her call as to what to tell him.

"Zarah has booked me a flight home." Her tongue tangled on the last word. LA had been her home for years, but now it may as well have been a million miles away. An awkward beat passed in which no one spoke.

"Yeah, uh, I think she said something about you coming back when she sent the news. Sorry. You know how distracted I get."

"I do. Anyway, I should get in late tonight." Feeling disheartened by the ever-widening distance between them, she grasped for conversational straws. "When are you heading east?"

"Day after tomorrow." The dullness in his tone told her he wasn't looking forward to making the trip, even if it meant he returned to the West Coast a billionaire. "I got the files you sent for the bedtime meditation series. Good stuff."

This was about as effusive as Tom ever was about the content she provided. Usually his persona of a disengaged, flighty genius amused her, but she found she was not in the mood to be dismissed. "Should be good for another ten million or so downloads," she said, affecting the same offhanded tone.

"What?" Tom coughed, then chuckled. "Oh, yeah. At least."

Irked by the stilted conversation, she decided to introduce a whole new topic. "Hey, did you also hear some guy tried to kidnap me at gunpoint?" she asked in a mockingly bright tone. "With a real gun and everything. Guess you can believe some of the stuff you read on the forums after all."

"Cara, I'm so sorry about what happened," he said in a rush of words. "I mean, you know I'm happy you're okay. I'd hate for you to get hurt—"

His verbal stumbling and bumbling only angered her more. He'd never been the most socially adroit guy, but this was beyond ridiculous.

"Can't kill the cash cow." She smiled as she said it, but a cold knot formed in her belly. Needing to end this torture, she leaned in, her face close to the phone. "I'll see you in New York, Tom. Safe travels." She ended the call with an angry jab of her forefinger.

When she looked up, she found Wyatt staring at her, brows raised. "And he's the one you're closer to?"

"He's…Tom. His mind is always miles down the road, you know?" She took a steadying breath. "I'm mostly used to it, but sometimes it would be nice if he could at least try living in the present."

Wyatt nodded. "There's this great meditation app I use…"

She gave an appreciative chuckle. "When he said the files I sent for the new series are good, I can guarantee he was talking about the audio quality, not the content." The corner of her mouth kicked up in a smirk. "Tom considers sleep a waste of productive hours."

"But Chris has to know content is king," Wyatt argued. "I mean, he's the guy out there pushing for investors and users, right?"

"Oh, yeah. Chris likes to say I'm the best impulse buy he's ever made."

"Whoa." Wyatt blinked and fell back in his chair. "Please tell me he's joking."

"I'd say it's about eighty-five percent joke," she conceded.

His brows drew down. "Do you ever think about leaving? Selling out and going off to do whatever you want to do?"

"Sure, I think about it." She shrugged. "The question is, what would I do? Actresses have a much narrower window when it comes to breaking into the business. Mine's pretty much closed. There's off-screen work, but there my success with LYYF may work against me."

"How?"

"Well, my voice is fairly recognizable now." She gave him a wan smile. "Having a familiar voice can be an advantage for men—look at Matthew McConaughey, Morgan Freeman or James Earl Jones. But women doing voice-over work? Sure, you get the occasional celebrities pushing perfume at Christmastime, or splash-washing their fully made-up faces for some beauty brand, but they're mainly hired for the on-camera work, not to be the voice of the product."

"And you're already inherently entwined with another brand," he said with grim understanding.

"Exactly."

She was saved from further discussion of her personal and professional choices by the buzzing of her phone. A peek at the display showed Chris's number. She smiled grimly and stretched a hand out to accept the call. "And now contestant number two."

She swiped the screen and called out, "Hey, Chris," before Wyatt even straightened in his chair.

"Cara, holy cripes," her longtime business partner gushed. "I'm so glad you called. I've been worried sick ever since Zarah told me what happened."

"What happened a couple days ago, or what happened last night?" Cara prodded.

"Last night? What happened last night?"

She looked up and met Wyatt's eyes. Chris sounded truly perplexed.

"Someone set my house on fire."

"The house where you're staying in Alabama?" he asked, sounding genuinely aghast.

She and Wyatt shared an amused smirk. "Arkansas. And no. I meant my house in LA," she corrected.

"No way! The little place in Los Feliz?"

"Yes." She leaned in closer. "You hadn't heard? I thought maybe Zarah—"

"Oh, she may have," he interrupted. "I've been running all

over New York taking meeting after meeting," he said in a rush. "But you weren't there, right? You're in, uh, Arkansas?"

"Zarah booked me on a flight to LAX this evening." She held Wyatt's stare but said no more.

"Hey, Cara, you think you might consider hiring some security," Chris suggested. "At least until all this stuff blows over. I think we may have been a bit…"

In her mind, Cara filled the empty air space with a few choice adjectives: *condescending…dismissive*?

"I mean, you never know when to take the trolls seriously. Am I right?"

"Right," she replied flatly.

She stared at the phone screen, wishing they were on a video call. It was hard to get a read on this version of Chris. She'd grown so used to thinking of him as little more than her business partner. She'd almost forgotten they were once good friends.

"So, yeah, maybe it's time for us to be more proactive about security. For you, and maybe all three of us?"

Cara couldn't remember the last time Chris's innate confidence had seemed so shaken. Now she wished she could have her old cavalier Chris back. His obvious worry made her feel all the more exposed. Picking up the pen Wyatt abandoned, she twirled it through her fingers like a baton.

"Maybe. I'll look into it," she promised, her gaze darting back up to Wyatt.

"Let me know how things are when you get back to LA," Chris insisted. "When are you coming east?"

Not wanting to be pinned down to anything resembling a schedule, she kept her answer as vague as possible. "I'll be there a day or two before to do any media you want me to handle and will probably beat a path out of there right after. You know I'm not a New York girl."

"Some actor you are," he teased, echoing an old refrain. "Aren't you all supposed to claim to want to have a serious stage career?"

"Not me," she answered, trying to muster some of her old bravado as she tossed out the line he expected from her. "I never said I wanted to be an actress. I want to be a star."

"You are a star," Chris replied. "The investors love you. We all do. Be careful and I'll see you next week."

Three long beeps sounded to indicate the end of the call. She pressed her lips together to stave off an unexpected rush of emotion. Dropping the pen to the table with a clatter, she pushed back and escaped the dining room before Wyatt could get a word out. She didn't know what to say anymore. Everything seemed to be the opposite of what it should be.

Roscoe lifted his big, square head and let out a soft woof when she pushed through the screen door onto the porch. She stood at the rail, her arms crossed tight across her chest, staring out at the spot where the old house once stood. Her jaw clenched tight, she shivered when the crisp autumn breeze cut through the cotton sweatshirt she wore. Tugging the sleeves down over her hands, she scowled down at the discount store athletic wear. Why hadn't Zarah included some regular clothes? Did she think Cara would be practicing sun salutations and Savasana while on the run from her tormentors?

Cara clamped down on her uncharitable thoughts, her fingers biting into the thin cotton fabric as she hugged herself again. Zarah had done her best. She'd found clothing and other necessities at a store with delivery while sitting in her snug home office over a thousand miles away. She should be grateful for the ease and comfort of the clothing. For her safety. She should be happy there were other people who were glad she was alive. And she was.

"Cara?"

The quiet, husky timbre of Wyatt's voice sent a different sort of shiver through her. Roscoe, who'd settled back in his customary repose, did little more than open an eye. Her cheeks flamed as she heard the hinges on the screen door squeak. She didn't dare turn to look at him.

"You want me to grab one of your mom's jackets?"

"I'm okay."

She clearly wasn't. Cara could almost feel him struggling to suppress the urge to argue the point. But to his credit, he retreated, the hinges creaking again. "How about I put on a fresh pot of coffee?"

A sob rose in her throat. Cara bludgeoned the knot of emotion with a short, sharp laugh. "I thought you were worried about spinning eyeballs."

"I'm a cop. I'm trained to withstand torturous levels of overcaffeination. I was worried about your eyeballs."

She turned to look at him, hoping he'd assume the color in her cheeks came courtesy of the wind. "Thank you. I wasn't quite up to my eyeballs yet, but didn't want you to feel emasculated."

"I appreciate your concern," he intoned gravely. He reached out to the side, pulled a fleece-lined denim jacket from the hall tree and popped the screen door open wide enough to thrust it at her. "I'll be in the kitchen when you're ready to talk."

She gave herself no more than five minutes to stew, sulk and otherwise sort through the swirl of conflicting emotions before she headed back into the house. Roscoe opted to relinquish his sunny spot in favor of shelter as well. She shrugged out of the jacket and hung it on its customary hook before following the old dog to the kitchen.

Wyatt was measuring grounds into the basket when she entered the room. Rather than jumping in to help him, Cara stopped at the table and watched. His movements were economical, but fluid. Almost graceful. He was comfortable moving around her parents' kitchen. She'd never pictured herself bringing a man home. Not that she'd brought him there in any sort of romantic way. But she'd never pictured it at all.

She'd never invited Chris or Tom to accompany her on trips home. Like most people from the coast, they considered anyplace west of Philadelphia akin to traveling to the outback. Tom had been offered an obscene amount of money to speak at a prestigious convention in Chicago and refused. To her partners, the middle of the country was an unappealing wilderness filled with dangerous creatures and backward people.

As Wyatt poured water into the coffee maker's reservoir, she felt an unexpected twist of sympathy for them. They would never know the pleasure of waking to the scent of strong black coffee and fresh-baked biscuits. They'd never know what a relief it was to have conversations with people who spoke slowly, choosing their words with thought and ending their sentences declaratively, rather than as questions. And there was no doubt in her mind which rock they needed to kick over next.

She gripped the back of her father's chair. "I think you're right. We need to take a closer look at Chris and Tom."

Wyatt stilled for a moment, then reached for the dishcloth hanging beside the sink to wipe his hands. When he turned to face her, his eyes were full of sympathy and a familiar resolve. "Ryan Hastings said the same thing. He says the threat almost always stems from a source close to the vic— uh, person of interest."

She gave him a wan smirk. "Thanks for not calling me a victim."

"You aren't one." He pulled a coffee mug closer. "Maybe we need to look at Zarah too."

Cara shrugged. "She doesn't have anything to gain from getting rid of me, though."

"True." He hit the button to start the coffee brewing, then gestured to the kitchen table. "But she seems to be in the middle of everything."

Cara conceded the point. It seemed more and more of her communication with her partners ran through Zarah these days.

Wyatt nodded. "We'll start with a brain dump of everything you can come up with concerning your partners." He hung the towel back on the hook, then fixed her with a look. "I asked Emma to rebook your flight for morning. If anyone asks, you can say you couldn't make the drive to Little Rock on time. Either way, it'll buy us a little more time on the going-to-California story."

"Good call." She nodded, impressed.

"I'd have handled it myself, but I couldn't be sure the connection would be there. I've crashed and burned more since we've been here than any time since I was in high school," he said with a grimace.

Cara laughed. "I'm sorry. And I have to say, I doubt you crashed and burned much in high school or since."

"Thanks, but either way, tomorrow we're driving into town to get a 5G gateway. I can't rough it with this faulty connection any longer."

Cara hid her smile as she moved to pull a fresh mug from the cupboard. Apparently, even the most down-to-earth men needed their creature comforts. "Sounds good." And it did. As good as it was to feel safe and secure on the ranch, she was starting to feel restless. It would be good to get out for a little while.

Chapter Thirteen

The following morning, the two of them drove north in search of a more reliable source of internet access. It was clear that if Wyatt was going to dig into the financials of three tech titans, he was going to need more speed than the spotty satellite could provide.

They rode in companionable silence, sipping coffee as they wound their way into Boone County. Wyatt glanced over at Cara as they approached the outskirts of Harrison, the next town of any size along the highway. "I should be able to get what I need at any cellular store, but if they don't have one in stock, we may need to head up to Branson or Springfield."

She shrugged. "Fine with me. My calendar is open all day."

"We can pick up anything else you might need while we're here," he offered.

She plucked at the front of her hoodie. Leaning against the door, she turned toward him. "My mom used to take me into Harrison to do my school clothes shopping. I didn't realize people bought clothes anywhere but JCPenney until I was about eleven and discovered the joys of a store called Goody's. They had all the cool stuff."

"My mom liked to drive up to North Little Rock so she could wander around the mall."

"Lucky you, shopping in the big city."

He rolled his eyes.

They crested one of the rolling hills and Cara's phone sprang to life with a series of texts from Zarah coming through in rapid succession.

Zarah: I went to pick you up and you weren't on the plane.

Zarah: Checked and saw you rebooked for AM. Hope all is okay.

Zarah: You're not answering my messages. Hot cop got your phone?

Her cheeks flamed as she read the last one, knowing at some point Wyatt would see it and know there'd been speculation about him. She was trying to formulate a response when a new message appeared.

Zarah: I'm picking you up at the airport. Hope you made your flight. Text when you land.

"Oh, crud," Cara muttered.

"What's the matter?"

"Zarah's waiting for my flight at LAX," she reported. She typed a response, then quickly deleted it. "You said Emma could do something to make it look like I got on the flight, right?"

Wyatt frowned. "Yeah. Why?"

"Zarah never picks me up from the airport. She lives on the other end of the earth," she mumbled, scowling at her phone.

"Hang tight." Eyeing a gas station ahead on the highway, Wyatt signaled his intention to pull over. Once he'd pulled into a parking spot outside a bustling mini-mart, he turned to look at Cara. "Tell me all about Zarah."

Her eyebrows shot up. "All about Zarah?" she repeated, punctuating the request with an incredulous scoff. "Where do I begin?"

"How did you meet her?" he prompted.

"Well, I hired her long before I actually met her," she said slowly. "It was at the start of the pandemic lockdown, and we couldn't turn out content fast enough."

Wyatt unhooked his seat belt and turned to look at her. "So your relationship has always been remote?"

"Yes. I mean, we've met since then, obviously," she said with a helpless wave of her hand. "But we've never shared office space. A lot of LYYF's staff works remotely."

"How did she come to work for you?"

"One of the programmers," she said with a frown. "They are cousins or something?" She brushed the fuzzy details aside. "Anyway, she was doing some travel booking for Tom, and then Chris. When we opened the offices in Mountain View, Chris and Tom took offices there and they have someone on-site. Being based in Southern California, it only made sense for Zarah to focus more on me."

"But she doesn't do stuff for you in person," he clarified.

"No. She didn't even want a desk at the production studio." She shrugged. "Like I said, she lives out in the Valley. It doesn't seem like a long way away when you look at a map, but when you factor in LA traffic…"

"And the airport?" Wyatt asked, making a winding gesture with his hand.

"Is even farther."

"Can you try to find out why she's picking you up? You know, subtly?" he asked, looking troubled. "Without giving away anything about where you are?"

She rolled her eyes. "Gee, I don't know," she drawled, settling into her seat. She typed out a message with her thumbs but before she hit Send, she turned the screen to him for approval.

CB: You're sweet, but it's too far away. Don't worry about me.

"Perfect," Wyatt said with a nod.

She sent the message and let out a long sigh.

The silence stretched taut between them. Finally, he broke it. "What are you thinking?"

She mustered a small, sad smile. "I'm thinking maybe I should give them all what they want."

"Who? And what?" he asked cautiously.

"Everyone. No one thinks I deserve my thirty-three-and-a-third of LYYF. Maybe I should sell out and go do something new. I mean, it's not like I wouldn't have options. I'd certainly have the money to coast for a while."

"Wait until after next week and you'd probably have the money to coast forever," he pointed out.

"Ah, but they don't think I've earned a big payday. People aren't assaulting innocent neighbors and burning down my house because they're hoping I sell after the stock offering. They want me out now. And what does it matter? Either way, I'll have more money than I need."

"What if selling isn't enough? From what I've seen and read, some people think you should be paying LYYF for the pleasure of putting together their award-winning content." He gave a little snort. "No. Don't sell out because they—whoever they are—want you to. If you want out, make sure you leave on your terms."

Her phone buzzed and she looked down. Another message from Zarah had arrived.

Zarah: It's no problem. See you soon.

"I have a feeling she knows I'm not on the plane," Cara said, her tone morose.

"Okay, so tell her." He gestured to the phone. "Let her know you talked to the LAFD and they said there was no reason to hurry back so you changed your mind."

"Tell her I stayed in Arkansas?" she asked, her forehead knit with concern. "What if someone's reading our texts?"

"You can make it sound like you decided to head to New York early. Might be the better idea," he added. "Let them try to find the needle in the haystack there."

Cara set her jaw. At last, she nodded and began to type.

CB: So sorry. Spoke to LAFD and they said no need to hurry back. Canceled flight. I'll deal with the house after the IPO. Probably head to NYC early. Go home. I appreciate the thought!

Then she turned the phone off and tossed it into the console. She caught his quizzical look and pulled a face.

"I'm starting to think all this technology is more trouble than it's worth." He chuckled and her expression brightened. "We could blow off getting your hot spot thingy. You know those phone places like to keep you trapped all day, and I know a place with the best onion rings you've ever tasted."

He let out a guffaw as he pulled his seat belt across his body and clicked it into place. "It's nine thirty and we finished breakfast less than an hour ago."

"I fail to see the conflict," she replied, straight-faced.

"How does this sound? I grab the gateway—it won't take long, the state has a contract with the carrier and it's all set up at the store." He sneaked a glance at her as he maneuvered out of the cramped parking lot. *Skeptical* wasn't a strong enough word for the look she gave him. "Seriously. All I have to do is show my ID and pick it up." She shot him a doubtful glance as he pulled back onto the highway.

"Fine," she conceded ungraciously.

"Then we can see what we can do about finding you some different clothes. You brought the cash Zarah sent?" She nodded and gave an affirmative hmm. "Good." He smiled as they picked up speed, hurtling toward the small city nestled in the Ozark Mountains. "Then we'll replenish with those onion rings, but I have to warn you, I've had some good rings in my time."

"In your time," she echoed with a snort.

He drummed his fingers on the steering wheel, smiling as he glanced over at her. "So tell me, who is this hot cop Zarah asked you about?"

THE PICKUP AT the mobile phone store didn't go as quickly or smoothly as Wyatt had hoped. When all was said and done, it ate through a full hour of their morning and layers of his patience.

"Come on, we'll get a ridiculously decadent cup of coffee, then I'll let you sit and watch the world go by while I try on jeans and pick up a few sweaters." She treated him to a wide, winning smile. "I've lived in Southern California for so long I've forgotten how great sweater weather actually is."

As they waited at the window to pick up overpriced coffees, Cara leaned across him to ask the young woman at the register for shopping recommendations. When he ruled out a trip to the Branson outlets, she insisted he drive her to the town square. Wyatt eyed the area skeptically. Like most small towns, Harrison had dried up when the highway bypass was built and commerce flowed away from the business district.

"There it is." Cara pointed to one of the run-down storefronts. "Sassafras," she announced, repeating the name of the boutique the woman at the coffee shop said had "real cute stuff" but was "kinda spendy."

The display window featured a single mannequin sporting a pair of slim black pants and an animal-print sweater with an enormous collar pulled down around its sculpted shoulders. Wyatt tried to picture Cara wearing such an outlandishly gaudy print but found he could imagine the tempting hollows of her collarbones all too easily.

"Maybe we should go up to Branson," he said gruffly.

She let out a tinkling burst of laughter. "Maybe, but I'll take a peek in here first."

When she reached for the handle, he placed a hand on her forearm to stop her. "Hang on. Let me go in and check it out first."

Raising a single brow, she asked, "You think whoever is stalking me somehow got wind of a random conversation I had with a barista through a drive-up window?"

"No," he admitted slowly. "But I'm, uh, responsible for, you know, keeping you safe."

The other brow shot up to match its twin. "Well, come on, Captain Responsible, we're going shopping. You can hold my keeper pile."

She bailed out of the SUV without another word and Wyatt cringed at the thought. He could have handled a trip to a mall. Department stores usually had chairs for people to wait in, at least. But this place looked to be about the size of a postage stamp and, from what he could see through the plate-glass door, was stuffed to the gills with glitter, fringe and frills. When Cara stopped on the sidewalk, crossed her arms over her chest and tapped her foot, he made a shooing motion before opening his own door.

"Go on. I'm getting claustrophobic lookin' through the window," he called to her.

Cara's triumphant grin lit her face. "I won't be long," she called, then sailed into the store without a backward glance.

He heard the jingle of the bell above the store's door as he climbed out of the car himself. Carrying his coffee, he strolled along the sidewalk, peering around the edges of brown-craft-papered windows into vacant spaces, and stopping to admire the neon marquee of the historic Lyric Theater. Not wanting to stray too far, he settled on a wooden park bench across from Sassafras. He'd responded to three work emails and was sipping the dregs of his coffee when she backed out of the store, shopping bags pulling on both arms.

The yoga pants, T-shirt and sweatshirt she'd been wearing were nowhere to be found. Instead, she wore wide-legged bleached denim jeans with a preppy-looking sweater. She still wore the thick-soled canvas sneakers Zarah had sent with the other supplies, but he could see the distinct shape of a shoebox in one of the bulging bags. Tossing his cup into a nearby trash bin, he hustled to the car to help her stow her haul.

"Wow. I guess this worked for you?" he asked with a laugh.

"Such cute stuff. Fun but functional. They have a whole

section of jeans called 'sassy pants,'" she informed him as he pried the handles of the shoppers from her fingers.

"I would expect nothing less," he said soberly.

"I'm going to tell my mom about this place. She'd love it too," she called as she headed for the passenger seat.

Wyatt had a hard time imagining practical, efficient Betsy Beckett shopping anywhere with so much sass, but he refrained from saying so. When he climbed back into the driver's seat, he could practically feel the buzz emanating from her. Her excitement was so infectious, he had to smile.

"I guess you needed some retail therapy?"

"I needed to make some of my own choices," she countered without missing a beat. She looked over at him. "I've been wearing clothes someone else picked out, sleeping in a bed I haven't felt comfortable in since I was seventeen, riding around in a car I don't own, with a guy I barely know, and eating random vegetables scrounged from the depths of my parents' deep freeze." She flashed a shaky smile. "I'm pretty sure there are jars of pickles in the cellar older than I am."

Wyatt blew out a breath, his shoulders drooping as he took in her words. "Man, Cara, I'm sorry—"

"No." She held up a hand, cutting him off. "I'm grateful. For all of it. Grateful I got away from Gerald Griffin, grateful to have friends and financial wherewithal to do this. Not everyone has a soft place to land…a place to call home no matter how long they've been away. I'm so lucky and I know it," she said earnestly. "But today, I needed a few minutes to just be me, you know?"

"I get it."

"It feels like all I've been doing for the past few weeks is reacting." She looked him directly in the eye. "Honestly, I don't know how much longer I can do this. I can't live my life according to rules other people make up for me."

"I understand."

And he did. Wyatt knew he'd be champing at the bit if he were in her shoes. Shock and sheer terror had carried her for days. She'd bounced from one blow to the next like a boxer pinned against the ropes.

But now she was coming around.

This punch-drunk powerhouse outfitted in her brand-new sassy pants would soon be ready to come out swinging, and he was going to be the guy to hold whoever was responsible for terrorizing her up for her to pummel.

She reached for her abandoned cup of coffee and took a healthy slug. She wrinkled her nose as she dropped it back into the cup holder. "Not so tempting when it's tepid."

"We can get a fresh one for the ride home," he offered, reversing out of the parking space.

"Nah, I promised you lunch, remember?"

"I rarely forget about onion rings," he intoned gravely.

She jiggled her knee, clearly still hyped up on her taste of freedom. "Excellent. Head out to Highway 7 South. There's a dairy bar down the road a piece."

"I love a good dairy bar." He hit his turn signal and headed in the direction she indicated.

A few miles outside town, Cara contented herself with an order of hand-battered onion rings while he wolfed down a ridiculously sloppy barbecue bacon burger the woman at the order window claimed was the best thing on the chalkboard menu.

Cara crunched into a ring the circumference of a softball and hummed her appreciation as she chewed, her gaze fixed on a point in the middle distance.

"Everything okay?" It was a ridiculous question, given their circumstances, but he was dying to know where her mind was.

"Do you mind if we stop by a grocery store on our way back through town?"

The request jarred a laugh from him. "Worried about your next meal already?"

"Always," she replied without missing a beat. "I was thinking I could pick up some fruit besides apples and oranges, and I'd sell an internal organ for a bean burrito."

"Wow. Quite a refined palate you have there. I'm not sure your internal organs would fetch a good price on the open market if all you're eating are bean burritos."

"Oh, I eat other things. Given something other than plastic-wrapped American cheese slices, I can put together a grilled cheese sandwich deserving a Michelin star," she boasted.

"I believe all grilled cheese sandwiches deserve a Michelin star, but you can be snobby if it makes you feel better."

"Some feta, nuts and quinoa would make me feel much better about eating the bagged salads my mom bought me." She took a noisy slurp of the chocolate milkshake she'd ordered, then let her head fall back against the seat. "And I could get some Brussels sprouts to grill."

He shuddered then reached over to swipe an onion ring from the paper bag. "I can't believe you're even thinking about Brussels sprouts while eating these."

"What can I say? I'm multidimensional," she said, gesturing for him to finish the last ring off. "And I can't go on eating potatoes, onions and okra. I'm going to turn into gumbo."

"Well, we can't have that." He crumpled his own wrapper, gathered their trash and reached for the door handle. "I'll go toss this and we'll be on our way. We need to get back. I have work to do."

While Cara shopped, Wyatt called her parents to let them

know they were in town longer than expected, but the call went to voicemail. Forty minutes later, they were sailing down Highway 65 hauling a decent sampling from Cara's favorite food groups—cheese, frozen burritos, snack crackers and breakfast pastries.

"Why don't you try calling your parents? Let them know we're heading back," he suggested, nodding to the phone she'd tossed into the console on their way into town.

"Dad said he needed to replace some wire on the western fence," she said as she powered the phone on. "Mom's probably helping him."

Wyatt frowned. "I could have helped him."

Cara glanced over at him, a faintly amused smile tugging at her lips. "You think my mom doesn't know how to stretch fence?"

"I think your mom can do anything," he replied without missing a beat. "I'm only saying I would have been happy to help."

"And I'm sure they'd appreciate the offer, but they know you're here on other business."

She jolted and they both looked down as the phone in her hand emitted several short bursts of vibration. "Someone was looking for you," he said grimly. "Was it your folks?"

Cara's lips thinned into a tight line. "No."

She snapped the word off so sharply, he checked her again. "Do I need to pull over?"

"It's nothing. More text messages from my biggest fans," she said, her voice tight with bitterness.

He reached over and took the phone from her hand. A quick glance showed a string of text messages from a variety of area codes. A surge of anger pulsed through him. He wanted to pull over to read them, but the stretch of road they were on had little to offer in terms of a shoulder. So he opted for the second-best thing. He pressed and held the power button as he maneuvered a curve one-handed.

"What did they say?" he demanded in a growl.

"I only saw the notification windows, but they looked to be more of the same. I don't deserve my share of LYYF. I should leave the company to the real geniuses. Blah blah blah," she muttered, turning to look out on a broad swatch of pastureland. "I'm so tired of it all," she whispered.

Without thinking, he dropped the phone back into the console and reached across to place a steadying hand on her leg. The moment his palm landed she tensed and he froze for a beat. Then he jerked his arm back, gripping the steering wheel like a fifteen-year-old angling for a learner's permit.

"Sorry," he breathed. "I didn't mean—"

"It's okay," she said, trampling his apology. "And I know. I appreciate you being here. I appreciate everything you're doing, Wyatt." She angled to look directly at him. "I hope you know I do."

"I do."

A horn blared and he glanced up into the rearview mirror. "Holy cow, this guy needs to slow down," he muttered, inching the SUV to the right as a sleek silver sports car swerved into oncoming traffic to pass. "Double yellow, dude," Wyatt complained, gesturing to the markings on the road.

"Missouri plates," Cara observed as the car dropped back into the lane in front of them.

The driver immediately ran up on the bumper of the next car ahead of them. The coupe was so low-slung the driver was barely visible over the headrest. Cara gripped the door handle. Wyatt tightened his hands on the wheel, half-expecting to witness a terrible accident as the erratic driver overtook car after car, heedless of the rules of the road.

"Wanna throw your cop light up onto the roof and go after them like on TV?"

He shot her a wry smile but kept their speed steady as the other car disappeared over a hill. "Sadly, this ride didn't come equipped with a cop light."

"So sad."

Wyatt shook his head in wonder as the line of traffic shaken by the aggressive driving of the speeder settled into a more sedate pace.

They rode in silence for a couple miles. Then turning her attention back to the road, she pointed to a blur of a highway sign. "If you turn off on 14, we can come in the back side. It's hilly and curvy, but it's a pretty drive and we could check to see if Mama and Daddy are in the west pasture on our way to the house."

"Sounds good."

They drove into the small town of St. Joe in tight silence. The *click-click* of the turn signal sounded almost laughably loud to his own ears. Ryan Hastings's warnings about getting too attached to a primary while on protection duty reverberated in his brain. Then again, Ryan knew the dangers firsthand. He'd fallen for Kayla Powers while trying to protect her from a murderer, given up his career with the state police and moved to Bentonville to help her raise the baby she hadn't known was on the way at the time of her late husband's death.

"Cara, I shouldn't have—"

"Please don't, Wyatt," she cut him off, the words quiet but firm. She reached over and placed her hand on his arm. "I don't want things to be awkward between us. I feel… Can't we...?" She stumbled to a stop as he slowed to make the turn onto the narrow secondary road. "I didn't mind. Okay? It's... Wow, things are complicated right now, and I don't—"

"You don't have to say anything more," he interrupted.

"Well, it seems like one of us does," she countered. "Sheesh, I mean...how 'bout them Hogs?"

He laughed, amused by her use of a native's shorthand for, *Let's change the subject, please.*

"How about those Hogs?" He smiled and let off the gas as they wound through a series of curves. "I don't know if they'll make it to a bowl game this year or not."

"You realize I have absolutely no idea how the Razorbacks are doing this year, don't you?"

"I do, but I'm willing to roll with it if you are."

"Okay then. Give me the midseason highlights," she invited. "It is midseason, right? I think I remember football going until Thanksgiving."

"You aren't far off," he said encouragingly. "Okay, here's where we are."

He spent a good fifteen minutes giving her the rundown on how the University of Arkansas football team was performing, who their star players were, and a fairly in-depth analysis on the current coaching staff. For her part, Cara pretended to listen, interjecting the occasional hums and snorts where his commentary warranted response. He was about to launch into his views on the ongoing college athletic conference realignments when she held up a hand.

"Okay, uncle," she cried.

He glanced over and found her smiling at him, her eyes crinkling at the corners. He grinned back at her. "Bet you never pull the old 'How 'bout them Hogs?' on a guy again," he teased.

"Are you kidding me? I've been using that line to distract my father since I was trying to get around his no-dating-before-sixteen rule," she said with a smug smile. "Turn left up here, then we'll take a quick right on the farm road."

He did as instructed. A quarter mile down the dirt road, they came to the section of missing fence Jim had pointed out to him on their tour of the property. The ATV Jim used was parked near the opening. He could see the coils of new wire to be stretched in the bed of the utility vehicle, but Jim and Betsy Beckett were nowhere in sight.

A set of deep ruts was cut into the ground from the edge of the road, the far side of the ditch and through the gap in the fence. Either one of the Becketts had driven the farm truck out to the pasture, or someone had come to call.

Slowing to a stop, he reached for his cell phone, but Cara had beaten him to it.

Her mother answered on the second ring. "Cara, honey, is that you?" Betsy asked, her voice tremulous.

"Mama? Where are you? Where's Daddy?" Cara asked, panic rising in her voice.

"Why, we're up at the house, sweetheart," Betsy cooed, her tone a shade too bright. "Are you almost to Little Rock? You don't want to miss your flight again, sugar. I know you think you have more money than God, but those tickets are expensive," she added with a tittering laugh.

"Mama? What's happening?" Cara demanded.

"Nothin' happening here. Paul Stanton stopped by for a visit. You remember Mr. Stanton? I guess I should say Lieutenant Governor Stanton." Her mother gave a high-pitched giggle and the hairs at Wyatt's nape rippled. "He's so sad he missed seeing you. But listen, I'm bein' rude," she said, her drawl thickening in her rush. "You get on now, and be sure to call us and tell us when you've landed safely. Love you, honey. Your daddy and I love you so very much."

The call ended.

Cara turned to look at him wide-eyed. "She's acting like we're on our way to Little Rock to catch a flight."

He shook his head. "She knows we're not, but whoever is there with her doesn't." He scowled. "Paul Stanton is there? The lieutenant governor?"

She bobbed her head. "Mama went to prom with him back in the day, but Daddy hates the guy. Wyatt, something weird is going on."

"I gathered as much," he said gruffly. "But I have to get you away from here."

"I can't go off and leave them," she argued, shrugging out of her seat belt.

"You can't go in there. Not with whatever is happening," he shot back.

"Those are my parents," she said, agitation pitching her voice high and tight.

"I'm aware, but—"

The next thing he knew, the passenger door was hanging wide open and Cara was leaping across the ditch. He shouted after her, but she didn't look back. He was still fumbling with the clip on his seat belt when he heard the engine on the ATV turn over.

She took off like a shot, careening over the bumpy hill at the edge of the property, headed straight for the house. Cursing under his breath, he lunged across the seat and grappled for the handle on the open door. The moment it was closed, he threw the car into gear and cranked the wheel. The SUV hit the bottom of the ditch so hard his head smacked the roof. He aimed for the opening in the fence, squeezing his eyes shut as he plowed through, a piece of the broken fencing scraping the length of the passenger door.

He couldn't think about damage to the state-owned vehicle now.

He had to catch up with a woman who preached the gospel of staying in the moment, but was proving to be an expert at making a quick getaway.

Chapter Fourteen

Cara spotted the enormous luxury SUV parked in the drive from a quarter mile out. She fixed her sights on it, opening up the throttle and clenching her jaw to keep from clacking her teeth on every rut and ridge hidden beneath browning grass and fallen leaves.

Paul Stanton. Paul Stanton. She'd known the man all her days, but for the life of her, she could not form a picture of him. Brown hair—probably grayish brown now. Brown eyes? Probably. Her overriding recollection of the man was he was bland. Handsome enough in a conventional way.

Neat. For some reason, she recalled shirts pressed to a crisp, khaki pants with knife-edge pleats and loafers polished to a high gloss. In other words, the polar opposite of her ruggedly handsome if not a bit rumpled and work-worn father.

It was no wonder her mother had dumped Mr. Permanent Pressed for her father.

"Gah!" she cried when she hit a bump so hard the rear of the gator skittered to the side. She let off the gas until she regained control, then hit it again the moment she felt all four wheels were under her.

The pearly white SUV parked behind her father's mud-spattered pickup gleamed in the afternoon sunlight. She squinted when the shining chrome trim tossed sunlight back at her. She took pleasure in skidding to a stop right beside the hulking vehicle, sending up a plume of dust and gravel she hoped marred the sparkling paint job.

She killed the engine and leaped from the ATV. She was skirting the back of Paul Stanton's vehicle when she slid to an abrupt stop. Parked beside the massive car was another. This one low-slung and sleek. A matte silver with an all-too-familiar profile. Hurrying to the rear of the sports car, she knew what she would find.

Missouri plates.

The driver who'd been in such a hurry on the highway had been swerving in and out of traffic, endangering the lives of other drivers so he could get here faster.

Here. To her parents' little ranch in the Ozarks. Her safe haven. The place she could hide out without anyone knowing where she was. No one except Paul Stanton.

Cara reached into the back pocket of her jeans for her phone but came up empty.

Cringing, she darted a glance at the field she'd sped across to get to them. She had no doubt Wyatt would be hot on her heels, but he would have to come around via the farm and county roads. She couldn't wait for him. Wouldn't. She was the one who'd brought this madness to her mother and father's doorstep. She would be the one to stop it.

Rolling her shoulders back, she circled the corner of the house and came up the front walk. Only then did she register the steady stream of gruff, rhythmic barks. Roscoe, bless him, was standing at attention, his forehead furrowed with concern and the hair on his back standing on end, barking to be let inside to inspect the newcomers.

Walking softly, Cara crooned the old dog's name as she climbed the shallow steps. She scratched behind his floppy ears, then pressed her forehead to his to calm him. "Who's in there, boy? Bad guys? Guys with bad hair? Why was Mama talking all funny, huh?"

The dog sat at her feet, his hindquarters hitting the deck with a thump.

"Don't worry. I'll get 'em. You stay here and tell Wyatt where we're at, okay?"

Creeping off the porch, she circled around to the kitchen door. Her mother had hung sheets out to dry in the sun. Cara pictured the state-of-the-art washer-dryer set in the laundry room sitting idle while Betsy Beckett's linens snapped in the autumn breeze. She could make out the muffled hum of conversation coming from the kitchen, but was too short to catch a peek through the window over the sink.

As quietly as she could, she took the two steps up the back stoop and pressed the button on the screen-door handle.

The click of the latch opening might as well have been a shotgun blast.

Cara froze, tensing every muscle in her body. She listened intently, but no one inside spoke. She bit the inside of her cheek, figuring she'd give it to the count of five before she proceeded.

She only made it to three.

"Well, hello there, Cara."

She looked up to find Paul Stanton smiling down at her beneficently from the screened back porch. He looked incongruous standing there next to the chest freezer, amid a jumble of discarded boots, rain and cold weather gear and the motley collection of half-dead houseplants her mother refused to give up on entirely.

The man who greeted her lived up to her recollections. His hair was indeed brown, but the close-cropped helmet now sported sleek silvery sidewalls. The buttons on his starched shirt strained across a round drum of a belly. He smiled down at her, but no warmth reached his dark eyes.

"Your mama was under the impression you were headin' down to Little Rock to catch a flight, but my friend couldn't locate any information about a flight booked, so we thought we'd hang around a bit to see if maybe you'd changed your mind. Again." He pressed the flat of his palm to the screen door, and she stumbled back a step as it swung open. "Come on in. We've been waiting for you to get home."

She took two steps back, her sneakered feet crunching the leaves gathered along the side of the porch. "Who's we?"

He flashed a wide politician's smile. "Why don't you come in and we'll all chat a bit. Your mama has poured us all a glass of her delicious sweet tea."

Riled by his ingratiating tone, she stood her ground. "Who? What friend? What are you doing here?"

"We came to talk to you, is all. From what I hear, you can be a very difficult young lady to pin down."

"Cara, honey, you go on," her mother called from inside the house. "I don't want you to miss— Oh!"

The surprise and distress Cara heard in her mother's sharp cry set her in motion. Running up the steps, she brushed past Paul Stanton and his smarmy smile and charged into the kitchen. "Mama!"

Three steps into the room she drew up short. Zarah Parvich was standing in her parents' kitchen, her feet planted wide and her expression disconcertingly businesslike as she pressed the muzzle of a gun to Cara's father's temple. "Hello, Cara. Looks like you missed your flight again," she said without rancor.

Cara raised both hands in a gesture of surrender. "Zarah? Why are you pointing a gun at my father?"

"Hey, now, no one said anything about pointin' guns at

people," Paul Stanton said, his forced laugh ringing hollow in the tense room.

The other woman hitched her shoulder in a shrug. "I needed to get your attention."

"Okay. You've got it," Cara said. "Can you lower the gun now?"

She fixated on the semiautomatic pistol in the woman's hand. It was strange to see a gun out in the open after living in Southern California for so long. She wasn't far into her freshman year when she learned to keep her mouth shut about horses, heifers and handguns. Almost everyone she knew was virulently anti-gun. Everyone except Zarah, apparently. Thankfully, the other woman complied.

She choked down the sob of relief squeezing her throat. "You okay, Daddy?"

"I'm fine, sugar," her father responded, his voice even and steady. "Got work to do, though. Not that *he* would know a darn thing about an honest day's labor," he added, jerking his chin in Paul Stanton's direction.

"Hey, now—" Stanton began, grabbing hold of his tooled leather belt and hiking his pants as he stepped forward.

"How dare you, Paul Stanton?" Betsy Beckett said in a low, tremulous voice. "What kind of trouble have you brought into my home?"

"Elizabeth, I swear—" Stanton began, but Cara raised a hand to stop him.

"We can get into the hows and whys later." Turning to Zarah, she scowled at the gun then the sharp-featured young woman who held it. "What do you want?"

"I want what everyone wants," Zarah said as if the answer should have been obvious. "I want what people have been telling you for weeks. I want you out."

"What's it to you?" Cara shot back.

With a huff of impatience, Zarah rolled her eyes. "Oh, I plan to have a vested interest."

Cara looked everywhere but at the back door. The last thing she wanted to do was tip Zarah off to Wyatt's imminent arrival. She took in the familiar kitchen, the ancient wood napkin holder bracketed by salt and pepper shakers, the iron skillet wiped clean and waiting on the stovetop, the café curtains Grandma June had helped her make for a Mother's Day gift.

The refrigerator's compressor hummed, undercutting the tension in the room. Drawing a steadying breath, Cara forced herself to meet Zarah's gaze. "What interest?"

"She said she's engaged to Tom Wasinski," Paul Stanton chimed in. When her mother shot him a filthy look, the man took an involuntary step back. "I'm sorry, Elizabeth, but Wasinski could be a deep-pockets donor and if I run for Senate, I want him on my side. His company is about to go public."

The Beckett family turned to glare at him as one. If her expression was one-tenth as incredulous as her father's, Paul Stanton had to feel lower than an earthworm.

"I always knew you were about as stiff as a fence post, Stanton, but I never realized you were as dense as one," Jim Beckett grumbled. "Our Cara is an equal partner in their company. Her pockets are every bit as deep as either of those two fellas."

"Now, Jim," Betsy began, long accustomed to stepping between the two men.

"Not for long," Zarah said. She pointed the muzzle of the gun to a plain manila folder on the small dining table. "Cara's about to get out of the business."

Cara wanted to bask in the warmth of her father's pride, but the glint of sunlight off gunmetal made it difficult to enjoy the moment. "You are not engaged to Tom," she said flatly.

"Well, not technically engaged," Zarah conceded. "But once you sign these papers, I'll be able to hook up with him, you know, as an equal, and he won't have to worry about whether he's 'technically' connected to my employment," she said, using a single set of air quotes to dismiss the excuse Tom must have used to rebuff her.

But Cara knew the two weren't and never had been involved. In one of the few confidences they'd shared recently, Tom had confessed he was deeply, but quietly, involved with a woman he'd met on a tech-free weekend yoga retreat he'd attended months ago. One Cara herself had recommended and Zarah had booked. Could it be the mystery woman in Tom's life actually was Zarah? She racked her memory for a name, but couldn't recall him disclosing one.

Cara wondered if she'd missed something big in her old friend's life, or if the young woman she'd trusted with hers was delusional.

"How long have you and Tom been involved?" she asked, her approach cautious.

"We talk all the time." Zarah smiled smugly, pulling her long ponytail over her shoulder with her free hand and stroking it as if she was settling in for some girl talk rather than holding Cara's loved ones at gunpoint. "I know he feels like he can't let things evolve as they stand now, but together, we're going to take LYYF to the next level."

Cara could only hope Zarah had forgotten there was a special agent with the Arkansas State Police staying with them.

"What about Chris?" Cara asked, anxious to keep her engaged.

"Chris won't be a problem. Everyone knows he's going to take the money and run the minute he can cash in." She tipped her chin up. "You and Chris never cared about what it took to keep the company going. Tom is the brains behind it all."

"Tom doesn't create content," Cara pointed out.

Zarah gave an indelicate snort. "Like it's difficult." She rolled her eyes. "I've been helping you churn that stuff out for years. Besides, I'm a better actress. I've booked more roles than you have in half the time in Hollywood."

"I talked to you this morning," Cara said, stalling for time. "How did you get here so fast?"

The younger woman rolled her eyes. "It's not like it was difficult to figure out you were stalling. Plus, TSA's system is ridiculously easy to hack. I've been waiting to see if you boarded a plane going anywhere. When you changed your flight, I booked one to Dallas. When you didn't turn up, I hopped a flight to Springfield, Missouri, and drove down." She pursed her lips. "I guess it's pretty enough with the trees and all, but there's not much around here." She wrinkled her nose in distaste. "And it's so run-down." She glanced over at Paul Stanton. "You might get more people to visit if things didn't look so…poor."

Paul opened his mouth to protest, but Cara spoke first. "So what do you expect to happen here today?"

Without missing a beat, Zarah pointed the gun at Cara's mother's chest. "I expect you to sign over your partnership."

Her father half rose from his chair and Paul Stanton bumbled forward with a hearty "Hey, now—"

Zarah swung the gun from one man to the other and they both subsided, hands raised. Moving closer to the table, Cara placed herself between Zarah and her mother. She was the target here, not her parents. Cara had to make certain Zarah kept her eye on the prize.

"Who am I signing it over to? You?" Cara asked, trying to keep her tone curious rather than accusatory.

"Yes. Sign it over to me, and I will let Tom know we can be together now. Equal partners," Zarah said with a decisive nod. Her pretty face brightened. "I mean, it's not like this is what you wanted to do with your life, right? And if you still want to be involved, maybe we can pay you a salary or something."

Cara glanced down to see her father staring at her intently. He cut his eyes to the window, and it was all she could do to keep from looking over. Wyatt must be out there. *Please let him be out there.* She needed to buy time.

"It was you, wasn't it?" she said softly.

"What was?" Zarah asked, squinting as if confused by the non sequitur.

"All of it. The doxing. The messages. All the...stuff." She closed her eyes, willing herself to hold it together as the pieces fell into place. "You did it."

"Oh, that," Zarah said with a dismissive laugh. She shrugged. "I put some info out there, but the rest... I didn't have to do much."

"Except have me kidnapped," Cara interjected.

"Oh, well, technically, you paid for that yourself. Good thing you never look at your account statements, huh?" She wrinkled her nose. "Anyway, didn't go as expected. He was only supposed to take you somewhere and scare you into signing."

"Now he's dead," Cara said flatly.

"Yeah, well, not my fault. He shouldn't have taken the job if he couldn't handle the pressure." Zarah exhaled in a put-upon whoosh. "I guess I learned a good lesson on outsourcing."

Cara fixated on the gun dangling from Zarah's hand like

an afterthought. She didn't look like she had much experience handling firearms. She certainly hadn't been taught how to handle one safely. She was waving what looked like a small nine millimeter around like it was a water pistol. And what if Wyatt came through the door and startled her? She could accidentally shoot any one of them.

Drawing on every acting lesson she'd ever had, Cara forced herself to look into Zarah's eyes with what she hoped were eyes filled with hope and optimism. "You know this was never what I expected to do with my life," she began, faking a quaver into her voice. "I don't know how I got this far off track." She bumped her mother with her hip, signaling the older woman to scoot her chair away. She pointed to the folder on the table. "What is this?"

"It's an agreement to transfer your partnership shares," Zarah said, her customary chipper efficiency slipping back into place. "And you've always been really nice to work with, Cara. I'm not going to leave you high and dry. Once the public offering goes through and prices are up, I'll cover you. In today's cash value, of course," she added.

"Of course," Cara murmured.

Out front, Roscoe gave a woof of greeting and they all turned. Zarah swung the gun around when a floorboard creaked. "Sounds like your hot cop is still hanging around after all," she said, turning back to press the muzzle into the dusty folds of her father's Carhartt jacket. "Tell him to join us," she called out in a louder voice. "But be sure to tell him I'm holding your sweet daddy at gunpoint."

"Wyatt, if that's you, Zarah is here and she has a gun," Cara called out robotically.

"I'm coming in, and I am *not* holding a gun," he announced before stepping into the doorway, his hands raised. To Cara's disappointment, he wasn't lying. There was no sign of a weapon in Special Agent Wyatt Dawson's hand.

"Some cop you got yourself there," Zarah scoffed. "He's got a kind of hot-nerd vibe going on. Too bad he couldn't come in busting down the doors to save you."

Cara raised her eyebrows. "He's a cybercrime guy. I'm not sure kicking in doors is their thing. He tells me they barely leave the office."

She shot Wyatt an apologetic glance and he made a point of scowling at her. But the glint in his eyes was keen and bright. He wasn't insulted, nor did he seem to be worried. Which made exactly one of them. Had he somehow called for backup? How long would it take someone to get there? Their eyes held for a moment and a veil of calm settled around her shoulders. He wasn't freaking out over a woman who was clearly suffering some sort of break waving a very real gun around like a toy. She wouldn't either.

"So what's the situation?" Wyatt asked, his tone casual, almost disinterested.

"We're talking business," Zarah snapped.

"Talking business with a gun pointed at a person?" Wyatt asked smoothly. "Isn't asking someone to sign legal documents at gunpoint coercion?"

Cara shot him a quelling look. "Don't you worry about it. Wasn't I telling you I was thinking about doing something different with my career? Well, Zarah is here and we're talking about making a deal."

"A deal in which she fronts zero dollars, and you sign everything over?" her father asked with an incredulous laugh.

"I'm going to pay her once the stock offering is complete. Tom and I can combine our shares, pay Cara for her time and efforts to this point and still have controlling interest in the company."

"Sounds like you have it all figured out." Cara nudged her mother with her knee, but Betsy didn't budge. "Mama, you still keep extra pens in your junk drawer?"

When she looked down, her mother was staring at her with naked disbelief. When she spoke, all traces of syrupy sweetness were long gone from Betsy Beckett's voice. "You can't seriously be considering signing those papers."

Cara shifted so Zarah couldn't see the silent stare-down between her and her mother. "Mama, I know what I'm doing." She thought of the old handgun her granddad kept in the kitchen drawer of the old house. Cara knew it made the move to this one along with Grandma June's cast-iron skillet. She'd seen it in the back of the junk drawer. "I know you and Daddy have never approved of what I do. Here's my chance to start over. I can have all my time back to pursue acting…real acting. All I need to do is sign on the dotted line and this will be all over."

"How do we know?" Betsy demanded. "How do we know she won't shoot us all?"

Zarah looked aghast at the suggestion. "You think I like doing this? I hate it. I'm not one of you hillbilly gun nuts," she snarled. "All I want is my share of LYYF and I'll be out of here."

Cara grabbed the folder again and waved it like a flag of surrender. "Fine. You know what? I'm tired of this. I want my life back. My actual life-life. The one I plan on living." She flipped over the folder and dumped the papers out onto the table.

She took the seat across from her father and Zarah and pulled the papers closer. "Mama, please grab me a pen, would you? If I know you, you've got at least six or seven of them you swiped from Buck's stashed in there," she said, naming a local gunsmith's shop.

It was both a request and a prod. The moment she met her mother's fiery gaze she knew the message had been received. With a small nod, Betsy rose and walked stiffly to the drawer on the far side of the stove.

It was time to show her know-it-all assistant from California how hillbillies from run-down little towns in the Ozarks settled their disputes.

She pretended to reread the first page of the documents, her shoulders tensing as she heard her mother rustling through the drawer behind her. "So, how will you work the transfer of funds?" she asked, pitching her voice low so Zarah would be forced to focus on her.

"Crypto?" the other woman replied with a cheeky smile. Cara snorted. "Nope. Cash."

"I'll wire transfer it to you." Zarah flashed a dimpling smile. "It'll be easy. I already know all your account numbers."

"Yeah, I may need to rework some of those things," Cara murmured, keeping her head down as the rummaging continued behind her. "Mama? You find me a pen?"

"Hold your horses. I'm looking for one that works." To emphasize her point, Betsy tossed a cheap plastic ballpoint to the floor in disgust. "I have got to clean this mess out one day."

"Sounds like you need an assistant, Mrs. Beckett," Zarah chirped.

"Maybe so," her mother murmured. The sifting of clutter finally ceased, and Cara glanced over her shoulder to see her mother reach up and carefully tuck her hair behind her ear, clearing her peripheral vision. "I'm not finding a decent ink pen, but I did find this."

With one fluid move, Betsy Beckett swung around to face the young woman, her father-in-law's old service pistol in her hand and a grim expression hardening her pretty features. "Drop the gun."

Zarah's eyes widened. "No," she snapped, jabbing her gun into Jim Beckett's ribs so hard he let out a soft grunt. "This is my plan. We're going to do things my way," she insisted, her voice climbing with agitation.

"Oh, God," Paul Stanton blurted. Both of his arms raised, he turned toward the front door. Seeing Wyatt in the doorway, he stopped short. "This is too much. It's all too far out of hand."

"You think?" Wyatt asked, unperturbed.

Cara looked up as the lieutenant governor switched directions, then dithered, his arms flailing. "I have to get out of here. I can't be here. I was never here," he babbled.

"Could have sworn I saw you," Wyatt replied, his voice a life preserver of quiet and calm amid the melee.

"I can have your badge," Paul Stanton threatened, spittle flying from his mouth.

"You can try," Wyatt challenged. "But from where I'm standing, it doesn't look good for you, Mr. Stanton."

"You drop your gun," Zarah demanded, stepping back from Cara's father and training her sights on Betsy instead.

You chose incorrectly, Cara thought as her mother released the safety on her weapon.

"You terrorize my daughter, point a gun at my husband and track your muddy shoes on my kitchen floor and you think you get to give the orders here?" Betsy demanded, widening her stance. "I don't think so, honey."

Out of the corner of her eye Cara saw Wyatt lowering his hands. He was cool as a cucumber. It gave her the confidence she needed to end this farce once and for all.

Meeting Zarah's eyes, she spoke slowly and deliberately.

"Lower the gun now, or I will never sign this. Mama, you too," she added. "I mean it. Everyone, lower the guns now."

"You mean everyone but me, right?" Wyatt asked, drawing his weapon from its holster at the small of his back as he closed the distance between him and Zarah.

Zarah's head whipped around in surprise, but his aim didn't waver as he took hold of her wrist with his left hand, expertly squeezing at the precise pressure point to make her release her grip. The gun she'd been waving around dropped to the floor as he twisted her arm behind her back.

"Zarah Parvich, you are under arrest. You have the right..."

Cara sat frozen, unable to tear her gaze away from the sight of Wyatt holding both of Zarah's empty hands behind her back.

"Cara, can I ask a favor?" Wyatt asked politely.

"Uh-huh," she said, and nodded.

"I left my coat on the living room floor. I have some zip tie restraints in the inside pocket. Grab a couple for me?"

"Sure," she replied as she rose.

"I'm leaving," Paul Stanton announced.

He took two steps toward the front room and without thinking, Cara snatched Grandma June's skillet from the stovetop and swung. She aimed for his body and not his head, wanting to slow the man, not kill him.

But the lieutenant governor wasn't the least bit grateful for her forethought. Cursing a blue streak, Stanton fell against the fridge, then crumpled to the floor, clutching his right arm.

"Excuse me, Uncle Paul," she said with a sneer as she stepped over his legs. "I think we'd like you to stay a bit longer."

On the opposite side of the room, Jim jumped up from his

chair and hurried to embrace his wife. "Girl didn't know who she was messing with," he murmured into her hair.

Her mother gave a watery laugh. "I'm a regular Dirty Harriet," she said, burrowing in.

Cara carried Wyatt's coat back into the kitchen and her mother looked up, shaking her head. "Holy cow, girl, I can't believe you remembered this gun." Betsy wiped her eyes with the heels of her hands. "I doubt it's had a bullet in the chamber in the last twenty years. How did you know it was still there?"

"I saw it the other day when I was looking for a pen," Cara said with a smirk. "You've got everything in the world in there except a working ink pen." Holding Wyatt's jacket by the collar, she turned her attention to him. "What are you carrying in here? It weighs a ton."

"Nothing much. Flashlight, pepper spray, flex cuffs, extra magazines, a collapsible baton," he said offhandedly. "Standard desk jockey stuff."

She pulled two zip ties from the deep inner pocket and handed one over. Zarah stood, unresisting, her head bowed, her lips clamped shut. Once she was cuffed, Wyatt guided her to a spot on the floor against the wall where she sat silently weeping.

Cara watched as he used the end of the other plastic strap to pick the discarded gun up off the floor. He deposited the weapon on the kitchen table, then looked from Cara to the woman on the tile floor.

"I called for backup from state police and the sheriff's department before I came inside. They should be here shortly. You okay to keep an eye on her while I see to our esteemed lieutenant governor?" he asked.

"I am," Cara responded. And to her surprise, it was true.

Lowering herself to the floor in front of the woman who'd turned her world upside down, she whispered, "Okay. Okay. Easy. Deep breaths, Zarah. Breathe in…"

Chapter Fifteen

Within minutes, her parents' house was a complete circus.
Teams from both the state police and the Searcy County
Sheriff's Office jostled for jurisdiction, but everyone knew
in the end the county would have to give way.

"I knew I should have checked your financials," Wyatt
muttered.

"Most people don't hire their own kidnappers," she murmured, her gaze fixed on her former assistant.

"Would have saved a lot of time and grief," he replied.

"Next time," she promised.

They watched as Zarah was properly secured and led to
one of the trooper's vehicles for transport to Little Rock. A
short distance away, Cara's mother stood behind the EMT
checking Paul Stanton's arm to ascertain whether X-rays
might be needed, reading her onetime prom date the prover-
bial riot act. Her father stood off to one side, a faint smile
curving his mouth, his admiring gaze locked on his wife.

"She's something," Wyatt said to her father. "Nearly gave
me a heart attack when she pulled a gun out of her kitchen
drawer."

Jim Beckett looped an arm over Cara's shoulders and
tucked her into his embrace.

"My dad didn't like leaving my mother in the house alone

while he was out doing chores, but as he used to say, you can't keep the inside and the outside up at the same time. So, he kept his old service pistol in the kitchen drawer in case trouble came strolling up the road. She must have brought it with her when she moved in with us."

"She did," Cara said quietly. "She told me Granddad would want us to have it to hand."

Without peeling his eyes off the floor show, her father pressed a kiss to the side of her head in a gesture he hadn't made in years, but one she remembered so well it brought a hot rush of tears to Cara's eyes.

"And another thing, Paul Anthony Stanton," her mother said, shaking her finger in the face of the man who held the second-most-powerful office in the state. "The minute they haul you out of here, I'm not only calling your precious mama, but I'm also callin' Delia Raitt. By the time I'm done with you, you won't be able to get elected prom king in prison or dogcatcher anywhere else!"

"I know I should stop her, but it's so darn entertaining," her father murmured to no one in particular. "Better than any show on CineFlix."

"Agent Dawson?" A shorter, powerfully built man with a blankly sober expression stood in the doorway Wyatt had filled mere hours before. "Could we speak to you in private, please?"

Wyatt nodded. "Yes, sir." He glanced first at Cara, then her father. "Y'all okay here?"

"We'll be fine," her father replied, giving her a squeeze as he answered for both of them.

Wyatt hesitated, his gaze lingering on her. Her cheeks heated, but thankfully, her father remained enthralled by the dressing down her mother hadn't quite wrapped up. "I'm good. Go do what you do," she said with a little jerk of her chin.

When he was gone, her father said, "I like him. Decent guy."

"I do too," Cara said quietly.

Satisfied with what he found, the EMT turned to one of the troopers standing nearby. "Doesn't look to be broken, but he should have an X-ray to be sure there's no fracture."

"Too bad," Jim whispered to Cara as the troopers hauled the man up from the chair and out of their house. "Swing for the fences next time, sugar."

She giggled and gave him a playful elbow jab. "Daddy. Behave." She assumed a prim expression. "You know I'm a pacifist."

He pulled back enough to tuck his chin to his chest and glare at her. "What? You only eat fish caught in the Pacific?"

She rolled her eyes and groaned. "Even for a dad joke that was bad."

Betsy Beckett turned to face them, hands planted on her hips. Thankfully, she seemed to have expended her supply of vitriol. "What's so funny, you two?"

"Not Dad's jokes," Cara replied. She slid out from under her father's arm and hugged her mother. "You were fantastic today."

"I guess I learned more than I thought I had, watchin' all those depressing shows your daddy likes."

"I wasn't worried. I know my wife." He leaned in and pressed a smacking kiss to Betsy's lips. "She can take care of herself and everyone else around her." He turned and looked at Cara as he pulled on the heavy work jacket he'd shrugged out of when the first of the patrol cars arrived. "You get it from her, Care Bear. You're like your mama."

A lump the size of a boulder rose in Cara's throat.

"Where do you think you're going?" her mother demanded as he reached for the handle on the back door. "I have a house full of cops and robbers here, and the police are going to want to talk to you some more. If you think you're going to slink off—"

"I'm goin' to see to the feed. I'll be right back," he said, zipping the jacket up to his chin.

He was gone before either of them could say another word. Betsy exhaled an exasperated sigh. "I swear he breaks out in hives if he has to spend more than an hour of daylight indoors."

"Probably," Cara concurred. "Nothing new there." A crime scene team bustled in, and it quickly became clear they were in the way. She caught her mother's tired gaze. "Let's go in the other room?"

"Sounds good," Betsy replied.

But when they slipped into the living room, they found themselves caught in the cross fire between one of the sheriff's men and an officious-looking state trooper. Betsy steered them toward the dining room, but there they found several men and a young woman dressed in dark suits setting up laptops and pulling legal pads from briefcases. Before they could be spotted, Cara took her mother's hand and led her down the hall toward the bedrooms. She could hear the rumble of deep voices coming from the room Wyatt had been using, so they tiptoed down the hall into Cara's room, closing the door silently behind them.

Betsy leaned against the closed door as if bracing against an approaching horde. "Good gracious, there's a lot of people in my house," Betsy said, patting her chest. "I hope they don't look too close at my floors. I haven't swept in days and Roscoe sheds enough for us to build a brand-new dog twice a week."

"Poor Roscoe," Cara said, peeking out her window at the front porch. Close to a dozen patrol cars and SUVs were parked haphazardly in the driveway and on the lawn, and the poor old dog had felt duty bound to greet every one of them. "I hope he's—" She scanned the porch until she spotted a familiar lump parked next to the rail. "Good, he's sleeping." She let the blind fall back into place with a chortle. "Wouldn't want him missing his middle-late-afternoon-pre-supper snooze."

"Supper," her mother groaned, stepping away from the door and dropping heavily onto the side of the single bed Cara had dutifully made before leaving the house.

Dropping down beside her mother, Cara patted her knee. "I think we're going to open the fridge and call whatever falls out supper."

Betsy tipped her head onto Cara's shoulder, and the simple reversal of their usual roles made Cara feel more centered than she had in years.

"Mama?"

"Hmm?"

"I think I am going to sell," Cara said, the words coming out as the thought took hold.

Her mother didn't move a muscle. For a moment, Cara wondered if Betsy had fallen asleep, or simply hadn't heard her, but then she stirred. Sitting up, she took both of Cara's hands in hers and held them tight as she gazed deep into her eyes.

"Don't decide anything now. Whatever you do, you do it in your time and in your way. No matter what anyone says, you created something special. You created it. You are the one who gets to decide what's right for you, and your creation."

"Well, me and Chris and Tom," Cara said with a self-deprecating little laugh.

"No, Cara," her mother said, giving her hands a squeeze. "Only you. Partners can help and support each other, but they can't dictate how we live our lives. You can walk with them, follow your own path or figure out a way to blaze a whole new trail. Make sure, in the end, you choose which it will be." Her mother let go long enough to sweep Cara's hair from her brow. "I imagine it's like a marriage. You have to be your own person, but together. Every day, choosing to be together."

Cara gave a snort of a laugh. "If my business partnership were a marriage, it would be illegal in most states."

Betsy rolled her eyes. "You know what I am saying. I'm only saying not to make any big moves until after this whole stock thingamajig is done. I have no idea if those fellas you're working with were actually involved in all of this mess or not, but I say let the truth come to light. You hang on and get everything you have coming to you, because it's yours and you earned it. After, well, then you can make your choices and your daddy and I will support you. One hundred percent."

Cara flung herself into her mother's arms. "Thank you, Mama."

They rocked as they held one another, Betsy alternately humming and shushing her. Cara was so happy to be assured of her parents' approbation to worry about the mixed messages.

With a snuffle, Cara pulled back a bit. Her gaze landed on the boy-band poster. "Mama, why didn't you ever take that poster down?"

Betsy spared the yellowing print a half glance, then pulled Cara close again. "As long as I kept it up, we'd both know this would always be your room. Whenever you came home, you'd feel…at home."

Cara squeezed her mother tight again and they stayed locked together until someone rapped lightly on the door.

"Who's there?" Cara said, dashing fingertips under her damp eyes.

"It's Wyatt," he replied without attempting to open the door. "Are all three of you hiding in there?"

Cara and Betsy laughed. "Jim has gone out to be with his cows," Betsy called back.

When he still didn't open the door, Cara asked, "You want to hide out in here too?"

The door opened slowly, and Wyatt poked his head in, a sheepish smile crinkling his eyes. "Hey."

"Hi," Cara returned, a single eyebrow raised. "You in or you out?"

His smile dissolved into a wince, and he raised a hand to the back of his neck in a gesture so familiar to her now, it made her chest ache. His gaze dropped to the floor and he shifted his weight from one foot to the other. "Listen, Emma is here with some guys from the FBI and the Department of Justice. It looks like we're talking state and federal charges for, uh, well, both of them and they want to talk to you."

"Okay." Cara rose, smoothing her hands down the front of the jeans she'd been so happy to acquire earlier in this endless day. "Let's do it."

Wyatt took a small step back, then glanced down the hall before turning back to her with an apologetic smile. "Actually, I have to go."

"Go?" she and her mother asked in unison.

Then Cara noticed the packed duffel at his feet. "Oh."

"The guy I was talking to is my section chief, Simon Taylor. He's heading back to Little Rock now and wants me to give him my full report on the way."

"Oh," Cara repeated, the bottom dropping out of her stomach. "Should I...? I'd like to meet him. Thank him."

Wyatt shook his head. "No need. Plus, he's not exactly

a people person, you know?" He wrinkled his nose. "Trust me, you aren't missing anything."

The silence stretched several seconds too long. Thankfully, her mother stepped into the breach. "Jim and I can't thank you enough for all you've done," she said as she rose to say her goodbyes. "Let me call him in from the barn—"

"Oh, no. Thank you, ma'am," Wyatt said with a quick, hard shake of his head. "I didn't do much more than try to tug on a few loose threads."

Her mother wrapped an arm around Cara's waist and gave her an encouraging squeeze. "You brought our daughter home safely to us."

Wyatt met Cara's eyes at last, then gave her a lopsided smile. "No. I didn't even do that. Jim was right. Cara took care of herself and everyone else around her. I was nothing more than the guy who got to drive her home."

"Dawson?" a man called from down the hall.

"I have to go." Wyatt raised a hand in farewell. "Take care, okay?" He gave her a winsome smile. "Make sure the guys let you be the one who rings the big bell next week. You deserve it."

He turned away, hoisting his bag onto his shoulder in one fluid move. Cara and her mother followed him down the hall, but stopped short of the living room. Wyatt didn't seem to want to linger. The stern-looking man holding a leather computer bag nodded to her and her mother, then followed his agent—her agent—out the front door.

Cara wanted to call after him, but she couldn't make any sound come out. Besides, what could she say? He was with his boss. She was with her mother. Surely they'd have a chance to catch up later. She sucked in a breath when he stopped to give Roscoe a pat as the other man made a bee-line for a marked state police SUV.

"Ms. Beckett?" the young redhead she'd seen setting up equipment said as she strode toward them, her hand extended. "Special Agent Emma Parker. It's good to meet you in person."

"Oh. Yes. Emma." Cara mustered her best smile, but knew it probably came across several watts weaker than usual. "Thank you for all you've been doing for the case." She gestured to her mother. "This is my mom, Elizabeth Beckett."

"Betsy," her mother supplied as the two women shook hands.

"If you don't mind, we'd like to ask you a few more questions," Emma said, gesturing to the dining room. "Wyatt said it would be okay for us to set up in your dining room, Mrs. Beckett, but I promise we'll be out of your hair ASAP."

Cara stiffened as a flash of headlights strafed the front of the house. She blinked a couple times, then saw the taillights on the SUV flash bright as the driver tapped the brakes. Her heart lurched. For a second, she thought maybe Wyatt had forgotten something and was coming back. Maybe the thing he'd forgotten was her.

Then she saw the vehicle dip as the driver maneuvered onto the rutted gravel lane and picked up speed.

"You go on with Agent Parker," her mother said in a gentle tone. "Do what you need to do. I'll fix up a mess of sandwiches for whoever wants something." Cara hesitated and her mother leaned in to kiss her cheek. "Go on now. Maybe later I'll tell you about the guy who drove me home from the prom."

Cara took a half step away before her mother's teaser fully registered. "Drove you home from the prom? You said you went to prom with Paul Stanton," she said with a puzzled frown.

"I did," Betsy said, a serene smile curving her lips. "I went with Paul. Danced with him a couple times too, but he was more interested in sneaking drinks with his football buddies." Her smile turned enigmatic as she started toward the kitchen. "Your daddy was the one who drove me home. It's been him ever since."

Epilogue

Cara Beckett strolled through Arrivals at Bill and Hillary
Clinton National Airport without a single person recogniz-
ing her, and that was exactly the way she liked it. She tossed
a glance over her shoulder to be sure her companions were
right behind her.

"You're in the fast-paced capital city now. Try to keep up,"
she called over her shoulder.

"There's seriously only one terminal?" Chris asked, quick-
ening his pace to fall in beside her.

"Yep."

She smiled as they approached the single escalator down
to the baggage claim area. Cara paused to allow Chris to go
first, waiting for Tom to catch up. With his ever-present computer bag hanging off one shoulder and a small carry-on in
the other hand, the man was craning his neck as if the small
airport was one of the wonders of the modern world.

"Come on, Captain Moneybags, you can put an offer in
on the place another time," she teased.

"It's weird. I guess I've only ever flown into larger air-
ports," he observed, stepping on the escalator behind her.

"When you've flown commercial," she qualified. "We
won't count general aviation."

Tom frowned as he pondered her take. "You know, if

you're serious about this, maybe we should look into invest-ing in a company plane after all," he mused.

"Yes!" Chris thrust his fist into the air, garnering the at-tention of the passengers around them. He didn't shrink from the spotlight. "I've been saying so for years."

"Yeah, well, we haven't been able to actually afford one," Tom shot back.

"And now we can," Chris said, his smile smug.

At the foot of the escalator he hooked a hand through Cara's arm. Tom flanked her left side, and they walked three abreast through the sliding doors into bright autumn sun-shine. The late-November breeze swirled around them.

Beside her Chris gave an exaggerated shudder. "I thought it was supposed to be hot in the South?" he complained.

"We're due east of Los Angeles," she reminded him.

"Do I need to call a car?" Tom said, sliding a phone from his pocket.

"No, I have a friend picking us up," she said as she scanned the line of cars depositing and scooping up passengers. She spotted the plain black SUV with the state tags parked in one of the diagonal pull-through spots with a five-minute limit. "There she is."

As they approached, the driver's door opened and Emma Parker stepped out. "You made it," she said, meeting them at the back of the vehicle.

"We made it," Cara called back. "Tom, Chris, this is Spe-cial Agent Emma Parker. Be polite. She has a gun."

But it was Emma who was enthralled by the sight of the tech whizzes. "Wow. I'm so thrilled to meet you." She shook each man's hand, then turned to Tom. "I've been hacking multi-player games since I was eleven. Like you." A pretty peach blush colored her cheeks. "I mean, I know you used to—"

Tom cut her off there. "Don't tell anyone, but sometimes I still do."

"He never had the patience to beat them legitimately," Chris chimed in.

"Me either," Emma said with a grin.

"Some of us actually have skills," Chris said pointedly.

"Okay, okay." Cara waved them both toward the doors. "You can flirt with her while we drive."

Once they were all settled into the vehicle, Emma joined the steady flow of traffic circling the small airport. Cara pointed to the parking deck. "The garage where I got carjacked," she said, using her best impression of a tour guide.

"Not funny," Tom muttered.

"I'm not kidding," she retorted.

"Cara's Trauma Tours," Chris said with a peevish edge. "Not a great selling point for your plan."

Cara turned and found both men scowling at the concrete structure as if it were responsible for the incident. "I don't have to sell you on my plan," she reminded them gently.

"We're still partners," Tom argued.

Smiling, Cara nodded, pleased too with the way they'd reconnected in the two weeks since Zarah Parvich and Paul Stanton were arrested and LYYF had a record-breaking launch on the stock exchange. When Cara told them she was heading back to Arkansas to spend Thanksgiving with her parents, the two men seemed genuinely sad to end the ongoing celebration.

"I can tell you the whole cybercrimes crew is really excited to have you drop by," Emma informed them as they merged onto the highway. She shot Cara a sidelong glance. "Wyatt in particular."

"Well, we appreciate all you did to help Cara," Chris answered. "A quick stopover to thank you in person is the least we could do."

Cara watched the highway signs zip past. This was the same route Gerald Griffin had forced her to take mere weeks before, but looked completely different with her two oldest friends along for the ride. Just a few miles down, Emma signaled her intent to exit. Arkansas State Police Headquarters was located in an old shopping mall on the city's south side.

Within minutes, Emma had wheeled the SUV into a spot designated for official vehicles and killed the engine. "We've got about an hour before I'll need to get you back to check in for your flights out."

"Let's do this then," Chris said, reaching for the door handle and discovering it was useless. He was trapped in the back of the police SUV. "Or not."

"Cop locks," Emma informed them. "Hang on, we'll let you out."

"Yeah. Makes sense," Chris muttered as Emma opened the rear door for him.

Cara smiled at Tom as he stepped out of the vehicle.

"Should I take my bags?" he asked.

Emma wrinkled her nose, then shrugged. "Up to you. This is not a great area, but if they're not safe in this vehicle, they aren't safe in any."

"Good point."

Emma made a point of chirping the locks as they walked away, and they all laughed.

A chuckle tangled in Cara's throat when one of the glass doors leading into headquarters opened and Wyatt Dawson stepped into the sunlight. His hair glinted gold and his shoulders looked broader than ever as he crossed his arms over his chest and waited for them, his lips curved into a smile he was clearly keeping on a tight rein.

Cara hung back, allowing Emma to make the introductions between the men. When Wyatt reached for the door and held it open for them, she hesitated on the sidewalk. Wyatt clocked her position with a glance, then let the door swing shut behind the others.

"Hey," he said, his gaze locked on her.

"Hi," she returned.

Then, unable to hold back a moment longer, Cara flung herself at him. He caught her up easily, strong arms winding tight around her as she buried her face in his neck.

"One minute you were there, and before I could even… you were gone," she mumbled into his skin.

"I wanted to stay. I wanted to stay with you, but I didn't know what you wanted and I couldn't… I love my job, Cara. I didn't know—"

"No. Right, I know," she said, her voice choked.

He held her fast, one hand sliding up her back to hold her to him even tighter. "Breathe," he whispered into her ear.

She gave a soggy chuckle and inhaled deeply. Maybe she got drunk on the scent of his soap, or perhaps he was exuding some kind of pheromone that made rational women lose their minds. She didn't know exactly why she pressed her lips to the exposed skin above his collar, she only knew it was absolutely necessary.

Wyatt froze for a second, and she wondered if she'd gone too far.

Then, the next thing she knew, he gripped the back of her head in his big, warm palm and his mouth was on hers. His lips were warm and firm, the bottom slightly chapped from his habit of gnawing on it, but all in all, the kiss was perfect. Long, lingering and packed with promise.

She pressed her slick lips together when he drew back for air. The last thing she wanted was to do something stupid like apologize. Not when she was not the least bit sorry he'd kissed her.

"I've wanted to kiss you a long time," he confessed, his voice slightly hoarse. "But this probably isn't the best time and place."

"Feels right to me," she said, her voice breathy.

"Complicates things," he said gruffly.

"Not for me," she answered, pulling back to look him in the eye. "This is by far the easiest decision I've made in weeks."

"Is it?"

She nodded. "I'm heading up to my folks for Thanksgiving," she informed him.

To her chagrin, he loosened his hold on her. "Sounds great. I'll be working on shift for the holiday, but probably head down to see my family over the weekend."

"Oh. I see."

She was unable to mask her disappointment, and he was as perceptive as ever. "Why? What's happening?"

"Oh, nothing." Cara flashed a shaky smile, her nerves ratcheting up as they circled one another. Taking a calming breath, she dove in. "I was wondering if you might have some free time this weekend."

His eyebrows rose. "Well, sure. I mean, I didn't have anything set in stone. What did you have in mind?"

"I thought you might like to come with me to check out a piece of property," she suggested, hugging herself as she braced against the stiff wind and possible rejection.

"Property?"

"There's a couple places out near Pinnacle Mountain State Park." His eyes lit with interest when she mentioned the recreational area just north and west of Little Rock. "You know, I was thinking someplace far enough out to have some land to build a studio, but close enough to enjoy the perks of high-speed internet."

"The perks of high-speed internet?" he repeated, his smile stretching wide. "What kind of perks?"

"Oh, you know, cop shows on CineFlix. And maybe, if the connection is as reliable as I think it is, a certain cop might possibly show up at my door to watch cop shows on Cine-Flix?" she suggested with a hopeful smile.

"I'd love to come look at property with you," he said, looking her square in the eye.

"I'm not going back to California," she told him. "I mean, at least not permanently. I'm sure I'll have to go out there someti—"

He cut her off with another kiss, this one swift and sure.

They jumped apart when someone hit the crash bar on the door with a little extra force. "Hey, Dawson," a gruff voice called out.

Cara laughed, pressing her forehead to Wyatt's shoulder as she tipped her head to the side. Trooper Masterson stood grinning in the open doorway, a small knot of people gathered around Chris and Tom behind him.

"You planning to hold the poor woman hostage or something? I wouldn't try it. I hear she's slippery."

Looping an arm across her shoulders, Wyatt kept her close as he turned toward the door. "Oh, I know. Cara Beckett can take care of herself and everyone else around her," he informed the older man. "Believe me, I plan to stay on her good side."

* * * * *

Don't miss the stories in this mini series!

ARKANSAS SPECIAL AGENTS: CYBER CRIME DIVISION

Shadowing Her Stalker
MAGGIE WELLS
January 2025

Catching A Hacker
MAGGIE WELLS
February 2025

MILLS & BOON

INTRIGUE

Seek thrills. Solve crimes. Justice served.

Available Next Month

Missing: Baby Doe B.J. Daniels
Wilderness Hostage Janice Kay Johnson

....

Cold Case Murder Mystery Nicole Helm
Catching A Hacker Maggie Wells

....

Protecting The Pack Julie Miller
Killer In Shellview County R. Barri Flowers

Keep reading for an excerpt of a new title
from the Romantic Suspense series,
THE TWIN'S BODYGUARD by Veronica Forand

Chapter One

For as long as Zoe Goodwyn could remember, she'd put the needs of her twin sister, Allison, first, even if it meant sacrificing her own needs. She'd given up career opportunities and even let go of a boyfriend or two to remain in their hometown to care for their father. Her latest sacrifice seemed mild by comparison—abandoning plans with friends to catch the ferry from Nantucket and watch her sister's dog.

Stepping off the bus into the heart of Boston, Zoe shielded herself from the city's loud energy, a sharp contrast to the meditative qualities of waves breaking on a sandy beach and the call of seagulls darting across the sky. The salt air in Boston felt invigorating, but the bags of trash waiting for pickup added a somewhat sour city smell that wrinkled her nose. Although Zoe enjoyed visits to Boston, she preferred when Allison traveled to Nantucket so Zoe could remain in her zen place. Not that she entirely disliked the city. Just city people. People acted differently in large groups. They had more of a survival of the fittest mentality. She preferred any groups around her to be under the age of ten. In fact, her third-grade students were her favorite people. Everyone else brought too much with them. Too much noise, conflict, gossip, expectations, and superiority. She slipped away from the crush at the bus station while texting her dad that she'd made it into the city.

Zoe relaxed as she reached her sister's neighborhood. Few cars ventured down the one-way cobblestone road to the three-story brownstone. Pausing in front of a florist, she bought a bundle of white and pink peonies before traveling the final block to her destination. Flowers always made everything a touch brighter and more fragrant.

A woman, dressed in a pale blue shirtdress and walking a large white dog, waved from across the street. "Allison, I loved your report on stolen pets. Keep up the good work." As a young and energetic investigative reporter for a local news channel, Allison had minor celebrity status in the city. She thrived among people and could persuade anyone to hand over their most personal stories. She also loved getting in the middle of complicated issues.

Normally, Zoe would ignore people confusing her for her sister, but she couldn't make her sister appear unfriendly. Trying to explain that she was not, in fact, Allison, was always too much of a chore. Not many people knew about Allison's sister, and Zoe liked it that way. Her baseball cap, ponytail and sunglasses should have kept her identity hidden. This was her sister's neighborhood, however, so perhaps, people could see through a disguise here. She waved and mouthed thanks to the woman, who smiled and continued down the street with her dog.

Once inside the building, Zoe heard howling. Marlowe. Mrs. Peterson, an older woman with a tousled, pewter bob and a charming disposition, never disciplined Marlowe when she watched him. She preferred the bribery method in restraining him. Zoe entered the apartment and was greeted by one very excited beagle. As soon as the door closed behind her, she let go of her suitcase, kicked off her red Mary Janes, never allowed on the perfectly waxed floor, and headed to the kitchen to put the flowers in a vase. Marlowe's intensity didn't slow. His tail wasn't wagging. Instead, he appeared distressed. He was always happy to see her, so his behavior caused her to pause and crouch down to his level.

"What's the matter, little man?" Zoe asked the shaking beagle. Normally, he'd greet her between blistering romps around the foyer, into the kitchen, over the living room furniture and right back to her side. Now he didn't leave her side.

She dropped the flowers on the counter and scanned the room. The kitchen and living room seemed as sterile and minimalist as always, but quiet, except for Marlowe.

"Mrs. Peterson?" she called out, as Marlowe continued his barking. He nearly tripped her as she tried to walk into the room. "Go to bed." She pointed to Marlowe's bed and looked around for Mrs. Peterson. She paused and stared him down. He popped into a down position on his bed, but as soon as she walked further into the apartment, he bounded to her side.

Turning away from him, she took a deep breath.

The energy inside the apartment felt unfamiliar. Something was off. Whatever created the tension in the room lifted the hair on her arms and made her almost turn around and run back out the door. But Mrs. Peterson had to be here because Zoe could smell hints of the jasmine perfume she always wore.

Marlowe rushed ahead, barking and winding up again. Zoe stalled at the door to Allison's study. Papers and drawers and files had been tossed all over the floor. Marlowe skittered back into the hall away from Mrs. Peterson, who was face down on the floor.

Zoe rushed over to her. It appeared as though she'd fallen or maybe collapsed. A good-sized gash was on the back of her head, matting her hair with blood.

"Mrs. Peterson, are you okay?" she asked, knowing she wasn't. Marlowe rushed toward her, barking louder. Zoe wanted to comfort him but had to focus on the unconscious woman in front of her.

"You're here?" A gruff voice came from behind her.

Before she could turn, the stranger's hand reached around and covered her mouth with a cloth. She tried to push him away, but his grip was strong and her ability to fight was fading. Her eyes closed, the barking grew faint, and everything went black.

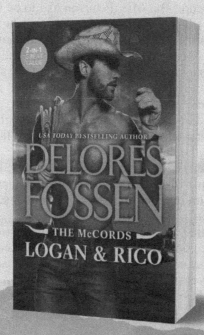

Subscribe and fall in love with a Mills & Boon series today!

You'll be among the first to read stories delivered to your door monthly and enjoy great savings.

MILLS & BOON

JOIN US

Sign up to our newsletter to stay up to date with...

- Exclusive member discount codes
- Competitions
- New release book information
- All the latest news on your favourite authors

Sign up at **millsandboon.com.au/newsletter**